MEAN HIGH TIDE

JAMES W HALL

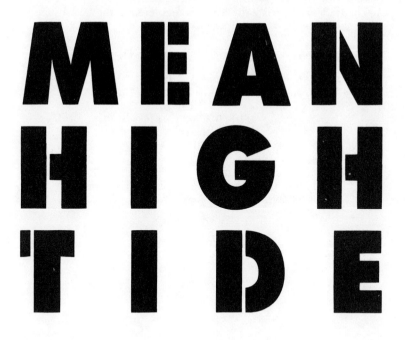

MEAN HIGH TIDE

Delacorte  Press

Published by
Delacorte Press
Bantam Doubleday Dell Publishing Group, Inc.
1540 Broadway
New York, New York 10036

Library of Congress Cataloging-in-Publication Data

Hall, James W., 1947–
Mean high tide : a novel / by James W. Hall.
        p.   cm.
        ISBN 0-385-30798-5
              I. Title.
        PS3558.A369M4   1994
813'.54—dc20   92-6226
                                                  CIP
Manufactured in the United States of America
Published simultaneously in Canada

April 1994

10 9 8 7 6 5 4 3 2 1

For Evelyn
with all my love

Thanks to Mike Picchietti for his generous help with information about tilapia and fish farming, and to Dr. Jeffrey Rosen for his very useful medical insights, and to Dennis Lehane for starting me out in the right direction.

Let the waters bring forth abundantly.
—Genesis

When you shall these unlucky deeds relate,
Speak of me as I am; nothing extenuate,
Nor set down aught in malice: then, must you
   speak
Of one that lov'd not wisely but too well;
Of one not easily jealous, but, being wrought,
Perplex'd in the extreme; of one whose hand,
Like the base Indian, threw a pearl away
Richer than all his tribe.
                    —*Othello*

CHAPTER 1

IT WAS A CLEAR HOT AUGUST MORNING, SPACIOUS AND EASY, THE KIND OF day when absolutely nothing bad could happen. The Atlantic as calm and tepid as day-old bathwater. All that stillness caused by a high-pressure ridge, Darcy said, perched over the Florida Keys, keeping the lid tight on the bell jar. Not a trickle of breeze, just the same air that was here last week and the week before. Getting a little muggy, maybe, but Thorn considered it good air. Damn good summertime air. Air with substance, heft.

The sky with a fresh coat of flawless enamel. A plush blue, the color of blood in the veins. Out on the eastern horizon, the gulls and herons, the frigate birds, even the distant tankers gliding along the shipping lanes were each in exquisite focus. Only a few stringy clouds hung motionless in the west like ripples in marble.

Saturday, six miles offshore of Key Largo, Thorn and Darcy anchored over a patch of sand a few boat-lengths east of Broken Conch Reef, just minutes south of the boundary of Pennekamp State Park. It wasn't quite noon, but already they'd put three good-size lobsters in the cooler. Twice Darcy had glimpsed a gigantic one, but she couldn't get close enough for a swipe at it. Now they were taking a break, finding their breath. Thorn stood at the console and watched Darcy clean her mask.

"You ready for lunch?"

"No," she said. "But don't let that stop you."

She smiled at him and went back to work on her mask. Thorn cocked a hip against the console, leaned his weight against it, and watched her rub the glass with the corner of a towel.

In the last couple of years, he'd spent a hell of a lot of time watching Darcy Richards. Watching her do little things, or nothing at all. Sleep or read, hang out laundry, brush her hair. He'd watched her mince the tough meat of countless conchs, then drop the breaded balls into simmering oil. He'd seen her cast her fishing line a thousand times, and watched her waiting while her bait sank, that expectant look in her eyes, and almost every day he watched her soap herself in the outdoor shower, watched her towel off then wrap the towel around herself and sit down on one of the Adirondack chairs and throw her damp hair forward over her head, presenting it to the sun. In the two years they'd lived together, he'd watched her do a few thousand things, and she'd never failed to fascinate him.

Lately she'd begun to cut her hair the way she had in high school. All the perm had grown out from her days as a Miami TV weather forecaster, and now her hair hung simple and straight to her shoulders, with her bangs just brushing her eyebrows. The dust of the city almost all blown away by the island breezes.

Her hair was the shade of honey with a ruby blush, one of the rare sunset colors. Her eyes were a rich avocado-green, but sometimes when Thorn moved close they seemed to play tricks with the light, run up and down some personal color spectrum. Suddenly a vaporous gray, or maybe an aquamarine.

"How'd you know about this place, anyway?" he said. "That there'd be so many lobsters left?"

She looked up at him a moment, then went back to her mask.

She said, "You know I can't reveal my sources, Thorn."

"Yeah," he said. "It's one of the six hundred things I like about you. Integrity. Confidentiality."

"Only six hundred?" she said. "That's it?"

"Six hundred to the tenth power," he said. "Multiplied thereafter by a repeating factor of four."

"What the hell's a repeating factor of four?"

Thorn shrugged.

"I heard it somewhere. I'm not sure. Maybe I made it up."

"All right then," she said, her pout fading, becoming a smile. "That's better than six hundred."

He bent down and dug through the cooler till he found what surely was the coldest Budweiser south of Anchorage. Thorn in his cutoff jeans, a T-shirt advertising a local tackle shop, his polarized sunglasses. His bare feet and the rest of his exposed flesh a dark chestnut. His hair these days was straggling past his collar from the last time Darcy had cut it a couple of months back. Summer blond, dry and brittle as hay.

"You ever consider," he said, "the crawfish population keeps thinning out at the rate it has, today might just turn out to be the last time we find any at all. Next summer the only ones left could be the deep-water critters, down a few hundred feet. You ever think like that?"

"I try not to."

Her voice was flat, and she didn't look at him, just exhaled on the glass of her mask and rubbed at another blur.

Thorn looked at her for a moment more, and when she didn't look up, he sighed, stretched his shoulders, then stared down into the clear water.

It was twenty feet deep here, but the water was clear enough that he could make out the wavy orange of elk horn coral, a small fluid school of damselfish down a dozen feet, a couple of sergeants major hanging near the surface. Business as usual on the reef. The come and go of thousands of iridescent minnows, pecking at the living rock of coral, clouds of purple and oxblood and crimson staining the water momentarily with their glitter. A gaudy mural that wouldn't hold still.

Thorn squinted out at the blue-diamond water, then slowly scanned the calm sea. Hardly any boat traffic today. A single open fisherman a half mile away, idling in their direction. Looked like a Grady White.

One boat, where just a couple of weeks ago there would've been a hundred, maybe a thousand. All of them full of tourist divers down for the four-day weekend, the annual opening of lobster season. It was a four-day horror show, a grim onslaught of thousands of strangers, cramming the narrow islands, carrying their nets and tickle sticks and cases of beer and loud radios, armadas of more tourists rolling down U.S. 1 in bright rental cars.

In the evenings, with their sunburns glowing, and decked out in T-shirts with pictures of lobsters and funny sayings printed on them, they crowded the restaurants, overwhelmed the bars and motels, and for four days they rented all the available boats, clogged the marinas and boat ramps and dive shops, and each morning they headed out to sea in rowdy groups to comb every inch of seabed they could locate.

Most of the local merchants loved that weekend, and advertised heavily throughout the state and the nearby states to lure more and more of them down. But for Thorn it was an agonizing time. For four days, everywhere he turned there were strangers and more strangers, all of them in a frenzy of gluttony, looting every cranny, dislodging rocks, sloshing along the shoreline through the fragile sponge beds, spearing and grabbing, overturning whatever was in their path.

And as usual, this year the Marine Patrol caught a few of the violators. Two men from Georgia who exceeded their six-lobster-per-day limit by several thousand. Heading back to Valdosta with their U-Haul chock-full of undersize crawfish on beds of ice, and a few hundred pounds of elk horn coral they'd snapped off to sell as souvenirs.

But that was two weeks ago. Now the waters were still again, the surviving lobsters left to the men and women who made their living trapping them in wooden cages for the restaurant trade, and to the few locals who had the patience to hunt down a last straggler or two to make a meal.

August half over, Labor Day ahead, another small invasion of tourists would swell the island again on that weekend, then the Keys would be quiet, left to the locals for several months till the winter season began and the rich Yankees began to arrive again. That's how it was going in the Keys. One cycle of locusts, then another; swarming for days or months, they stripped whatever succulent tidbit the last wave had left behind, then at some magical signal, they all whisked away in one voracious cloud to the next fertile field that struck their fancy.

Thorn was sick of it, getting sicker every year. Not sure exactly what to do. He was no political type. He couldn't give speeches, or organize the locals against the pillaging of what was theirs to safeguard. Lately, he had toyed with the idea of leaving the island, sailing farther out into the Caribbean, where the swarms might not be as large or ravenous.

But like it or not, Key Largo was his home, had been for all his forty-two years. Cursed as it was by its own willingness to sell itself, spreading its legs by the hour or the week. Renting its soul. This was his home. And since he could not save this place, he did what he could to save himself. He hunkered down. And when that didn't work, he hunkered down lower.

Thorn opened the cooler and drew out one of the tuna-and-cheddar sandwiches they'd made before sunup this morning. Heavy on the mustard with a leaf or two of lettuce and an inch-thick slab of fresh tomato. He climbed up on the observation platform above the engine, opened the wax paper, and began to eat.

Today they'd come out to sea in the eighteen footer, his Hewes bonefish skiff with a six-inch draft, made for skimming over dew and windowpanes of water, not for the big rollers of the Atlantic. Ordinarily, this far offshore, he would've used the thirty-foot Chris-Craft, the old teak-and-mahogany boat he'd inherited. But with the water so smooth, the horizon as precise as a snapped chalk line, hell, he and Darcy could've paddled a kayak out there today, kept going if they'd felt like it, across the Gulf Stream, made it to Nassau by happy hour.

He watched that open fisherman idling closer. The person cut the engines four hundred yards away, and went forward and threw the anchor over, then a red dive flag on a white float.

"What's the bottom like over there?" Thorn motioned toward the Grady White. "You know?"

"Some rocky patches," she said, "nothing else."

"Maybe that guy knows something you don't."

"Not likely."

Darcy stared at the boat, squinting, but didn't say anything. In a moment or two she looked down, spit into her mask, rubbed the saliva across the glass, and as she rubbed, she once again brought her eyes to that boat.

"You ever bring anybody here before?" he asked.

She looked over at him, put her mask aside, folded her hands in her lap, and shook her head.

"It's my secret place," she said. "You're the very first to know about it. And you're sworn to silence."

"Really?" he said. "Nobody? Not even that Roger, what's-his-name? Your prom date?"

She gave him a mildly caustic look.

"Well, can I at least tell Sugarman?" he said.

"Sugarman already knows about it."

"I thought I was the first."

"You are."

A smile tinged her lips.

"What is this? A riddle?"

She said, "Sugarman brought Gaeton and me here. Though I'm sure he wouldn't remember, it was so long ago."

She leaned back against the gunwale, reached out and dangled an arm overboard, her fingers trailing through the water.

She said, "I was ten years old, maybe eleven. Which would've made Sugar and you and Gaeton seniors. The two of them were just playing around that day, exploring. Grouper fishing, as I recall. I don't know where you were, probably home tying flies or something. But I remember Gaeton and Sugar didn't catch anything here, so I suppose they didn't file the place away. But I snorkeled around that morning, and I never forgot it. The size of the lobsters here. I didn't tell them what I'd seen, kept my mouth shut and my poker face on, but I snuck back every year I could after that. Never told anybody. Not my brother, not Sugar, nobody."

"Till today."

"Yeah," she said. "Till today."

"Why now?"

"I thought it was time," she said. "You never know, there could be an asteroid with my name on it, a Greyhound bus flying down U.S. 1. Stuff you don't see coming. I don't want to die carrying around a lot of valuable secrets."

She looked over at him for a long moment, while that lingered. Thorn stared back at her, waiting for her to laugh, hoping by god she would; but without any sign that she was kidding, she dropped her eyes and ran her fingers again through the water.

She'd been saying things like that lately. In the middle of a joking conversation, lurching suddenly into an ominous tone. He'd known her all his life, had been best friends with her older brother Gaeton, and for the last two years had been sharing his house and bed with her. But in all those years, it was only in the last month Darcy Richards had been taking these swerves in her mood. Like a soprano suddenly breaking into a hoarse bass.

Thorn thought it might be something biological, maybe the ache of childlessness resonating up from somewhere inside her, making her wistful. Or perhaps it was just her age, the winding down of her thirties, forty hovering dangerously on the horizon. One morning she gets out of bed, the calendar has dropped another page overnight, and right then some prickly dread hatches deep in her bowels and begins gnawing its way out.

He ate his sandwich and watched her. When he was done, he

climbed down from the platform, threw the wax paper into the garbage bin, and came over to her and sat down. She was staring off at the horizon.

"So who stood you up back at the docks?"

She brought her eyes back from the distance, and though she smiled, and held his gaze firmly, something was moving in her eyes, some shadowy form ducking away to hide behind the brightness of her smile.

"Just somebody I wanted you to meet."

Earlier, when they'd gassed up at Snake Creek Marina, Darcy had paced the dock looking for someone. Making Thorn hang around another ten minutes after the tank was full. Finally giving up and heading on out to the reef.

"Tell me about it, Darcy. What's going on?"

She lowered her eyes, studied the back of her right hand.

"Tell you about what?"

"You know what. The way you've been lately. Moody, quiet. The asteroid thing, the Greyhound bus."

"Moody? Me?"

"Is it something medical?"

A reluctant smile surfaced on her lips. She looked at him, shook her head, and Thorn felt the blood that had been massing in his throat begin to seep away. At least it wasn't that. Thank god, not that.

She took a measured breath, let it go, and said, "Oh, I don't know. It's nothing really."

"Why can't you tell me?"

She leaned overboard, looked down into the water, a single finger touching the surface, moving across the transparent skin as if she might be writing something there.

She wore a yellow bikini with dabs and splashes of greens. Her hair clenched in a ponytail; her skin sheened with seawater evaporating, sweat appearing. Brine going and coming.

He cleared his throat and spoke her name. But she kept her eyes on the message she was writing.

"Oh, just something I stumbled onto at work," she said. "I

don't know exactly what it means, so I thought I'd poke around a little on my own, see if I could figure it out."

"What kind of thing at work?"

"I don't want to talk about it."

She looked away from him, watched a cormorant slant in from the east, pass low overhead, then splash into the water a few yards away. It bobbed to the top and turned itself in their direction, waiting for food scraps.

"You know, Thorn," she said. She took a long breath and let it go, watched the cormorant swim closer. "I like how we are together. I like our rituals. All of them. I do. The fishing, the wine. No phone, no newspaper. Up at dawn, out in the boat every day. The good life. The uncomplicated life."

She sighed, touched a strand of damp hair at her temple. She looked over Thorn's right shoulder, gazing intently as if someone were sneaking up on him. Thorn swung his head around, but nothing was there except the flat blue water.

When he looked back, she was staring down at the deck.

"But see, it's your life we're leading, Thorn. You lived exactly the same way before I came along. I've adjusted to your rituals, your schedule, made your preoccupations mine. And lately, I've been feeling like I want a few of my own again. That's all. Simple as that."

Thorn set his beer down. Tried to find words, but failed.

She lifted her eyes to his.

"This isn't a criticism, Thorn. Our life together is fine."

"But you want more. Something more."

She sighed.

"Oh, Thorn, now you're hurt."

"A little," he said. "What'd you expect?"

"I'm just talking about having something that belongs to me alone. You have that. Things you keep private. Worries. Fantasies, things you don't tell anybody about."

"No, I don't."

"Tell the truth."

He thought about it, watching the cormorant grow bored with

them, then launch itself up and flap away toward the Grady White.

"I guess there's some stuff I don't tell you. Nothing major."

"Well, that's all this is, Thorn. Nothing major. A small problem I want to handle on my own. That's all. Okay? Like you have with your bonefish flies. Your own creations."

"I see," he said.

He watched the cormorant splash down next to the Grady White. He couldn't see anybody on board it anymore.

"Thorn," she said, standing up now, coming to him. Sweat sparkling on her shoulders and the tops of her breasts. "I love you exactly how you are. And I'll love you when we're ninety years old, sitting in our rockers on that porch, watching the sun sink into Blackwater Sound, swatting mosquitoes, drinking white wine. I want to be with you till the day I die. You got that? Is that clear enough for you?"

He stood up. Darcy Richards reached out, and with a single finger traced the ridge of his collarbone.

"Just one thing," he said.

"Yeah?"

"Does it always have to be white wine? Can't we make it red occasionally?"

She smiled and stepped into an embrace. He could taste the sea salt on her lips, and could feel the heat and hunger that hadn't slackened in years of kissing. Eyes closed, a lush darkness in Thorn's head as if his eyeballs had rolled back and might stay that way permanently.

When they were finished, she stepped back and smiled drowsily. Thorn reached out for her, but she shook her head.

"Not now," she said. "When we get back in. Okay? Right now, I really want to get that lobster before it sneaks off."

"Sure," he said. "But find it quick."

She bent down, picked up her flippers and began tugging them on. Thorn went back to the cooler, got another beer. He watched a flying fish break the surface and sail past the bow of their skiff. It stayed aloft for thirty yards, then sliced back in.

Sitting on the wide gunwale, her back to the water, Darcy said, "I keep meaning to ask you, Thorn. Have you ever run across a fish called a red tilapia?"

He popped the cold beer, slid it into the insulator cup.

"Doesn't ring a bell," he said. "Why?"

"Oh, I was just curious. It's nothing. Somebody mentioned it the other day, and I thought you might've heard of it. You're such a fish guy."

"Is that what's bothering you? Some fish?"

Darcy formed a careful smile.

"Thorn," she said. "Don't."

Before he could say anything else, she pressed one hand to her mask, waved at him with the other, and fell backward into the water.

It was after one o'clock, and for the last hour while Darcy snorkeled around the elk horn and brain coral, still in pursuit of the monster lobster, Thorn fished off the other side. Twelve-weight fly rod with 850 grain shooting head and fifteen-pound tippet-heavy tackle. Using a tarpon fly he'd invented recently. Red Mylar wrapped in intricate figure eights around a plug of ram's fur. A short purple skirt that hung down over the spray of fur, and for a head, a pearl button from one of his ratty cowboy shirts.

He'd plucked the fur from a stuffed ram's head Sugarman's wife, Jeanne, had bought on impulse at a garage sale. When they got the thing home it was just so big it overpowered every wall in their house, so Sugarman hauled the ram's head out to his car, drove over to Thorn's, and offered it to him.

And sure, why not? Thorn liked using oddball materials. Mixing hundred-year-old fur with space-age plastic strips. And surprise, surprise, a week after Thorn sold his first dozen of them, one of his friends, a tarpon guide down in Lower Matecumbe, stopped by the house to tell Thorn the ram's-head fly was snagging a good crop of tarpon, an occasional permit. So today he'd decided to field-test it for himself.

He'd never been a match-the-hatch fly-tier. The match-the-hatch guys believed fish would only bite replicas of the insects that were hatching during that time of year. They believed fish were programmed to avoid anything their biological almanacs told them was out of season. Made them jittery if it didn't jive.

But for Thorn, verisimilitude wasn't the point of fly-tying. Hell, the truth was, he wasn't interested in catching some goddamn fish with no more imagination than that. Far as he was concerned, the only fish worth catching was one willing to strike something it had never seen before. Willing to take that risk, that leap of impulse, crazy faith in its own abilities.

He glanced over at Darcy, floating on her stomach, peering down into the water. He could hear her breathing through her snorkel. That raspy breath coming in spurts as she moved around for a better view of things below.

Okay, so Thorn's quiet retreat wasn't holding Darcy's full attention anymore. She was right, of course. Thorn's daily script was unvarying. Had been for years. Tying bonefish flies each morning to make his borderline income, a nap in the hammock after lunch, out in the skiff at five to catch yellowtail, grouper, trout for supper. Dusk reserved for a couple of glasses of wine, lighting the grill, studying the fluid patterns of birds in flight, and the nights were for reading novels, or charting the long slow passage of the moon and constellations. An occasional splurge at a Key Largo restaurant.

For Thorn, none of the vitality had leaked away from the rituals. He did what he did, then did it again the next day, but it never seemed monotonous. Always a familiar newness, a steady, growing pleasure. He thought of his routine as an endless perfecting of what was already very, very good.

He watched Darcy dive into the calm waters. Watched her fins wave in the air for a moment as her body sank. Hearing again what she'd said a few moments ago. Wanting her own turf, her own private challenges. He'd cringed when she'd said it. Sounded like the preamble to a parting speech. But now, he felt fine. Her kiss had done that. There was no doubt in that kiss. No uneasiness. None whatsoever.

Thorn turned away and cast again, planting it delicately in front of a large shadow. He watched the fly sink slowly through the surface of the brilliant water. He watched the shadow approaching, quickly taking shape, becoming bright silver, a tarpon, a massive fish, whisking past the bait, past the bow of the boat, on its way out to sea.

He watched it go, then watched it begin slowly to veer to the right, ten yards ahead of the boat, peeling off its course into a wide arc. Beginning a cautious circle back.

Apparently Thorn's fly had registered somewhere inside the great fish, a small prick of curiosity. A faint hunger. Growing as the fish turned, as it fought against its suspicions, the itch deepening in it, becoming something else perhaps, a craving, a desire so strong, it could only be satisfied by gulping down that object of its fascination, that bright, tantalizing tuft of fur with its gleaming, hidden hook.

CHAPTER 2

DARCY FLOATED ON THE SURFACE AND WATCHED THE LOBSTER'S ANTENNAE wiggle at the base of a big mound of brain coral. Twenty feet of water between her and the critter. At that depth, she'd have about thirty seconds to tickle the lobster out of its cave and get it into her bag before her breath ran out and she'd have to kick back to the surface.

She seemed to recall a time when she could have lasted more than a minute down there, twenty years ago, a girl of fifteen, many afternoons like this one, out on the reef with Thorn and Sugarman and her brother Gaeton, everyone staying down it seemed like hours on one breath. But no doubt that was a trick of recollection. Nostalgia giving things an expansive glow.

The hard truth was she'd never been able to hold her breath long enough to catch the wiliest lobsters. Two grabs was about all she could manage, then it was back to the surface for another gulp of air. Though Thorn was something else again. When he dived, he never seemed to gulp any extra air, just nonchalantly ducked his head under and dove and stayed down and stayed down and stayed down some more. Darcy would go back to the surface, gasp a few times, drag in another breath and come down again, and that damn Thorn would still be down there from the first breath, snaking his arm deep into some hole, coming out with another crawfish.

She could never match that, but then neither could Sugarman or Gaeton. Thorn had something special, a gift, some biological quirk that let him stay under longer than anybody she'd ever met. None of them ever put a clock on him, but she guessed he could manage somewhere near two minutes, like those pearl divers in Japan or something.

When they kidded him about it, Thorn would just shrug. Give some silly explanation. Once Sugarman claimed that Thorn didn't have to hold his breath like normal people because the guy'd eaten so many fish, he'd mutated into one, grown gills in his armpits. He'd take a stroke, extract some oxygen, take another stroke, more oxygen. *Hey, Thorn, raise your arms, let's check this out.* And Darcy could picture it. All of them on Gaeton's boat, gathering around Thorn, while slowly, theatrically, he lifted his arms, everybody coming in close, and Sugarman poked through the hair under his arms. Then Gaeton gasped. *Holy shit, it's true, look!* Darcy screamed, and everybody broke up.

When they were calmed down again, Thorn said, "Okay, if you must know. The secret of staying down so long is just not to think about it. Do it, but don't think about it."

As soon as he said that, Darcy knew it was the answer. And now that she understood Thorn a whole lot better, she saw there were a lot of other things Thorn didn't think about, and usually they turned out to be the exact things he was good at. Awfully good sometimes. A skill she'd never had, turning off the thoughts, doing something with her mind dead silent.

Maybe she should try it just then, just glide through that twenty feet of water, leisurely fetch up that damn lobster, the one that was waving its antennae at her, beckoning her down, and no matter how long it took, she wouldn't think once about the pressure, the burn in her lungs.

She raised her head, looked over at Thorn on the skiff. He was casting his fly off the other side. Giving it that wave, that elegant loopy undulation he had, whipping it back and forth like snapping a bullwhip in slow motion, then floating the fly out onto the still water, and though she couldn't see from here, she bet the line drifted down so quietly, it wouldn't leave a ripple.

He turned slightly, and noticed her watching him, and called over to her. Asked if she'd seen anything down below.

"That big bug again," she said. "Hiding in a crevice under some brain coral."

"Well, whatta you waiting for?"

She snugged her mask into place, still looking at him.

He raised his arm and made a sweeping gesture toward the horizon, smiling out at the amazing day. She nodded that she saw it too, then she fit the snorkel in her mouth, took a bite on it, looked back down through the water to get her bearings.

It was slack tide, so she hadn't moved, still hovering above the same patch of brain coral. From her right, a school of violet wrasse closed in on her, ten thousand inch-long fish, moving in one sinuous cluster. They swam toward her, parted, turned the water lavender, and slid by. She felt the tickle of their passing.

Christ Almighty, no matter how many times she came out here, every day was another amazement, always new configurations. Thousands of flecks of color endlessly shifting and rearranging. The light sliding up and down its brightness scale. Forever unique, a motley dance of tints and shapes, tranquil motions and blurs of speed. The fan coral stirring, the schools of angels, grunts, and mackerel, butterfly fish, and snapper, a lone shark cruising past, the gold and yellow twists of elk horn and fire coral and basket sponge.

For the million million fish in these warm clear waters, this hundred miles of reef was mating ground and feeding ground and stalking ground, a place of grace and danger and endless energy. Of course, these days everyone knew the reef was dying. Darcy had watched it decline for three decades now, its vivid colors dulling, the fish not nearly as dense or varied. The water cloudier. Too much traffic out here, jerks dropping their anchors on the fragile coral, more jerks breaking off in a second what took a century to create, too much sewage runoff fertilizing the algae growth, too many humans cramming the shoreline, dribbling their oils into the bays and canals and sounds that led out to sea.

She floated on her belly, watching those antennae wave, a small school of jack crevalle and blue runners, a medium-size nurse shark, a leopard ray fluttering along the sandy patch below, angelfish and hogfish and warsaw grouper—and yes, it was true, the reef seemed healthy enough. At moments like this, listening to her own breath rasp in and out of the snorkel, watching the million winks of color, the possibility of losing the reef seemed like some incredibly distant concern. On par with the death of the sun.

That was the problem. It happened so slowly, it was hard to register. An antler of coral gone from one spot, and months later some yellow tube sponge turning white and shriveling in another place, and a while after that, the filter-feeding gorgonia, a soft relative of the coral, began to droop, and its thousand filigree pieces fell slowly away.

You had to come here every day for years. You had to have a sharp memory, an eye for detail; you had to continually match the past against the present. So, for a tourist diver, out for an hour or so for one afternoon, there was no way to detect the loss or sense the immense calamity that was taking place. To them it all seemed marvelous, rich and plentiful.

Lifting her head, she looked back at Thorn, still fishing, contented. Then as she peered down again at the lobster, she sensed something passing by her, some large presence just out of the edge of her narrow peripheral vision. She jerked her head to the right, then left, scanned the water slowly all the way around her, but saw nothing.

Blowing out a hard breath, she turned onto her back, spit out her snorkel, floating for a moment to calm herself. Because this had happened before. In fact, almost every time she'd come to the reef lately she'd had another mild panic attack. Perhaps it was just another feature of middle age, some new tendency to imagine the twelve-foot white shark stalking her from behind. Time's finned chariot. Wherever it came from, it pissed her off. It wasn't like her to be spooked. Not like her to feel anything but peacefulness out on the reef.

She pressed the mask back into place, took the snorkel in her mouth, and turned back onto her stomach. She located the antennae again, then, without hyperventilating as she usually did, Darcy simply slid her face below the water, trying to imitate Thorn, see if that had any effect, and she coasted downward through the water with a slow easy flutter of her flippers.

She had a nylon net tied around her waist, a measuring caliper tied to that. She wore thick-weave yellow gloves on both hands, and she carried the same tickle stick she'd used for the last few lobster seasons, a two-foot aluminum poker with a slight bend at the business end. And as always, she wore the eight-inch Medlon knife in a plastic scabbard at her ankle. She'd taken a lot of kidding about that knife over the years: Darcy, the Navy SEAL, off to slit some throats. But she couldn't count all the times it had come in incredibly handy, those same people suddenly grateful she'd worn it. She'd used it to cut a ton of fishing line wrapped around propellers, or to pry anchor lines from craggy rocks. She'd sliced fishing plugs from mangrove limbs, performed numerous minor shipboard surgeries. Not to mention opening countless bottles of beer.

Now as she swam downward, she kept her eyes trained on those two large antennae sticking out from beneath the brain coral. If it was the same monster she'd seen twice this morning, then this time it was a hell of a lot more exposed than it had been. Getting overconfident maybe. Swaggering.

The thing was big enough, it could have been ten or fifteen years old. Which meant it was crafty—had to be to survive that long, to avoid the hordes of divers, and all those lobster pots. It knew the tricks, knew which pulse of water was friendly, which was deadly. She was certain she wasn't the first diver to spot it and try to snatch it out of its watery world.

As she reached the sandy floor, she pinched her nose and cleared the pressure in her ears. And then gave two strong kicks and was just above the antennae. Her flippers swirled up a little sand, made the water milky. But the critter seemed to have lost his earlier caution. Sleeping maybe, digesting some piece of gristle it had scrounged.

In any case, she didn't wait for it to sense her, but angled the tickle stick to the lobster's front end and eased her free hand in behind it. She poked it with the stick, and just as it was supposed to do, it skittered backward into her hand and she gripped it hard, and then just as suddenly it kicked free.

She pushed away from the rock, her chest beginning to ache. She twisted around and swam down against the buoyancy to see beneath the coral. It was there. Wedged backward as far as it could go inside a small crevice in the rock, its antennae working hard now, waving like a pair of fencing foils.

She let the buoyancy lift her, kicked once on the way back up. In no hurry really, but when she broke through the surface, she spit out the snorkel and dragged down a long gasp, and another. That was her limit these days, less than a minute. Lifting her mask up to her forehead, she treaded water, got back her breath. Glancing over at Thorn, his back to her, something big on his line. Good for him.

She snugged her mask back in place, bit down on her snorkel, found the fit. This time she used her own method. She took three measured breaths, blew them out, and sucked in a bigger one and curled over and swam through the silky water toward that wall of limestone beside the brain coral.

The wall was honeycombed with shadowy openings, and it took her some moments to locate the crevice the lobster had chosen. As a squadron of angelfish floated past, she gave a couple of strong kicks and plunged her right hand into the lobster's hole, a narrow, ragged slot in the rock, going inside it up to her elbow.

And she had it. Gripping it hard this time, she held on against its thrashing and began to draw it out. But the hole was too narrow. It wouldn't pass through. The lobster knew the way in, but there was some subtle tilt and slant required to pass through the narrow notch. The critter flipped in her hand as she twisted it this way and that. The flesh at her wrist burned each time she scraped her arm against the rim of the hole.

Like trying to work a house key free of a difficult lock. Some mesh existed, she was sure of it, but she was never good at that problem, had to step aside a few times over the years and let the man do it. Resenting it, but it was simply not a skill she had.

Darcy felt the pressure growing in her chest. She tried to extract the thing twice more, but it wasn't going to happen. And now a large moray had come out of its hole, showing three feet of itself, mouth open. Probably just display. Puffing itself up to frighten this invader from the other world, this creature that was stirring up the bottom.

Darcy let the lobster go. And began to slide her arm out of the slot, but her hand caught. She paused, fought back a stab of panic. Willed herself to relax, to soften the tissue and muscle, to ease her hand out of that slot of stone. For after all, it had gone in. But it didn't work. Her hand seemed to have swollen to twice its size. She couldn't find the fit.

This had happened to Gaeton once when he was just a kid. His hand caught in a cleft of rock; he was badly skinned, but had worked himself free. Afterward he'd said the trick was to be as limp as possible.

So she willed herself to go slack. The ache in her chest was growing. She tried every angle, every push and pressure, but her hand was trapped, numbing now, and a mist of darkness was rising from the lobster's hole. Her own blood leaking into the water.

She'd been down more than a minute, approaching two perhaps. She fought the terror rising inside her, twisted around, brought her feet against the rock, planted them, tried to straighten her legs, wrench her hand free, but the edges of her vision began to wrinkle and darken from the pain.

She blew out the last bubble of air in her lungs, and stared helplessly at the bright surface above her. A small hammerhead cruised overhead, its eyes moving on the stalks. It dallied for a second, sampling her blood, then in a rush it disappeared.

Darcy bent forward, reached her left hand to her right leg and drew her knife from the scabbard. Again she tried to calm herself, bringing a shoulder down, trying to glimpse the opening in the rock where her hand was caught. Her blood beginning to rise from the hole in darker shades. And her hand was completely numb. There was no more time.

She hacked with the knife at the rock around her wrist, broke small pebbles of it loose. She pulled hard, but still she was caught. She stopped. Stilled herself. Brought her face close to the rock where her arm was stuck. Peered into the opening, and nearly fainted at what she saw.

A white-gloved hand gripped her fingers, holding them in some strange handlock. Then above her she saw the thin trail of bubbles from an air tank rising from the other side of the lobster's hole.

Fluttering her fins madly now, she tried again to wrench herself from this grip. But it didn't budge. And in a flood of panic, she brought her feet back, once again planted them against the rock, and with all her strength she thrust upward, tried to straighten. But the person behind the wall simply found a tighter clasp.

Again, she brought her face to the hole. Sighting on the white-gloved hand, she lifted the knife blade and stabbed. Slashed across the knuckles of the glove, drew a cloud of blood. But she wasn't sure, it might've been her own.

A large burst of air bubbles rose from the other side of the rock, and the diver pulled Darcy's arm even deeper inside the hole.

The light had begun to dim. And Darcy felt a sudden rush of calm. Her muscles relaxed. Overhead, she watched a hogfish swim through her blood, its lips working. She stared up through that twenty feet of water toward the luminous surface, and she saw a large tarpon on Thorn's line, running from the boat, launching itself into the air, and then a splash almost directly above her.

She swallowed back the pain in her chest, focused her eyes on the brightness above. She composed a short, wordless prayer, and looked around her one more time at the bright colors, the delicate, twisted corals.

With all her strength she jerked against the grip, straining so hard she took an involuntary breath. And choked. And it was as if the sun had passed behind a thick mass of cumuli. The water darkening, and suddenly cooler. Everything slowing, as her body stopped writhing, gradually went slack. And long empty moments passed until finally she realized she was free.

Free from the tight fit, free from everything. Her lungs full of rich, cool seawater. And as she rose, yellowtail snapper, grouper, soldierfish, angels and spadefish, and glasseyes schooled around her. And then a cluster of strange red fish she'd never seen before swarmed past. The water filled with fish. Every color, shape, and size stitching back and forth, amazing numbers of them. Their eyes watching her as she rose and rose through the bubbles of air, as she rose through a bright mist of glassy minnows, millions of them, millions, the sea crowded with fish, and everywhere there were eyes, transparent, like bubbles in blue water, eyes watching her as she rose, as Darcy Richards drifted up toward the impossible sky above.

CHAPTER 3

TO THE WEST THE GRADY WHITE MADE A SLOW, WIDE CIRCLE, THEN SURGED up onto plane and headed back toward shore. Thorn watched it go, watched its wake spread out, come in slow, shallow ripples in their direction. The skiff rocked lightly. The ice shifted in the cooler.

Then something told him to look over his shoulder. Some nagging peripheral awareness that things weren't right. The tarpon at that moment making still another run in front of him, taking almost all the line, heating up the bearings in his reel, then exploding out of the calm water, a spiral of silver, a gush of brilliant water, the fish standing on its tail for an extraordinary instant, and at that second Thorn pulled his eyes from the marvel of the fish suspended in air, and behind him he saw Darcy on her back in the water, mask askew. It was clear she was not basking in the sun after a long dive.

As the tarpon splashed back down, he dropped his rod. The fish sped away, pulling the line taut, and the rod clattered across the deck, smacked the rail, and flew overboard, the big fish taking it under. Thorn stared at Darcy, waiting for her to lift her head, start to tread water, smile over at him, hoping this was not what it looked like. But none of that happened, none of it, and Thorn sucked down a breath, took a quick step, and dove over the gunwale toward her body, toward the spreading shadow of red hovering around her.

He lay her body on the bow deck, tipped her head back, pulling her jawbone down, peering inside her mouth for obstructions. Then he pinched her nose, his lips to her lips, blowing into her as hard as he could. Blowing as he tried to calm himself, make sure this was right, the way he'd seen it done. Then leaning his weight heavily on her chest to make the heart squeeze blood, and repeating it, repeating it, gradually finding a rhythm, adjusting to a more and more natural cycle. He kneeled beside her, the blood from the gashes on her wrists spreading across the deck.

For some absurd reason while he worked on her, while he fought off the panic, he pictured the tarpon swimming away, hauling his rod and reel, towing it out miles and miles through the peaceful ocean, the water rushing over the big fish's gills, bubbles of oxygen churning in its wake, as the fish turned downward, sounding into the dark depths, towing Thorn's graphite rod behind him, this man-made thing, this unnatural, preposterous thing chasing the fish deeper into the cold water, into the rapturous channels of the sea. Thorn following the tarpon in his head while he breathed into Darcy Richards, while the fish dove into bleaker and bleaker water, trying to break free of the terrible weight it dragged behind it. All the while the fish breathed the water. Breathed the water.

And something happened in Darcy's throat, a hitch, then a sloppy cough. Thorn pulled away in time, and she gagged up a quart of seawater. And when she was through, he brought his face back down, sealed her mouth with his, breathed in, and with both hands pressing against her sternum, he forced her chest down hard. Got another trickle of water from her lips, and she began to breathe on her own. A troubled rhythm, feeble. But she was managing it herself.

He waited a few seconds, watching her continue her meager breathing. When he was fairly sure she didn't need him anymore, he hustled to the console, switched on the VHF to channel sixteen, and called Mayday. After half a minute he raised a charter captain and gave him a quick picture of the situation, and lined up an ambulance for the docks at Snake Creek Marina, the closest landfall, and he dropped the microphone and hurried back to her body.

Her chest had gone still again. And Thorn dropped to his knees and again he breathed into her. Mouth to her mouth, very careful, as if he were making love to the dwindling life inside her, as if each wary breath were exhaled against some fluttering flame. Too much wind would blow it out, too little would starve it. Trying to coax that glowing wick, bring it back.

Five minutes, ten. Dizzy, sweating heavily, he pulled away, checked the pulse at her throat. Watched her chest for any movement. But there was none. Her lungs wouldn't restart, her heart was quiet.

He pressed hard against her chest and spoke her name, stroked her cheek, but she gave no sign she heard. Her eyes were closed, the muscles in her face lax, as if she were listening intently to some blissful inner choir. Music more alluring than anything this world had to offer. Almost a smile on her lips.

In Thorn's throat a hot swell had begun to ripen as if an enormous blister were growing on his larynx. His head was heavy and he felt like he'd gone for days without sleep. He spoke her name again, trying for the tone he'd used once or twice to awaken her from nightmares. Darcy. Darcy.

But it had no effect. No effect at all.

At Snake Creek Marina, Sylvie and her father, Harden, relaxed at a stone picnic table at the outdoor grill. Fish sandwiches, cole slaw, fries, draft beer in plastic glasses, that kind of place. Both of them wearing bathing suits, Sylvie's a black one-piece,

Harden in dark green baggies. A pair of binoculars lay on the table. Sylvie was sitting backward on the bench, leaning against the table as she watched the excitement.

The EMS truck with red light whirling, the stretcher, the two young paramedics, and the tall, rangy blond man hurrying after the rescue guys as they wheeled the stretcher from the blond man's boat to the ambulance. Sylvie took a sip of her beer and watched the guys load the stretcher in the EMS truck.

The blond man was good-looking in a rough-and-tumble way. Scraggly Prince Valiant hair, dark tan. He had a fluid, athletic way of walking, agile and limber. And with that kind of coloring he probably had blue eyes, though Sylvie couldn't tell for sure at such a distance.

"Tragedies," she said. "There's no escaping. They're everywhere. You can't sit down, have a beer without death rolling past."

Sylvie watched the blond man climb into the ambulance and kneel beside the stretcher.

Her father glanced at her, had another sip of his beer and set it down. He picked up the binoculars and brought them to his eyes, focusing on the one-story concrete building across the channel.

After the EMS truck was gone, Sylvie turned around on the bench and followed Harden's gaze across Snake Creek. At this distance all she could make out was the comings and goings of the commercial fishing boats, big lumbering dirty things, and men rolling loaded dollies up and down the concrete ramp, a small winch regularly lifting crates of lobsters and fish out of the boats and swinging them up to the dock. There was a sign hanging above the double back doors. In bold black letters it read, ALBRIGHT'S FISH HOUSE. SUCCULENCE FROM THE SEA.

"And you," Sylvie said. "You're another tragedy. A grown man, obsessing like this. It's embarrassing. It's goddamn sad."

He lowered the binoculars for a second and gave her a long, empty look.

"Someday may you be so lucky to love someone as deeply as I love her."

"Is that what you call it? Love? Hell, it looks more like the heroin jitters to me."

Sylvie was twenty-five years old, though people regularly mistook her for seven, eight years younger. She had black hair, which she hacked off every week or two with pinking shears. Short like a boy's, or Mia Farrow's back in the old days. Looked like she ducked her head into a food processor, turned it on puree.

Nothing a normal woman would do to her hair. But then, Sylvie wasn't a woman, normal or otherwise. She didn't fuss with her nails. Had no interest in dresses or skirts, clothes of any kind. Mainly wore Harden's old castoffs. Though some nights she'd slip into something one of her boyfriends gave her and head out to the bars. Trolling clothes. She wasn't any kind of cook or house cleaner either. Didn't crave a baby, sure as hell didn't have any appetite for a husband, a man snoring away next to her every night the rest of her days. Lipstick, eye shadow, mascara, hell, she hardly knew one from the other. Never played with dolls, never wanted to ride a horse.

But on the other hand, she wasn't any tomboy either. Hell, she had no desire to be a man, some snot-slinging, boozing, vine-swinging ape. Sylvie Winchester thought of herself as a brand-new evolutionary development. Sylvie, the missing link, an early stage of what was coming. Neither sex. Sexless.

She'd never even had a menstrual period. The years when all that should have started were just too stressful. Her body seemed to know she couldn't handle one more problem. So no fat accumulated, her breasts never budded, her hips stayed narrow. Sylvie, the girl with no sex. Yet somehow certain men found her irresistible. Sylvie could make them steam. Could make ribbons of drool hang from their mouths. God only knew why.

Harden had enough sexual energy for both of them. Still burning for that one woman from years ago. Something between them once, something hot and dangerous, but finally she'd run off. But that didn't seem to matter to Harden. Here he was, fifteen years later, still devoting himself to her from afar. Making the hundred-mile trip from the Gulf coast to Key Largo twice a month to sit at this same marina, or down the street from her house, waiting to get a glimpse of her. Pathetic.

Harden was handsome enough, he could've had almost any woman in the world. He kept himself in damn good shape for sixty-one, his balding head tanned as dark and gleaming as a coffee bean, with a fringe of gray hair he kept bristle-short. An inch or two over six feet, lean, wide shoulders. When he worked, the muscle strands rose and twisted in his arms and stomach, like snakes crawling for cover, hard and sinewy.

Back home on the farm, he went without his shirt all day every day, working outside, and his shoulders and back were a coppery gold. He let his beard grow just long enough so it wasn't stubble, the same silvery gray as the hair on his chest and arms. There was a glitter in his gray Scottish eyes, and he had a roguish smile that Sylvie had watched him use to bring ladies to their feet across a crowded barroom. He was the kind of man who knew how to touch a woman, how long, and where. Sylvie knew that because she'd seen all those women come out of Harden's bedroom in the morning, float into the kitchen, the mellow looks on their faces, hear the slow, honeyed voices they spoke in, not at all how they'd acted the night before.

Her father claimed he had no real interest in those women. "Keeping in practice" was what he said he was doing. Keeping his blade sharp, his technique up-to-date, to stay ready for Doris Albright.

Married, single, rich, poor, he could talk any one of them out of her cocktail dress or blue jeans in a Miami minute. He could be trashy or a gentleman, whatever was called for. And there were probably a thousand women who would've gladly taken Doris Albright's place. But no, Harden couldn't manage that.

"She's wearing pink today. She always looked good in pink."

Sylvie groaned.

Harden said, "Has her hair pinned up. Same way she used to wear it when I'd come home on leave."

"You see her husband over there anywhere?"

Harden lowered the binoculars and glared at her.

Sylvie stood up, ran a hand through her butchered hair.

"I'm ready to go back to the motel. I'm tired."

Harden lifted the binoculars again, steadied his elbows against the stone table, and trained the lenses on the fish house.

"Pink shorts and a pink jersey top," he said. "Pink's definitely her color. Soft, feminine."

"Pink," Sylvie said. "The color of open wounds."

"Don't talk like that."

"What you're seeing, it's a ghost, Daddy. A pink ghost."

Harden ignored her, kept the binoculars trained on the fish house, his breathing changed now, slower, deeper, a quiet vibration filling the air around him.

"You want to look, Sylvie? See your mother?"

"Maybe some other time. About ninety years from now."

Sylvie downed the rest of her beer. Looked around the dock for something to capture her attention. Just tourists coming and going, people renting boats, starting them up, heading off to the reef. A couple of the ponytailed riffraff sitting on the seawall, drinking beer from cans, ogling the pretty tourist girls. One of them kept glancing her way. God help the poor bastard.

She looked back at her father, still spying on the woman in pink. His body throbbing like a plucked string. All around him, the air filled with something like the hum of a frayed power line.

If that was the look of love, Sylvie wanted no part of it. She'd settle for something less hazardous, something that didn't turn the blood to vapor. Love was just going to have to be another thing she'd miss out on, one more major life experience she'd have to get along without. Like some paradise everyone raved and raved about, but that would always remain a blank continent on the map inside her.

"I'm ready to go," she said. "You coming?"

Sylvie got up and walked across the parking lot to the red '83

Oldsmobile and got inside it. And though it was in the mid-nineties, with the humidity about there too, she left the windows rolled up. She didn't mind sweating. It felt purifying, her body distilling away the unessential fluids.

Maybe if her father took a very long time getting back to the car, she might even sweat away entirely, like a Popsicle held up to the sun. Maybe that was possible. Death from sweating. Harden comes to the car and Sylvie isn't there. No sign of her. Only a small oily puddle on the floor mat. Hell, when she thought about it, considered the other options, it didn't seem that bad a way to die. Just melt and evaporate. Turn into a cloud.

Now, there was a good idea. A cloud. Every few seconds Sylvie could assume a new shape. And all around the world people would be lying out in meadows looking up at the sky as Sylvie rolled by, all of them seeing a new thing every few seconds. Now look, it's an alligator, now it's a moose, now it's Santa Claus, now a rocket ship.

Yeah, that was good. Sylvie the cloud.

Sylvie the cumulus.

CHAPTER 4

"YOU SHOULD EAT SOMETHING, THORN. GET SOME GREASE IN THERE, SOAK up some of that tequila."

Sugarman slid the plate of conch fritters in front of him.

Thorn looked down at the plate for a second, the eight round doughy balls gleaming with oil, the small paper cup of cocktail sauce, another of mustard, all of it arranged neatly on a bed of lettuce. Thorn slowly raised his hand, caught the lady bartender's attention and twirled his pointing finger in the air. She came over. A young woman, late twenties, black hair to the middle of her back.

"Another, please, ma'am."

When the bartender left, Thorn let his head loll to the side and pressed his nose to his shoulder and took a long sniff. He choked out a cough and felt his stomach begin to empty. He sat up abruptly, took hold of the bar, straightened his spine, and willed it back down.

"You okay?"

Thorn swallowed, looked at Sugarman.

"I don't smell like myself."

"Or look like yourself, or act like yourself."

Thorn pressed his nose again to his shoulder.

"I stink," he said, "therefore I am."

Sugarman patted him on the shoulder.

"Shake it off, Thorn. Come on, let's get out of here."

"Hey, look, Sugar. When you lose the one goddamn thing in your life you care about, then maybe you can tell me something. Okay? But not till then. Till then, leave me the hell alone."

It was Sunday afternoon. Thorn had been drinking steadily since two o'clock yesterday, right after Darcy had been pronounced dead at Mariner's Hospital. Drinking at the Lorelei in Islamorada, drinking through the afternoon, through the evening, drinking, falling asleep with his head on the bar. Nobody bothering him. Waking up that morning at sunup, two other guys passed out at a picnic table nearby. Maybe the loves of their lives drowned as well.

The bar opened again at eight, Thorn washing his mouth out with a draft beer, then starting back with Cuervo Gold. In no hurry to go home, where Darcy's clothes hung in his closet, where her things mingled with his.

Sugarman was staring down into his draft beer, shaking his head sadly. He was dressed this morning in a peppermint-striped seersucker shirt, short-sleeved; tan pants; sandals. No longer wearing the uniform of the Monroe County Sheriff's Department, Sugar was out on his own, making clothing choices for the first time in a long time. Not real good at it yet either.

He was a handsome man. Sometimes, from the right angle, the guy was almost pretty. His father was Jamaican and his mother Norwegian. Thorn never met the father, but he clearly remembered Sugar's mother, a thin woman with wispy blond hair, pale, almost translucent skin. She'd given Sugarman her delicate face and long lashes. And he'd split the difference between mother and father in skin color. A golden toffee. In open sunlight, arm against arm, Thorn's tan was darker than Sugar's.

So there he was, Thorn's friend, that sleek, exotic, simple

man, drinking beer at the Lorelei Bar in his seersucker shirt, middle of the day, middle of August. Trying to console his inconsolable friend. His friend of more than thirty years. And at that moment, Thorn was fighting off the urge to push his old pal backward off his bar stool. To throw him to the ground, jump on his chest and pound his fists on Sugar's body, force his old friend, his great good buddy, to retaliate, to hit him till the blood came, batter and slam him till bones broke, flesh tore, till Thorn's body began to feel again.

A couple of teenaged girls passed by in scanty bathing suits. Thorn turned and watched them pass. One of them with red hair almost Darcy's shade, worn in a ponytail, bangs cut close to her eyes. Thorn wanting to shout out a warning to her, stay close to the shore, don't swim alone, don't stick your arm inside crevices of any kind. You can get your arm caught in there, you can drown. Wanting to follow her, dedicate himself to her protection. Man, oh, man, catching himself just in time.

Sugarman's hand was on his shoulder.

"Okay, Thorn. Come on, now, let's take it on home, buddy. All right? You ready? Here we go."

Sugarman stood up, tried to nudge Thorn off the stool.

The bartender set another drink in front of him, gave Sugarman a what-can-I-do look, and walked away. Thorn shrugged off Sugar's hand, lifted the drink to his lips and had another sip, wiped his mouth on his shirtsleeve, and set the glass carefully back onto the bar.

"I was fishing." Thorn closed his eyes, seeing it all again, the tarpon running, the graceful, silver launch. "I was jerking myself off with my fly rod, playing that fish while Darcy was down there going through who knows what kind of holy terror."

"Come on, man. You've had yourself a good wallow. Let's just give that the checkered flag."

"One day? That's all the time I get to wallow? One fucking day?"

Thorn threw back the rest of the tequila and slapped the glass down.

Sugarman looked away and took a good pull on his beer, set it down, and wiped his mouth with a napkin. He swiveled around and faced Thorn.

"I didn't want to tell you this now. Not here."

Thorn banged the glass on the bar a couple of times and looked for the bartender.

"Something's not right about her hand."

Thorn hesitated for a moment, replaying the words, then he set the shot glass down and thrust his hand out and grabbed hold of Sugarman's shirt and dragged him forward. He sputtered something, not sure himself what he was trying to say. And Sugarman gripped Thorn's wrist, used one of those cop tricks he had, twisting it hard. Thorn's hand came loose and his eyes watered with the pain.

Sugarman looked down at the front of his seersucker shirt and brushed the wrinkles out of it. Took a long, exasperated breath and released it.

"The damage to Darcy's hand," Sugarman said. "It isn't consistent with her being caught. It doesn't seem right."

Thorn stared at him, tried to focus, but got a double image. He blinked but saw only a bleary version of Sugarman.

"Not consistent? Not consistent with what?"

"Well, it wasn't just scrapes. There were also bruises on her wrist and fingers. Knife wounds too. And two fractures."

"Don't do this, Sugar. Don't make this any harder."

"I'm just telling you what I saw."

"Look, she was lobstering," Thorn said. "She got her hand caught in a crevice. A fucking lobster hole. It happens. Hell, she panicked, she was struggling for her life. There'd be bruises and cuts all over the place."

"Maybe," Sugarman said. "But more likely what you'd get, a hand pinched like that between rocks, you'd get a glove avulsion. At least a partial."

"What!"

"Glove avulsion. You see it when somebody gets their hand caught in the gears of a machine, something like that. They're pulling so hard, the flesh tears. It comes off in one piece, like a glove, leaves the skeleton of the hand, that's all, some tendons dangling or something."

Thorn said nothing. He swallowed and kept his eyes on Sugarman's.

"Same with wedding rings. You see it all the time, somebody jumping from the dock to their boat, their ring gets caught on a nail on the piling. Their body is on the boat, their finger is back there on the dock. Skins the flesh right off. Leaves the bone sticking out. It's why you don't see many paramedics wearing wedding rings."

"What the fuck, Sugar?"

"I'm saying, if her hand was caught between two pieces of rock, caught so bad she drowned because of it, you'd get different trauma than what we saw. These injuries looked like something else. Something that when you're in law enforcement you see on a fairly regular basis."

"Say it straight out, man."

"Like the hands of some of the dirtbags I used to bring in. Ones I had to forcibly restrain. A hand lock, a grip on their fingers, bending them back. Same kind of injuries. Broken fingers, in two places. Not at all what you'd expect if someone caught their hand in a crevice."

Thorn shook his head, trying to clear his eyes.

"Let's walk around," he said. "I need some air."

They meandered past the restaurant and marina, Thorn leading with his head down, feeling the slump of his shoulders, the weight of hours of drinking settling there. He led them out to the small, pathetic beach. A few tons of dirty sand that had to be replaced after every serious blow.

There were a couple of Jet Skis tearing up the calm water just beyond a roped-off swimming area. A few teenagers splashing around in the shallow water.

"Hate those fucking things," Thorn said, staring out at the Jet Skis.

"Asshole machines, I call them," Sugarman said. "Either

you're an asshole already and that's why you want to ride one, or else as soon as you set your butt on one you become an asshole."

Thorn stepped into the shade of a sabal palm, put his back against it and slid down till he was sitting in the sand. Sugarman crouched down beside him. He scooped up a handful of sand and let it run through his fingers.

"You're telling me," he said, "somebody had hold of her? Someone drowned Darcy?"

"Were there other boats out there? Did you notice?"

Thorn thought about it, trying to picture it again.

"One," he said. "A few hundred yards away. I didn't get a great look at it. A Grady White. Twenty footer, twenty-two maybe. Open fisherman."

Sugarman nodded.

"Now listen, Thorn. I may be way off base here. I don't know. But I'm just telling you how it looks to me. Her hand, that's all I'm basing this on. And I could be mistaken."

Thorn closed his eyes, listening to the blare of the Jet Skis, to the reggae coming from the tiki hut, to somebody's radio playing an old Beatles song down the beach. Someone screamed out in the water, a healthy libidinous scream. Someone thrilled by someone else. Someone tossing someone into the water. The kind of scream that was going to make Thorn hurt for a long time to come.

Before Darcy, Thorn had never known any kind of contentment with a woman. If it hadn't been for her he might never have discovered that delicate, tricky feeling where every body part, every bone and muscle and internal organ, was relaxed and poised at once. An intimacy with no games, no maneuverings, everything exposed. A sweet, sexy nirvana.

That's what she'd done for him. Two perfect years of her. The no-bullshit honesty, the luxurious ease in bed, the heat, a faultless fit of body and timing. Their mutual love of fish and sea. Their long conversations at night on the upstairs porch, wineglasses in their hands. The comfortable silences. A touch on the neck, mussing of hair. All that. Everything he had missed before her, he was now going to miss again.

"We gotta get you sobered up a little and over to the funeral home," Sugarman said. "Supposed to meet Ralph Mellon at two."

"Ralph who?"

"Dr. Ralph Mellon. Guy's with the M.E.'s office in Broward County. He and his family happened to be down in Big Pine vacationing this month. Old pal of Sheriff Rinks, apparently. So when I called Rinks this morning, told him what I suspected, he thought about it a second or two, then he said he'd call somebody he knew. Ten minutes later he phoned me back, said this Mellon guy was intrigued by the situation and agreed to help. According to Rinks, Mellon's one of the top pathologists in the state. Seen it all. He said if there's anybody who can give us an expert read on that hand, it's Dr. Ralph Mellon."

"Let's go."

"You sure you're up to it?"

"I'm a little drunk, is all."

"Well, hang on, Thorn, this isn't going to be easy."

"Sugar," he said, "I don't think any goddamn thing's going to be easy. Not for a long, long time."

CHAPTER 5

DR. RALPH MELLON WAS SIX FEET SEVEN INCHES TALL AND WEIGHED OVER three hundred pounds. Somewhere just past fifty, he had only a little of his curly blond hair left, but his beard was still prosperous. A tangled Mr. Natural growth, worn long enough to cover the knot in his tie, if he'd been wearing a tie and not the shiny flowered shirt opened to his gut. Garish pink hibiscus blooms covered the green shirt and the matching shorts. And when he waded into that dim mortuary vestibule, his big wife following in an identical outfit, the room suddenly seemed to be aglow in cheap neon.

Sugarman made the introductions. Sally Spencer, the longtime owner of the funeral home, was tall, blond, her face shadowy and sunken. Today in a white summer dress, pink Keds. When it came Thorn's turn, he put out his hand and Ralph Mellon swallowed it up in his big, soft catcher's mitt.

"I'm so glad I could be of help," he said in a grand and lazy Mississippi drawl. He stepped back, and one at a time, he made careful eye contact with Sally, Thorn, and Sugarman, as if he were taking their measure, cataloging each of them on some private rating system. "So," he said when he was finished. "Sandy Rinks tells me somebody has suspicions of foul play here."

"The victim's hand isn't right," Sugarman said.

"Oh, her hand's not right." The doctor smiled at his wife. A condescending grin for this layman's sloppy vocabulary. The two of them stood there beaming in their ridiculous flowered outfits, things she must've whipped up on her Singer for their summer holiday.

"So. Let's take a look, shall we?" the doctor said, and reached up and took a deep grip on his beard.

Sally led them down the somber hallway and pushed open the door at the end of it. Thorn had been there before. The small operating room lit to a painful brightness with fluorescent bulbs. The glossy white walls, the impeccable shelves lined with the materials of embalming, the stifling odor of antiseptic and exotic fluids. A chemical sting in the very cool air. And of course, the chrome surgical table, the body beneath the sheet.

As the group moved to the table, Thorn stayed behind the doctor's broad back and kept his eyes on Sugarman. Sugar's mouth was gritted hard, eyes blurred, looking down at Darcy as the doctor raised the sheet.

There was a difficult pause, then the doctor said, "Handsome woman."

"Ralph," his wife said, prompting him. And the doctor cleared his throat in a halfhearted apology.

He lifted Darcy Richards's right hand to the light, tipped his head at different angles, brought his eyes close. He flexed her fingers, mumbling to himself. Thorn kept out of range, shielding himself from Darcy's face with the big man's back. But he glimpsed her hand. The back of it was scuffed and bruised a bright yellowish purple. Five or six white puckers marked her wrist. Bloodless gashes where apparently she'd tried to hack herself free.

He felt his stomach turn.

"Well," the doctor said. "Well, well."

"What?" Thorn stepped around beside the man and got a sudden look at Darcy's face. It was bland and rubbery white, as though her skin had been scrubbed so hard it was cleansed of all traces of personality.

The doctor manipulated her hand for a moment or two longer, massaging it thoughtfully, feeling the structures below the flesh. Then he laid it down again, covered her over with the sheet, turned his back on the group and started for the door.

"Where the hell you going?" Thorn hustled over and put a hand on the man's beefy shoulder.

The doctor turned on him, looked down into his eyes. Despite the coolness of the room, the doctor's face was sweaty. A damp blond ringlet was glued against his forehead.

"I believe I'll make my report to Sheriff Rinks."

"What'd you see, Doc?" Thorn said quietly.

Maybe it was the hush he got into his voice, the lazy, feigned indifference of the dangerous lunatic. Or maybe the good doctor saw something in Thorn's eyes, some spike of lightning that was aimed his way. Whatever it was, it gave the big man a moment's uncertainty.

"What'd you see?" Thorn said again, almost whispering this time.

"Sir," he said, a thin mustache of perspiration growing on his upper lip. "There is fracturing in the condyloid joints and the phalanges of her two middle fingers. Multiple fractures, with what looks to me like severe socket damage. Does that mean anything to you?"

"She could do that to herself? Her hand caught in a narrow hole?"

The doctor studied Thorn for a moment as if looking for the faintest signs of intelligence, then raised his hand in the air and waved for them to follow. The group walked behind him down the narrow corridor into the foyer. When they had gathered there, Sally Spencer suggested they sit down in her office.

"Do you mind, ladies," the doctor said, "leaving us menfolk alone for a moment or two?"

When the men had shut the door behind them, the doctor settled on the big leather couch across from Sally's desk and motioned Thorn and Sugarman to nearby chairs, but neither of them moved. The doctor continued to sweat. His color was different. Whatever he'd seen in there was putting a kink in his bloodstream. His eyes were a pale blue, and seemed to have gotten vague and empty during the walk down the hallway.

Mellon combed his fingers through his beard and laid his vacant blue eyes on Thorn.

"You two boys vets? Spend time in the Asian jungles, did you?"

Neither of them spoke. Thorn giving the doctor the blankest look he owned. Let Ralph Mellon draw whatever conclusion he wanted. Thorn had been asked this secret-handshake question before, by men who used it as their sole measurement of worth. Was he one of those who wriggled down into the bowels of hell and were baptized in that slime and putrefaction? Because if he wasn't, he was not worth a thimbleful of their piss.

Thorn never tried to explain his lack of military service. He'd met enough Vietnam guys to know he'd missed the right war. Far as he was concerned, the ones who ran to Canada or burned their draft cards had earned themselves a statue in Washington just as much as the others had. As for Thorn, he'd not even known the war was going on until it was almost over, living as he always had, exposed to the weather and the seasons, focused on the migrations of fish and birds, but not the least aware of the dips and flashes of national events. So secluded, he had not even heard the name of that distant country until one night it came booming out of a jukebox in a bar down in Islamorada: *One, two, three, four, I don't give a damn. Next stop, Vietnam.*

They were dead wrong, of course, those vets who believed in the sacredness of what they'd learned in 'Nam. Hell, Thorn hadn't been to any wars, but he knew more than his share about civilian combat, the degradation, the savagery humans performed on one another. He knew betrayal and loss, he knew gore. He'd fought against an enemy he couldn't see, done it on battlegrounds without front lines, everyone out of uniform. He'd put himself in the line of fire. Felt the rip of lead through his flesh. He'd taken human life.

And he wasn't proud of any of it, didn't flaunt it, or test others with the grim knowledge he'd acquired. And he was absolutely certain of one thing—exposure to violence didn't confer any wisdom that mattered.

Dr. Ralph Mellon shifted himself on the leather couch.

"Am I to understand by your silence that you don't think highly of military service?"

Sugarman pulled one of the mourner's chairs away from Sally's desk, turned it around backward and straddled it. Thorn walked over to the office door and turned the dead bolt.

"You got anything on tap this afternoon?" he asked Sugar.

"Nothing pressing."

"Look, boys . . ."

Thorn said, "I don't believe I have any engagements till late next week."

"Ditto to that," said Sugar.

"Now, come on. Stop this."

"What'd you see?" said Sugar. In that cop voice he could still summon. Flat, empty, but with a little buzz hidden in it, like the sound of a dry fuse burning.

"I told you, boys, I'm going to have to speak to Sheriff Rinks about this."

Sally Spencer knocked on the office door. She called out their names, but no one responded. Ralph Mellon's wife came to the door and spoke his name with some concern, and the doctor called out that he was all right, just a minute more, staring bitterly at Thorn.

Five minutes later Sally knocked again. But no one moved. A few minutes after that Mellon's wife came around to the outside office window and rapped hard against the glass, pressing her nose to the glass. But Thorn went over and twisted the little rod for the blinds, and that was the last of Mrs. Mellon.

A minute or two later the doctor rose from the couch, and Sugarman stood up too, and he and Thorn blocked the doorway. Hands at their sides, giving the big man the unblinking stare. Mellon shook his head helplessly and took his seat again, saying as he sat that, by god, the sheriff was going to hear about this. False imprisonment, kidnapping. He'd make things rough on them if they didn't open the door right away. But Thorn looked over at Sugar, and Sugar looked back at him.

"You pissing on yourself?"

"Not yet," Sugarman said. "You?"

"Dry as bone," said Thorn.

Mellon harrumphed, wriggled his big butt against the leather, and seemed to settle in. Accepting the challenge.

It was three thirty-eight by Sally's cuckoo clock when they began their standoff. Thorn parked himself in her green leather swivel chair, rocked back, put his feet on the desk and his hands behind his head, staring across at Dr. Ralph Mellon. And he began to practice his well-cultivated skill of contemplation.

For over thirty years he'd been a fisherman of one stripe or another. He'd learned a lot about waiting. He knew how to disengage his mind, drift through a twilight of half-thoughts, a semidoze, while part of him was still wound tight and watchful. He knew how to sit, where to rest his hands, when to give himself the mild stimulations of memory or the stronger jolts of fantasy to keep the brain from shutting down completely.

For the first few minutes he let himself crave various forms of drink. And for a while after that he listened to the traffic out on U.S. 1. He thumped his thigh in time with different songs that played in his head. He kept his eyes on the doctor, the big man with his eyes on the rug, now and then shifting uneasily on the couch. And finally Thorn thought of Darcy Richards. Her body lying in that bright cool room twenty yards away. Her empty face.

Without destination he began to wander the time he'd known

her, before they were lovers, back when she was simply his close friend's tagalong little sister. Good with a spinning rod, mildly clairvoyant about locating fish, Darcy had been in his life for many years before she'd stirred his carnal feelings. He'd loved her as a sister before he'd loved her the other way.

At four fifteen Sally tried the door again, pleaded that she had a service ready to begin in thirty minutes and she absolutely needed to come into her office to get everything set up for it. Sugarman stood up, stretched, did a couple of toe touches. The doctor called out to Sally that he was being held hostage, and that Sally should call the sheriff and have him send help. When he'd finished, Sugarman told her to cancel that last message.

She was silent outside the door.

"You hear me, Sally?"

She hesitated a moment, then said, "I hear you, Sugar."

"We got to do this. Now, you help us, okay? Be cool."

"Okay," she said. "Okay, Sugar."

And Dr. Ralph Mellon crossed his arms over his big chest, settling into what looked a great deal like a teenage pout.

As the silence grew, Thorn thought some more about Darcy Richards. He snaked back through the last few weeks, began to prowl the hours, trying to locate the day, pinpoint as near as possible the exact moment when the worry had begun to settle in her smile and deaden it. At first he confused days with other days, then after much struggle he got things back in rough chronological order for a while. But a siren passed by out on the highway and Thorn lost his concentration and scattered the moments again into a crazy snarl. Finally, methodical and focused, he ticked backward through the last two weeks, day by careful day, narrowing it, and narrowing it some more, until at last, finally, he fixed it to a single weekend.

Yes, a weekend when she'd been very quiet. Uncommunicative. Thorn noticing but saying nothing. The first weekend of August. Lobster weekend, that madness happening all around them, the invasion of tourists, the gluttony, the orgy. Thorn in a cranky mood. Refusing to go out of the house till it was over. Yes. That was it, that weekend.

Thorn took a long breath. He watched Dr. Mellon sweat. He watched the light fluttering against the blinds. Listened to the big trucks boom past on the highway, carrying their heavy loads down those hundred miles of highway and bridges to Key West.

The first weekend in August. Darcy's eyes without sparkle, her head slumping a millimeter. Quiet, and at loose ends. Reading for a while, putting the book aside. Walking out onto the porch, looking off, searching the distances. Thorn with his flies, looping, knotting the bright strings, the tufts of fur and feather around the spines of steel hooks. Business as usual.

Darcy paced the house, picking up her book again, lying back with it propped before her, staring up at the ceiling. It was there in her face. It was so clearly there. She said nothing, but that shadow across her eyes, that nervous silence, it was unmistakable. So goddamn clear, now that he pictured it all again. He should have said something then, cut its head off before it grew huge around them and squeezed the air from their lives.

But no, Thorn had said nothing. Avoiding the problem. He'd had his lifetime dose of trouble already, and was in no hurry to whip up any more. And Darcy knew that. She knew he'd retreated again. Maybe she'd kept quiet about the problem not just because she wanted to solve it herself. Oh, maybe there was *some* of that. But some part of it had to have been to spare Thorn. So he could keep larking along.

At five twenty-five, with organ music and quiet singing coming from the chapel, the murmuring of voices from out in the foyer, Ralph Mellon took a long breath, blew out a harsh sigh, and rose to his feet in a great gush of primary colors.

"Okay," he said. "Enough is enough."

"So what was wrong with her hand?" Thorn said, bringing his feet down from the desk.

"You two," the doctor said. "You're crazy. Both of you."

"Good point," said Thorn. "Wouldn't you say, Sugar? We're all a little crazy down here in the Keys."

"It's the water," said Sugarman. "I think somebody's been dribbling something in the pipeline. Mescaline or something. It's turned us all into raving lunatics."

Mellon stepped out into the middle of the floor. He seemed to have grown softer in the three hours of sitting on the couch. To have lost some height, gotten pudgier, glands withering inside him.

"Okay, goddamn it."

"So tell us what you saw, Doc. In her hand."

"All right, all right," he said, veins crosshatching his temples. "Well, for one thing, your friend's assailant was not some ordinary, generic killer."

"How's that?" said Sugarman. Interested, not pressing too hard. Didn't want to frighten him into another three-hour pout.

"This particular hand lock," the doctor said. "I believe it could be the signature of someone who's had training."

"Go on," Thorn said.

"The killer crossed your friend's fingers very precisely, her two middle fingers. Then pressure was applied, probably with the killer's thumb, to the motor end-plate that lies between the scaphoid and the semilunar bones."

The doctor reached out for Thorn's hand, and Thorn stepped over and extended it. Mellon gripped his hand lightly, and pressed his thumb into a tender wedge of flesh just behind his knuckles, and Thorn winced as a jab of heat ran up his arm.

"Yes," the doctor said. "Something like this, I suspect, but executed with considerably more force and precision. All of which severely damaged the major efferent nerve fiber, the motor nerves that run the muscles in the hand and arm. In other words, gentlemen, the killer effectively paralyzed her right arm."

Thorn glanced at Sugarman, met his eyes. He wasn't sure about this guy. Like Thorn, Sugar didn't seem certain how much the doctor was playing with the truth here.

"What're we talking about?" Sugarman said. "A professional? Is that what you're saying?"

"Better than a professional," Dr. Mellon said, giving a tut-tut click of his tongue. Thorn drew his hand away from Mellon's grip. His fingers numb, tingling. "This is state-of-the-art. This is the kind of subtlety that is taught only at the very best schools. And I don't mean Harvard."

He tried an ingratiating smile, but it didn't catch on with either of them and gradually shriveled on Mellon's lips.

"So tell us, Ralph, just how do you know so goddamn much about state-of-the-art killing?" Thorn said. "You get a lot of that up there in Ft. Lauderdale, the old fogies knocking each other off with hand grips?"

The doctor took a long, slow taste of air, looked back and forth between Sugarman and Thorn. Then wistfully at the door. Stood there, hovering for a moment, sweating heavily now, his gaudy beach outfit starting to give off a faint reek of synthetic fiber B.O.

"Let's just say it's something of a hobby with me, studying martial art technique, the physiology of it."

Thorn smiled bleakly.

"Long day at the morgue, you come home and sit down with a martini and a good book on high-tech murder techniques."

Thorn looked over at Sugarman, shook his head in wonder. Then back at the doctor.

"Who're we talking about here, the CIA?"

The doctor clamped his mouth, glanced again at the door. He shook his head several times. Trapped by wackos. Muttering something to himself.

"Or maybe NSA, FBI," said Sugarman, the helpful cop. "Or one of the lesser-known abbreviations."

Thorn took a step, came within a short right jab of the doctor.

"Is that what you do, Mellon? You work for these guys? Show our boys where the pressure points are? Teach them how to be quick and quiet? Invent some new tricks, do you?"

"I consulted once or twice," he said. "Back in the sixties. Almost thirty years ago. That's all, nothing more than that."

"You fucking prick."

"Easy, Thorn," said Sugarman. His voice hypnotically slow, as though he were trying to coax a cobra back into its basket. "The doctor's just helping us out here. He's taking time off from his vacation to share with us his scientific expertise."

"This asshole trained people, Sugar. For all we know he taught this little finger trick to the guy that killed Darcy."

"That's not true," the doctor said. "I certainly did not teach anyone this hold."

He stepped past Thorn and moved to the door. Six seven, three hundred pounds of hibiscus. Thorn made a move for him, but Sugarman put a rough hand on his shoulder and held him.

The doctor unbolted the door, opened it. He turned around then, his face beginning to fill with color again, running through a small series of facial tics as if he were hastily reprogramming all those mannerisms of browbeating and pomposity he'd abandoned in the last few hours.

"I never saw this grip before," he said. "Because we didn't teach it. We weren't that sophisticated. Things have progressed since then. Apparently they've progressed quite a bit."

"Get out of here," Thorn said. "Get out of my sight."

The big man snorted, tasting freedom again, the old ways, and he eased out the door and pulled it closed behind him. Thorn kicked it the last inch shut, turned around and went over to one of the chairs and dropped into it. He stared up at Sugarman.

"Is he full of shit, or what?"

Sugarman shrugged.

"Rinks claims he's the best around. Major authority on all things postmortem. And hell, the government's been known to use medical people that way. Not that surprising, really."

"I'd like to make that asshole into something postmortem."

"Well, for right now," Sugarman said, "we got to get you home and halfway cleaned up. Wake's supposed to start at eight thirty. Unless you want to just call the whole damn thing off."

"No," he said. "I can handle it. I just need a drink or two; I'll be all right."

Just then the organ music swelled, vibrating through the cheap walls of the funeral home. They looked at each other and listened to it. A requiem Thorn didn't recognize. A slow gray hymn in a minor key. A melody some maestro had composed a century ago, for just such a day as this.

CHAPTER 6

SUNDAY EVENING, NINE THIRTY, AND SYLVIE WAS DRESSED IN ONE OF HER two bar outfits, the Key Largo one. Red spandex dress, hem at mid-thigh. So tight it looked like she'd been dipped in warm blood. Wearing a black five-gallon Stetson with a turquoise band, black cowboy boots that had red scrollwork, and earrings made of green stones, which dripped like candelabras from her ears and clicked when she turned her head. Looking cute. A bronco rider. A girl who could hang on tight, and given the chance, could dig in the spurs.

The country band was finishing a set when she walked into Snappers, a wood-frame bar and seafood joint two miles north of Tavernier on the ocean side. On her way across the empty dance floor heads turned, and male voices fell into the sex warble, sizing her up, her availability, her squirm potential. Coming to favorable conclusions, it sounded like to Sylvie.

She walked down the length of the bar, peering at their hands till she found what she was looking for. She stopped in front of two beefy ones in T-shirts and sunburns, and asked if the stool between them was taken. They made room for her.

The two of them had matching sunglasses hanging from leather straps around their necks, and each pair of dark glasses had those blinders on the sides. Easy prey. A couple of fishing guides, spending the night in a dark bar trying to get the sun-dazzle out of their eyes.

Sylvie perched herself up on the wooden stool, looked across at her reflection in the windows behind the bar. Gave her cowboy hat a slight tilt to the left. Smiled.

The lady bartender eased in front of her, gave the two fish guides an eye roll, then asked to see Sylvie's ID.

"Twenty-seven years old."

"I need to look at it, honey."

"You show me yours, I show you mine."

"Yeah," one of the guides said. "Let's see yours, Sharon."

"Twenty-five in October," said Sylvie. "October twelfth."

"She's legal, Sharon. Don't hassle the lady."

The blond fishing guide leaned his forearms against the bar and made eyes at the barmaid.

"Shot and a beer," Sylvie said. "Budweiser, Wild Turkey."

The bartender considered her for a moment, leaning forward and peering at her like she was trying to see if Sylvie had any breasts, which she didn't, even though the spandex was designed to push up all her extra chest flesh into the bra cups. That still didn't produce enough mass you could call breasts.

Down at the other end of the bar a waitress started calling out drink orders, and the barmaid frowned and went down there.

"You take that thing off just for tonight, or was it for good?"

"What?" the blond one said.

Sylvie tapped a fingernail against the guy's ring finger. A white fleshy stripe where his wedding ring used to be. The dent of the band still visible.

"Oh, that," the blond guy said. "That's gone for good."

"Damn right," his buddy said. "Fuck the bitch. Gone for good."

"What'd you do?" Sylvie said. "Screw around with other women? Drive her off?"

The two fishing guides glanced at each other; the dark-haired one shook his head and gave some kind of warning look to his buddy. Then the blond one muttered something back that Sylvie couldn't hear and his dark-haired buddy swigged the last of his beer, shook his head at his friend, glanced once more at Sylvie, and moved on down the bar to a group of rowdy guys throwing darts.

"Frank Witty," the fishing guide said.

"And I'm Sylvie," she said.

Frank put out his hand and they shook.

"And just how witty are you, Frank?"

"Not too," he said.

"Good," said Sylvie. "I prefer being the witty one."

He was looking at her with a mild heat growing in his eyes. Her outfit doing its job, her eyes holding on to his. Sylvie let her mouth come open a crack. Moved her tongue around inside her mouth just a little, exploring her teeth. The guy adjusted his breathing.

"You from around here?"

"No," she said. "I'm not from around anywhere."

"I sure haven't seen you in this dump before."

"Till tonight I hadn't sunk this low."

Frank smiled and Sylvie smiled back.

The bartender set Sylvie's shot glass and beer mug down in front of her, and the fishing guide reached into his wallet and pulled out some bills and gave them to her and she left.

"So why'd she leave you?" Sylvie said. "You unfaithful?"

"Hey, I just met you. That's personal stuff."

"I go for the throat," Sylvie said. "That bothers you, maybe you should play darts with your friends."

The blond guy glanced over at his buddies for a second or two. Then brought his face back around and looked right into her eyes and said, "She found another guy."

"Hurts you to admit it, doesn't it?"

"Damn right it does."

"You do anything to the guy? Fight him, anything like that?"

"I did, as a matter of fact."

Sylvie hummed her appreciation.

"You hurt him?"

"Not very much, no."

"He hurt you, Frank?"

"A black eye. Broke a tooth."

"Let me see."

Frank pulled back his lip with a thick finger and showed her an incisor that had lost its point. She took a sip of her beer.

"He must've cut his hand pretty bad on that tooth."

"Yeah, I guess I hurt him after all."

They both smiled. Getting along. On the same side.

"So what do you like, Frank Witty?"

"What's that mean?"

"You know what it means. What do you enjoy doing in your secret life?"

He thought for a second, then very quietly he said, "What? Like in the bedroom?"

"Any room. Doesn't have to be just in the bedroom. You can enjoy things all over the house. Outside even. Haven't you ever enjoyed a woman out in the tall grass before?"

Frank Witty didn't say anything. Overloaded. Brain on the fritz. Eyes getting hazy.

"So what do you enjoy, Frank? Come on, tell Miss Sylvie."

"I like lots of things."

"Name one."

He had another sip of his beer. Looked to his left and then his right. Brought his voice down.

"Something I do to her or something she does to me?"

"A thing she does to you. Something none of the other girls will do for you."

He had another swallow of beer, looked over at his friends again, then back at Sylvie, and leaned close to her.

"How much is this going to cost me?"

Sylvie drew in a patient breath.

"Frank, Frank, Frank. Is that how hard up you are? You looking to pay for some love and affection?"

"I'm sorry."

"You should be."

"I feel like an idiot."

"So tell me, Frank. What do you like her to do?"

Frank ran his finger around the rim of his beer glass. He
swallowed back a small belch.

Frank said, "Well, she could put her finger . . . You know.
Wiggle it around."

Sylvie looked at him for a moment. The guy trying to smile.

"A finger up your butt, that's what you like?"

He swallowed. Things happening too fast for Frank Witty, but
just the right speed for Sylvie. Two nights, three, that was all this
guy was going to take.

She said, "That drives you crazy, does it?"

Frank Witty stiffened and glanced around to see if anyone
had heard. Apparently not, because he leaned in again, getting
into Sylvie's breath stream. Taking her eyes off his, she reached
out, picked up her Wild Turkey, had a sip, and then a slug of
beer. Let go of a gasp of pleasure. Came back around so she was
smiling into his face.

"We have to talk about this here?" he said. His face with some
extra color now. Sweat growing on his forehead.

"This is where we are, Frank. Couldn't very well talk about it
somewhere else, 'cause this is where our bodies happen to be at
the moment. It's a law of physics, I believe."

"I meant, do you want to go somewhere else? Place where we
could . . . you know, talk private."

"Is that what you want, Frank? You a big talker, are you?"

"I can talk fine. I can do other things too."

"I bet you can. A big guy like you."

"Damn right, I can."

"Is that why she left you for the other guy? He a better talker
than you?"

Frank tightened his eyes.

With both hands Sylvie lifted off her cowboy hat and put it on the bar.

Frank Witty stared at her hair for a moment, then said, "What happened to you?"

"Nothing happened. That's my style. You don't like it?"

She mussed her hair.

"It's unusual. It's different."

Frank's buddies were looking over at the two of them now, and Sylvie leaned out around Frank, smiled at them, made guns of both her hands and fired off a half dozen rounds at them. The guys looked away.

Up on the stage, the country music group started in again. Some banjo music, then some guitar, a little bass. A fiddle. Noise building up.

"So, Frank, now you decided you don't like Sylvie anymore 'cause she's got an unusual haircut?"

"I didn't say that. It's just, I never saw hair like that before."

"I got a personal style," she said. "It's not your everyday look."

"No, it's not."

"What kind of hair do you like, Frank? Long, straight? Short, curly? Red, black, blond? What's your ideal?"

"It doesn't matter, the color."

"Black's okay? Like mine?"

"Black's good. Black's fine."

"How about length? What's your fantasy woman got?"

He thought about it for a moment, taking his eyes out of action. Then he swung back around, looked at her again and said, "Bangs across the front, and real long and straight, like hippie-chick hair, down to her butt. That's what I like."

"There's that butt thing again. You're a real butt-crazy guy, aren't you, Frank Witty? Just anal as hell."

Frank reached out abruptly and finished his beer. He set his beer glass down and rubbed a finger down each side of his nose like he was wiping the oil away.

"If Sylvie were to grow her hair down to her butt, would you like that? Would that turn you on?"

"It'd take a long time for you to do that."

"Oh, I'm young. I got years and years to grow my hair any length I want. It wouldn't take that long to get it to my butt. A few years, maybe. It grows fast. You like fast hair, Frank?"

"You're making fun of me," Frank said. "You asked me what kind of hair I liked and I told you and then you twist it around to call me an asshole. Mock me."

Sylvie smiled at him, put her left hand over his right.

"Are we arguing, Frank? Are we having our first big fight already?"

"Maybe I should go play darts."

But he didn't move his hand out from under Sylvie's.

"How about we go off somewhere, Frank? You and me and my finger? Somewhere out in the dark?"

"You're doing it again, making fun of me."

"I'm asking you if you want to go with me. Out into the night. Do you? Into the tall grass."

"Yeah, okay," he said. "I guess so."

"Okay? You guess so?" Sylvie shook her head. "You're a real passionate guy, Frank, aren't you? A real hot-blooded type."

Sylvie's hand was still resting on top of Frank's.

"I can be passionate."

"Sure, Frank, whatever you say. You're the expert on Frank Witty. I'm just learning."

"I don't like sarcasm," he said. "My wife was sarcastic and it drove me crazy. I could never tell for sure what she was saying. The bitch."

Sylvie slid her pointing finger between Frank's fingers. Drew it out again, snaked it back in, rubbing against the crotch between his fingers.

"Okay, then, I won't do that again. I won't be sarcastic with you. I respect your wishes. That's the kind of girl I am. You tell me what you like, what you don't, I can change to suit. Kind of like a cloud, Frank. Like a cumulus. Your own personal cumulus."

Frank looked at her, eyes drifting down her red spandex, then coming back up. The doubt dying away. No curves on Sylvie, just a stalk of a body. But it was doing something to Frank Witty.

He stared forward at the window that looked out at the small marina. He seemed to be looking into her reflection over there. Then he said her name aloud. Sylvie. Said it like he was getting used to the word in his mouth. Preparing himself to say it a lot more.

"But before we get any further along," she said, "you got to know one thing up front."

Frank cranked his head around, put his eyes back on hers. Looking anxious, probably thinking she was going to tell him she was diseased. The bluegrass band was starting to pick up speed and volume, so Sylvie leaned in close to Frank's ear and said, "I got a father."

He drew back, uncertain.

"So?"

"I thought I should tell you."

"A father?"

Sylvie nodded ominously. Sliding her finger back and forth between Frank Witty's fingers, increasing the pace.

"Everybody's got a father."

"Not like mine."

"He strict with you or something?"

"Strict," she said. "Yeah, you could call it that. Strict is a good word for it."

"Fuck him," Frank said. "Fuck your old man. You're an adult. You can do whatever the hell you want to."

Sylvie took her hand off Frank's. Two nights, three at most. This guy might even be willing to take a stab at it tonight. But hell, she didn't like to push things. Sex first, then when she had the guy drowsy and warm, she'd begin to whisper more about her daddy.

"You know how you can get rid of that thing?" Sylvie tapped the white rim of flesh where Frank's wedding ring had been. "There's only one surefire way I know of."

"How's that?"

"Get somebody to suck it," Sylvie said. "Have her suck and suck that finger till it's all tight and smooth again."

He looked at her for half a minute without breathing.

"Let's get out of here."

"Lights, camera, action." She smiled brightly, coming down off her stool, stepping away from Frank. She made her left fist into a camera, held it in front of her left eye, peeping through the opening in the middle of it, and with her right hand she pretended to crank the thing. Focusing it on Frank Witty. He stepped away from the bar, looking directly into her lens, then glancing nervously around at his pals.

"You coming, or what?"

"Oh, no, I'm not coming yet, Frank," Sylvie said, still cranking, squinting through her fist at him. "But believe me, once we get started, it won't take Miss Sylvie long."

She opened her hands and made the camera disappear. Then put her cowgirl hat back on, and followed Frank Witty across the dance floor and outside to the gravel parking lot to his blue Ford Bronco. Lights, camera.

Action.

CHAPTER 7

WHEN THORN WOKE MONDAY MORNING, HIS CEREBELLUM WAS TRAPPED inside someone else's skull. Way too tight a fit. And his bed was canted to the side, almost spilling Thorn onto the floor as he lifted himself upright to survey the room. Too much sunlight, too much heat, nothing in focus. He clenched his eyes and eased back down on the mattress. Chunks of brick filled his pillow, and overhead, the beams of his ceiling sweated dark insects. His mouth was caked with what felt like bits of clay and iron and his tongue had been breaded and left too long in the sun.

Groaning, he rolled onto his side, opened his eyes cautiously. Directly ahead of him outside his north window, there was a mockingbird on the branch of a sea grape. It was hopping in place, making small bleats of rage. As Thorn watched, the bird noticed him, and it turned, set itself firmly on the branch, leaned in Thorn's direction and shrieked like the rusty brakes of a locomotive.

Thorn sat up, dropped his legs over the edge of the bed. He leaned forward, lowering his head into his hands. He was naked, his clothes dumped in a pile near the door. Around him, his sheets were soaked and smelled as rank as old grave clothes. His hair was sticky. And now a helicopter had appeared inside his skull, and was trying to lift off with too heavy a load, its blades *whupping,* chipping at bone.

He kneaded his temples, and with the quiet focus of prayer, he willed the chopper away. He breathed carefully, holding himself still, groaning a mantra of self-loathing. And when he thought he had everything settled back into place, he stood.

All around the bedroom, their possessions were laid out neatly, exactly as they had been when the two of them had left this room Saturday morning. A shelf of books, fishing gear, clothes on hangers, lamps with nautical lamp shades, a horse conch they used as a door jam.

He gazed at it all as he padded toward the john. Everything in its normal place, but today the heartbeat was gone from it.

Behind him, the mockingbird screamed one more time and exploded into flight, off to torment some other late-morning sleeper. The helicopter, its *whup-whup* fading, also moved away into the soundless distance.

In the bathroom he swayed before the mirror, staring at his image. Eyes bloodshot and swollen. Deep gullies grooving his cheek, his flesh puffy, with a jaundiced tinge. His hair was wild and matted as if he'd gone for weeks without touching a comb to it. Looking wretched and unwell, but still better than he felt.

His hands wavered to the edges of the lavatory to steady himself, and he upended a plastic drinking cup. Looking down at the countertop, his hands crabbed and palsied, Thorn with great concentration managed to set it right.

And there beside the cup was her roll-on deodorant, her glass ashtray full of bobby pins, a clear plastic box crammed with lipstick and makeup. And next to the toothpaste was her hairbrush, with a tortoiseshell handle, dark bristles.

He stared at it for a moment. And when he gripped it by the handle and picked it up, and held Darcy's brush out before him, a cold shadow spread through his bowels. He felt the silence in the house, its pressure straining against his eardrums as though he'd sunk suddenly into the depths of a dark sea.

Snarled in the bristles were three strands of her honey-red hair. While he studied them, the hush deepened. And after a moment more, with numb fingers, Thorn plucked one of the hairs free. He set the brush down and pinched each end of the hair and stretched it taut. He held it up to the light coming through the transom window. The hair so sheer it might have been made of glass. Sheer but strong.

He wrapped it two, three, four times around his first finger, wrapped it as tight as it would go. Then closing his eyes, he rubbed that finger against his cheek and he tried to call up one sensation of her, the sound of her voice in the bed beside him, a snapshot of one of her many smiles. But there were too many moments jumbled, too many exquisite mornings waking warm beside her in the half-light, too many afternoons out of sight of land, the water stretching away brilliantly in every direction, and far too many evenings, grilling their catch, wine on the porch, books in bed, their shoulders touching as they read, and later, on so many nights, the books tumbling to the floor. Staying there till morning.

He unwrapped the hair from his finger, set it carefully on the counter. He picked up her brush again, lifted it, and ran it tentatively through his coarse hair. His eyes blurred and began to burn, and all at once he was there again in the skiff on that hot noon two days ago, fighting the tarpon, flushed with the pleasure of a tricky catch, turning around and seeing her, fifteen yards to the east of the boat, Darcy floating faceup, lifeless in the still water.

It was not the first time Thorn had been grazed by death. Oh, no. Apparently, he'd been born under the star of calamity. On the very day he was born, his parents were forced off the road by a drunk, and drowned in Lake Surprise. Though somehow baby Thorn had managed to survive. And then, just a few years back, his adoptive mother, Kate Truman, was murdered by a gang of jackals who had wanted to bulldoze the last hundred acres of wilderness in Key Largo. Kate fought them hard and openly, and lost her life in the process. Thorn hunted them down, exacted his bloody revenge.

And then only two years ago, Darcy's brother, Gaeton, was killed. Thorn's oldest friend, tortured then shot while working undercover with the FBI. Again Thorn untangled a snarl of corruption and lunacy. The only good to come from that incident was that he'd fallen in love with Darcy Richards. And she had fallen in love with him.

His life had been nothing but a long succession of violent episodes, and each of them in turn had shaken Thorn down out of his stilt house and thrown him back into the turbulent and chaotic world. More violence than was his or anybody's due. Yet one tragedy had not vaccinated him against the next. Today he was still as susceptible, still as unprepared as he had been each time before. No authority on pain, still a goddamn amateur, flailing wildly, dragged down helplessly into a whirlpool of rage and desolation.

Thorn stared at himself in the mirror, and brushed and brushed at his scalp till it was hot and raw, until for the first time in years a rumble of anguish rose up through him too powerful to oppose, and it broke into his throat. His eyes burned, but he clamped his jaw tight and swallowed it back, his face turning to iron.

It had happened once too often. He had let himself love one more time, let himself grow soft, vulnerable. But that would not occur again. When this was finished, he would climb up into his house, nail the door shut. And, by god, he would keep his Smith & Wesson oiled and cocked, his heart as cold and dense as marble.

"You look like shit, Thorn. Week-old shit."

Thorn took a sip from the bottle of seltzer water he'd brought along and gazed at young Andy Stutmeyer. Months ago, Jeanne had insisted that if Sugarman had to hire a secretary, then by god it was going to be a guy. And the only male who'd answered the ad was Stutmeyer, a gangly kid who hovered somewhere in his early twenties, but who was usually as snotty as a boy half his age.

"I seen eighty-mile-an-hour, head-on collision victims look better than you," Andy said.

During his first couple of years out of high school, Andy had ridden shotgun on the tow truck for Wheaton's Texaco, and now he looked back on that time, all the carnage he'd witnessed, as a touchstone, his version of war experience.

Andy had a magazine spread open on the desk in front of him. Black-and-white photos of heavy metal stars. Skinny guys with faces painted in gruesome masks. For a moment Andy squinted up at Thorn, shaking his head at what he saw, then he drummed his fingers on the desk and turned back to his magazine.

"Sugar in?"

"He's with somebody." Andy flipped to the next page.

"Buzz him, tell him I'm here."

"He told me never to bother him when he's with a client unless it was urgent."

Andy scowled up from the magazine, and Thorn could feel his headache begin to tighten again, his eyes resuming their dance of pain. Andy's desk was placed squarely in front of Sugar's office door. The boy was big-boned enough, and Thorn was just frail enough at this moment, to put them on equal footing.

"Do me a favor, Andy, okay? Buzz him, tell him it's me, and let him decide if it's urgent."

Andy stared down at an ad for punk paraphernalia; spiked bracelets, studded suspenders, nose and nipple rings. He bent the corner of the page over and flipped to the next.

"It's not how it works," he said without looking up. "You gotta tell me what it's about, and I decide it's urgent or not."

Thorn took a step backward, glanced around the cheap paneled office. One green leather couch across from Andy's desk, old copies of *Florida Sportsman* on a table beside it. There were three underwater photos on the wall, and Sugarman's high school diploma and his degree from junior college. A couple of his police citations, some photographs of presidents vacationing in the Keys, and a few war heroes. Sugarman's civic pride collection.

When the shopping plaza was new, this storefront had been a loan company for a year or two, then it became a dive shop briefly, then a check-cashing business. Two years ago it was part of the beauty salon that was still next door. About the time the beauty business started shrinking, Sugarman was looking for office space. So now he was there, sandwiched between the salon and a store that sold inflatable rafts shaped like exotic animals.

Quidnunc Enterprises. That's the name Sugarman had chosen for his private investigation agency. A *quidnunc* was, as Sugarman explained it, a busybody, someone who needed to know everything that was going on. Sugarman liked the word, how it sounded, ever since he'd come across it in one of his vocabulary books. Thorn said at the time that nobody would know what the hell it meant. Especially in the Keys, where the average vocabulary was about twenty words, most of them having to do with fish, sex, or booze. I want something unique, Sugarman had said. Something with spice. I don't want to be just another boring private cop. So, you're going to be a quidnunc? Thorn said. And Sugarman, getting huffy, said, Yeah, goddamn it, that's right. Quidnunc Enterprises. So there.

Sugar and Darcy had been business partners. Sugarman quitting the Monroe County Sheriff's Department after ten years of service and starting up Quidnunc. About the same time Darcy had left her job as meteorologist for Channel Six in Miami. A TV weather lady. She'd returned to Key Largo, fallen in love with Thorn, and moved in. But she found the noiseless routine of their days didn't fulfill her. Up early, Thorn tying flies every morning, fishing the back country in the afternoon, reading at night by lantern light. Lots of sky watching, cloud meditation. Hammock time. An occasional drive deeper into the Keys to fish new flats. It had been good for Darcy for a while, but finally one day she informed Thorn that she wanted action, noise, something to get her blood pressure back up. So she'd gone in with Sugar, and had been spending a lot of time in the last few months driving her car up and down the Keys, pitching their services to the small businesses. Less than a year she'd been at it, but Thorn had detected a new heat in her. An improved disposition. She was back in the world, and her blood was flowing again. Until that problem came up. Something she wanted to handle on her own.

Andy Stutmeyer was bent lower over his magazine, bobbing his head in time to the rock and roll noises he was making in his throat.

Thorn glanced over at the underwater shot, one of Sugarman's wide-angle attempts at capturing Carysfort Reef on a sunny day. A school of grunts, some wrasse, the shadow of a large barracuda hovering in the background behind a mound of coral.

Thorn stooped over, took a grip on the bottom edge of Andy's oak desk. He gathered himself, drew in a long breath, blew it out, and straightened up, bringing the side of the desk up with him. Andy's pens and radio and magazine spilled onto the floor. Thorn lifted the desk all the way up with as much force as he could muster, and he heaved the goddamn thing toward the cheap paneled walls. It tumbled to the right and nearly took out the side window. Came to rest on its side, drawers hanging open.

"Shit, Thorn. Look what the fuck you did."

With a wild, disheveled look, Andy was sprawled in front of Sugar's office door. Before he could say another word, the door to the inner office swung open, bumped him in the back of the head, and a woman stepped out. Early forties, striking. She looked down at Andy, then turned her large blue eyes on Thorn. White-blond hair, milky translucent skin. Her eyebrows thick and darker than her hair, with a slight arch over her right eye that gave her a skeptical but amused expression, as if she'd just heard some outrageous lie that was nevertheless charming and clever.

She wore a burnt-orange sleeveless blouse with wood buttons. A matching pleated skirt that was short enough to display her chiseled calves and narrow ankles. A dancer's legs and a supple, powerful body. A woman who looked like she could spring into the air and hold herself there as long as it suited her.

She stood there for a moment, two yards from Thorn, then gave him a faint smile and walked out the door.

"Boy," Sugarman said when the door was shut. "Now, there's a woman who deserves life's finest pleasures."

"Yeah," said Thorn. "Looks like she may have enjoyed one or two of them already."

Still looking at the door she'd shut behind her, Sugar said, "That's Doris Albright. Albright Seafood."

Then Sugar glanced down at Stutmeyer.

"Hey, Andy. Could I get you to keep your work area a little neater, please? Makes a bad impression on our clients, things all thrown around like this."

Sitting in the chair across from Sugarman's desk, Thorn said, "Darcy was upset about something. She said it was something she'd run into at work. It was making her act strange: serious, very quiet. Not like her at all."

Sugarman ran his eyes over Thorn's face and was silent. He was wearing a white shirt today, and an orange madras plaid tie that seemed to jangle when it caught the light. Sugarman rested his forearms against the edge of his desk and leaned his weight on them. He toyed with a silver letter opener, tapping it against his green ink blotter.

"Upset? She was upset?"

"That's right. But she wouldn't say what it was about."

Thorn looked around at the walls of the office. The same paneling as outside. A wooden hat rack in one corner with some of Sugarman's baseball caps on it. On one wall were some trophy fish: trout, a nice sailfish, bonefish. And a watercolor Darcy had painted of Thorn's house, with the four of them, Gaeton, Sugarman, Thorn, and Darcy, all sitting on the upstairs porch.

Behind Sugarman was a large, dark gray tinted window. It was positioned so it gave them a view down the row of swivel chairs of the Hairport, the beauty shop next door. The window was a remnant of the beauty parlor's better days, when the previous owner of the shop sat where Sugarman was now, adding up her profits and keeping an eye on her workers through the one-way mirror.

Sugar's office smelled of perm solutions and dizzying acrylic fumes from the nail-sculpting cubicle at the back. The noise seeping through the wall was always fierce, a dozen competing voices, blow-dryers and razors, the phone ringing and ringing. Yet Sugarman had decided not to wall-in and insulate the cutout section. He said the mirror helped him pass the slow hours, looking in at the ladies in dryers, the shampoos, the constant snip-snip. And, as he'd confessed, there was something mildly sexy about it. No nudity or anything, but a chance to look at a world he'd never witnessed, not to mention the fact that he could hear through that pane of glass a lot of very high-quality gossip. Sugarman believed he was now better informed about certain aspects of Key Largo social life than any man in town. Something any quidnunc would value.

"Well," Sugarman said, his eyes searching the air just above Thorn's head. "I don't know what the hell it could be. I only have the two clients. Murtha's Liquors and First Federal Savings. And all they are is employee surveillance. Watching rolls of videotape to make sure nobody's stealing. A bullshit job. She was out on the road, passing out brochures and talking to people, trying to drum up business, and once or twice a week she'd watch some of the videos we shot. That's all it was."

Sugarman tapped his letter opener against the blotter, and looked off at a mounted bonefish on the wall.

"That's it? Two clients?"

"Yeah, sorry to say."

"That woman just walked out of here? She one of the two?"

"No, Doris just walked in today. I haven't decided if I want to take her on. It's a strange case. Wants me to find her ex-husband. I'll tell you about it sometime."

"Okay," Thorn said. "I want to know every store she's been in the last few weeks, and then I want to see those videotapes."

"You're kidding."

"If that's what Darcy was doing with her time, then I want to know about it."

"You want a list of every business Darcy went into to hand out business cards and brochures?"

"That's right."

"That's nuts, Thorn. I don't have any idea where she's been. We didn't keep a log or anything like that. She just went driving. Stopped at places, chatted, like that. Totally random."

Thorn tapped his foot fast against the tile.

"The videos, then. I'll start there."

"You want to sit in my living room and watch Milly Pickles and Jane Etheridge cash social security checks? Watch Murtha sell Chivas Regal to Republicans? That's what you want to do?"

"I'll be by tonight."

"It's hours, Thorn. Hours and hours of the same bullshit, grainy film, nothing happening. If you want to do it, hey, fine. But I'd bring something to read."

"When's a good time to get there?"

"All right," he said. "Come at seven. Jeanne's got her bonsai class tonight."

"Bonsai?"

Sugarman said, "You know, clipping the roots off these trees and plants and stuff. Making midgets out of them. She's doing that now. The house is full of these teensy oak trees and stuff. I'm starting to think I should shop around for a steel jockstrap."

Thorn forced a smile. Sugarman didn't.

"What happened to her ballet class?"

"Jesus, where you been? That was months ago. Since then we been through guitar, organ lessons, and candle making. Last month it was writing limericks. Hell, she even won some goddamn contest. The International Limerick Association sent her a certificate. Honorable mention. You sure I didn't tell you about this?"

Thorn shrugged. He hadn't heard it before and didn't want to hear it now, but Sugarman was tapping the letter opener fast, taking stabs at the ink blotter. Ventilating.

"The contest was a goddamn scam," Sugarman said. "These people tried to sell her a copy of the book her winning limerick was going to be published in. Fifty bucks. You believe that? Buy one for each of your friends, share the gift of limericks."

Thorn was watching things in the beauty salon over Sugarman's shoulder. Shirley Marx wearing a white robe, leaning her head back into a shampoo sink. A young man in a flowered shirt washing her hair.

"Assholes trying to get rich off limerick writing, for godsakes. I guess I'm lucky Jeanne didn't have two dozen friends to buy them for. As it was, she bought three copies."

Thorn made a commiserating noise.

Sugarman said, "There was something else after the limerick phase, but hell if I can remember what. I mean, that woman's had more hobbies than the Pope has beads."

Thorn glanced again at the watercolor. The four of them, old friends, laughing, sipping wine, Thorn stretching his hand toward the last shreds of an extraordinary sunset dying on the horizon. A real day. Not something imagined. Not some romanticized event she'd dreamed up for a painting. A real day, a true sunset. Probably even those particular laughs had been real.

Sugarman looked over at the painting with him. Then lowered his eyes and shook his head.

"Sooooo," Sugarman said, drawing the word out, clearing away all the memories, ready to get back to business. "Where do we start?"

"You're the detective."

"Don't bullshit me, Thorn. Which way you headed?"

Thorn stood up quickly and felt his headache take a sharp

whack at his frontal lobe. He walked over to Sugarman's side. Sugar was looking up at the plastic replica of a ten-pound trout he'd caught early one rainy morning back in Tarpon Basin. Thorn had been there that morning. Thorn had been there for all the fish on the walls in this room.

"Thought I'd run back out to the reef. Have a look at the scene of the crime. You want to come?"

Sugarman said no, then turned from the fish. There were wrinkles in his forehead where usually it was smooth as toffee.

"Now, look, Thorn. You keep me in the loop, man. I know you're upset. You're grieving. So am I. But don't get rash on me, run off and do something without talking to me about it first. Let me be your designated thinker, okay? Can we agree on that?"

Thorn nodded.

"Say it, say it out loud."

Thorn stepped over to the office door.

"I promise," Thorn said. "I won't be rash."

"Okay, then I'll see you at seven. We'll watch those videos. Sugarman Cinematic Productions. No car chases, no buildings exploding, no bodies riddled with bullets. Just life at the bank in Key Largo, Florida, a few weeks in the nine-to-five lane. You never know, Thorn, you might learn something about the real world."

"I'll bring the popcorn."

Sugarman gave him a long look, and said, "Nothing rash."

"Rashless," Thorn said. "Completely rashless."

Sugarman shook his head sadly while Thorn held his gaze for a moment, then left.

On the way across the parking lot, Thorn flattened a beer can under his shoe, and kicked it along ahead of him for a few paces. Then he took a hop-step and sailed the thing into the scraggly grass behind the Amoco station.

Okay, so he wouldn't do anything rash. He'd promised. But what he didn't tell Sugar was, he didn't know exactly what rash was anymore. In fact, he doubted there was anything he'd consider rash as long as it helped him find the bastard who'd clutched Darcy's hand until she had no choice but to draw in a lungful of seawater.

CHAPTER 8

A FIFTEEN-KNOT BREEZE OUT OF THE SOUTHEAST WAS MUSCLING UP THE swells. To the west the sky was thick with ash and smoke from a fire smoldering in the southern Everglades. Overhead the clouds had turned to a gritty iron, stealing the sharp blues and greens from the sea. Herons, egrets, gulls floated over the mangrove islands as Thorn idled out the main channel past Pennekamp Park.

Taking the thirty-foot Chris-Craft today, partly to handle the rougher seas, but mainly because he wasn't ready to board the skiff again, didn't want to stumble across some stray object still haunted from that morning. He didn't want to remember anything about that day. Or for that matter take any unexpected detours into the past, relive another moment with Darcy Richards. She was gone. He'd had his chance and had failed her. Now, goddamn it, those memories were going to have to stay shut inside the heavy book in his heart.

As he wheeled the sluggish Chris-Craft around the last turn of the channel and wallowed out to the open water, gulls screamed close overhead and dove into his wake. His passage had stirred to the surface a school of minnows, ripe for the taking. Thorn glanced up at the dizzy gulls, listened to their hungry screams, watched them streamline themselves and plunge on their silver prey. He turned his eyes away, focused on the markers before him.

It took half an hour, idling back and forth across Broken Conch Reef, before Thorn found the spot Darcy had led him to. He anchored, and the boat swung around, bow into the wind. It rocked against the current, but the anchor held.

He looked off at the shallows where that other boat had approached, and tried to picture it again. To see the shape of its hull, any markings, a name perhaps, bringing it out of the fuzz and static of memory. But he could recall only the sleek lines of the Grady White. Twenty or twenty-two feet. Must be a few thousand identical fishing boats registered in these waters. Nothing unique about that particular vessel. One person aboard, throwing an anchor over. Nothing more than that.

Thorn stared out at the water, falling into the lull of the rise and fall of the sea. He thought he might hypnotize himself, sink into the past, recapture that moment, haul up some trifling detail, anything. Getting down deep where the chemistry of remembrance fermented, where the foaming cells kept everything alive, every piddling second. Every scent, fraction of gesture, each smile and word and darkening of eye. All of it passing endlessly through the circuitry of consciousness.

But try as he would, there was nothing more he could see of that single boat. A vague anonymous craft piloted by a faceless, sexless person who had kept himself exactly far enough away.

Thorn stripped to his bathing suit, put on his mask and flippers. And without further thought he scooted over the side and went feetfirst into the water.

He swam for over an hour, tracing back and forth, trying for a methodical mapping of the reef. He dove, and each time he stayed down for as long as his breath allowed, poked his arm into the walls of rock and coral, looking for a spot where she might have been caught. But nothing looked right.

Back to the surface for another breath, then ducking and going down again for a minute or two, coasting along the sandy bottom, the water dim today, the colors drained from the coral. Seeing a few lobsters, shorts, and some schools of yellowtail and wrasse, but little else.

He was rising up for another breath, when he saw at the base of a mound of brain coral an object that broke apart from its surroundings. Something black and inert.

And though he was almost out of air, his chest beginning to tighten, he turned back from his ascent and churned his fins, and dug back down through the water. When he was near the object, he recognized it, and felt a sharp twist in his chest. He pushed himself deeper and as he was reaching out for it, he noticed to his right a lobster, twice as large as any he'd seen till then. It was looking at him from a cleft in the rock, waving its antennae, daylight showing through the latticework of the rock behind it. The lobster's escape route was a slot where a human arm might fit, might grab at the succulent creature, might become lodged, might be gripped tight from the other side of the high wall of rock.

In his temples Thorn felt the warning pricks of oxygen starvation, the yellowing dusk of his consciousness beginning to fade. He held himself still in front of the lobster's hiding place and waved his hand at the lobster, watched it disappear into its hole. Then he pushed his hand in after it, felt the snag and burn of the rock jagged against his flesh, but he shoved deeper, up to the elbow in the rock, his hand feeling nothing back there. No sign of the lobster, nothing solid.

Then he drew his arm out, came close to the opening and peered in. And yes, there was an opening back there, a cave of some kind that was large enough for a diver to swim into unnoticed from his position. Large enough for the diver to turn and wedge himself into place and grip the hand that clutched at the lobster.

Thorn turned and found the black object in the sand beside the hole, and picked it up and angled himself upright and waved his fins at the floor of the sea, rising through the water as Darcy must have risen, feeling the shriveling of his veins, the last vapors of oxygen being consumed. Rising up through the gray sea to the boat rocking above.

As he swam, he held out his left hand and peered at the black plastic scabbard Darcy had always worn around her right ankle. Its buckle was twisted, the strap mauled as though from repeated scraping against the rough rocks of the reef. It had broken free, fallen into the sand, and lay there like some last note she'd dashed off to him in her desperation. A final message to him from across the void.

Sugarman parked his Mustang in a vacant lot next door to the Albright residence and got out. Doris and Philip Albright lived in a concrete stilt house at 16 Seahorse Lane. Behind it was a canal that led out to Rodriguez Key and the Atlantic beyond. It was one of several canals hacked into the limestone of that treeless neighborhood behind the Winn-Dixie. Tidal canals, straight as rulers, crisscrossed the whole island, laid out by the same mindless bastards who built the houses.

All through the Keys, that's what they did. Tripled real estate values by hiring a midnight bulldozer to clean out stands of mangroves that obstructed views. Or over several nights gouged a trench from a landlocked piece of property direct to the sea. Never mind that it was illegal, or that doing it sent chalky silt far out into the bay, destroying the sea grasses. And never mind that all those canals had fatally weakened the land mass, so one day when Key Largo got its inevitable hurricane, there was a damn good chance the storm would shred the land to rubble and carry it far away.

Their house was white with yellow trim. Two cactus plants in ceramic pots shaped like burros sat by the bottom of the concrete stairway, and the yard was full of glossy Carolina river rock. Like so many on the island, it was a low-maintenance place. The kind of house you could lock up and walk away from for six months and not have to ask anyone to water anything or feed anything you'd left behind. Like walking away from a bus locker.

Throughout this subdivision all the houses were the same. The half-million-dollar ghetto. Most of them with yachts tied up out back, big sloppy boats that were at least as expensive as the houses. The architecture had all the grace of a federal prison. Big concrete rectangles up on big concrete pilings. Flat roofs covered with pea rock, screened-in porches that stared across the canals at other screened-in porches. Every house with the same concrete slab driveway, concrete stairway, concrete picnic table. All of it hard and permanent and painted white to reflect the sun. There was probably so much damn sun being reflected in that neighborhood that the migrating birds had to veer miles out of their way to keep from being blinded.

Standing out in the street, Sugarman couldn't tell which houses were inhabited and which weren't. In neighborhoods like this the lights came on and went off, radios poured out endless strains of Benny Goodman, but no one ever seemed to come outside. Even the cars in the carports could be misleading because a lot of these folks left their vehicles behind when they returned north. Apparently they kept duplicate Lincolns back in Muncie and Rochester.

Sugar didn't know anybody for ten blocks in any direction. That's the way it had become in Key Largo. He'd lived on this island all his life, a town with only ten thousand permanent residents, and still, he was a stranger in certain neighborhoods, and might easily have been mistaken for one of the hitchhikers who from time to time ambled in off U.S. 1 to see if they could find an open door.

Nothing stirred inside the house when he rang the bell at the bottom of the stairs. And when he climbed them and hammered on the front door, no one answered. So he paced along the wraparound porch, peeking in at the edges of blinds, seeing only glimpses of a powdery pastel living room.

He was about to give up and leave when he saw the man in the wheelchair down by the seawall.

It was Philip P. Albright in a blue terry cloth shirt and matching shorts and a pink terry cloth hat. The man was gripping a fishing rod, and as Sugarman approached he gave the line a practiced pop. Snapper fishing.

Sugar said hello, but Mr. Albright didn't turn his head. So he pulled up a bench from the picnic table and sat down beside him and looked down into the dark canal water. A black-and-white angelfish was hovering next to Albright's shrimp, the fish flipping its side fins to stay still in the incoming tide. Philip Albright didn't seem to notice.

Twenty-five years before, Sugarman had been deeply intimidated by this man. The owner of the island's only seafood market, Albright had been a commercial fisherman of great renown. And from time to time when Gaeton, Thorn, or Sugar made a catch of yellowtail or grouper that was more than they and their families could immediately consume, they peddled their surplus at Albright's Fish House. Which meant they had to stand up to the hard bargaining of Philip P.

Only Thorn was good at it. Gaeton took whatever Albright offered first, and Sugarman halfheartedly stayed in the contest for a round or two. But Thorn was always icy tough with the tall, gaunt Albright. Stood up to his disparaging remarks, his withering putdowns of their fish and fishing abilities. Once, Thorn hauled a thirty-pound warsaw grouper off the scales of Albright's Fish House and carried the dead fish out onto the dock and pitched it into Snake Creek rather than accept the price Albright was offering.

Now Philip P. was partially paralyzed from a stroke. And he'd apparently lost the muscles in the right half of his face. The corner of his mouth turned down, a glisten of drool shone there, and his right eye was drooping, pulled south by gravity and the weight of the atrophied muscles in his cheek.

With some effort, Philip looked over at Sugarman, grunted quietly, then turned his face back to his fishing.

"Hello, Mr. Albright."

The man grunted again, and labored over a word that got lost in the useless muscles of his tongue.

"I'm Sugarman. I used to sell you fish once in a while, a long time ago."

Again Albright sputtered and Sugar leaned close to hear. Some glottal malfunction, a garble of larynx and phlegm, but through it all, Sugar managed to decipher the word.

"Philip," said Sugarman.

And Albright nodded his head, yes, yes, call him Philip. And the man unfastened his right hand from his fishing rod and offered it to Sugarman. He shook it. Boneless and cool.

"Good to see you again, Philip."

The man nodded. Same here.

Sugarman felt a fleeting wave of vertigo, the images of the two Philip Albrights failing to merge. The one from long ago, the rawboned, aggressive, penny-pinching fisherman who stayed out at sea for weeks at a time in the *Ocean Fox*, his old Hatteras, and only came back to land when the ship was about to sink under the weight of his catch. That man who took those thousands and thousands of pounds of fish and from them built, over thirty years, one of the largest businesses in the Keys. That Philip Albright, and this new one, the terry cloth man, who glowed with triumph when Sugarman understood a single word he uttered.

"I came by to speak to Doris," Sugarman said after a while.

Philip slurred out a word and Sugar leaned close.

"Work?" Sugarman said. "Doris is at work?"

Philip turned his head and gave Sugarman a lopsided smile.

For the next hour Sugarman sat with him in silence. The angelfish nosed around his bait, but did not strike. It never would. The angel was a filter feeder, from the low end of the food chain. It ate only what it trapped in the web inside its gills. Algae, or tiny particles that the meat-eating fish had left behind.

At a quarter after six a small mangrove snapper showed up, zipped in and stole the shrimp from Philip's hook. He didn't seem to notice, but kept on popping his line every few minutes, a motion he did with such effortless grace that Sugarman knew he was in the presence of one of the truly great ones.

When Doris Albright hadn't returned by six thirty, Sugarman asked the old man if he was ready to go back inside the house. Albright shook his head no, and kept his eyes on the water.

Then the old man warbled something deep in his throat, something which Sugarman took to mean that Philip P. Albright, master angler, was convinced that now as the sun was setting the fishing was about to improve dramatically.

As Sugarman was settling into the seat of his Mustang, Doris wheeled into the drive in her gold Eldorado. He got back out and met her as she parked. Opened her door for her.

She drew herself out and they stood there in the gravel drive. She'd changed into white shorts and a denim shirt. The faint scent of fresh fish clung to her clothes.

"Mrs. Albright, I've decided I can't take your case. I came over to tell you in person."

"Very sorry to hear that."

"It's not that I couldn't use the work. No, ma'am. But something's happened, a personal thing, and until I clear it up, I can't see how I can spend time on anything else."

She peered past him, looking at Philip by the canal. Her eyes emptying.

"My husband," she said. "He's very ill, you know. And there's no more money. The fish house is almost bankrupt. The health insurance isn't covering the bills."

"I'm sorry. I really am."

"But if you could help me, help me find this man," she said, "I think he might be willing to lend me money. Keep me afloat."

"This man, he was your first husband."

"Yes," she said, and drew her eyes away from Philip Albright and settled them on Sugarman. "Will you come inside?"

"Out here's fine."

She walked over to the front steps and sat down. Her legs

glistened coppery in the amazing light. Sugarman walked over to her.

"I'm crazy, aren't I? Thinking the man I abandoned would loan me money. That's kooky, isn't it?"

"Well, I'm no great judge of kooky."

"I married him when I was very young, not even out of high school. He was very dashing, a military man. Our marriage lasted a while, but it was terrible. He suffocated me; I was his prisoner. So I ran. Fifteen years ago, it was. Then just a few weeks back, there he was on my doorstep. Saying he'd made himself into a rich man, and asking me to return to him. Fifteen years, and the man is asking me to come back to him like it was only a week or two had gone by."

"You said no."

"I said more than that."

"But you changed your mind. Now you want to find him."

She hugged her knees and said, "I appreciate your coming over, Mr. Sugarman. But it's just as well. It's a stupid idea. It wouldn't work. I was just desperate, not thinking straight."

Something splashed in the canal and Sugar glanced back and watched as Philip labored over his reel, cranking up a small blue runner.

"Well," he said. "I suppose I could call around a little. I got time to do that much. Get in touch with some people I know. See if they can locate him."

"Would you do that?"

"I'd need his last known address, full name. Social security number, military records, if you have them. Anything like that."

"When we were married we lived on a farm over near Naples. No telephone, no mail delivery out that far. Very isolated, no neighbors or anything. We got our mail in town. That farm's the last place I know he lived. But I doubt very much he's still there. It was so long ago. I just don't know where to start. I guess I could drive over there, ask people. See who he sold the farm to, maybe they'd know something about him. But I'm just so busy with Philip. I don't know what to do."

"When your ex-husband was here recently, he didn't leave an address?"

"No," she said. "I didn't give him a chance, I threw him out so fast."

"You try calling Information over there, see if he has a phone now?"

"I tried that, yes. No listing for him. He could be anywhere."

She caught Sugarman sneaking another look at her legs, and managed a tired smile.

"Hell, I guess I could give it an hour or two, call around, see what I can find out."

"You're a kind man, Mr. Sugarman."

"Right now I think I better help Mr. Albright get that fish off his hook. He seems to be having a little problem."

She held him with her intense blue eyes for a moment more, then she let the light go out of them, and by god, Sugarman felt like the sun had suddenly dimmed by half.

CHAPTER 9

IT WAS JUST AFTER ELEVEN WHEN THORN MADE IT TO KEY BISCAYNE. HE parked his VW outside the Rosenfeld Science Building and went through the double glass doors into the harsh refrigerated air. Ten minutes later, after being passed to four different offices, Dr. Paul Ludkin's secretary assured Thorn that if her boss didn't know what a red tilapia was, nobody this side of Saturn did.

The professor didn't look up from his computer when his secretary introduced Thorn, and he kept staring into the screen while Thorn explained what he wanted to know.

"There's no such thing," the doctor said, his eyes still fixed on the monitor.

"What do you mean?"

"No such thing as a red tilapia. There's a black tilapia and there's a white tilapia. But no red. It doesn't exist. It's as if you came in and asked me to tell you about a red shark. I'd have to say the same thing. A red shark doesn't exist. I could tell you what a shark is, just as I could tell you about a tilapia, but if you put the word red in front of it, then no, I can't say a thing."

"Okay," Thorn said. "Then tell me about a tilapia."

"Now, that I can do."

Dr. Paul Ludkin was a small man. Five four, not more than a few pounds over a hundred. Wearing a white shirt with a red bow tie, a blue sport coat. His horn-rimmed glasses looked like they weighed more than his entire muscle mass. A good finger-poke could break through his chest wall. Thorn had begun picturing that possibility. Obviously the guy hadn't been keeping up with his interpersonal skills exercises. Sitting behind his army-surplus green metal desk, tapping a few keys, lifting his head to listen to Thorn while he kept watch on the screen.

Ludkin was head of the University of Miami's marine science program. Professor emeritus, his secretary told Thorn. Apparently that meant Ludkin was so used to speaking to a hundred and fifty people at a time, he'd lost the ability to talk to just one.

Thorn tranquilized himself by glancing at the long view out Ludkin's window. Looking north from Key Biscayne out across the green-blue shallows to the brash skyline of Miami. Even on that hot, hazy day, the city looked energized. Wired on Cuban coffee, giving off a jittery light.

"What is this about anyway?" Ludkin said. "You walk into my office, barely introduce yourself, and I'm supposed to give you unlimited quantities of my time."

"What it's about," Thorn said, "is a murder."

That got two seconds of Ludkin's attention, then his eyes lost interest in Thorn and drifted back to the screen.

He pecked in two or three words, kept his eyes on his work.

"Well, to begin with," he said, "we're not talking about one particular fish here. There's about a hundred and fifty known species of tilapia. *Oreochromus aurea, hornorum, mossambica, nilotica,* on and on. They are lake fish, a species indigenous to the Middle East, Israel, Egypt. Supposedly the Pharaohs raised them for food.

"And they're mouth breeders. Which means the mother fish holds the eggs in her mouth for protection. Even when they get bigger, at the first sign of danger, the fry come swarming back into the mother's mouth, swim in through her gills, however they can manage it. And when the fish get larger, their fathers stand guard over them. The net result is, these fish survive at rates a great deal higher than normal fish. Much, much higher rates."

"Like what?"

Ludkin looked over at him again. His eyes were shrunken and watery behind the thick lenses.

"A murder?"

"A friend of mine was killed. I think it had something to do with a tilapia."

"Now, that would be very odd."

"You were saying these fish survive at higher rates."

"Yes, well, for instance, take a grouper," he said. "At each cycle, your average female grouper produces five thousand eggs. Out of that, maybe two or three survive to adulthood. Two out of five thousand. Not a very good production rate, though it is fairly normal for most fish. But with tilapia, because of the mouth breeding and their general genetic resilience, out of that same five thousand eggs, you'll have roughly three thousand surviving. Three thousand adult fish. Which, of course, works out to be a thousand times more productive than normal fish in the wild. All of which makes them very desirable fish for aquaculture."

"Aquaculture?"

Ludkin typed a few sentences into his computer.

"Fish farming," the professor said. "The fastest-growing form of food production in the world."

"I didn't know."

Ludkin took a short, exasperated look at Thorn, then ducked his eyes back to his work.

"Some cultures have been farming fish for thousands of years, while in the West we are just discovering it. Raising some salmon, some trout, catfish, trying to use our high-tech skills on it. But we're still very much behind in the field. Someday soon, most of the fish we consume will be farm raised. Billions and billions of pounds of fish growing up in breeding ponds. There's a worldwide race going on at this moment to see who can patent the best aquaculture techniques, market the best fish."

"But there's no such thing as a red tilapia."

"That's what I said."

There was a knock at the door, and Ludkin grumbled his permission to enter.

A woman in her twenties with pert blond hair and a button nose opened the door and stuck her head through the crack, and told Professor Ludkin it was eleven thirty. His graduate tutorial was waiting.

"Yes, yes," he said, and went back to typing.

The young woman kept her head in the doorway.

"Maybe there's somebody else I could talk to," Thorn said.

"Professor Ludkin," the young woman said. "The tutorial was supposed to start at eleven."

"Red tilapia are a myth," Ludkin said. "Stories have circulated about them for years like fairy tales. People turning lead to gold. But it can't happen. You can't change a black fish into a red fish. You can't turn a white into a red either. It's hogwash. Scientifically ridiculous."

"Why would anybody even try?"

Ludkin looked up at Thorn. The man took his glasses off, drew a handkerchief out of the breast pocket of his sport coat, and began to polish the lenses.

"Why would anybody try?" The professor smiled, his eyes a milky blue, probably not seeing much beyond the edge of his desk. "Why do actresses dye their hair blond? Why do car manufacturers spend millions of dollars experimenting with new paint colors?"

"Why don't you just tell me."

"Because, my dear fellow, a red tilapia would be far more popular than a black tilapia. It is that simple. Popularity. Go to a fish market, go to a restaurant. Watch what people buy. They want redfish, red snapper, those are the commercially popular fish."

"That's ridiculous."

"Ridiculous?" Ludkin looked up at Thorn. "Yes, I suppose it is. But it's true nonetheless. Red fish are more sought after than black or white. Strange but true."

"Wait a goddamn minute. What about salmon, grouper, trout? They're popular. And they're not red."

Ludkin peered coldly at him for the count of five.

"Are you dense, young man?"

"Yeah," Thorn said. "Murder has that effect on me. Makes me very dense. Dense and violent."

Ludkin dwindled an inch or two in his chair, lost a couple of shades in skin tone.

Finally he cleared his throat, and said, "Salmon, grouper, trout, those are established fish. People know them. They order them off menus, buy them at fish markets. Their parents ate salmon, their grandparents, and they eat them too. But unfortunately, the natural supplies of all those fish are dropping drastically. We'll see the end of commercial salmon fishing in our lifetime. The time is ripe for alternatives.

"But Americans don't know tilapia. It's an unfamiliar name. And even though they breed at fantastic rates, have flaky white meat, have all the right commercial properties, fish farmers have resisted raising them simply because they're ugly. But if they were red, a color Americans clearly prefer, if this red fish were lying on beds of ice in fish markets all over America, it wouldn't matter what its name was, the results could be staggering. If someone had a breeding stock of red tilapia, I daresay that person would control a very large share of the market on farm-raised fish in a year or two."

"Lead to gold."

"Oh, yes," Ludkin said. "Everyone agrees. If such a fish existed, it would be extremely lucrative."

"So what're we talking about? Genetic engineering? Fiddling with DNA to turn black to red?"

"Unfortunately, it can't be done. We've played around with it ourselves here in the lab. They tried at Seamark for years. Utter failures. It's just wishful thinking."

"Seamark?"

"A government facility near Florida City. Marine research."

"The government is doing this, trying to change fish colors?"

"Agriculture, engineering, chemistry. Everything. Government people have their careers to justify, just like anyone else. Promotions to make. If someone came up with a red tilapia in a government lab, they could write their own ticket from then on."

The man showed Thorn his small yellow teeth.

"Professor Ludkin," the young woman said. "Should I just go call off class?"

"Then, of course, there's Peter Lavery," Ludkin said. "A gentleman farmer, runs a tilapia farm in Thomasville, Georgia. He's been claiming to be close to a red tilapia for years. But he's a crackpot. Like they all are. Winchester, Lavery. All of them. Dilettantes, amateurs. Not unlike the perpetual-motion crowd."

"Winchester?"

"Has a farm over on the west coast of Florida," Ludkin said. He put his glasses back on, squinted at the woman in the doorway. "What do you want, young lady?"

"Your eleven o'clock graduate tutorial," she said.

"I'm canceling it," he said. "I'm too busy."

"Yes, sir."

She shut the door quietly.

"Students!" he said. "Damn *students*."

"This Winchester," Thorn said. "He's also working on a red tilapia?"

"All I know about Winchester is, he's stopped in here a few times in the last couple of years. Asked me questions, picked my brains like you're doing. And from the nature of the questions, I would assume that was his interest. Yes. Red tilapia."

"Anybody else?"

"Those are the main ones. The main crackpots."

"Lucrative," Thorn said. "Just how lucrative?"

Ludkin stared blankly into Thorn's eyes for a moment.

"Lead to gold," Ludkin said. "How lucrative would that be?"

"Can you put a dollar sign on it?"

Ludkin sighed, completely drained of patience. He took off his glasses and turned his blind eyes on Thorn as he wiped the lenses again with a dirty handkerchief.

"Billions of pounds of fish consumed each year," Ludkin said in a metronome beat. "Tilapia sell for five dollars a pound. Red tilapia would certainly be more. And you could figure that with the color change, tilapia might account for a significant percentage of the total fish market, say ten percent, twelve percent maybe. Now you do the math, Mr. Thorn. Tell me, what's ten percent of a billion dollars? Put a dollar sign in front of that, and what do you get?"

Thorn rose, stood behind his chair, and looked down at Ludkin.

"What I get," said Thorn, "is a goddamn good motive."

It was quarter after one when Thorn stopped at a bait store in Florida City and asked the three-hundred-pound woman behind the counter if she'd heard of a place called Seamark. She looked up from the shrimp tank where she was skimming the dead ones off the surface.

"We got beer, we got worms. Which will it be?"

"I already had lunch."

"Well, then, if you're lost, there's maps for sale across the street at the Shell station." Miami manners creeping south.

They'd never heard of Seamark at the Shell station, not at the Texaco either. It wasn't on the Homestead–Florida City map. Thorn checked a phone book under *United States* and found nothing.

He drove west, crossed through the shabby intersection that was the center of Florida City. He pulled into a strip shopping center. A pet store, a TV repair shop, a doughnut place. Two stores on the end boarded up. Florida City's main shopping district. He tried the TV and doughnut shops first. Empty looks.

Then went into the aromatic pet store. Breathed in the ammonia of damp kitty litter and the spoiled-fruit smell of snake.

"You turn left on Silver Palm." The teenage girl with black punk-rock hair was cleaning out a parrot cage. "Keep going west till the road gives out. Put it in four-wheel drive and keep on going down that gravel road till it peters out. And you'll be just about there."

"Sounds like a place they don't want you to find."

"Only way I know about it is me and my boyfriend go dirt biking and we ran across the place. Six months ago, I guess. Something like that. We never went back. Not friendly people back there. Not friendly at all. What do they do in that place, anyway?"

"I don't know," Thorn said. "Alchemy maybe."

She looked at him and nodded.

"I thought it was something like that."

The VW convertible didn't have four-wheel drive, so when the gravel road turned to dark mush, he pulled off to the side, parked under a gumbo-limbo, and walked. He was wearing a long-sleeved blue T-shirt and gray jeans and three-year-old white Keds that were spattered with engine grease and fish guts. As close to formal wear as Thorn owned. His going-to-town clothes.

The mosquitoes weren't hampered by the T-shirt. They lit up welts of warm flesh on his back and neck as he wandered down the trail, deeper into the dense hammock. The live oak and slash pines were covered with strangler figs, and a dense thicket of mahogany, stopper, buttonwood, some rogue Florida holly grew close to the path. A cypress or two, bromeliads sprouting in the crooks of branches. The ground was sloppy wet just off the gravel, a slough, or the eastern edge of the Glades. Birds squawking out there, the click and chirr of animals Thorn didn't recognize. Thorn had a brief and eerie chill, as if he were being observed by something big and fast. A panther perhaps.

There was a lush sulfury smell of freshly turned earth, and the air around him had a vague greenish hue. He saw motorcycle tracks hardened into the trail, running up the slight rise. Beyond the rise, the pathway dipped into a gully filled with dark water, and beyond the ditch, it led up into the woods again. Thrill hill.

He stopped and listened, but heard only the piping whine of mosquitoes at his ear. He waved his hand in front of his face, and stepped down into the knee-deep water, plunging ahead toward the opposite bank where the trail seemed to resume. Slogging through the soft mud, a tangle of weeds around his ankles, the water rose to his thighs. Thorn forged on and grabbed the limb of a sapodilla and dragged himself up the slippery bank. When he'd caught his breath, he pushed aside a low branch of a Brazilian pepper and headed on into the deep brush.

"Hey, there," a man said behind him. And Thorn felt the hard thrust of a rifle barrel at his spine. "Now, where in hell you think you're going, boy?"

Thorn didn't move. The man patted Thorn down, ran his hand skillfully up and down the legs of his jeans. Then came around and stood before him. A few inches taller than Thorn and maybe a hundred pounds bulkier. The man had kinky gray hair tied back in a ponytail. Except for a pair of muddy cowboy boots, the man was naked.

His big gut spilled down over his pubic hair and almost hid his nub of a penis. He had the meaty upper arms of a man who'd never done any serious exercise but could still clean and jerk a pickup truck if he had a mind to. His bolt-action Remington looked freshly oiled. Walnut stock, large-barreled .375. A safari rifle.

"Well," the man said. "You ain't a butterfly collector, 'cause you don't have a net."

"You think you could point your friend there a little off to one side?"

"I could do that," the big man said. "But I won't. Not till I find out what the fuck brings you snooping around back here."

"I'm looking for a fish," Thorn said.

"Yeah? And where's your pole?"

"Red tilapia. That's the fish I'm looking for."

It didn't mean anything to the man. His eyes remained wary, but nothing flickered.

"You're naked," Thorn said.

"I'm a sun lover," the man said. "Haven't worn any clothes to speak of since nineteen sixty-five."

"And the mosquitoes?"

"They've given up on me."

"You live out here?"

"Hey, who's on trial here, buddy boy?"

"Look," Thorn said. "I was told there was a research place back here. A place where they're farming fish. I have an interest in the subject. I thought I'd try to find it."

"You thought you'd try to find the place."

"That's right."

"An interest in fish."

"That's right. An interest in fish."

"Shee-it."

"Now, listen," Thorn said. "I don't give a rat's ass what you're up to back here. If you got a still, you're growing marijuana, fine. I'm just trying to find this place. Seamark."

"Seamark? Well, hell, why didn't you say so?"

The big man lowered his rifle, turned and waded through bushes, and Thorn followed.

There were two dozen of them. From sixteen to seventy. All of them naked. A volleyball game was in progress on a sandy square near the swimming pool. A few people lounged on chaises and watched the game. A man was doing slow, arduous laps in the pool while a radio on a wooden picnic table played a Lawrence Welk polka. More women than men. More blondes than brunettes. Nobody paying any special attention to Thorn, and Thorn trying not to pay too much to them.

Circling the camp were a dozen small cabins each with a

screened-in porch. SUNNY PALMS was painted on the lintel over the main gate.

"Sweaty palms," the big man said, pointing at the sign. "That's what they call us in town. They think this place is about sex. Orgies and all that. But it isn't. It's about being natural. That's all."

"You get a lot of Peeping Toms? That's why the gun?"

"It ain't loaded," the man said. "But it does the trick ninety-nine percent of the time. We get a lot of kids out here. Coming out on dirt bikes, three-wheelers. Got their binoculars. Irritates the hell out of me. I take a pass through the woods every now and then, see who I come up with."

The man led Thorn into the main cabin.

"Hey, Shelley," the man said when they were inside. "Found this one out on the east perimeter. Says he's looking for Sea-mark. You have any trouble, call out."

The big man gave Thorn a cautionary stare and walked out the door, left Thorn looking at a dark-haired woman about his age. She was tanned as dark as pumpernickel. Dark eyes, long lashes. Her breasts were large and hung so far down, her nipples were hidden behind the large oak desk.

"You looking for Seamark?"

"That's right."

"Well, you found it."

Thorn glanced around at the office. Orange cypress paneling. Bookshelves covering two walls. Some drawings thumbtacked to the wood, kid's renderings of birds and alligators.

"This?"

"It used to be. Seven months ago. The government was leasing the land. Now we're leasing it. Moved right into the cabins they used. A nice little piece of property. Out of the way."

"I guess my information is out of date."

"I guess so," she said. And she stood up, showed him her slim athletic build, a wild snarl of pubic hair. She came around the desk and stood in front of him.

"Who are you?"

"I'm a guy," he said, "who's trying to find out what happened to the woman he loved."

She looked at him for a moment, and he thought he saw a small flame come to life deep in her dark eyes.

"I'll show you around. Would you be more comfortable without your clothes?"

"If it's all the same," Thorn said, "I think I'll leave them on."

"Suit yourself."

"This is where they found the bodies," Shelley said. She'd taken Thorn to the shell of a concrete-block building fifty yards to the east of the volleyball game. The building had been gutted by a fire. A couple of stainless steel tables gleamed in the rubble. Some broken beakers and a twisted Bunsen burner, what looked like a half-melted microscope, the remains of some wooden furniture.

"Bodies?"

"Twelve of them. The complete staff of Seamark. One of our Sunny Palms members, Andy Beam, was on the volunteer fire crew from Homestead. They answered the call out here, so he saw the bodies while they were still stacked up."

"I don't follow you."

"Crisscrossed. Like Lincoln Logs. Ankles on throats. A little log cabin of corpses. Andy said it was the creepiest thing he'd ever seen. Somebody's idea of a joke. No sign of blood. No gunshots, no stab wounds. Just these dead people stacked up."

"I never heard anything about it."

"Oh, no, you wouldn't have. The good stuff never makes it into the paper. The truly interesting news, somehow they manage to keep it quiet."

"Unless you have a friend in the fire department."

Shelley turned away from the building and led Thorn down a narrow sandy path into a clearing.

"We haven't decided what to do with this yet. Seems like we could use it for something."

In the middle of the clearing there was a concrete pool the size of half a basketball court.

"This was where they raised the fish," she said. "A breeding tank."

"The tilapia."

"Whatever they were."

"And what happened to them?"

"Andy said he'd never seen such a thing. So many fish in there you could walk across their backs. All of them floating upside down. Poisoned."

"By any chance did Andy say what color they were?"

"Color?"

"Is Andy here today?"

"Playing volleyball," Shelley said.

"Mind if I talk to him a minute?"

"Sure."

Andy Beam remembered it vividly. Standing there with the volleyball in his hand, trim and tanned. The other members gathered around looking curiously at Thorn's clothes, and Andy Beam said, "Red."

"You're sure? You're positive?"

"Yeah, red. A bright ruby-red."

CHAPTER 10

THAT MONDAY NIGHT JEANNE SUGARMAN RETURNED FROM HER BONSAI class at nine, looked at her husband sitting beside Thorn on the yellow sofa, a big bowl of popcorn in front of them, watching a videotape of First Federal Savings, and without a word she shook her head and stalked back to her bedroom.

"She hates my job. Says it disgusts her." Sugarman's mouth twisted into a pained smile.

"Why?"

"Well, for one thing, it doesn't pay anything. We've been living on savings for the last six months. And for another it has no spark."

"No spark?"

"That's her word. She got that from ballet class, or somewhere. All of a sudden one day she's talking about spark. What has it, what doesn't."

"And your job doesn't."

"My job. Me. My whole life. According to her I had more spark when I was a regular cop. Now, out on my own, I lost what little I had."

Thorn watched the flicker of the digital time display at the left-hand corner of the tape. It was running through the hours of the day at triple speed, making an eight-hour workday into a two-hour silent movie. Bank customers strutting about like awkward penguins, making spastic gestures, tellers spitting out sentences to customers, giving them fleeting smiles, then ripping up the phone and chattering into it.

Earlier in the evening double-speed was all the pace Thorn could manage, so untuned were his eyes to video. But now, after only a few hours of this, they'd adjusted and he was starting to crave a souped-up VCR, six times faster than real time, ten times. Anything to get through these tedious days faster.

"I bet I'm low on the spark totem pole myself."

"No," Sugarman said. Then lowering his voice he said, "Jeanne says you got lots of spark. But you're an ascetic."

"Ascetic?"

Thorn watched the customers, three of them in line waiting to cash their social security checks, chatting with each other. Little jerks of their head, the twitches and spasms of human interaction. People Thorn knew, people he didn't. The teller they were waiting for, a young woman he'd dated once or twice in high school, Judy Mueller, looking gaunt and hard-edged after three husbands and two kids, a short stint in jail for transporting a few kilos of grass up to Miami.

Sugarman said, "According to Jeanne, you keep your spark hidden inside. Like a monk. You're greedy with it. Use it on inner pursuits."

"That Jeanne. She's got some ideas in her, doesn't she?"

"Yeah, she keeps me on my toes." Sugarman drained the last of his Coke and set his glass down on the coffee table. He scooped up another handful of popcorn, and Thorn leaned forward and did the same.

With his mouth half full, Sugarman said, "Fact is, I'm up on my goddamn toes so much I about forgot what it's like to walk around normal."

Thorn patted his knee.

The walls of their living room were hung with the legacies of Jeanne's hobbies. Macramé, crocheted samplers with cute slogans, some black-and-white photos of bugs. Her bug phase. A whole wall devoted to religious icons: crucifixes; virgins; dark, somber carvings of saints. And beside them some framed awards she'd won selling cosmetics door-to-door, some others that her glee club won, and a plaque for honorable mention in a local art show. She'd been doing this for years, cycling through a new distraction about every six weeks. Nothing ever taking root.

"You have any adventures today?"

Thorn said no, nothing of any note. He could feel Sugarman looking at him, but he didn't glance over.

They watched the videotape, talking occasionally about the people who passed through them. People they hadn't seen around town in a while, ones they knew stories about. People they'd been friends with once, still were in most cases. They'd covered the last three weeks of banking business and absolutely nothing had snagged Thorn's attention.

Sugarman got up to put in the first Murtha's Liquors tape.

"You up to any more tonight?"

Thorn said yeah, he was still wired.

"Well, I'm fading fast myself, but I guess I could go maybe one more round."

"Tell me something, Sugar. What in the hell did these people expect you and Darcy to find looking at all that tape?"

"Oh, it's just standard procedure. They got these miles of tape sitting around, they invested all this money in it, they can't just throw it away, right?"

"So they pay more money to have somebody look at it."

"Not a whole lot more money, no."

"Ever find anything?"

"Once," Sugar said. "A month ago Darcy was watching, she spotted some young guy, a teller, he was palming a packet of bills from a cash drawer when another teller's back was turned. Close to five hundred dollars. He put it on the edge of his drawer, then about five minutes later he slipped it into his lunch sack. Had it down to a science. I had to watch the tape five, six times before I could see what he did. But Darcy spotted it right off."

"She never told me about it."

"Maybe she thought you wouldn't be interested."

"Yeah, maybe."

"Well, Bill Getty was thrilled. I took him the tape, showed it to him. He just wanted to look at it over and over. Finally, he'd caught one of these shitheads stealing from his bank. He's been running short once or twice a month for a year or two and couldn't tell how it was happening. Thought it might be some kind of conspiracy, everybody in the whole bank in on it. But then, there it is, in black and white. He loved it. And renewed his contract with me for a year."

"And Murtha?"

"Murtha's a different story. Old guy, seventies. Liquorland, you know his store, across from the high school."

Thorn nodded. He knew the place. He'd gone in there once or twice, though he didn't remember meeting the owner.

"Well, Murtha's all alone in that liquor store, no employees, so there's nobody to steal from the register. But he's got the camera going every minute of every day. Set to turn on at nine sharp and shut off at five."

"What's the deal?"

"Guy's paranoid," Sugarman said. "He's sure some of the lowlifes coming in are stealing bottles from him. A fifth here, a quart there. And Murtha's become goddamn obsessed. Has me mark every frame where any long-hairs or poor brothers could be slipping something inside their shirts, and he has the frames blown up, studies them with a magnifying glass. Makes these wild statements, threatening people, saying if he catches one of these assholes he's going to tear their fucking nuts off. Old guy like that, it's a little scary."

"Let's have a look."

Thorn settled back on the couch, put his feet up on the coffee table, aimed the control at the VCR, and began to speed-watch a day in the life of Roy Murtha.

For a while it was a relief after all those hours in the bank. But pretty quickly the routine became obvious. Murtha was a short, stocky man, dark complexion. He had large features, Mediterranean, Turkish or Greek. He wore dark clothes, strangely out of character for the Keys. He was in his early seventies, with thick white hair and a fragile step. He moved with slow caution, as though he was expecting any minute a trapdoor to spring open beneath him.

Murtha unlocked the store at nine, came in, went right into the back room. A minute later he came out with his apron on. He took a swipe at all the bottles with a feather duster, and when everything was clean, he went to the safe, opened it, filled the cash drawer.

By ten he had downed two cups of coffee and checked his hair three times in the mirror on the west wall. He unlocked the door, propped it open, looked around at the parking lot, and came back inside. He settled into a chair behind the counter and began to read the *New York Times,* section by section, not skipping a page. At about eleven thirty each day he would pull from below the counter a plastic bag of junk food. Cheez Doodles, pork rinds, Thorn wasn't sure. The man would feast on them for a while as he finished the paper, a splurge of gluttony, and when the bag was empty, he wadded it into a small ball and tried a basketball shot into the can that sat near the front door. More often than not, he missed.

Thorn worked through the last week in July, watching the same white-haired crowd buying the same gallon jugs of vodka, the same construction guys plunking down their sweaty bills for fifths of rum and bourbon. On one Friday night a group of black teenagers descended on the store. They seemed to have something more than liquor on their minds. But one of them looked up and spotted the camera and all of them turned and stared at it and began to primp and mug for the video. Probably as close as they were going to get to their fifteen minutes of fame. A moment or two later they left without buying anything.

And then a day after that, a skinny young woman came into the store. She had short black hair and a pale complexion. She was pretty in a raw, mishandled way. She and Murtha talked for a few minutes. A longer conversation than Thorn had witnessed till then. Thorn punched the button and slowed the speed to normal.

Something had happened to Murtha's face, a stiffening that looked very much like fright. The girl edged around to the end of the counter, and bent her head to the side provocatively, eyes fluttering. Murtha came up to her and the girl reached out and touched him. The touch was hidden behind the counter, but it looked to Thorn from the way Murtha flinched that it was an intimate groping. At that point Murtha grew very agitated and hustled the girl toward the front door and practically pushed her out onto the sidewalk. She stood there for a moment smiling at him, then left.

Sugarman was snoring softly beside him on the couch. Thorn watched a few more uneventful days go by in Liquorland. Then one Saturday morning at the blip of ten, the first customer through the door was the same skinny young woman, early twenties, wearing black jeans and a black T-shirt, a straw bag over her shoulder.

Murtha put aside the bag of Chee·tos he was working on and came out from behind the counter and stood close in front of her. She spoke a few words to him. Then Murtha squinted at her, standing very still as if he were having trouble digesting what she'd said. She came up on her tiptoes, leaned in, and kissed Murtha on the cheek. Then she reached into her straw bag and as she turned her back to the camera, she withdrew something and held it out to him. Murtha shook his head, sad but firm. Refusing with deep discomfort.

The young woman spoke again, stepping forward and setting the object on the counter. It was a black snub-nosed .38. At that moment Murtha seemed to remember the camera, for he glanced at it, then hurried over, reached his hand out toward the lens and the film turned black. When it came on again, the thin young woman was gone, and Murtha was again the methodical store owner, going about his routines. Gone was the amiable look that had taken him over when the young woman had appeared.

Thorn was sitting up, watching intently. But there was no more of the skinny girl on that Saturday. At five the camera blinked off, and came to life again at nine Monday morning. Nothing unusual on that day, and still no sign of the girl.

That tape ran out, and Thorn got up and inserted the next one. It was Tuesday, again the same routine. Then Wednesday turned out to be normal as well, and Thorn was about to file away Murtha's encounter with the girl as irrelevant. Then came Thursday, and the first person through the door was Darcy Richards.

Thorn picked up the control and backed up the tape. He slowed it to normal speed and watched again as Darcy entered the store. Murtha stood behind the counter, and Darcy spoke to him for a moment. In her blue jeans, white jersey top, her slouchy red jacket, the sleeves rolled up to her forearms. Over her shoulder her crocheted cotton bag with leather trim. A thumb hooked in the strap of the bag, holding it in a stiff pose.

She spoke a few sentences, and Murtha came out from behind the counter, bringing his bag of chips along. He stood before her. As she continued to speak, his eyes dropped, and his head began to sag. She kept speaking to him, talking to the crown of his head. Then she stopped. She shifted her stance, leaning toward him. She said something else, not more than half a sentence, something fierce and final. And his face bobbed up. He stepped away from her, shaking his head, then shaking it faster, speaking now for the first time, working himself up, showing his teeth, a snarl, then lowering his head and tilting it to the side like a boxer slowly boring in. He kept speaking, edging forward, and Darcy took a step backward. She said something more, then stumbled briefly, and as she did, Murtha dropped the plastic bag of chips and drew back his right hand and slapped Darcy Richards hard in the face.

Thorn hit the stop button.

He took a breath, blew it out. He backed up the tape. He hit *play*, then punched *slow-mo*. Took another careful breath, looked over at Sugarman sleeping. He turned back to the screen and watched Murtha bulling in on her, saw Darcy stagger, Murtha reacting, taking advantage, jerking his hand back and flashing it open-handed against her left cheek. Thorn froze the frame. Caught Darcy's face flinching, head snapped back, hair flying.

He stood up, walked around the coffee table to the TV. It was perched at eye level on a fake wood wall unit. Thorn stood close before it.

The house was soundless, only the quiet hum of the VCR, and the fizz of electrons bombarding the TV screen. Darcy's image fired at the silver-coated glass, some of the electrons penetrating, making it through, some of them crossing the space between screen and Thorn, across those seven, eight inches of air. Electrons sending Darcy's image beyond the tube, beyond the screen. Firing her into Thorn, into his body, lifting the hair on his neck.

CHAPTER 11

ROY DAVID MURTHA, 218 SANDPIPER BAY ROAD. THORN FOUND THE LISTING in the kitchen phone book.

He sprinted out to his car, drove furiously through Sugarman's neighborhood and the two blocks out to the highway, mashed the gas pedal to the floor and drove the VW straight across the northbound lanes, bounced across the median, swerving out in front of a southbound Greyhound, which honked and flashed its lights, Thorn holding the pedal down, past real estate offices and banks, hardware stores and pizza shops, restaurants and sea-shell shops, through downtown Key Largo, the shopping center dark and empty, past motels and dive shops, flashing past the Burger King and bait shops, bars and condo developments, the warm air blasting through the car, picking up old papers from the backseat, swirling them up into the night, Thorn holding the pedal down till the speedometer grazed eighty. Hurtling down the long straightaway past the Sheraton and Popp's Motel, the Stoneledge, holding it down around the big bend into Tavernier, swinging out to pass late-night cars and trucks and then braking hard, tires squealing, the VW tipping briefly onto two wheels, as he swerved into the parking lot of Sandpiper Bay Village. Thorn wrestled the car back under control, aimed it at a concrete parking marker and jolted to a stop against it.

He switched off the ignition and threw open the door. Half past eleven. The place quiet. Only a scattering of cars in the lot. Most of the condos owned by Miamians or snowbirds. The Canadian crowd. All the signs in French.

Sugarman would definitely consider this rash. He would've wanted Thorn to sit down and nonchalantly discuss things, decide together the best way to proceed. Maybe if Thorn had woken him they would've decided to wait till business hours tomorrow. Chill down. Then both of them would walk in, confront Murtha in his liquor store, in the doorway where he'd slapped Darcy. That was probably the sensible thing, the rational, under-control thing.

Thorn took the stairs three at a time, was in front of 218 before his conscience could mutter another word. He hammered the door. Eight times, ten. Rattled the knob, then turned around and kicked the door with the heel of his shoe. Seven, eight, nine. Spun back around and banged it with both hands. Pounding in time with his heart.

The door to the apartment next to Murtha's came open. Eyes appearing in the crack above a gold security chain. Thorn hesitated, his fists raised.

"Thorn?" A woman's voice.

He lowered his hands, his heart lugging down.

"That you, Thorn?"

The woman's door closed. Thorn stood there for a moment, then the chain rattled and the door came open again. Rochelle Hamilton stepped into the outdoor hallway in a long white T-shirt with Snow White circled by the dwarfs on the front of it. The shape of Rochelle's body was a shadowy presence beneath the thin cotton.

Rochelle had been several years behind him at Coral Shores

High, closer to Darcy's age than his. A cheerleader and home-coming queen. Class president, valedictorian. Won an academic scholarship to Harvard. But something mysterious happened to her up there. Thorn never heard what. After only a year in Boston, she'd come home full of dark jokes about the world out there, off the island. Now she and her parents ran a yogurt joint in one of the strip shopping centers. Beautiful and smart, Rochelle had begun running wild, drinking herself rubber-legged in public places, getting a reputation around the island for her willingness to snuggle up to any yahoo with a pickup truck and money for a six-pack. He'd spoken to her a few times across the counter of her shop as he and Darcy bought yogurt sundaes, but those were the only words they'd ever exchanged.

Thorn slid his gaze away from her, out toward the empty parking lot.

"You looking for Murtha?"

Thorn said yes, he was.

"What? You run out of Scotch? Can't wait till tomorrow?"

Thorn turned his head and looked her in the face, disciplining himself away from the shadow of her body.

"Sorry I woke you, Rochelle."

"Oh, you didn't. I don't sleep. I'm one of those. I lie down, close my eyes, but it doesn't happen. I go over things instead. While everybody else is rejuvenating, dreaming, I'm going over things."

"Well," he said, "dreaming's not always what it's cracked up to be."

She smiled and fingered the hem of her T-shirt.

"You're here about Darcy, aren't you?"

"Why do you say that?"

"I heard about it, about what happened to her. I assume that's why you're so wild-eyed."

"Whatta you know, Rochelle? Tell me."

She looked out into the night, buying a moment or two. Thorn's hands twitched. He felt the sweat trickle down his back.

"Talk to me, Rochelle."

"It's nothing really," she said. Looking back at him, doing something behind her eyes, a calculation, as if she were deciding just how honest to be. "Murtha asked me about her, that's all. Asked me what I knew about her."

"Oh, did he now?"

"And about you too. Who you were, where you lived."

"When was this?"

"I'm not sure. Little while back. Two, three weeks."

She stepped across to the aluminum railing, leaned against it and looked down into the parking lot. As she bent over the railing, the T-shirt rose to reveal the back of her thighs.

"He's not home," she said, turning back to him. "If his red Firebird isn't there, then he's out somewhere."

A hundred yards away, a transfer truck rumbled past on the highway, and beneath their feet the concrete shook.

"You know where he takes his Firebird? Where he hangs out?"

"From what I can tell, he has something of a sleeping problem himself," Rochelle said. "I gather he likes to drive. Go on little road trips at night, up to Miami, places up there."

"What kind of places?"

"He doesn't confide in me. I just hear him through the wall, coming in just before dawn. And I've been out walking a couple of times real early, and I saw him park, get out, he's all dressed up, coat and tie, shoes polished. So I assume Miami. I mean, down here, if you wear a suit and tie like that, you're risking a fistfight. Right?"

"Maybe he's been to church. Midnight mass."

Rochelle smiled. Her eyes wandering out to the dark and back to Thorn. She took a breath and let out a husky sigh. She arched her back against the railing, propped her elbows there. Thorn allowed himself a look. Purely clinical. His entire sexual apparatus was shut down cold. But she was still a beauty queen. Still the voluptuous and brainy woman who'd carried the town's banner off to the bleak Northeast to fight the big fight. Which she'd somehow lost.

"Okay, Rochelle. Sorry I bothered you." He turned to go.

"Why don't you come in? Have a beer. I might remember something else."

He turned back around.

"If you know something else, Rochelle, I want to hear it. But beyond that, no."

Rochelle straightened. She crossed her arms across her breasts. Her face, her body, a wild mix of signals. Defiant, coquettish, embarrassed.

"I wasn't propositioning you, Thorn. I just invited you in for a beer."

"I'm sorry if I misunderstood."

"You did. You misunderstood."

She held his gaze for a moment, then something collapsed in her eyes. Her face twisted as if she'd gotten a sudden whiff of something foul.

"Well, good night, Mr. Eagle Scout. Sleep tight."

Thorn said nothing.

She marched to her door and shut herself back inside her apartment. He counted four locks snapping shut. He turned and walked back to his car, limp and dazed. The afterglow of his adrenaline buzz vaporized in the flash of Rochelle's rage.

Thorn drove home, eyes heavy, feeling the accumulated lack of sleep from the last few days weighing down on his shoulders. Turning his blood to a numb syrup. Even picturing again Murtha's slap didn't revive him. What he needed was to sleep till three tomorrow afternoon. Eat a healthy breakfast, and sit down at his desk and draw up a plan of action.

Maybe it wasn't as bad as it looked. It was possible the slap was about something else entirely. Maybe Sugarman even knew about the incident already. A disagreement over a bill, or something else totally unrelated to her death.

Thorn drove north along the overseas highway, watching the black asphalt unroll before him.

No. That slap was not about any late payment. That slap wasn't something that would've slipped Sugar's mind. Absolutely not. Not even mild, saintly Sugarman could have pardoned Murtha for that.

He drove the return trip well below the speed limit. And even with his eyes burning with weariness, something snagged his attention a half mile before the gravel entrance road to his house, and he jerked his head to the side before he even put a name to what he'd seen. Parked at the side of the Little General Food Mart was a glossy red car. Thorn lifted his foot from the gas, craned that way for a better look. And yes, by God, it was a Pontiac Firebird.

He hit the brakes, downshifted and swerved across the median, bumped down the steep gully, up the other side, across the road, and slewed into the parking lot of the convenience store.

When Thorn threw open the double glass doors, Abner Fellows looked up from behind the counter. Abner, a black man in his mid-seventies who Thorn vaguely knew through Sugarman. Same church, same bowling league.

Abner closed the magazine he'd been leafing through. Hollywood gossip.

"Hey there, Mr. Thorn," Abner said. "You up early or out late?"

"Little of both."

Thorn marched across the front of the store, looking down each aisle. The place gleaming, and empty. But he pushed on, prowled down every aisle, went to the rear of the store and shoved open the gray swinging doors into the storage area. Nothing back there either.

He walked slowly back to the counter, Abner giving him a pleasant smile.

"That Firebird out there. It belong to you, Abner?"

"Sure wish it did. Car like that, hell."

"Whose is it, you know?"

"Not by name, but I can tell you what he looks like."

"Old-timer?" Thorn said. "Short, stocky man with thick white hair? Greek-looking. Swarthy."

"That's right, that's the very one."

"When'd he leave the car there?"

"Little while ago."

"You see where he went?"

"North along the highway."

"Toward my place."

Abner stared at him and scratched his gray chin stubble.

In the lot outside, an old white van pulled in, and three men piled out, long beards and scraggly hair, leather hats and tattoos.

"Don't worry," Abner whispered. "They's regulars. Been smoking some reefer over at their clubhouse, now they gonna have themselves a Twinkie or two."

Thorn watched the motorcycle guys come in and spread out up and down the candy aisle.

"You still friends with Sugarman?"

Thorn said yes, they were still friends.

"That boy still with the police?"

"No, he's on his own now."

The Hell's Sweet Tooths began lining up behind Thorn, hands full of M&M's and Snickers. Thorn stepped out of their way and Abner began to ring up their booty.

"Well, now, you say howdy to Sugar for me, okay? I haven't seen him down at the church now for 'bout a year."

"I'll give him your regards."

"He still married to that same white girl?"

"Jeanne, yeah."

One of the motorcycle guys was giving Thorn a toothy smile like they were in on some gag together. The universal dope joke.

"Well, now, that's too bad," Abner said, ringing up more candy. "Yes, sir. That boy's taken on one heavy cross to bear."

"You should tell him that. Maybe he'd listen to you."

"Hell. Don't nobody listen to me. No, sir. Don't nobody listen to an old black man, not even another old black man."

The biggest of the motorcycle guys chuckled, and that set off the other two. Laughing, with their beards quivering, big bellies shaking inside their dirty T-shirts. Abner laughed, too, as he rang up some Reese's, a carton of doughnuts. The motorcycle guys laughing their wide asses off. Everybody looking at Thorn, waiting for him to join in.

He nodded solemnly to Abner and left.

Thorn turned in at his drive, angling the car to the right, blocking the entrance. He set the brake and got out and walked slowly through the grass at the edge of the gravel, eyes scanning the undergrowth. Nothing moving out there. At least nothing he could see. The three-quarters moon was hidden inside a bank of heavy clouds. The bay was about as dark as it ever got.

Thorn picked his way quietly to his wooden stilt house. He stepped beneath it, stood there for a moment listening. A light breeze was chattering in the silver palm, and there was the breathy whisper of the tide against the shoreline. Nothing else.

He edged over to the stairway, probing the dark, searching the hibiscus and oleander on the perimeter of the property. Nothing there either. And nothing passing by out on the water.

Above him rose his darkened wood house, his own creation, built painstakingly from boards scavenged at the shipyards in Miami. He'd spent months there dismantling packing crates from the Far East and Africa. Entire forests of exotic wood were being sacrificed to cradle the heavy goods shipped to the great gulping maw of America.

Thorn had constructed his house entirely from those scraps of wood, intercepting them before they could be burned at the dump. With the help of one old ship-building carpenter, Thorn had fit every board to every other board, dovetailed and pegged them, shaved them, planed and milled them. And as a result, he knew his house intimately, its sounds, aromas, its barometric feel. Its rhythms and dispositions.

Staring up at the floorboards, he listened now for the scuff or quiet creak of human presence. He made himself as still as he could, made himself a part of the dark. Holding back. Skulking there beneath his own damn house without a weapon, nothing but his wits. And they were so fired and quickened just now, it was a wonder he didn't glow.

He waited and heard nothing. No paper sack rustling, no gun being cocked, no swarthy man rattling in the woods nearby. He waited some more. Gave it a good wait. Fifteen minutes, twenty, twenty-five. And then there it was. Upstairs. An almost inconspicuous noise. The quiet rasp of grit beneath a leather sole.

He edged to his right, reached out and touched the knotted end of the hawser hanging there. A thirty-foot length of anchor line that had been tossed overboard from some passing tanker. A month ago the heavy rope had washed ashore somewhere alongside the roadway down in Islamorada. Darcy spotted it and lugged it home and found the right limb to attach it to. It was her joke. Tarzan, Jane, their tree house, the mighty yodel performed from the swinging vine. But only once since Darcy hung it from the oak limb off their bedroom had Thorn used it. Crocked on Chianti, he'd swung out from the balcony, done his squawking Tarzan call, and rope-burned his hands sliding down.

Now, hand over hand, cold sober, he pulled himself up into the trees. Ten feet, fifteen, his triceps and back muscles burning. He stifled his heavy breath, going higher, past the first low branches and then hauling himself up, eye level with the wraparound walkway. He paused, his palms on fire, then dragged himself higher until his waist was even with the wood railing.

He rocked his weight and gradually pushed the rope into a gentle swing. Wider and wider till he could touch the house with his toe, then one more arc and he was there. His foot on the mahogany rail and he stepped off onto it.

He took a long breath, stared at the side of his house. He picked his spot. And without further thought, he jumped down hard onto the porch, took a half second to set his feet, and dove headlong through the open bedroom window, ripped through the screen. Ducking as he flew, he meant to execute a judo roll, hit the mattress on his left shoulder and get to his feet and come up swinging.

But her scream changed all that.

The woman he landed on shrieked again, and began to claw and clamber out from under him. In his shock Thorn balked for a moment, then tried to grab her wrists and quiet her, but after only a second or two she twisted free. She was strong, all sinew and gristle, and her flesh seemed oiled. When she'd squirmed out from under him, she broke a leg loose and just as he sensed what she was about to do, her knee drove solidly into his crotch.

Thorn rolled away onto Darcy's half of the mattress. He groaned and tried to find a breath. Opening his eyes, flooded with nausea and wavering light, he watched helplessly as she got to her feet and stalked around the foot of the bed, down the aisle beside the window he'd crashed through.

The woman was panting, coming closer.

Thorn swallowed back the agony in his groin, tried to ready himself. Tensing as she came nearer. This girl from the video, from Murtha's liquor store. With her hair as short and dark as panther fur. Wearing a man's long-sleeved white shirt rolled up to her elbows, the tail hanging outside her cutoff jeans.

She held her hands out before her like someone fending off furniture in a darkened, unfamiliar house. Long, thin fingers. No rings. Nothing in her hands.

She came closer, and as she peered at him through the dim light, her breathing slowed. Until she was just beside him.

"You always come in like that? Or you just trying to impress me?"

He snorted. Raised himself onto his elbows and shot a hand out for her shirt. He took a handful of it and dragged her forward. She didn't fight this time, but gripped his wrist with both her hands, holding on for balance.

"Who the fuck are you?"

When she said nothing, he tightened his grip, holding her there at the side of the bed.

"Sylvie," she said, glowering. "Sylvie Winchester."

Thorn let go.

And in the next second, a yard from where they stood, a fist-sized plug of wood exploded from the plank floor.

CHAPTER 12

AT FIRST THEY DIDN'T MOVE.

Just watched the bright beam of light aim up through the hole in the floor and shine against the naked rafters. Then another explosion of wood, a foot closer to Sylvie. She leaped onto the bed and lay flat on her back beside Thorn.

Beneath the house, he could hear the shooter scuffling in the gravel. Then the flashlight washed over the floorboards, bright light leaking through hundreds of cracks. Thorn craned over the edge of the bed, watching the light explore the planks until the man downstairs located the new hole, and held his beam steady against it.

Sylvie leaned close and in a hoarse whisper said, "Friend of yours?"

Thorn drew himself upright and kneeled at the foot of his bed, began estimating distances across the room. His .357 was wrapped in an oily rag, stowed on the top shelf of the front closet, in the farthest corner of the living room. Not likely he could tiptoe that far across the bare floor without the flashlight catching him. And Christ, he wasn't even sure he had ammo for the thing anymore.

"Why doesn't he just come up?" she whispered. "Get it over with."

"Maybe he's chickenshit," said Thorn. "Wants to kill us without having to face us. The fucking asshole bastard."

"Is that what you do?" She gave him a scolding glance. "Get gross under pressure? Some kind of new Hemingway thing?"

He turned and peered at her. This woman with her airy smile, bantering while lead shrieked around the room. Sylvie Winchester was lying back down now, resting her head on Darcy's pillow. Just enough light to see her grinning eyes, the glitter of her diamond studs.

"We could go out the window," he whispered. "The rope I came in on. Surprise him."

"Boy, now there's a stupid idea. If he saw us coming down, it'd be a shooting gallery."

"You have a suggestion?" Saying it while he surveyed the room for a weapon. Seeing only soft domestic things, objects requiring hand-to-hand proximity. Angry at himself for growing so cozy, for forgetting the lessons he'd shed blood to learn.

"You could call 911."

"I don't have a phone."

"Well, hell, one thing's for damn sure," she said. "This mattress isn't going to give us a hell of a lot of protection."

Thorn watched the flashlight roam the cracks. In any other place in the world, his neighbors would have heard the shots and probably called the police. But along the Keys waterfront, with the quirky way sound traveled, it was impossible to tell where particular noises were coming from. The shots could be miles away, or could be coming from next door. And in any case, there was a certain south Florida tolerance for gunfire. A shoot-and-let-shoot covenant.

"I got an idea," Sylvie said. "Follow me, Hemingway."

She twisted to her right, reached up to the shelf above the bed and lifted a small queen conch that Darcy used as a bookend.

Looked back at Thorn, and began to nod her head in cadence and said, "On your mark, get set . . ."

On *go,* she pitched the conch shell onto the floor against the far wall, and in the same moment jumped to her feet and sprinted noiselessly to the door of the outer room. She stood in the doorway for a moment, studying her choices.

Out there was a twenty by twenty living area, with a wicker couch, two flimsy rocking chairs. And to her right, a minimal kitchen, a stove, refrigerator, breakfast counter, and two stools.

Thorn watched her make up her mind, cut to her right and disappear behind the wall. He hesitated a moment, then cursed and followed her. Three quick strides and he was through the door, the bare floor erupting behind him, one explosion then another chasing him across the room. He risked a look, stumbling as he did. Another blast a few inches from his left shoe sent splinters into his ankle. The searchlight from below continued to sweep across the slits between the boards.

He found her perched on the stove.

For a moment he stood in front of her while she waved her hand frantically, motioning him to the burner beside her. A yard behind him another plank shattered. And with that he climbed aboard the old Hotpoint range and squeezed in beside her.

"You call this an idea?" he said. Shoulder to shoulder with her, squatting there, he rubbed at his ankle. "Sitting on the goddamn stove?"

"Our gooses aren't cooked yet," she said, and smiled. "Lights, camera, action." Sylvie held her hands up in a pantomime of a movie camera. She panned the room and cranked her right hand in a circle by her left fist. The beam of light continued to roam the cracks, searching for the fresh holes. They could hear the grim metallic clink of the man reloading down below.

Sylvie dropped her hands from her face and leaned out and dragged open the refrigerator door.

"Now what the hell're you doing?"

Two more shots blasted up chunks of the living room floor. A paisley cushion on the couch ruptured, spewing a cloud of batting into the air. Some of it caught in a draft from the ceiling fan and began to float toward the kitchen. A few feet away one of the rockers was pumping furiously.

Leaning forward, Sylvie peered into the refrigerator, moved aside a carton of milk. She shifted a couple of other items and sat back, smiling with satisfaction and holding out before her a large jar of tomato sauce.

"This stuff is much better, you make it fresh."

Thorn wiped the sweat from his forehead and watched as she unscrewed the metal lid and put her nose to the edge of the jar.

"Myself, I'd never eat this junk," she said quietly. "I guess Darcy wasn't much of a cook, huh?"

Thorn took a breath, and bit back what he wanted to say.

Sylvie said, "Okay, so it's not perfect, but it should do all right for this circumstance."

Another shot smashed through the floor in the middle of the living area, then up, ricocheting off the ceiling fan. One of the fan blades shattered, dangled down, flapped for a moment as the fan turned, then fell. Out of balance, the old Hunter began thumping against the ceiling. It wobbled more and more until it twisted so far out of line, one of the remaining blades caught against the ceiling and the fan strained to a halt.

"Man, your place," she said. "It's coming all apart. Somebody better do something quick, or you won't have a house anymore."

Sylvie leaned out from the stove and held the lid of the tomato sauce out over the floor and gave it a flip, then drew back beside Thorn, flattening herself against the wall. The lid spun around two or three times like a coin on a countertop, and then another pistol blast hit nearby and sent the lid skittering across the floor.

"Yell," she whispered into his ear. "Yell, damn it!"

When Thorn said nothing, she sputtered, "He hit you. He shot you. Yell, you're dying."

Thorn gave it a try. Moaned. Dragged it out.

"That was lame," she whispered. "Very lame." Shaking her head at him. Shaking it some more, she said, "Okay, hold me."

She pointed to the rear waistband of her cutoffs, and after a moment's confusion, Thorn grabbed them as she began to lean out perilously from the stove.

Sylvie angled to her right, stretching her arm out as far as she could reach and dumped the contents of the jar into the newest hole. Shook the last of it out. And they watched the glop ooze through the opening. Suddenly the flashlight beamed on it. The light held still, focusing on the bright red drool.

"He tastes it, we're in trouble," she murmured, coming back to rest on the burner. Bringing her lips close to his ear, she said, "But if he's the chickenshit you think, he isn't going to dab his finger in the blood of his victims. Huh? You think?"

Thorn said nothing. He leaned away from the woman, looked at her, then back at the hole. The flashlight switched off.

"You think I'm a lunatic, maybe? Well, wait. See what he does, then tell me I'm crazy."

They were quiet, Thorn straining for any sound of the shooter. Feeling a hot whirl of anger rising from his gut. Pissed at himself for being so defenseless and unprepared, at the gutless bastard downstairs, and angry as hell at this woman next to him, grinning, pulling her silly stunt with the tomato sauce. Something a kid raised on cartoons might come up with. For all he knew she *was* a lunatic, with that nutty light in her eyes, the scatterbrained grin. Giddily leading them into disaster.

She leaned close and whispered, "He's staring at it, but he won't go near. Doesn't have the stomach for it. Not into gore. I hate people like that. Prissy shits."

Two more shots came in quick succession, the first a foot in front of the stove, the next skimming the oven door. Sylvie gasped and pressed her body back against the wall.

And Thorn jammed a rigid finger against her lips, then pulled it away and pointed the finger toward the creak of the stairway. The weight of a heavy man straining the teak. Thorn let himself down from the stove, slipped over to the silverware drawer, eased it open and took out the first knife with any size.

He halted at the edge of the living room, stood motionless. Another creak of wood outside. The shooter halfway up, eight, nine more stairs to go, taking it slow. Nervous, or crafty. Thorn wasn't sure he'd called it right, the guy a chickenshit. He could just as easily be a professional hitter, bored by the point-blank approach, looking for some new titillation.

Thorn edged across the room, sidestepping the gouges. Put a hand on the rocker to still it. Carrying the knife lightly, he inched to the doorway and flattened his back against the wall. Tense, shifting the knife to an overhand position. Thinking he'd hack the guy in a major muscle group, knock the pistol out of his hand. Trying to picture it, get the image clear, clean all the clumsiness out of it.

He set his feet, listening to the stairs creak, and to the sound of a man exhaling out there. A long gasp Thorn couldn't read. He glanced to his right, a quick check of the knife, and saw he'd chosen not only the largest one, but the dullest, most useless one. An antique from Darcy's hope chest. An ornamental scimitar of tarnished silver. Her great-grandmother's. Its blade would be taxed by a brick of cheddar. A damn jewelry store knickknack meant to be displayed in a glass breakfront. Unless the shooter's muscles were creamy soft, the thing in Thorn's hand was utterly worthless.

Outside, the stairs strained again. Thorn thought he could feel the subtle shift, the house registering the man's bulk.

"What're you going to do?" Sylvie whispered at his back. "Butter him to death?"

Thorn swung around, almost took a swipe at her. She tiptoed across the floor to the side window and stared out.

"There he goes down your driveway. Saw the tomato sauce and vamoosed. Just like I said he'd do."

Thorn hurried to the front closet. He pulled down the Smith & Wesson from the top shelf. His heart churning, a nasty headache sinking its claws through his temples.

"Man, you should get yourself a damn phone. You're going to make enemies like that, you should have a direct line to police headquarters."

He felt around on the top shelf, but there were no ammo boxes there. Sylvie followed him over to the desk, sat in his desk chair, hands in her lap. He ransacked the desk but found only one round, a .22 slug from god knew where. Useless.

Sylvie turned on the desk lamp, put out her hand, and said, "Hello, Mr. Thorn. Nice to make your acquaintance."

He held on to the round and looked at her in the light. She had a narrow face, with a sharp, angular nose and sculpted cheekbones. Gleaming black hair, boot-camp short, an inch or so on the sides, just enough length to keep some of it lying down, and a spray of cowlick bristles at the back. Her eyes were beetle-black, larger and more widely spaced than was glamorously correct. Her lips were plump for such a thin face.

It was a face with spunk, the vitality of the hybrid. Small-boned and elegantly chiseled, but with oversize features, as though she were the offspring of two clashing breeds that somehow had produced a daughter of jarring good looks. At another time, another place, Thorn might have been attracted.

She gave up and lowered her hand.

"Who are you and what the hell are you doing here?"

"I told you. I'm Sylvie."

"Look, goddamn it, what's going on?"

Sylvie stood up, brushed past him, stepped into the middle of the floor and surveyed the room as if she were assessing the rustic decor, the minimal decorations for signs of his character. When she was done, she brought her eyes slowly back to him. Her skittish grin was gone.

"You and Darcy, you weren't married?"

"What're you talking about?"

"You're not wearing a wedding ring."

Thorn looked down at his left hand.

"We lived together. We weren't married."

"For how long?"

"What the fuck is it to you how long I lived with her?"

"How long? A year, three years?"

"Two years."

"Good," she said. "That'll do."

"Now, what're you doing in my house?"

"Why I'm here," she said, glancing around at the bullet-riddled floor. "If you want to get right down to the basic truth, Sylvie is looking to find somebody who has the guts to step inside the ring of fire, get her out. She needs a hero."

Thorn was silent.

"You think you're up to that?" she said. "Think you can save Sylvie? Carry her out of the ring of fire?"

"What?"

"You gotta hear everything twice? I'm asking you to save Sylvie's life. I'm giving you an opportunity to slay the dragon, carry off the maiden."

Thorn stared hard at her. A smile flirting on her mouth.

Quietly, he said, "I don't know what you think you're doing, but I can tell you one thing, lady—I got all the fucking dragons I can handle at the moment. I don't need one of yours. Okay? Are we clear?"

She released a breath and closed her eyes briefly, and when she opened them again some of the radiance in them had leaked away. They were flatter and darker.

"You're sure?"

"I'm sure," he said. "Now, what did you have to do with Darcy?"

"Oh, I'll tell you," she said blandly. "I'll tell you all about it. But first, that guy, the one trying to kill us, remember him? He's getting the hell away. Aren't you going after him or anything?" Keeping her eyes from him, her shoulders slumping. She eased backward and let herself down into Thorn's desk chair.

"Okay," he said. "But you're coming with me."

"I think it's starting to hit me now," she said. "I'm feeling a little seasick."

"Stand up, you're coming with me."

"Look, I told you I'd wait for you. Don't worry. You can handcuff me to your bed if you want. Sylvie'll be here when you return. She wants to talk to you some more. Wants to make her case."

Thorn hesitated a moment, then turned and hurried to the door. Ran down the steps, out into the yard. Sprinted along the edge of the long gravel drive. But he saw no one. And out on the highway, breathing hard, there was no sign of anyone in either direction. He jogged back to the VW, drove to the Little General. The Firebird was gone. He sped the ten miles to Murtha's condo, parked in the lot beneath his apartment. No Firebird there either. He went up to 218, hammered on the door for five minutes, but got no response. Not even Rochelle came to the door this time.

Behind the rec center, he located the manager's office. A sour woman in her fifties wearing a flowered nightie, she wouldn't open her door to Thorn, keeping a half foot back of the gold security chain, telling him, no, sir, she certainly was not going to open Mr. Murtha's apartment, and to get the hell off the property or she'd call the cops, and come to think of it, maybe she'd just call them anyway.

Thorn marched back to the parking lot, stood for a few minutes looking up at Murtha's condo, wondering what the hell he could do, thinking of absolutely nothing, then got into his car and drove home.

All the lights were off inside his house.

He stood below the porch for a moment, but heard nothing this time. As he was starting up, he glimpsed something on the bottom stair. In the moonlight it seemed to glow. He stooped and picked it up, held it out to the light. It resembled a tiny human finger twisted by arthritis. A single Chee·to.

He flicked it out into the dark and walked soundlessly up the stairs. All the lights were out. He eased open the door and slid inside the darkened house. With his back against the wall of the living room, he listened carefully but heard nothing. After a few more cautious moments, readying himself for a dive and roll for cover, he flipped on the overhead light.

But the room was empty. He went carefully into the bedroom, opened the closet doors, the bathroom, the small pantry. Sylvie Winchester was gone.

He walked around turning on the rest of the lights, even lit a couple of kerosene lanterns. For a few minutes he examined the damage. Then he made himself a drink. Just enough Coke to darken the rum. He sat down at his fly-tying desk, swiveled the chair around, and looked again at the gouges in the floor and roof.

After he'd finished the drink, he stood up, turned the chair back around, and pushed it under the desk. And there on the desk was a sheet of lined tablet paper. In purple ink was a childish drawing. A stick-figure girl in a triangle skirt stood inside a flaming circle of ragged lines with her arms stretched out through the flames as if waiting for an embrace. At the bottom of the page a single word was printed in the same clumsy hand.

Please.

CHAPTER 13

IT WAS WELL AFTER MIDNIGHT, AND HARDEN WINCHESTER SAT ON THE front porch of his motel cabin at the Largo Lodge, mile marker 102. The cabin next door was vacant; on the other side was a small beach and beyond that Tarpon Basin, glimmering black in the moonlight. Same room they always stayed in. Twice a month they'd been making the trek over to Key Largo. Harden's hunger to glimpse Doris Albright seemed to be growing stronger every hour.

Tonight he was in gray running shorts, no top, his old white Adidas running shoes. Smoking a Havana cigar. A box of them came once a month from a friend of his still out in the field. A friend who owed Harden his life. One of many who did.

Minutes earlier, when Sylvie returned, she'd refused to speak to him. She walked past him into the cabin, showered and changed into her sleeveless nightgown, and now she was sitting in the wicker chair beside him, fanning the cigar smoke away.

"So where'd you sneak away to?"

"Took a walk in the starlight. Communing with the interstellar radio waves."

"Where'd you go, Sylvie?"

Harden blew a stream of smoke toward the screen, toward a moth that was battling to get inside, wanting to hold itself close to the porch light and set its flimsy wings on fire.

"Down the highway is all. I had a cup of coffee. Walked back."

"I can tell when you lie. I can always tell."

"Well, then," she said. "You're so psychic, let's hear it, Daddy —where've I been?"

Harden had another draw on his cigar. Let the smoke drift out of his mouth.

"The police won't help you," he said. "You should know that by now. You've lost your credibility, girl. Your crazy stories. The most that'll happen, they'll come talk to me, it'll end up the same embarrassing way as always. They take a look at your record, they'll be apologizing for disturbing me, backing out the door with their hats in their hands."

"You always underestimate me, Daddy."

"It won't work, Sylvie. None of it will. I'm going to put the Winchester family back together again, and nothing you can do is going to spoil that."

"I'm in love," she said.

He looked at her.

"The thunderbolt struck tonight, came crackling out of the heavenly dark. I found my own sweet prince."

"This is something new?"

She said, "Now I can be as obsessed as you. Hide in the trees, spy on my lover with binoculars. Spend all my waking hours plotting to get him in bed beside me. Like father, like daughter. Wackos of a feather."

"You don't need to keep doing this, Sylvie. You can spare yourself the trouble."

"It's no trouble, Daddy. No trouble at all. It's my job as your daughter to make your life hell."

She rose from her chair, walked to the edge of the porch, and looked out toward the black water. Harden thought of her long, arching neck, her throat, the bones in her cheeks, the soft shine of her eyes. With her back to him, he could see the shadowy ridges of her spinal column, her lumbar region's gentle sway.

As she stood looking out at the black-jelly shine of the bay, Harden pictured the shape of her vertebrae, the neural arches, the cartilaginous joints, the tender notches of bone that shielded the spinal cord.

And though she was only twenty-five, prison-camp thin, her hair black and shorn with savage disregard for appearance, despite all that, in the pale light, she was as striking as her mother. Powerful chromosomal echoes. The same bones floating under that same moon-white flesh. The same liquid light in the eyes, the same steam in her voice.

Another kind of man might have used Sylvie to rehearse the strokes and nibbles and caresses he would someday soon lavish on her mother. But Harden Winchester would never do that. He treasured the sanctity of his own family. He was no goddamn child molester. It was one of the few inhibitions he knew.

Two o'clock, then two-thirty. Harden sat on the porch in the dark with his cigar, watching the moths fluttering at the screens. Hearing finally the drone of Sylvie's snore, barely more than a purr.

He stood up, eased out the screen door, loped across the gravel parking lot, up to the highway, then out along the empty road, a loafing pace, through the tall grass of the median over to the northbound shoulder, then heading south, cutting onto the bike path, and opening up his stride for a mile, another, his breath coming easy and free, running a little over half speed, feeling light, fluent, increasing his pace gradually for the last mile till he was up on his toes, sprinting into her neighborhood, onto her street, and at last slowing and coming to a stop in front of her house.

His breath fast but not labored as he gazed up at the place. Standing in a swatch of shadow outside the range of the streetlights, he listened to the soft trill of an owl in the mangroves, to a distant dog barking at some stray scent.

When he had attuned himself to the resonances of the neighborhood, he came out of the shadows and climbed the stairs of her house. Her front door was simple. A useless Yale lock, no dead bolt, his wire key scratching in the slot, finding the cams, smoothing them all into place. Opening the door, stepping into the dark hush of her living room.

Harden stood there for a moment breathing her air. Trying to detect any sound of her. But the house was still.

Lathered from his run, Harden thought now as he crossed the living room rug that tomorrow when Doris woke, this house would be full of his evaporated sweat, filling her lungs, his invisible fragrance entering her, maybe even evoking in her some brief recollection of him.

He slipped down the hallway to her bedroom door. Stood there and listened to her snore, a duplicate of Sylvie's. Harden thinking how easy it would be simply to push open her door, force himself onto her, enjoy one momentary ecstasy. But no, he would not do that. For he wanted more than some fleeting gratification. Much more than that.

Touching the cool wood of her door, he let his fingertips linger for a moment, leaving behind his oils, his scent, then he let go of his breath and moved silently to the guest room, where the man slept. Doris left all the doors slightly ajar, probably so she could hear the old man if he woke in another fright. But Harden wasn't worried. He'd stolen into rooms where highly trained guards sat on full alert, and he had sifted across open spaces while a dozen eyes searched for any sign of him. Part training, part instinct, he knew how to take the gravity from his step, move without footprints, breathe soundlessly until he was as dark and unreflective as the shadows.

Nudging the door open, Harden eased into the man's bedroom. Came close to his bed. A slash of brightness lay across his quilt, shining from the security spotlight across the canal.

From the small back pocket of his shorts, Harden took out the paper envelope. No bigger than a single packet of sugar. He opened the flap, moistened his finger, and dabbed it inside. Felt the grains adhere to his fingertip.

The man's eyes came open. He looked up at Harden. In the dimness Harden could not be sure, but the man seemed resigned to this. Finished struggling, knowing by now that it was no use.

This was his third dose. And it was almost as if the man were welcoming Harden back, perhaps even wanted him to make it a lethal amount this time, wanted no more toying around, no more delay, have done with it.

But no, Harden had measured it precisely, knew exactly what one dab would accomplish. He didn't want this man dead. He wanted him to suffer. To feel some portion of the pain Harden had experienced because of him.

He leaned over the old man, and with his left hand he gripped Albright's lower jaw and pulled open his mouth. He inserted his right first finger into the man's mouth, wiped the grains across the old man's tongue.

As he was pulling away, Albright lunged upward and bit down hard across Harden's knuckles. Gnashing while a sound rose up in the old man's throat, a pathetic growl.

But Harden fended off the pain, kept silent, disciplined. Calmly found a pinch on the old man's carotid artery, shutting off his blood for a second, two, three, till the man relaxed his bite, lay his head back against the pillow, and closed his eyes.

He was still for a moment or two more, seemed to be falling asleep, eyelids fluttering. Harden watched, inching backward toward the doorway. He paused at the threshold, pressing his bleeding hand hard against his hip, stanching the flow, as he stared at the old man in his striped pajamas. Watching him for a minute, a minute more, until finally the first convulsion began.

"Where you been?" Frank Witty said. "You said midnight."

"I'm here, Frank. What's the problem?"

Frank rubbed his eyes and turned his back on Sylvie and padded into his bedroom. A little concrete block house on Sunset Drive. A nothing house. Smelling like a bachelor pad. Sweat socks and booze.

He sat down on the edge of his unmade bed. Smelled like sex in this room. Sex and sweat socks. Sylvie started unbuttoning her white shirt. Doing it slow, getting Frank's attention as it came undone.

"You said midnight."

"Are you whining, Frank? Is that what that was, a whine?"

"I was all pumped up. That was hours ago."

"It was my father's fault," Sylvie said. "He was standing guard over me and wouldn't let me leave."

"Your fucking father, man."

Sylvie got to the bottom button, hesitated, then undid it, drawing the shirt open very slowly. Frank's pajama bottoms starting to rise.

"Is that a tent pole I see, Frank?"

"Why you still live with your father, anyway?"

"I have no choice."

Sylvie unzipped her jeans, slid her right hand down into her crotch, wiggled it around down there. Guys liked that, a girl touching herself. God knew why.

"Your fucking father."

"He's awful, Frank. You have no idea."

This one was so easy. A definite yes. Thorn, on the other hand, she didn't know for sure about him. Worth another try, but probably not going to help her. You had to keep thinking down the road though, be with one, line up the next. No rest for the weary.

She stepped out of her blue jeans and put a finger between her lips and licked it wet.

"I'm getting ready, Frank. I'm lubricating myself. How about you, Frank? Are you ready for the long flight out of here, ready to push the envelope, Frank?"

He stood up, slipped his pajamas off. His thing was erect. Pointing at the ceiling. Frank was a done deal. So easy.

"Lights," Frank said, and smiled. "Camera." He made a camera out of his hands and cranked it at Sylvie as she walked naked toward him.

"Action," said Sylvie. "Action, Frank."

It was after three A.M. when Sugarman drove his Mustang down Thorn's gravel drive, honked three quick times, his usual signal, parked next to the VW, walked up the stairs, knocked on the doorframe and came in. Without a word to Thorn, he walked around the house, examining the gashes in the floor, the ceiling. When he was done, he stopped, looked over at Thorn for a moment, shaking his head like he was disappointed he'd missed the action, not sure when the next time would be.

"You left the TV on like that. I woke up, there was Darcy. Her face right in front of me. Christ, I thought I was going to have a seizure."

"You run the tape back?" Thorn said. "See what happened?"

"Most of it, I guess. Enough to send me on pretty much the same path you've been on tonight."

"You went to Murtha's place?"

"His condo, yeah. Just came from there. He wasn't home, but I saw Rochelle Hamilton." Sugarman picked the fan blade out of one of the rocking chairs and sat down, held the blade for a moment, not knowing what to do with it. Finally just dropped it on the floor. "Jesus, Thorn, what the hell did you do to Rochelle to piss her off so bad?"

Thorn glanced up at the ceiling, then back at Sugarman.

"You don't seem particularly curious about all this." Thorn waved at the wreckage.

"I knew we'd come to it."

"It was Murtha. I spotted his car parked a half mile down the road. Abner at the Little General described him too. I even found one of his Chee·tos on the stairs."

"Not exactly covering his tracks, is he?"

Thorn squatted down, broke some splinters off the floorboards and dropped the pieces through a bullet hole.

He said, "Maybe Murtha never got his doctorate in the fine

art of criminal behavior. Doesn't know you're supposed to wipe down your prints, leave a spotless crime scene."

"Maybe."

Then he told Sugar about Sylvie, the tomato sauce, all of it. He showed him the drawing she'd left, repeated the words she'd used.

When he was done Thorn sat down across from him. Sugarman was rocking thoughtfully, his eyes on the rafters.

"You should've held on to her, Thorn. You shouldn't have run off like that. That's what I meant about being rash. You weren't thinking, man. You weren't being level-headed."

"Hey, look at this place, man. A couple dozen slugs through my floor. Damn right I wasn't thinking straight."

"Don't get weird on me, Thorn. Don't go spinning off."

"I'm fine now. Just fine."

"So'd you call the law?" Sugarman waved his hand at the riddled house.

"No."

"Then we should do that next."

"Suit yourself," Thorn said. "Talk to them all you want. I'm not up to dealing with police bullshit at the moment."

"Wait a minute, hoss. I know what you're thinking."

"Yeah? What would that be?"

"Take the .357, go have a high-caliber conversation with Roy Murtha."

Sugar met his eyes, and Thorn said, "So tell me, buddy. The hell would you do in my place? Somebody shot up your house, trying real hard to kill you, the same guy slapped your loved one around a couple of weeks before she was murdered. You'd give all that to the police, let them decide how to proceed?"

"Yes, I would. I have that much respect for the law."

"Oh, I respect the law just fine," Thorn said. "It's the fucking people who execute the law I got serious doubts about."

"Stay here, Thorn. Talk to the police. I guarantee you, the two of us, we'll be at the store at nine o'clock. We'll have a talk with him first thing."

"Yeah, civilized chat," said Thorn. "Take your Miranda card along, make sure everyone's lawyer is present."

"Thorn," Sugarman said, getting some bite in his voice now, a little of that sternness that lived deep down in the hollows of his viscera and rarely made it up to the light. "Believe me, Roy Murtha's going to have to supply a good explanation of why he slapped her, and an absolute airtight alibi about where he was tonight to keep me from taking him out to Blindman's Pass and cutting him up into pieces so goddamn little even the crabs wouldn't have to chew."

Thorn looked at him a moment longer. His buddy leaning forward, elbows on knees, eyes fully charged.

"Okay, okay. We'll talk to your old comrades. But I'm goddamned if I'm going to rely on those shitheels to take this where it needs to go."

Sugarman held Thorn's eyes for a moment, the creases gathering in his forehead. He and Thorn'd had this argument before, back when Sugarman was on the force. Now that he was private, it seemed that Sugar had lost only a fraction of his old rigidity. There was just something in his nature, all those indelible habits learned by the light-skinned black kid who was an outsider in both worlds. The kid who'd used his rawboned strength and his quiet ferocity to become a high school football star, a skinny fullback who won the grudging admiration of his redneck teammates. And later, the young man who fought for years to penetrate the rigidly orthodox, all-white world of the sheriff's department. Through it all, his habits of strictness and adherence to the rules won Sugarman respect and earned him rank, helped him up the ladder. And though he was a free operator now, he wasn't free of all that. Still wanting to solve things within the narrow lanes of the cop world. A rule book stored at cell level.

"Tomorrow, I'll loan you my jigsaw," Sugar said, getting out of the rocker, squatting down, touching his finger to one of the gouges. "You can cut plugs for these holes, use Liquid Nails, glue them in, be good as new. Maybe even better. Give the place a nice polka-dot effect."

"I don't think this is funny, Sugar."

"No, it isn't funny."

Thorn stood up, went over to the fly-tying desk, looked down at the crude drawing Sylvie Winchester had left.

"Ring of fire, dragons, carrying off maidens," Sugar said. "This lady sounds like she's read one too many fairy stories."

It taxed him considerably, but Thorn smiled.

The Monroe County deputies had a good prowl around the house and property, took their sweet goddamn time poking through Thorn's things, showing considerable enthusiasm, even taking measurements of the holes in his floor. One deputy invited Thorn onto the outside porch and asked him a few dozen questions. Then asked them a second time. Thorn didn't give them Murtha's name.

"So, you go out drinking with the boys tonight, Thorn? Tip a few too many. That what happened?"

The deputy leaned close, into range of Thorn's breath.

"Aw, shit, Earl, you caught me. That's just what I did. Snorted a quart of rum, came home and filled my house full of lead, then called in the mounties as a prank."

"It happens," the deputy said. "I've come across stranger goddamn things than that."

Thorn turned around, went back inside, sat in a rocking chair, and didn't speak again.

After they'd gone, Sugarman hung around, drinking one of Darcy's diet Cokes.

"You satisfied now?"

Sugarman said yes, he was.

"So go home, sleep. I'll be by early, pick you up."

He took a minute or two more to finish the Coke, keeping his eyes fixed on Thorn. Then he got up, dropped the can in the recycling bin, patted Thorn on the shoulder and left.

Thorn lay down on Darcy's side of the bed, still dressed. With

the empty .357 cradled against his chest, he listened to the chit-
ter of insects, and the distant burr of fishing boats far out in the
back country. He lay still, eyes open, hearing the quiet dissolve
of seconds. Listening to each minute becoming the next, the
hours making their dark arduous passage. Crickets becoming
frogs, frogs becoming silence. And finally, with his head against
the pillow, his eyes still open, Thorn listened as the stillness
melted away into the gray hum of dawn.

CHAPTER 14

AT SEVEN HE PUSHED HIMSELF OUT OF BED, SET THE SMITH ON THE dresser, stumbled into the bathroom, and in ten minutes he was showered, shaved, and dressed. Gray jeans, blue work shirt, his grease-spattered Keds.

He picked up the pistol and carried it into the living room. He lifted it, felt its weight, took a grip on it, then aimed it at the front door. He kept that pose for a moment, then turned and panned across the room till he was pointing out the front window. He cocked the hammer, sighting on a gumbo-limbo near the shore.

Held his focus for thirty seconds, then a minute, held it until a quiver came into his muscles and grew to a shake. Out of shape. Lost his edge. Grown a flabby husk of domesticity and pulled it around himself like some comfy sleeping bag. But now it was time to wake up, crawl out, start some brutal weight training again. Lift the pistol, aim, hold it steady. Fight back the quiver. Lift, aim, lift, aim. Till it all came back. Till he was hard again. Hard and cold and merciless.

When finally his muscles began to fail, he set the pistol on his fly-tying desk. At the front door he stood for a moment and in the full daylight examined the damage. There were a dozen fist-size punctures in the ceiling, spears of sunlight coming through. Probably tore the hell out of the wood shingle roof and ripped up the tar paper all around it. The floor was worse, ragged splinters punched up, and twisted shards of wood everywhere, the ground fifteen feet below the house was visible at each step. Next decent rain, the room was going to be one large colander.

He went downstairs, climbed into the VW, and drove to Sugarman's house. When he arrived Sugar was standing in the front yard in his pajamas, pressing a piece of plywood into one of the wooden frames of his double hung windows.

"I had a visitor last night too," he said, glancing at Thorn. "Guy apparently forgot his key, had to climb in through here."

"When?"

"While I was off looking for you."

"Jeanne all right?"

"She was sleeping. Snoozed right through it."

Sugarman hammered on the edge of the plywood with the side of his fist until it was wedged tight in the window frame.

He turned around and Thorn saw the anger had taken hold in his eyes.

"The fuckhead rifled through my video collection. Threw around all those great Disney classics. Shit, he even broke my *Fantasia* cassette."

"He find what he was looking for?"

"No," Sugarman said. He waved hello to one of his neighbors, a fishing guide trailering his skiff to work. "I took all the work tapes with me in the car. Seemed a little paranoid at the time."

Thorn followed him inside. Sugarman told him to help himself to breakfast if he wanted, and he walked back into the bedroom to get dressed.

Thorn found a loaf of rye bread and made himself a couple of pieces of toast. Buttered them and poured a cup of coffee. Some kind of Irish mint creme with a hint of chocolate almond. Jeanne's doing. Closer to candy than coffee.

Thorn sipped the stuff and sat at Sugar's dinette and watched two squirrels chasing each other up and down the side of the oak tree in Sugar's backyard. One finally caught the other and mounted it from the rear. Their tails switching, immobilized for a few moments. As he watched them, caught in their moment of animal bliss, the chocolate coffee turned to acid in his belly.

Thorn explained what he wanted to do, and they took Sugar's Mustang to Largo Park, one mile north on the ocean side. A row of expensive new houses were down by the sound, but the rest of the subdivision consisted of small two-bedroom jobs, working-class houses with old pickups out front, rusty Keys cruisers; Cadillacs and Chevys, lumbering dinosaurs from the sixties, with barge bodies and menacing grills.

He pulled in the driveway of a small white house. Red shingle roof, two shabby palms, a rusty tricycle on its side in the yard. Thorn got out, went to the door, hammered hard enough so there was a remote chance he might be heard over the TV cartoons.

Sugarman stood on the porch beside him, holding the two cassettes.

A black woman in her thirties came to the door. She was wearing a motel maid's uniform and her hair was straightened into a Doris Day flip.

"Well, if it isn't Mr. Thorn and Mr. Sugarman," she said. "What you boys want so early in the morning?"

"Hey, Tonasha."

Thorn said, "We'd like to use Eddie for something."

A young black kid appeared behind Tonasha and wedged in beside her hip. Seven, eight; large eyes.

"What you want with my Eddie?"

"We want him to look at a movie for us."

Beside her, Eddie bobbed his head up and down, eager for the job. Tonasha moved aside to let them in.

"Now, what kind of movie would that be?"

"A silent one," Thorn said.

Eddie sat on the couch, watching the video of Murtha and Darcy. He lip-read and signed to Tonasha, who sat on the arm of a velveteen La-Z-Boy and interpreted aloud for her guests.

"He need to look at that part again," she said. "That man's talking too damn fast for Eddie."

Thorn aimed the remote zapper at the VCR and backed it up.

The boy had already translated the first minutes of Darcy's visit. Right away Darcy had asked Murtha who the girl was. The girl who'd handed him the pistol. Murtha didn't answer, just stared at her. And she told him she wanted to know what their conversation meant. Murtha was speechless. Darcy asked him where the girl was now. And Murtha dropped his head, stared at the floor. Darcy told him that she wasn't going to let this slide. She was going to locate that girl, talk to her, find out what was going on. Murtha raised his head. Looked at her.

Tonasha concentrated on Eddie's lightning hands and said, "The man say it don't be none of Miss Richards's business what he said to anybody in his store. He call Miss Richards a bitch and says he's not paying her to spy on his personal affairs. And sure as shit he's going to cancel his contract."

"Maybe this is too strong for Eddie," Thorn said. "We should get somebody else to do it."

"He's heard worse," Tonasha said. "Every day of the week."

Sugarman turned his back on the TV.

"Right there the man's telling her to get on out of his store and to never come back," Tonasha said.

Eddie continued to sign, reading Murtha's final angry speech.

"The man is asking her who else she told this trash to. He call it slander. He ask her if she'd said anything to Sugarman." Tonasha paused and watched Eddie sign. Then said, "And Miss Richards, she answer him. She say something about you."

"Me?" Sugar said, turning around.

"No, him. Thorn."

On the TV screen, Murtha advanced on Darcy, she stumbled, and he slapped her. Thorn stepped over and turned off the TV. He stood in front of the blank screen and looked at Tonasha. He was sorry he'd done this now. Hearing Darcy's words come alive from Tonasha's mouth, bridging that impassable distance.

Tonasha shifted in her chair, watching Eddie's hands.

"Miss Richards telling the man she hadn't said nothing to her boyfriend about any of this, 'cause if she did, Thorn'd probably rush over and whop that man upside the head to get the truth out of him. Then Thorn be the one in trouble. And she say she didn't want that to happen. That's when the man smacked her."

Thorn took a long breath, and ejected that tape and slid in the other. He turned the TV back on. It took a minute to find the place, then Thorn stepped away from the screen and they all watched Murtha and Sylvie speaking to each other. Sylvie reaching behind the counter to touch Murtha. Then him hustling her out of the store. A moment later Sylvie was back and handed Murtha the pistol, Murtha shook his head in refusal, then reached up and switched off the camera.

Eddie didn't sign through either scene. Tonasha stared at Thorn.

"What's wrong?" Thorn said. "What's going on?"

"We already saw those," Tonasha said. "Couple of weeks ago."

"You did?"

"Thought you knew. Darcy brought it over, had Eddie read the lips just like you doing. We looked at that tape over and over, maybe twenty times. Liked to burned out my eyes watching the damn thing. 'Cause of how they got their faces turned, you can't tell exactly what they saying. Just a word now and then."

"What words?" Sugar said.

"The weird girl, the first time, she say that man is cute. A real attractive man. Coming on to him, like. Then he got her out of there. The second time, the girl say something about money. A lot of cash money."

Thorn backed up the video and they watched Sylvie's second visit replay in slow motion. Eddie signing now.

"Eddie say that girl is saying the man can have a whole lot of cash money if he just use that gun on somebody."

"On who?"

"That's exactly what Darcy wanted to know. But from this direction, Eddie can't tell."

"Anything else?" said Thorn.

"Yeah. What's that word, Eddie? That word she say when she talking about money."

Eddie spelled it out with his fingers and Tonasha said, "T-I-L-A-P-I-A."

"Tilapia," said Thorn.

"Yeah," said Tonasha. "*Red* tilapia. She say something about red tilapia and lots of money."

Sugarman stood up and snapped off the TV.

"And what in hell's name is a tilapia?"

"It's a fish," Thorn said. "An exotic fish."

Thorn and Sugarman rode in silence to the strip shopping center across from Coral Shores High School where Murtha's Liquors was wedged between an Ace Hardware and a small video arcade. There was a jewelry store on the far end of the strip and an empty shop on the near end. It was nine thirty when they pulled into the parking lot. Murtha should have been halfway through his opening up ritual.

"He's not here." Sugarman turned off the motor.

"Why am I not surprised?"

"Well, I guess we wait, see if he shows."

"Let's go to his apartment," said Thorn, "kick the damn door down."

"Already went there. This morning before you came over, Thorn. Thought it might be interesting to speak to the man, just me and him. Close and personal. Ask him why he had to break my *Fantasia* tape. When he didn't come to the door, I went and found the manager, convinced her to open his place up for me."

"How'd you manage that?"

"I believe I gave the lady the erroneous impression I was still with the sheriff's department, working plainclothes now. She was very helpful. Full of respect for the law." Giving Thorn a meaningful look.

"I'm glad to see you're loosening up a little."

They sat for a few moments watching customers go in and out of the hardware store. Roofers with long, snarled hair and well-dressed retirees, housepainters and women in silk blouses. All the social classes waiting in line at the cash register, everybody forced to mingle for a few uncomfortable seconds.

Thorn asked him what he'd turned up at Murtha's apartment. And Sugarman took a long breath and blew out a cheerless sigh.

"Guy lives like a slob. Place smells like rotten fruit and mildew. I thought, based on how shipshape he keeps his store, you know, he'd be a neat freak. But no, he's taken untidiness to a whole new level."

"That's it?"

"I found something else, yeah."

Sugarman reached across him, opened the glove compartment, and drew out a small pulp magazine. *Captivating Lassies.* Fifteen pages of naked girls not yet in their teens posing in various sexual positions with adult men. Grainy black-and-white photos, all of them shot against harshly lit backdrops. The girls ranged from ten to maybe as old as twelve. The men were in their forties, most of them sporting pompadours and lamb chop sideburns. The magazine had a musty smell and the edges of the pages were yellow and crumbled in Thorn's hands. There was no date stamped on the cover, but the thing had to be nearly a hundred years old.

"I was in there an hour," Sugarman said. "Dug around in the drawers, did a major snoop."

"All without a warrant," Thorn said. "Man, you must be feeling guilty as hell right now."

"I feel fine," he said. "Except for wanting to tear Murtha's dick off, I feel just fine."

"This magazine," Thorn said, paging through it carefully. "It's some kind of collector's item. Antique porn. These girls, by now they'd be in nursing homes."

"Yeah," Sugar said. "If any of them made it past childhood."

They watched a woman walk by on the sidewalk in front of them. White hair, shorts, and a sleeveless blouse. She went to the door of the liquor store, tried the handle, peeked into the dark, looked at her watch, tried the door again, and gave up.

"Take another look at page six."

Thorn glanced at Sugarman for a moment, then opened the magazine again, found the page. A young girl standing against a white curtain, black hair, thin, no breasts, her arms behind her head, while a naked man crouched before her and explored her crotch with his mouth.

"Look familiar?"

Thorn stared at the photo.

"Jesus."

"I thought so."

"I mean the body's similar, the nose, even her cheekbones, yeah. But the eyes are completely wrong. Sylvie's are bigger, wider set."

"But she's close, you'd agree. Striking resemblance."

"What the hell? This magazine is a hundred years old."

"So maybe it's just a coincidence. A guy sees a girl he's been staring at in a magazine for years. His bell goes off. He's got to have her."

Thorn shook his head, kept looking at the girl. Her eyes staring off at the ceiling. The look on her face, one part phony ecstasy, one part horror. Her lips were shaped into a sultry smile, but there was no real heat behind it. As if she'd plagiarized the expression from somewhere, practiced before a mirror until she'd trained her muscles to portray an emotion she'd never known.

She looked painfully emaciated against that stark background, but there was still something compelling about her. An excitement in her eyes that Thorn associated with animals in the wild, a jittery look as if she were forever mapping out the geometry of escape.

Thorn lay the magazine on his lap, and they watched some high school kids in baggy shorts and T-shirts walk into the video arcade. Another kid arriving on a bicycle yelled to the group, dropped his bike on the sidewalk and followed them inside.

"Care to connect the dots?"

"I don't know," Thorn said. "I got to digest this."

"Well, we know a few things anyway," Sugar said. "We know Darcy watched the tape of Murtha and Sylvie. Sylvie hands him a pistol, Murtha shuts off the camera. Darcy must've sat up straight when she saw that. So, she thinks about it, then off she goes to Eddie and Tonasha. Sounds to her like Murtha and the girl might have been discussing killing somebody or something.

"But Darcy can't be sure. Lot of ambiguity here: So she shows up at the liquor store, confronts Murtha about it, and he slaps her. She leaves, and then maybe she starts worrying that Murtha has a right to be pissed. She can't be sure the thing she's witnessed is criminal. Could be a murder conspiracy or it could be nothing at all. Eddie can't read all the words, so it might be something else entirely. They could be talking about killing roaches, for christ sakes. Who knows?"

With his eyes still closed, Thorn said, "So Darcy's confused about the whole thing, maybe a little guilty she may have lost you guys a client. Fifty percent of your business. And she's decided she wants to do this completely herself."

"What? Where'd you dream that up?"

"Darcy told me. Out on the boat the day she was killed. She implied she was investigating something on her own."

"Why didn't she tell me?"

"She wanted some independence, I guess. Wanted something that was all hers."

"Oh, man."

"So, anyway," Thorn said. "She confronts Murtha about

what's she seen, and if that truly was what he was doing, planning to murder someone, then Darcy put herself in some significantly deep shit."

Sugarman was staring at Murtha's liquor store, breathing hard. Thorn looked again at the skinny girl in the photo. All her ribs visible, the shadow of her skeleton.

"Goddamn it to hell," Thorn said.

"What?"

"This is my fault. I knew something was wrong. But I couldn't get it out of her. I didn't say the right words."

"Oh, sure, that's good, buddy. Blame yourself. Twist it around, put yourself on the old emotional rotisserie, get a good guilt burn going."

Thorn opened the glove compartment, pitched the magazine inside. He stared out the windshield at Murtha's front window.

"One thing that bothers me," Sugar said. "How the hell did the killer manage it? How'd he know you and Darcy were going out in your boat at that particular time, that Darcy was going to go swimming underwater? I mean, it's all a little too convenient."

Thorn looked off at U.S. 1, the endless stream of traffic.

"She was supposed to meet somebody."

"What?"

"She'd made an arrangement to meet somebody at Snake Creek Marina the morning we went out to the reef. I don't know who, but they didn't show. So somebody knew where she'd be and when. The rest was probably just free-form, make it up as you go."

Thorn looked out his window at a car pulling in beside them. A white-haired gentleman in long madras pants and a bright green shirt got out, headed into the hardware store. Living the colorful life of retirement. Socially secure.

Sugarman tapped his fingers on the steering wheel, both of them watching a fifteen-year-old boy standing at the doorway of the video game arcade, peering in.

"Now, look, Sugar. Does Roy Murtha strike you as a guy

trained at some advanced military school? A Green Beret type. Scuba tanks, lethal hand grips. I mean, come on, the guy's doddering around his store, looks like a training film on heart attacks."

A young couple in blue jeans and matching plaid shirts strolled up the sidewalk, his arm over her shoulder, her arm around his waist. They walked the length of the shopping center, stopped in front of the jewelry store and looked longingly at the window display. Thorn turned his eyes away, stared at the traffic out on U.S. 1.

"Something else I'm curious about," Sugar said, "is why you forgot to mention this tilapia thing to me." He leaned forward, lay his cheek against his hands gripping the steering wheel. Thorn looked over, met his gaze.

"Just before she jumped in the water that last time, Darcy asked me if I'd heard of red tilapia. When I remembered it later, I wasn't sure, but I thought maybe it could be related to what was bothering her. So yeah, I needed to do something, so I dug around, studied up on tilapia. I did it yesterday."

"But you weren't going to share any of this with me."

"I didn't know what it all meant yet. If it was relevant."

Sugarman sat up, pointed a finger at Thorn.

"No Lone Rangers, Thorn. We're on the buddy system. Looking out for each other. You hear what I'm saying?"

Slouching lower in the bucket seat, Thorn reached out and pressed the glove compartment button, opened it, then snapped it closed again. He cleared his throat, stared out at Murtha's store. Then he began to fill Sugar in about Ludkin, Seamark, the dead bodies stacked up. He repeated what the professor had told him about red tilapia, lead to gold, giving it all to him, word for word, moment by moment, as much as he could remember.

When he was done, Sugar said, "All right, okay. Interesting stuff, but where's the tie-in? Sylvie, tilapia. Murtha. I don't get it."

"Well, for one thing," Thorn said, "there's Sylvie's name. It's the same as some guy who raises tilapia over on the Gulf coast. Sylvie Winchester."

"Well, well, well."

"As for Murtha, I don't know. Maybe that's just an anomalous return."

"A what?"

"One of Darcy's terms. From her weather forecasting days. Some kind of false echo from the radar bouncing off big office buildings. The radar screen shows thunderstorms that aren't there."

"Murtha's a false echo?"

"Maybe."

"But what about the Chee·to under your house? That doesn't sound like any false echo."

"Okay, Sugar, then you follow the Murtha thread. I'll take Sylvie."

Sugarman started the car and backed out of the space.

"You're getting that look again, Thorn."

"Which look is that?"

He found a break in the traffic and headed out onto the overseas highway.

"That look," he said. "Like somebody better start praying."

"They can pray all they want," said Thorn. "Believe me, Sugar, it won't help them one goddamn bit."

CHAPTER 15

BACK AT SUGARMAN'S OFFICE THORN CALLED JIMMY PAT CRISWELL, A friend of his with the Florida Marine Patrol, but no, Jimmy Pat knew nothing about fish farming, tilapia, or the whereabouts of anybody in the business, but he did give Thorn a number of a guy at the Department of Interior he knew up in Atlanta, main number of the Richard Russell Federal Building. Jimmy Pat believed Interior was the agency that inspected aquaculture farms anyway.

But Jimmy Pat's guy wasn't in, and his secretary told Thorn it was U.S. Fish and Wildlife he wanted, and she gave him the number for the southwest regional office, a guy named Jones in charge, so he called that number, but Jones had transferred two months earlier to the Sarasota office, and the woman on the line asked Thorn if maybe she could help. The raspy voice sounding distantly familiar, but Thorn couldn't place it. Telling the woman who he was, what he wanted. She hesitated a moment, then said, Thorn? Fly-tying Thorn? The Key Largo hermit? Thorn, the hundred-yard-dash man?

Well, he said, I haven't been doing much sprinting lately, but yeah, the rest of it's accurate. You're not going to believe this, she said, but this is Judy Nelson. Used to be Judy Murphy. Then paused for him to respond, but hell if he could place her. After an awkward silence, he said, oh, yeah, Judy Murphy, of course. Hi, Judy. Still having no idea who the hell she was. Yeah, yeah, she said, I married some no-account named Nelson, thing lasted a year and I dumped him, but kept the name, don't ask me why. And, hell yes, she knew Winchester. She'd even drive Thorn out to his place if he wanted. Catch up on old times on the way out. When did he want to come over? Tomorrow, he said. First thing Wednesday morning. Fine, she said, I'll be ready for you. And Judy, he said, I'd like to drop in on this guy unannounced. Is that all right with you? Judy considered it a moment, then said, You gonna tell me what this is all about? Tomorrow I will, Thorn said. Tomorrow.

"Now, that's weird," Thorn said as he set the phone down. "You remember a Judy Murphy?"

Sugarman looked up from his desk.

"Judy? Yeah, sure. Of course. Come on, Thorn, you don't remember her? Left defensive tackle."

Thorn had to work at it, but finally the image came to him.

"Oh, god. That Judy."

"Yeah," Sugarman said. "Big Jude."

Judy Murphy had been the only girl in Key Largo history to try out for Coral Shores varsity football. She'd been cut just before the first game of the season. By then Judy had knocked half a dozen of the starting offensive line on their butts. The coach decided it was too demoralizing to the boys to keep her around. Thorn and Sugar and a couple of the others said Judy didn't demoralize them. They liked having her around. But the coach had decided. Judy didn't squawk. She'd made her point. And afterward she went to all the games, sat in the last row of the bleachers, watched intently, but never cheered.

Sugar's phone buzzed. He picked it up and listened, then said, yeah, sure, Andy, send her in.

Thorn sat down in the client's chair and watched as Rochelle Hamilton came through the door. She wore a dark green cotton T-shirt and baggy white jeans, suede sandals. She had her hands in the pockets of the jeans, looking back and forth between Thorn and Sugarman.

"Rochelle," Sugar said.

"Hi," she said, and stood awkwardly in the doorway a moment before turning and shutting the door. "Hi, Thorn."

He gave her a neutral hello.

"I came by," she said, " 'cause I started thinking about the other night. How I was. I wanted to say I'm sorry."

"It's okay," Thorn said. "Forget it."

"You want to sit down?" Sugarman said.

"I brought something. I don't know, but I thought it might be useful."

She hesitated briefly, looking at Sugarman, then the office, as though something was dawning on her she hadn't expected.

"I don't know if I should."

"What is it, Rochelle?"

She pulled a newspaper clipping from her pocket and stepped forward and handed it to Sugarman. Then she stepped back, her eyes wandering to Thorn, then cutting away to the wall.

"You might need a magnifying glass," she said. "I did."

Sugarman looked at the clipping, read it, looked up at Thorn. Then he opened his desk drawer, pawed through it for a while, came out with a magnifier. He grunted, leaned close. And without looking away from the clipping, he reached out for the desk lamp and hauled it over, switched it on.

"What is it?" Thorn said.

"Where the hell'd you get this, Rochelle?" Sugar's head still down.

"I knew you were going to ask."

Thorn got up, peered at the clipping. There was a photograph of a man fallen forward into his plate. Face turned to the side. The headline said, THIRD MOB KILLING IN FOUR DAYS.

"Try the magnifying glass, Thorn, tell me what you see. The guy in the pasta, face toward the flashbulb."

Thorn took the glass, angled the light at the newspaper, found the best distance and bent close.

"No . . . no way," he said. Then, "Well, wait a minute."

"So? Which is it?"

The man's hair was darker and fuller, his face a few pounds thinner. But with the same jowls, the lump of a nose, same eyebrows. That coarse, dark complexion. Roy Murtha.

"Raymond Bianetti, is what he's called here, shot seven times while he was eating his fettuccine Alfredo."

Thorn set the magnifying glass aside.

"Would you all tell me something?" Sugarman said. "Why the hell do they always do that? Get so specific in the newspaper about the pasta or whatever. I mean, hey, it's degrading. Sounds like some kind of reporter's joke, is what it sounds like. Those cynical pricks. Mr. Sugarman was found dead of a stroke, his head floating in his Campbell's alphabet soup. An *A* and *C* stuck to his cheek. It's a cheap shot, is what it is, making fun of some guy who's dead, for christ sake."

"This guy, though," said Thorn, "he isn't dead. This one got up and walked away."

"Not according to the *New York Times*. Pronounced dead at Cedars Sinai at four thirty-eight A.M., January ten, 1975. Also known as Raymond the Clink. Sources say he had something like twelve human beings on his life list. Old Ray was a busy guy, punched a lot of tickets."

"Where'd you come by this, Rochelle?"

"Murtha and I . . . ." She took a breath, and shook her head in disgust.

"You had a thing," Thorn said. "You and the liquor store guy."

"Yeah," she said. "When he first moved into the condo. It didn't last long. A week."

"And you found this in his apartment?" Sugarman said.

"I was looking for an aspirin one night," she said. "Murtha

snoring in the bedroom. I was in the guest bathroom, opening drawers, not finding anything, then there it was, in this cabinet underneath the towels and facecloths. A scrapbook. Dozens of clippings, same story from different papers. I pulled one out, started reading. It was just starting to register when I heard him moving around in the bedroom. I got flustered. I mean, all I had to do was shove it back with the rest of them. But I didn't. I slid it in the pocket of my robe. It was so stupid, but Jesus, I was scared; I didn't know what the hell I was doing."

Rochelle closed her eyes, bowed her head.

"Raymond the Clink?" Sugarman said, looking up from the article. "What kind of goddamn name is that for a mobster?"

"I don't know," said Thorn. "Clink, like in jail, maybe."

"Well," Sugar said. "Doesn't inspire much terror in me. Just sounds dorky."

"Guy had to've paid plenty to fake something like that," said Thorn. "Hospital staff, police, restaurant people. Had to spread around a shitload of cash."

"Or maybe he's in witness protection. The feds might've staged this. One of those deals."

"Do you know anything about that, Rochelle?"

"No," she said. "I never got that close to him or anything. We barely talked."

"Man," Sugar said. "Only the federal goddamn government would do something like that. Good old U.S. of A. Kill a dozen of your fellow citizens—hey, no problem. All you gotta do, testify against somebody for jaywalking, we'll set you up in a sweet little liquor store down in the Florida Keys, purge the old record. Shit, even the Pope wouldn't stand for that kind of absolution."

Thorn took a last look at Murtha in his fifties and pushed the clipping back across the desk.

"Doesn't really matter, does it? If he staged it himself, or the government did it. He's still in the middle of this."

Sugar said quietly, "No, it doesn't matter. Not at all."

Rochelle said, "I guess I better get going."

Thorn stood up, came over to her.

"Thanks, Rochelle. Thanks for bringing this over. I know you didn't have to."

"Could I be in trouble?" she said. "I mean if he misses the clipping, figures out who might have it."

"If there were a lot of others just like it in the album, I doubt it. And you took it a few months ago," said Sugar. "He hasn't missed it yet."

"He's the one in trouble," Thorn said. "Don't worry about it. Just keep your door locked. If he shows up, call Sugar."

"All right," she said. "Well, I guess I'll get on to work."

"I'll drop by later," Thorn said. "Check on you."

"Will you?" she said. Then she caught herself, lowered the emotional volume and said, "Don't bother, Thorn. I'll be okay."

"I said I'll drop by, so I'll drop by."

Rochelle smiled vacantly. Heard that one a few times too often. When she'd left, Thorn sat down again in the chair across from the desk.

"It could explain why he shot up your house the other night. Guy thinks Darcy is on to him, going to reveal his real identity. He murders her, then he comes after her boyfriend."

"Bullets through the floor? Doesn't sound like Mafia to me. Sloppy, unprofessional."

"Guy's in retirement. Been out of the game awhile. Lost his thirst for blood, maybe."

"Maybe," Thorn said. "But anyway, I still want to tug on the Winchester thread. It feels like it's woven deeper into this thing. Think you can handle Raymond the Clink?"

"Oh, yes," Sugar said. "I believe that's entirely within my capabilities."

Sugarman swiveled his chair to the side, leaned back, glanced into the beauty salon where a pretty young black woman was getting her hair frosted a few feet away.

Watching the woman, he said, "I want you to know, Thorn, I'm hurting too. I loved Darcy. Maybe not the same way you did, but just as much, in my own fashion. Just as much. And trust me, buddy, there isn't a thing on god's earth I won't do to set this right. Within the law."

He filled his lungs and held it for a few seconds, then let it back out. Turning back to Thorn, a complicated smile rising to his lips. Serene, but urgent. A dark burn in his eyes.

This was a man who'd never been a hater. Apparently born without the necessary organs to support bitterness or spite. About the most Sugar could manage was a mild huff, a growl of displeasure now and then. Rage and fury were beyond him.

Thorn often recalled a particular Friday night in October, twenty-five years before, Sugar and him pinned helplessly to the grassy turf at the bottom of a tangled pile of football players. Sugar with the pigskin in his arms after squirming for yet another first down. They'd looked at each other through the grids of their face masks, the fans cheering, the referee's whistle screaming above them, and they'd smiled at each other, giddy, never been happier.

And just at that moment a big white hand had appeared through the churning mass of bodies, and it reached down and located Sugar's face guard, and some rawboned linebacker named Langstaff from the sugarcane fields around Clewiston dug a bony finger into Sugarman's right eye. Gouged him deep. Thorn grabbed for the arm to take a bite out of it, but it wriggled away and was gone as the bodies unpiled.

With his eye bloody, Sugar kept on playing. Didn't seem angry, just more focused. More precise. Until late in the fourth quarter, he broke through the line and into the open field, and Langstaff was there, taking a bead on him, galloping head-on, big guy, six three, outweighed Sugar by thirty pounds, and this time Sugar didn't swivel his hips, didn't feint, even seemed to slow his stride, torquing down to a lower gear, and both boys lowered their shoulders as the point of collision approached, but somehow Sugar got his the necessary fraction lower, and planted his helmet in the linebacker's gut, stood him up straight, then ran the hell over him. The hayseed was unconscious for twenty minutes, Sugarman sipping Coke on the sidelines. Not mad, not celebrating. Just playing by the rules.

Sugarman rested his elbows on the ink blotter. Eyes still severe.

"Promise me, Thorn, when you get thrown in jail over in Naples, use your one phone call on me, okay?"

Thorn stopped at the office door.

"You know she loved you too, Sugar. You know that, don't you?"

Sugarman looked down at the ink blotter, took a breath.

"Yeah," he said from a long way off. "But somehow, at this moment, that's not a whole hell of a lot of comfort."

"Maybe not," said Thorn. "But it's all the comfort we got."

Thorn spent that Tuesday afternoon patching his roof. Working out in the August sun, ninety-four degrees. The humidity so thick he could've taken a few swipes through the air with a drinking glass and collected enough water for a healthy sip.

He tore off each wooden shake that had been splintered, pried off the others above it till he'd exposed a clear patch of tongue-in-grove decking. Then with galvanized siding nails he hammered each new shake into place. Twenty-three bullet holes. Sixty-eight cedar shingles. Four hundred and twelve nails.

He worked through the afternoon and sweated away pints of tequila and beer. He knew that wasn't biologically correct. The liver disposed of the booze, but all that sweat seemed to cleanse him nonetheless. And when he was finished with the work, his house watertight again, the sun just starting to bleed into Blackwater Sound, he barely had enough strength to climb down from the roof. He felt like he'd been running wind sprints in full pads for weeks. A flulike achiness.

In the kitchen he drank a gallon of water, then drank another. Carried a glass out to the porch and watched the sun ignite one isolated cloud, which sprouted from the horizon like a great sugar maple going through its fall colors. A mild blush of pink, then the harder reds, and in a while the cloud turned silver, then finally a dark leaden gray before it disappeared into the thick forests of the night.

Thorn drank more water, but couldn't quench his aching throat. He drank water until the stars came out, then lay down in the porch hammock, his eyes open, his mind ringing with the sound of his hammer driving each siding nail home. He lay in the hammock all night and didn't shift positions, and he didn't sleep.

CHAPTER 16

DORIS ALBRIGHT WAITED BESIDE THE PASSENGER DOOR OF THE GOLD ELDO-
rado while Billy and Don Malton lifted her husband out and set
him in his wheelchair. Boss man still coming to work no matter
how sick he was, how feeble and out of it.

The Malton brothers had worked in the fish house, cleaning
lobsters, shucking oysters, filleting fish, whatever needed doing,
for close to fifteen years, a hell of a long time on this island for
anybody to stay with anything. Working for Philip that many
years, they still spoke to him with the same careful deference
they'd used before his stroke reduced him to this limp sack of
flesh.

Philip had once been as gruff and scathing as any man Doris'd
met. But not long after she met him, she began to see that the
surliness was simply camouflage for a deep sentimental streak.
Secretly he treasured Billy and Don, thought of them as sons,
just as he loved all the men and women who worked for him,
who like Philip had gashed and mangled their flesh for years to
haul fish after fish from the cold depths.

Doris walked behind Billy as he rolled Philip's wheelchair up the cement ramp and into the fish house. She exchanged greetings with the half dozen employees she could still afford to keep on. None of them knew it yet officially, though most probably suspected, that their place of work was up for sale. A million three, the asking price. Barely enough to pay off the two mortgages, the mountain of medical debts, back taxes. A million three hundred thousand. An unthinkable amount.

As each of the employees wished Philip well, he replied in grunts, bobbing his head with great effort. She took over the chair and wheeled him into the glassed-in office, shut the door and locked it, then set about closing the several sets of venetian blinds.

She had to change into her work clothes before starting her day here. Doing all of Philip's work: balancing the books, dealing with the stream of suppliers, and the endless conversations with hard-luck lobstermen and shrimpers. Overseeing the cleaning and shucking, the packaging, endless grinding of chum, and the thousand other details of the retail fish market.

This morning it had been another trip to Baptist Hospital up in Miami, one more MRI. There'd been another seizure last night, and when it was over, Philip had described in his muddled and breathless way another visitation by the dream man who he claimed was slowly poisoning him. Routine, the neurologist said. In the feverish spasms of a seizure, it wasn't uncommon to experience hallucinations.

Doris was still in her city clothes. The white cotton gauze dress that tumbled in tiers of ribbon and lace trim. White canvas sandals on rope-covered wedges with laces that wrapped up her ankles. A garden-party outfit as cool and crisp as pineapple sherbet. She would've worn shorts and a jersey, but Philip liked the outfit so much she put it on every other day now. He'd bought the dress impulsively a couple of years ago on a Caribbean cruise they'd taken. Now, whenever she wore it his eyes brightened. And anything that accomplished that, Doris was willing to do. Anything at all.

She was down to her bra and panties, reaching for her denim sleeveless dress hanging from the hook on the back of the door when she noticed Philip was mumbling, leaning forward in the wheelchair, his face turned to her, eyes poring over her exposed flesh.

A broken smile disfigured his face, and he curled a finger at her, beckoning. She put the denim dress back on the hook and walked over to him, checking the blinds as she went. Smoothing a couple of slats into place, then moving close, standing in front of him, offering herself, till he lifted a hand and reached for the elastic band of her panties.

His fingers were crabbed and callused, brittle against her flesh as he pulled the panties down an inch or two, a contented croon working up from his throat. She felt a shiver pass through her, a complicated chill, love and regret, and though she hated to admit it, a mild aversion to this man who now inhabited a stranger's body. Philip bent forward, focused mightily on the job of tugging at her underwear. She dropped her arms to her sides, and let him slide his hands inside the silk and fumble between her legs. Where once he had been so smooth in delving her, now he was all bump and spastic flutter, a man in an iron glove.

In the years before his first stroke they'd made love Sunday mornings usually, and one night mid-week. He, a vigorous sixty-four, she, many years younger. All the attraction still there. The delight in each other's body unfailing in fifteen years of marriage. A reliable and powerful heat that kept the weld strong.

But now, some glitch in the wiring of Philip's cortex had made him horny day and night. Unable to manage an erection, yet he still had an inexhaustible fever for her, constantly gripping her, lifting her skirt, reaching inside her blouse to bump his mangled hand against her breasts so he could bring himself to another fruitless, imaginary ecstasy. And she complied whenever possible, giving him this, no matter how awkward and uncomfortable it often was. Giving him what she hoped was some echo, however faint, of what they'd known before.

Just this morning, with Philip deposited in the waiting room, Doris had questioned the neurologist about this new lustfulness, and the M.D., a woman about her own age, put down her notes and stared across her desk at Doris and said, "And you're complaining?"

Philip groaned to himself, one of his crooked fingers finding its way inside her, wriggling now, and Doris looked down at the top of his head while she stroked his thin hair. She could hear an argument rising in volume out on the loading dock, could make out something about the Orion scale weighing light.

Philip gripped her buttocks with his free hand, drew her closer, lost in the dreamy rhythms of his fantasy. His finger making short strokes along the familiar angle that always had given them such pleasure.

Outside on the loading platform, a fistfight had broken out, and Tilly called for Doris to come out and intervene. She knocked on the door and called Doris's name while out on the dock the men hooted and catcalled.

Doris turned her eyes to her husband's thin white hair. He was finishing now, with a shudder and a sad whimper. Breathing hard, he tipped his head up and looked into her eyes, squinting the way he always did when they finished making love, his silent question; Had she come too?

She nodded at him, yes, she had. No reason not to lie. And then stepped back out of his hold, drawing her panties into place. She took her denim dress off the hook on the door and stepped into it and buttoned it up.

Again someone knocked on the door. Several hard raps, a pause, then more.

She checked her face in the cut glass mirror that hung on the wall opposite the photos. Patted an eruption of hair over her left ear, and went to the door and opened it.

Roy Murtha stood in the doorway. An elderly man, his dark eyes smiling at her. He was wearing charcoal slacks, a gray shirt

with black stripes, shiny material, rayon or some other petro-
leum fabric that looked unbearably hot. Murtha always dressed
this way, more like your local bookie than the usual slovenly
Keys citizen. He was swarthy and his body was short and thick.
He could've been one of those powerful Soviets, a coal miner or
weight lifter. Lips puffy, jowls with a shadow of beard. White
wispy hair.

For the last few years he'd been coming into the fish house
four times a week. Their most loyal customer. Far as she knew
the man lived alone, but he bought food enough for twenty.
Always a smile for her, a special hello, always wanted to chat, talk
about news events, the weather. He'd given her the creeps when
he started coming in years ago, always that smile, that lingering
look. Now she was used to it, saw he meant no harm.

"Hello, Mr. Murtha."

He held out a small bag of Chee·tos, offering her one. She
shook her head.

"How can I help you?"

He drew the bag back, took a handful of Chee·tos and patted
them into his mouth, gave her a smile, then shouldered past her
into the room as he munched.

She drew a breath.

"What're you doing?"

"We need some privacy, Doris. You and me, we need to talk."

She hesitated for a moment, watching him browse her office.
Then she shut the door behind her.

"I been coming in here, what is it, going on six years now?"

"That sounds right."

He smiled and swung his head around the room, ticking off
every detail.

"Must've spent, a hundred, two hundred a week."

"Sometimes more," she said.

"But I never been inside here. In the inner sanctum."

He walked over to Philip, craned down for a look. Her husband's eyes were closed, his head slumped forward. A doze.

"He's not looking so good, is he?"

"What's this about, Mr. Murtha?"

He glanced over at her, gave her that familiar smile.

"Funny thing is, Doris, the honest truth, I don't eat seafood of any kind. Never have."

"What?"

"Hate the stuff. Creatures living underwater, I never could stomach them. Just the names for the things, gills, fins, scales, all that, it makes my stomach turn. No, ma'am, I'm more into snack food." He rattled the bag her way, giving her another shot at a Chee·to. But she made no move. "I tell you what, Doris, I always wished you were in some kind of other business. I don't know how many times I came in here thinking, Christ, I wished you had a flower shop, or a jewelry store. Almost anything but fish."

He was standing in front of the wall of photographs, looking them over while he shook more Chee·tos into his hand. Eating them now one at a time.

"The thing I have about fish," he said, "I guess it comes from my background. Father in the merchant marines, loved boats. One of his shore leaves, he took me out, wanted to teach the buckaroo how to fish. I was six, seven. I was afraid. The water, the waves, all the big boats passing by, rocking our boat, it was all new. It scared the piss out of me."

"Mr. Murtha, I'm really very—"

He put up his hands in a be-patient gesture.

"My dad and me, before we're even away from the dock I'm throwing up. The old man can't believe it. His own son. A pussy like that. I'm puking out my guts and he's there driving the boat going, *Raaaalph, Raaaalph*, making fun every time I vomit over the side. And hell no, he wouldn't take me back to shore, had to ride up and down all day in the New York harbor, all those swells making me sicker and sicker, my father going *Raaaalph, Raaaalph*. And he kept on fishing, kept catching these things, bringing them on board, fish flopping around, blood all over the deck—I'd see that, and then I'd get sick again. Spent all day at the rail, my knees bleeding. That had to be what it was, don't you think? A thing like that, it happens when you're a kid, it marks you. You never touch fish again, hate the idea of the goddamn things. That's how it is when you're a kid, impressionable. Making choices for the rest of your life. *Raaaalph, Raaaalph,* over and over. A funny guy, my father. Very funny."

"Please, Mr. Murtha. I'm truly busy today. Is there something specific you want?"

Still looking at the photographs he said, "Now, that's the big question, isn't it, Doris? Man my age, man of some means, I ask myself that question all the time. What do I want? I could buy this, I could get that. Nice car, speedboat. But what is it I really want? What's missing in Roy Murtha's life?"

He turned around, looked at her. Putting a finger in his mouth, sucking at the orange crust that coated it. She took an impatient breath, let out a sigh.

"Most people, Doris," Murtha said, licking the last traces from his fingers, "they work something out on this issue. They marry, have kids. Don't ask anymore what they want. They get preoccupied, find diversions. All that philosophical daydreaming, it goes to sleep. They don't have time for it anymore. Now they gotta make a car payment, gotta run out, get more milk, take the baby to the doctor. But me, it never happened, the marriage thing. Worked too hard, never had time for candy and flowers. So here I am, prime of life, time on my hands, and I'm asking myself that question all day every day. What is it I want?"

"Now, look here, Mr. Murtha. I don't mean to be impolite, but I'm afraid you're just going to have to leave."

He cleared his throat and said, "Me, I come from rough, simple people. Not big thinkers, my people. No education, except in the streets. Grew up in the Bronx, never what you'd call close to my parents. Didn't connect with them. Sounds weird to say it, your own parents, not feeling anything for them. But there it is. That's just how it went with me."

Doris opened the office door, held it open.

Murtha grew still, his stumpy body taking root in the middle of her office. He peered strangely at Doris as if she'd just materialized before him.

"You know what, honey? It's kind of spooky saying it, but you two, you got the very same eyes. Same cheekbones. I mean, yeah, sure, it comes together in different ways, but it's all there. Coloring, even that lift in your eyebrow."

Her hand wandered to her throat.

In a hushed voice, she said, "Same eyes as who?"

"Why, Sylvie," he said. "Your daughter, Sylvie Winchester. You two are dead ringers for each other."

Doris stepped back. She managed a breath.

Murtha turned away from her, went across the office, glanced at Philip, then brought his eyes to the wall of photographs. Black-and-white shots of fish hanging on the dock outside. The marlin and sailfish with their weights painted in white on their sides. Mexico, the Caribbean, California, Nova Scotia. Philip and Doris in all of them. Sunburned, giddy from another great day on the water. And there were other assorted characters on that wall, others from the many who flowed through their lives, holding their rods in one hand, drinks in the other. Faces without names now, afternoons floating timeless on the cedar wall.

"All these people friends of yours?"

"Yes," she said. Light-headed now, a tremble in her knees.

"That's good," he said. "Friends or family. Got to have one or the other. Preferably both."

Murtha came across to her, shut the door behind her. He reached out and brushed her cheek with the back of his right hand. Doris cringed as she felt the tickle of the hair on his knuckles. She stepped away.

"You see, Doris, I came in today—it wasn't to buy fish. It's because I decided it's time we get down to the nitty-gritty. I tell you about me, details of my life, you tell me about you, we exchange autobiographies, then we talk about the serious issues affecting our lives. How's that sound?"

Murtha dug out another Chee·to, poked it into his mouth. Doris was quiet, her pulse still wobbling from hearing her daughter's name on this man's lips.

"In my case," Murtha said as he chewed, "you add up the

years, and what I am is an old man. But the truth, Doris, I don't feel a bit old. I got no health problems, got a good heart rate, blood pressure's low. On the social front, I'm a fairly decent man. Oh, I may wind up still talking crude sometimes, but don't let that fool you. That just comes from spending too much time around the wrong people. Myself, I'm not crude. A *fuck* will creep into my speech now and then, a *shit*, like that. But believe me, this is not Roy Murtha talking. It's 'cause of the men he's been forced to associate with over the years; it's those guys rubbing off on me."

With a dark ache swelling up from her groin, Doris walked over to the blinds and began to open them. The fistfight was over now. Everyone back to business out there. A few eyes cut her way as she opened more blinds.

She stood with her back to Murtha, looking out at the stark gray concrete interior of the fish house. And feeling inside her the solid wall she'd built so carefully beginning to crumble. That high, hard partition between her old life and her new one, between the pain and confusion she'd known as a young woman and the fairy-tale joy of her life with Philip. Hearing Sylvie's name on this man's lips. Hearing her name after all these years.

She turned and walked over to stand behind her husband, rested her hands on his shoulder.

"Here's how it is," Murtha said. He took a single Chee·to from his bag and looked at it fondly as though it were some fine cigar. "I came in here six years ago, it wasn't to buy fish. Like I said, I hate fish. Every day I leave here, I go right away to the Snake Creek Bridge, unwrap that fish or shrimp or whatever, and throw it in the water. No, sir, the reason I came in here was to see you. Talk to you. Be close to you, Doris."

Her voice wavering, she said, "I'm not following you."

He put the Chee·to in his mouth, chewed it as he walked over to Philip's wheelchair. He looked down at Philip's head, which had dropped forward, chin on chest. A rasping snore.

Still staring at Philip, Murtha said, "Let me put it like this,

Doris." His eyes rose up casually and held hers for a moment. "I'm Sylvie's grandfather."

The room swayed. Doris took a breath and felt a cold wind begin to whistle in her veins.

"See, Doris, your actual mother, your biological one, she was a nightclub singer. Torch songs, you know. Her name was Jenny Marciano. Pretty woman. Tall, slinky, could even be elegant, you know, if the mood took her. Jenny sang at the Copa for a while. That's where I saw her first. Wonderful voice, cross between Billie Holiday and Eartha Kitt."

"What're you doing? Why're you saying these lies?"

"Doris. I wouldn't lie about something like this. I'm no villain. It's true. I'm your father. Your old man."

Doris swallowed. Swallowed again.

Fiddling with a Chee·to, Murtha said, "So when Jenny got pregnant, I gave her the cash to get it fixed. Instead, without discussing it with me, she ran off, disappeared. Hid out in Tahoe is what I found out later, had the baby. You, Doris. Then, it turns out, when you were a year old, Jenny decides motherhood isn't her thing. Decides she wants her career back. So she put her little girl up for adoption. And that's how you wound up with Mr. and Mrs. Glenn R. Carter in Tennessee. They told you, didn't they, that you were adopted?"

Doris nodded yes, they had told her.

Her mouth was open but the dry words gagged in her throat. Murtha circled the office, studying the photos, glancing across at Philip, touching things as if he were committing it all to memory.

"In my heyday," he said, "I had a few men working under me. Guys. It was within their abilities to locate people, so, you know, I had them find Jenny, then after that, it wasn't hard to track the Carters down in Clarksville, Tennessee."

Doris waited, watching this stocky old man circle the office.

He said, "I never let the Carters know about me. I saw right off they wouldn't approve of who I was. What kind of life I was leading. But over the years I managed to pull a few strings, help your daddy's business dealings. I made sure he got himself that bright, shiny new car dealership he wanted so bad.

"Stayed in the background, discreet. But I kept watch over you, Doris. I kept watch. Clarksville, Fort Bliss, Lejeune, then the farm over on the Gulf coast, and finally here. I'm not bragging about it—I mean, I feel guilty I didn't do more. Guilty I didn't reveal all this to you long ago. But I did what I could from a distance."

She let herself down heavily in the salesman's chair beside Philip's desk.

"When it came time to retire, I decided to move down here. How I pictured it was, maybe I'd pass by you in the grocery, catch a whiff of you now and then, the post office, wherever. Little moments of togetherness. Watch you, make sure you were doing okay. Maybe someday, when the moment was right, I'd come up to you, reveal myself. But I never actually worked up the courage for that.

"Then a month ago, who walks into my liquor store, wants a pint of Ronrico dark rum? Yeah. None other than Sylvie."

"In Key Largo," Doris said, "Sylvie."

"That's right. I saw her, and I almost fell over. Looked so much like you. So much like my mom, too, you want to know the truth.

"I'm staring at her, standing there behind the counter of my store, listening to her ask for a bottle of rum, but I couldn't move. Just stared at her. And what does she do? She sees me looking funny at her, and very slow, she comes around the counter. Wiggles up close to me. Starts whispering things. And Christ Almighty, I can't believe it, but she's flirting with me, batting her eyes, reaches out her hand for my leg. My own granddaughter, not even knowing who I am, standing there running her hand up and down my goddamn thigh.

"I cool her off, get her out of there soon as I can. But then she calls me at my condo. We talk. She calls five, six times. We get chummy, a little bit anyway. Talking about ourselves a little. Then a day or two later, she shows up at my store again. Turns out she thinks I can help her with something, a personal matter. She's been looking for somebody, like a knight in armor kind of thing. Thinks I might be it. Even offers me money, a whole lot of money. Wants to pay me to help. Names some goddamn fish that's worth all this cash; Christ, I didn't know what the hell she was talking about.

"My first reaction was, I was dumbfounded, you know, her being who she was and me being who I am, and I said no, I wouldn't do it. I shoved her out of there. Now I look back, I reflect on that day, what she was asking me, and it's clear, I treated it too casual. She got angry and that's the last I saw of her."

Doris couldn't speak. Just kept staring at this man, trying to hear what he was saying through the static growing in her head.

"What Sylvie said was, she said her father, this man you married, Harden Winchester, he was forcing her into things of a sexual nature. Making her do things to him. Deviant stuff. She couldn't get away. Would I help somehow? Walked up to me, a random guy in a liquor store and makes this kind of statement. Would I help her escape this monster?"

Doris was shaking her head.

Murtha said, "So after I have a moment to consider it, I see I gotta do something. But to get going I need to know where she is. A current address for her. That's why I'm here. Why I had to tell you who I was."

"Lies," Doris said. "Lies, lies."

"The truth," Murtha said. "The plain simple truth."

"Harden wouldn't do that. He would never do that. You're lying to me. All this. These horrible lies."

Doris couldn't seem to lift her arms, a ghostly spread of numbness through her limbs.

"Where's Sylvie, Doris? Just tell me where she's living. That's all. I can check this out, come back and tell you what I found."

"I don't know where she is," she said. Her voice not her own, a flimsy imitation.

She dragged herself to her feet, looked out the window at the work area. Another load of lobster arriving on the south ramp. Rough men drinking beer, others shoveling ice into their huge coolers for another week at sea. She turned and faced Murtha. Philip was awake now. He burbled to himself like a two-year-old chatting with an invisible playmate.

"I haven't seen Sylvie in fifteen years, not since I left the farm."

Slowly, he brought his eyes back to her, stared for a while as if he were trying to rearrange her words, find some good news hidden in them. Then he frowned and said, "You're her mother. You gotta know where she is."

"I stopped being Sylvie's mother a long time ago. If you've been spying on me like you say, surely you know this."

"Okay, Doris. That's how you want it to go, I'll just have to find her some other way. But hey, look, now this thing is in the open between us, there's no way around it, we got to converse some more. You calm down, think over what I been telling you, and we'll speak again, work it out between us in some fashion. Okay, can you do that? Calm down?"

"Get out. Get out. Get out!"

One of the big lobster boats rumbled to life out in the creek, and Murtha turned his head and listened. He peered out at it for a few seconds. Then turned back to Doris. She was holding open the office door.

"You should know, honey, only reason I stayed away from you all these years, only reason I didn't come to you sooner, tell you all this, it was 'cause of the life I led. I didn't want you thinking you were poisoned, had bad blood flowing in you. This was the only reason. To protect you, Doris. Protect you."

When he was gone, she locked the door and walked over to the window. She watched the big lobster boat making the cramped and tortuous turn out in the narrow channel. Backing the engines, then forward again, and back. It was the *Deep Pleasures,* run by Jody Marcus, a young woman from down in Big Pine Key. Doris watched her work the silver throttles back, then forward, the streams of silver bubbles rising from her props.

Doris stared hard at the young woman working the controls until her vision blurred and the tears began to run freely and painful sobs cramped her stomach. She sat at Philip's desk, lay her head against her arms, and gave herself over to it.

CHAPTER 17

IT WAS JUST BEFORE NOON AND HARDEN WAS EATING THE LUNCH SYLVIE had fixed, sitting at the round oak table, bare-chested, in his bright yellow gym shorts and old sneakers, stuffing down the turkey and Swiss sliced thin and stacked high on pumpernickel, heavy on the mustard, lettuce, a wafer of tomato, hamburger dills, a handful of Ruffles potato chips on the side, washing it down with Perrier from the bottle, making little grunts of pleasure between gulps. Sylvie was at the sink washing her plate, her eyes on her work, not glancing out the side window, not even allowing herself so much as a peek at the clock.

She set her plate in the drying rack, wiped off her fork and knife on the dish towel, keeping her back to Harden, her eyes hidden from him, doing the routine things, the every-day-at-lunch things. Trying to move with a leisurely pace, keep the fidgets out of her hands, though she could feel the warm tension in her chest, the radiance of anxiety, the double-time tick of her pulse as she put the mustard and lettuce and the sliced turkey back in the refrigerator, let the door *whoosh* closed.

She sponged off the white tile kitchen counter, keeping her actions slow, lazy, uninspired, rinsing the sponge and squeezing it out. And then, Jesus Christ, she almost squealed when she heard the rumble of the truck, and the next second its two quick honks.

Harden scraped his chair back and stood up. When Sylvie turned from the sink, he was already at the back door. He tugged a blue work shirt off the peg by the doorway, put it on.

"Who is it?" Sylvie said.

"UPS truck."

"Oh, goody," she said. "A package from somebody."

"Did you order something again, Sylvie? Is that what this is?"

His voice was cold and he didn't wait for an answer. He was already out the back door, heading across the fifty yards of sandy yard to the front gate.

Sylvie followed, keeping a distance, already feeling the stink of failure growing on the moment.

The UPS man got down from the truck with a small box in one hand and his clipboard in the other, his brown uniform fitting tight over his wide shoulders, deep muscular chest, a brown baseball cap over his thick blond hair. Looking authentic.

When she got within earshot, the man in the UPS uniform was saying, "You folks live a long way out."

Harden was silent.

"You Harden Winchester?"

"I am."

Sylvie stepped back, kept her eyes away from the UPS man's, looking at the package in his hand, at Harden's hands, hanging easy at his sides. Her father seemed relaxed, unsuspecting.

Frank Witty handed the clipboard to Harden for his signature. Frank Witty, the fishing guide from Key Largo. Turned out Frank had been in the U.S. Marines, served in Desert Storm. A halfway worthy opponent for a change.

Sunday night, Monday night, and last night Sylvie had fulfilled Frank's sexual fantasies and then fulfilled them again. Hours together, hours of sweat. Last night Frank had come all the way to Naples. Sylvie snuck out and met him. Both of them naked on the motel sheets, sweat drying in the air-conditioned air, Sylvie asked Frank Witty if he liked her well enough to step into a ring of fire for her. Would he step in and rescue her?

And he said yes, of course he liked her that much. More than that. Sure, she said, that's what they all say.

"What kind of ring of fire?" Frank Witty asked her.

"Never mind," she said. "Don't promise Sylvie something you can't deliver."

"Try me," Frank said. Blond hair, sincere eyes. His ring finger with that white rim of fresh flesh. Three nights together and Frank primed and ready. A record for Sylvie. Three nights. The previous record was six. That was Mr. Joseph McCabe. Or was it Mr. Tommy Matkov? She wasn't sure anymore. It was such a blur lately. Men, men, men.

Try me, Frank Witty said.

So then, just last night, Sylvie told him about Harden, described things he'd done to her. Years of coming into her room in the middle of the night, lying beside her, stroking her flesh, entering her, making her scream.

Frank Witty said nothing for a minute.

Sylvie, the cumulus, becoming the abused daughter for Frank, see if that registered on his scale. Made him mad. If not, she'd keep on searching until she found the story that stirred him. Men were so easy that way. They had no trouble believing in other men's evil. They knew that every dark imagining was possible. It was part of what made them men. For Sylvie it was only a matter of time, hunt and peck, probe and listen before she found Frank Witty's button. But this was quick, superquick.

"Your father raped you?"

"For years," Sylvie said.

"The fucking bastard."

"Since I was four. Maybe even before that."

"We'll go to the police."

"I already have. They're scared of my father. He has some powerful connections. Judges, senators. It's no use."

Frank was quiet, staring up into the dark. Sylvie had caught the fishing guide on the first cast.

She told Mr. Frank Witty how remote the farm was, how easy it would be to do anything out there and hide it. Her father without any social life. No friends coming to look for him, see where he was when he no longer drew breath on this earth.

"You want me to kill your old man?" Mr. Frank Witty said in the dark, naked on the sheets beside her. "That's what you're asking me to do?"

And Sylvie touched him again between his legs, let her fingers rove.

"I'm not asking you to do anything, Frank," Sylvie said. "Long as you don't mind sharing me with my father."

He was silent, lying still beside her. But his penis was thickening in her hands.

And then she told him, even if he wanted to help her, there was one very big complication. Her father was a trained killer. The United States Government had sent him to special training camps to show him the best ways to do it. Then for twenty years he'd traveled around the world to erase people who threatened the American way of life. He worked undercover for the State Department most of the years Sylvie was growing up. Libyans, Iranians, Saudis, Nicaraguans, Iraqis, Vietnamese, Cambodians, French, even British. He killed them all. Harden confiding in Sylvie once in a drunken moment. Nineteen people. *"I reshaped history, girl. These hands reconstructed the world. Kept it from going off in the wrong direction."* Sylvie mixing truth with the rest of it, giving the story a smooth, consistent texture.

Sylvie told Frank Witty that Harden liked to brag that he and a dozen other men like him had more effect on world events than all the presidents and bullshit senators and congressmen put together.

"Jesus," Mr. Frank Witty said in the dark. Sylvie's fingers working down there. Finding his hot places again, finding the squirm trigger, the rigid-as-iron trigger. "I knew guys like your father in the Marine Corps. Gung-ho, first hand in the air. Do anything for the old U.S. of A."

"He's an old man now," Sylvie said. "Feeble, slowed way down."

"I hated those guys."

"Think you could handle it?" Sylvie said. "Kill a sixty-year-old man? Shoot him when he wasn't expecting it. Rescue Sylvie from a monster." Sylvie nuzzled close, her hand riding up and down his slightly curved penis.

"Why don't we just run off? We could go tonight," Mr. Frank Witty said. "He'd never find us."

"He'd find me. He would. He always does. It's like I got a little radio beeper planted inside me, he follows the waves, finds me, brings me back. Believe me, I tried and tried."

"We could get on a plane. Pick a destination at random. Disappear."

"My father isn't going to let you have me. No man is going to take me away from him. He's like that. He doesn't mind if I screw around with guys. But he'll never let me move away, live with somebody."

"He can't do that. You're an adult."

"Oh, he can do it, all right. He does whatever he pleases."

Sylvie went quiet. Spent the next hour using her mouth, her fingers, her ass, to give flesh to Frank Witty's dreams.

"I have a deer rifle," he said when they were lying still again. Saying it quietly, his voice different. "A deer rifle with a scope," he said.

Sylvie rolled up on an elbow.

"No good," she said. "It has to be close range. I know my father. You wound him, anything but a through-the-brain head shot, he'll manage to slip away. Then both of us will be dead."

"And how the hell do I get that close?"

Sylvie said nothing. Let him answer his own problems. They lay there for a half hour without talking or touching. She could hear Frank thinking. Finally he rolled over to her.

"I have a friend, a high school buddy," Mr. Frank Witty said.

His voice was solid now. He was there finally. Sylvie bringing him to that decisive point, making a hero out of him. "My friend drives a UPS truck in Key Largo. I think he'd loan it to me if I asked him."

"Whatta you gonna do, try to run over my daddy with a UPS truck?"

"No, I got an idea."

"When're you going to do it?" Sylvie said.

"I don't know. When would be good?"

"My father has sex with me every single day," she said.

She could hear Frank swallow in the dark.

"Tomorrow then," he said. "I'll have it tomorrow."

"You sure?"

And now under the hot noon sun, Sylvie watched as Harden signed his name on the clipboard, and Mr. Frank Witty kept his eyes down, watching Harden's hands. Over and over Sylvie had warned him whatever he did, not to look at her, warned him to keep his eyes nailed to Harden. Like Lot's wife, don't don't don't, whatever you do, don't look back. Don't, don't let my father see what's in your eyes for me.

But as Sylvie watched, Mr. Frank Witty did exactly that. The fishing guide from Key Largo ticked his eyes her way and smiled, and at that exact second Harden glanced up and caught the look, and Mr. Frank Witty sensed what had happened and stumbled back and twisted his arm behind him, grabbing for his handgun wedged in the small of his back, but it was too late, another tragedy, because Harden had seen what was in Frank's eyes, the desperate love, registered it, and he reacted a millisecond faster than Frank Witty, flashing his hand out and gripping the man's upper arm, twisting to the left, and at that moment, the muscular man with the blond hair, the thick chest, Frank Witty, the marine, the recently divorced fishing guide who had kept himself in shape, running, lifting weights, the man who had lived out all his sex fantasies with Sylvie in three nights together, this man sagged in Harden's grasp, knees relaxing, going down. The Vulcan death grip. Bones giving way, muscles loose, Mr. Frank Witty's face slack and empty and bloodless. His eyes on Sylvie as he drooped.

And what happened next, Sylvie had seen many times before. Her father making a quick step, a dance move, turn your partner, do-si-do, behind him, lift his arm, a tango of death, Harden's gristly wrist pressing across Mr. Frank Witty's Adam's apple, throttling him, the man's eyes going groggy, then her father bending the celery stalk that was his neck, snapping it, and Frank was dead. The pistol fell from his hand, the man in the UPS suit dropping motionless at her feet.

"Sylvie, Sylvie, Sylvie," Harden said, looking down at the heap. "Jesus God, girl, this poor bastard was so slow, he never had a prayer. Like a goddamn lamb to slaughter. You should be ashamed, Sylvie. Ashamed."

He walked over to the storage shed and came back with a shovel. Sylvie stayed there and watched as her father raised the point of the shovel above Mr. Frank Witty's head. Then she lifted her eyes to the large clouds rising over the Glades. Cumulus. Forcing herself to look for shapes, Santa Claus, rocket ship, gorilla, sailboat, as Harden brought the sharp-bladed shovel down on Mr. Frank Witty's throat, again and again.

CHAPTER 18

WEDNESDAY AS THORN WAS ON HIS WAY OUT HIS DRIVE, SUGARMAN'S MUS-
tang pulled in off U.S. 1, blocked his path. They both got out,
met at Sugar's car. Without a word Sugarman spread a file
folder open on the hood. A hot breeze off Blackwater Sound
riffled the pages, but Sugar held them in place.

"It was right there in the file cabinet," Sugar said. "My two
clients, First Federal and Murtha's Liquors. Then there was this
one. My third client, the one I didn't know about. In alphabeti-
cal order and everything, the Winchester file."

On the top were photocopies of two library articles on tilapia.
Both were written by Dr. Paul Ludkin. After that was a sheet
from a yellow legal pad. A list of words in Darcy's hand, *tilapia,
Ludkin, Seamark, Winchester*. Then on another yellow page was an
ink drawing, what looked like a map of the Naples area. At a
location well inland from the Gulf she'd drawn a star.

"She went over there?"

"Must have," Sugarman said. "Look at the next one."

The second page was filled with Darcy's shorthand prose,

notes to herself as she tried to sort out the situation. *Sylvie claims ongoing incest. Vague about encounter with Murtha. Angry at him. Doesn't want to talk about it. Very excited someone would take interest in her. Strange girl. Funny, quick, but scatterbrained. Checked with Health and Rehabilitative Services, Naples office. Dorothy Hobson, caseworker. Had a file on Sylvie. Won't reveal contents, but implied the file is extensive, and Sylvie may have "reality problems."*

" 'Reality problems,' " Thorn said.

"Hell," Sugar said. "That may be what I got."

Her notes ended with a brief description of Harden Winchester. *Charming man. Smart. Manipulative? Early sixties, seems younger. Extremely revved up. Shocked at mention of red tilapia, tried to cover his surprise, but it was there. Claims he knows nothing about such a thing. If Sylvie is being sexually abused, why couldn't she just leave? Answer: that codependent thing. Sounds bullshitty, but I guess it could be true. Some women can't leave. Scared, weak. Dependent. But which one to trust? Father or daughter? And what about the pistol in the videotape?*

And the final line was, *Whole thing starting to feel like a dead end. Maybe misconstrued everything. Probably should bring Sugar in. Have him look at video. See what we do from here, if anything. Quit fantasizing, playing Nancy Drew.*

Thorn stared at the page, brushed his fingers across her elegant handwriting, so controlled, so neat. Then he lifted his head and looked out at the dark sparkle of the empty bay. A single brown pelican drifted ten feet above the water, giving its cumbersome wings a single flap, then sailing on out of view.

Thorn drove the VW twenty-odd miles north to pick up Krome Avenue, then to Tamiami Trail, and made the peaceful hundred-mile drive west across the Everglades in a little over two hours. He found his way to the Fish and Wildlife office by three. They had a room in a Holiday Inn near the entrance to Alligator Alley.

He sat in the parking lot of the hotel, his mind going back to Broken Conch Reef, hand exploring the lobster hole, another part of him back in his stilt house, still feeling the numb and hollow anger, the last vibrations of two dozen bullets blasting through his floor. Then out on the skiff last week, the tarpon taking his fly, running, Thorn turning and seeing her body.

His veins were clogged with a thick brew of rage. He knew he was no Sugarman. He didn't give a goddamn about the fine points of sportsmanship. This wasn't a matter of chivalry or table manners. When he found Darcy's killer, he was going to knock him on his ass and if he got the chance, cleat him in the face. And if the son of a bitch came back to consciousness, he'd put him down again, keep him pinned till the man was gone. And when that was done, maybe Thorn would just drive the VW up the road a way and locate that linebacker, Mr. Langstaff, the eye gouger. See what he was up to. Have a polite chat with him too.

Judy Nelson, assistant investigator for U.S. Fish and Wildlife, was over six feet tall, weighed fifty pounds or so more than Thorn, and as they were shaking hands in the doorway of her office, she informed Thorn that just last month she'd acquired a false nose.

The doctors had to slice the real one off, it was so eaten up with skin cancer. The new nose was gel-filled, she told him, and could fool most people if she took the time to get her makeup right, caulking around the edges of the thing, then feathering the hypoallergenic cream so it blended with her skin tone. None of which, Judy said, she'd bothered to do this morning. She hoped Thorn wasn't too grossed out by it. He said he wasn't.

She was wearing a green government uniform with gold patches. A small silver badge. She had her dark brown hair tucked up under her hat, no jewelry, quick, probing eyes, and a voice full of rough sand. A three-pack-a-day rasp. Maybe Coach Hardy had been right, after all. Judy had a brawny, intimidating manner that would've demoralized any number of Thorn's jock buddies, past or present.

They took the elevator downstairs and Judy led him outside and they got into the green government pickup. Windows down, no air conditioner, they rumbled east along U.S. 41, the afternoon sun baking the oils from the asphalt, sending wavy undulations into the air in front of them. Ten minutes out from her office, Judy cleared her throat significantly, and asked if Thorn minded if she took her goddamn nose off for a while. The thing was hot, like wearing a toupee she guessed, and he said, hell no, she should be comfortable, he didn't mind a bit.

So she squeezed hard on the bridge of the artificial nose and Thorn heard a sharp plastic snap. She pulled it off and lay it on the seat between them, and while she adjusted her sunglasses, she kept her face forward. Thorn did too.

They turned off 41 and headed north along a county road, the asphalt rougher back here. RV parks, sod farms, a few avocado groves, a deserted industrial park, a dilapidated honkytonk, houses with windows boarded up, the highway stretching long and empty before them.

"Well," Judy said. "Want to have a peek? Get it over with?"

Thorn paused for a moment then said, okay, sure, let's get it over with. And Judy took off her sunglasses and turned her head slowly and let him have a good look at the trapezoid-shaped scar tissue in the middle of her face. A complex white plastic fastener poked up in the middle of the trapezoid; the skin was raw at its edges. A single hole about the size of a dime had been cut through a patch of gleaming flesh just below the snap.

"Now we got that behind us," Judy said.

"Doesn't look that bad."

"Hell it doesn't," she said. "Looks like one of those goddamn Star Wars monsters, that bar scene with all of them drinking radiator coolant. It looks like shit."

Thorn thought about it for a moment, gazing out at a tree farm, long arcs of water shooting out over the rows of palms.

"You gonna be sick?" Judy said.

Thorn said no.

" 'Cause I had that happen, you know. Guy from Washington, down here two weeks ago to audit the hardware, make sure none of the agents had stolen any typewriters, that kind of thing. So we were riding along like this, and he kept pestering me to see what I looked like without my nose. I showed him and a second later he puked all over the dashboard. We got him cleaned up, and the asshole spent the rest of the day trying to make it up to me, ended up asking me out for a date. Wanted to take me dancing, for christ sake. I said, 'Look, honey, you think I'm going dancing with a guy, he pukes when he looks at me? Come on, get serious.' "

She glanced over at Thorn again.

"You sure you aren't about to be sick?"

"I'm fine," said Thorn. "I was thinking about something else."

"Sure you were, honey. Sure you were."

"I was thinking of all the sun I've gotten. No sunscreen, no hat."

Judy Nelson was quiet.

"And how they used to tell us in school, all that sunshine was making us healthy, the darker our tans, the more vitamin A."

"Vitamin melanoma is more like it," Judy said. "Hell, I spent so many years in the sun, I didn't even know I was a natural brunette till this nose thing happened and I started staying in the shade. I thought I was real blond. What a goddamn disappointment."

Thorn chuckled along with her.

"Lucky for me," she said, "I never was a slave to men's approval."

She was quiet for a moment, pulling out to pass a tractor that was hauling a large water tank. When they were back in their lane, she said, "So, you gonna tell me why you want to meet Winchester?"

"I've got an interest in fish farming."

"What? Thinking of going into the business?"

"Maybe."

"And you want to spy on the competition? That it?"

"Not spy, exactly. I just want to see if the whole operation is too complicated for a guy like me to take a chance on it."

He could feel her staring at him, but he didn't look her way.

They watched another mile go by in silence. Traveling east now, beyond farm country, the land growing soupy, more barren, trees sparse, sawgrass and palmetto, the brown distances opening up. That wide empty plain of the Everglades.

Its beauty was so subdued most people had trouble savoring it. Plenty of times Thorn had run into tourists who'd driven across the Glades for hours looking for the spectacular views, and not seeing anything special, wound up thinking they'd been on the wrong road.

True, it was no Grand Canyon. But then, any damn fool could get out of his car and stand on the rim of that incredible gorge and look down and have an easy rush. But this broad empty space was a hell of a lot more demanding. A stark place, monochromatic at first glance. It was a place you had to wade out into. Had to train your ears to uncover the faint sounds, sharpen your eyes enough to tell one vague gray from another. That was one of the problems. People were so glutted on the garish, the loud gimmicks of Disney World, the neon extremes of the new Florida, they didn't appreciate grays and browns anymore. The nuances of dull greens.

The result was, a lot of people were willing to part with what they took to be nothing but a colorless mosquito breeding ground. Willing to let the machines gobble away at it, mile by mile, drain it, pave it, let the cardboard housing developments sprawl farther and farther into that place where most of south Florida's rainfall and half of the wildlife was spawned. That sweet fertile heart of the state.

Thorn looked down at Judy Nelson's gel-filled nose.

"So tell me about this particular fish," he said. "What the hell's so special about it that the government has to send their crack agent out to inspect?"

She smiled at that, reset her hands on the steering wheel, glanced out her window at an old yellow school bus straining to pass them. It was full of sleeping laborers.

"These fish are getting to be a damned nuisance."

"How's that?"

"They're too successful," she said. "Flood canals down here are chock-full of them these days. A lot were released by Florida Freshwater Fish and Wildlife Commission people a few years back. They thought tilapia might fill a niche in the ecosystem. Eat some of the algae that's choking the waterways. Instead, that goddamn fish turned out to be worse than the algae. Filled the whole system. Now, ten years later, it's the tilapia that's choking the canals. They're the goddamn kudzu of marine life. Weeds with eyeballs is how I think of them. Crabgrass with gills."

"And Winchester? What's he like?"

"Harden Winchester," she said, and smiled at the windshield. "Hell, some days when I'm bored, my brain getting sluggish, I make the drive out here just to spend some time around Harden. Man has these slow, Texas manners, even drawls a little, but he's got a damn power plant for a brain."

"He married?"

She turned her head to him, her eyes with that look people sometimes have when you've come too close to their secret stash.

Judy shifted her eyes back to the road.

"You'd have to be a special woman to live with Harden," she said. "The man gives off a hum, day and night. Being beside him, it's like standing next to a couple hundred pounds of uranium, he's buzzing away all the time."

Slowing for a sharp curve, Judy said, "I never been real sensible when it came to picking men. But let me tell you something, if Harden Winchester was available, I'd be on him like a cat on a lizard. Unfortunately, the man's eyes are fixed on the horizon. He's after something a lot bigger than Judy Nelson."

"Sounds like a crush to me."

"More than a crush," she said. "More than that."

Thorn watched a flock of ibis banking south above a line of slash pines.

Judy was silent for a mile or two. Slowing down a little, forty, thirty-five. There were cattle on both sides of the highway now. Big Angus bulls sunning in the grass with white egrets standing on their backs pecking happily at the insects fastened to their hides.

She slowed the pickup even more, braked, and guided them off that narrow two-lane onto a narrower side road heading deeper into the Glades. A soft sandy road with deep tire tracks.

"People call tilapia the Jesus Christ fish. You know that?"

Thorn said no, he hadn't heard.

She looked over at him and said, "You religious, Thorn?"

"I can be. Under the right circumstances."

She smiled, her face softening.

"Folklore has it that tilapia was the fish Jesus used to feed the five thousand. The multitudes."

"A miracle fish."

"Yeah. Some people seem to think so."

Thorn looked out the windows. Nothing synthetic in any direction. Just those slash pines, loblolly pines, stoppers, palmettos, sawgrass, a few twisted cypress trees, the long slow glide of hawks. Clouds mushrooming in the east, darkening at the edges.

"I think what it is," Judy said, "like with a lot of things, tilapia do fair to middling in their native environment, average, not great, not bad. But soon as you move them away from home, all the rules change. The checks and balances they had back home are all different. New temperatures, new ultraviolet light rates, whatever. So, in the new place, they either wither up and die or they flourish. With tilapia in Florida, it's the second. These fish are growing like mold in a hothouse. Nobody really knows what impact they're going to have, long-term. That's why we gotta watch them so careful."

Thorn watched her steer the pickup around a sharp bend, the sand getting deeper, darker. Mixed with the loam and marl, the crushed seashells. This enormous piece of real estate so recently risen from the sea.

"You ever eaten one?"

"I have." She picked up her nose from the seat between them, gave Thorn a warning glance—a chance to look away. Then she snapped the nose back into place.

"They any good?"

"You've probably eaten them too, and didn't know it. Tastes enough like snapper, they get away with substituting it in restaurants these days. Flaky white meat, broils up nice, not much flavor really. Kind of like tofu. Tilapia's so bland, whatever seasoning you put on it, that's how it tastes."

"I've never worked up much excitement for tofu."

"Oh, well. Nothing wrong with a little bland now and then. It's the American way. If you can make it taste enough like chicken, you can make a million bucks off it."

Thorn looked out his window, at the expanse of federal land. Cypress and pine, palmetto scrub. Clouds growing dingy in the east. A stand of trees in the distance where a colony of ibis was roosting. The big white birds crowding the limbs like outrageous blossoms.

"I like my fish gamy," he said. "A thing grows up in a breeding pen, its gotta be dumber, slower than something in the wild. If I eat an animal, I want it to be one that died fighting."

"Hey, get with the program, Thorn. We all gotta start gearing up for the twenty-first century, my friend. It's going to be the age of man-made everything. You can just forget gamy."

He looked out his window at the brown sweep of empty miles.

"I haven't learned to stomach the century we're in yet."

"Well, let me tell you something, doll, you want to get along with Harden, I'd just keep quiet about that wild versus penned bullshit. He's a goddamn missionary for these fish. Talks them up all the time."

She slowed for a deep trench, slewed across it at an angle, but kept the pickup moving.

"So when you come out here," Thorn said, "what're you supposed to inspect for?"

"Pretty routine," she said. "Just gotta watch they don't add more ponds than their license allows for. Harden's licensed for seven. I forget the total water volume he's allowed, but it's considerable. The main thing, though, is to make sure the place is secure."

"Secure?"

"Oh, you know, some of these yahoo fish farmers, they get a crop of fingerlings that are running small, they'll lay a sewer pipe over to a canal, pump the runts out. Like flushing alligators down the toilet. Doesn't get rid of them, just gives the state something else to spend its money on."

"Florida's in the fish killing business now?"

"Not yet, but it keeps going like it is, someday we might have to. Trouble with fish toxicants is, they kill everything, not just tilapia. So for the moment, we gotta make sure the fish farmers dispose of their larvae properly, don't run any risk of letting fish get free, add to the problem we already got."

Judy wheeled them around a sharp turn, almost lost traction in the sand, but kept working the gas pedal through the corner. As they rounded a bend and looked down a short straightaway at a metal gate, Thorn said, "So, who am I supposed to be?"

"What?"

"Who am I going to pretend to be?"

"All right," she said. "Let's see." She slowed the car while she thought. Then swung her head around smiling. "How about district supervisor? You're in from the Atlanta office. Taking a day off from your desk job to see the lay of the land. Get oriented."

"In other words, I'm your boss."

"You think you're up to that, kiddo?"

"Judy, I don't think there's anybody could be up to that."

"You got that right, Thorn. You definitely got that right."

She pulled to a stop at the gate and got out of the car. In the shrubs beside the gatepost someone had nailed a small sheet of plywood to a poisonwood tree. Spray-painted in fading black letters it said, THE FUNNY FARM.

Judy Nelson pushed the gate open and walked back to the car and got in.

"Funny Farm?"

"These Winchesters," she said. "They're a laugh a minute."

Judy took them down a long bumpy road, the sand becoming something less than sand, and that becoming something closer to water. Finally, she slogged the truck through a sharp left turn, and all at once they were facing Sylvie Winchester and a man who had to be her father.

Sylvie in cutoff jeans and a black long-sleeved Raiders jersey and muddy cowboy boots. The shirtless man was thick-chested and bald, with a silver gristle of beard. He had a sunbaked boxy face, and what hair he had was skinned close. All he wore were yellow gym shorts and tennis shoes. He was holding a shovel at port arms.

As Judy turned off the engine, the man's face lost its tension and rearranged itself into a wide smile. Then a half second later, Thorn registered something else, some darting glance his way that diluted the man's smile by half. Harden Winchester seemed to have gone on full alert.

A hundred yards behind where the two of them stood, Thorn saw several earthen-banked ponds the length and breadth of football fields. And off to the west were half a dozen smaller tanks no larger than backyard swimming pools. Aluminum frames arched over the smaller pools like the rigging for a winter hothouse. And a complex system of white PVC pipes led across the surface of the weedy dirt from pond to pond, and eventually converged at an aluminum Quonset hut.

To the east, surrounded by a bright green lawn, was a small house built of gray weathered wood. Pioneer construction, a wood cottage with a Cape Cod design, probably hammered together a century ago from trees now extinct. It had a screened porch that ran the full length of the front, a high sloping tin roof with cupolas and dormers. And Thorn noticed that on the windows of a single room at the front of the house someone had attached a set of burglar bars.

Next to the house was a tall windmill of iron girders. Its blades turned lazily in an airless breeze. Further to the east the sky was filing with thick swipes of gray putty, the afternoon storm clouds, darkening and crowding together out over the heart of the Everglades. Though they were fifty miles away, they still flavored the light overhead with a silvery tinge.

Sylvie broke away from her father and walked jauntily over to Judy's window and said hello, and she pressed her cheek to Judy's, and gave Thorn a wink and a slow secret grin, then pulled her head back out the window.

"Daddy, come here," she called. "Look who Judy's brought with her."

Harden Winchester strode to the pickup, shifting the shovel to one hand. Judy and Thorn got out. Winchester went over to Judy Nelson and gave her a quick peck on the cheek, then aimed his eyes across the roof of the truck and settled them on Thorn. The man had washed-out gray eyes. His hide was as tough and weathered as the wood of that house. A handsome man, but with a shifty light in his eyes. His smile was blurred at the edges as if some fraction of it were a grimace.

"And who do we have here?"

Behind Harden, Sylvie smiled mischievously at Thorn. Letting him marinate for a moment or two more.

"Can't you guess, Daddy? Who is it we've been expecting?"

Thorn started around the front of the truck, his gut tightening. This big-jointed man took a new grip on the shovel. He watched Thorn approach.

"Don't be impolite, girl. If you know the man, introduce him." As Thorn stepped forward, Harden ticked his eyes up and down him with professional astuteness as if he were registering a dozen minor details that he'd ponder later.

"It's Mr. Lavery, Daddy," Sylvie said, grinning at Thorn. "Mr. Peter Lavery."

Judy glanced at Thorn, and he turned his face away from the Winchesters and gave her a helpless shrug. He turned back as Harden reached out his hand. Thorn shook it, a chunk of callused flesh as unyielding as any he'd ever touched.

"Well, you're a day or two early, Mr. Lavery."

Thorn drew his hand out of the solid grip.

"My plans changed," he said. "Things were a little slow in Thomasville, so I thought I'd come on down."

Sylvie jerked her head around, stared at him.

Thorn said to her, "I been doing my homework, Sylvie. You been doing yours?"

Harden glanced between the two of them, eyes uncertain.

"Two in one day, Sylvie?" he said. "Another UPS delivery?"

"Come on, Daddy, give me a little credit, okay? For once?"

Harden's eyes shied away from her as though he'd decided to let all this ride for the moment. He turned to Judy and asked her in a careful drawl if this was an official visit.

"Not really," she said. "I was just helping . . ." She looked at Thorn. "Helping Mr. Lavery find his way out here. He called the office, and I volunteered."

"Called the office, did he?"

"A courtesy call," Thorn said. "I always like to touch base with the local fish and game people."

"Well, I'm sure sorry he bothered you, Judy. Lavery was supposed to let us know when he'd checked into his hotel, and we were going to come get him, show him the way out here. At least that's how I recall the plan. But then, since Sylvie made the arrangements, I suppose things could've gotten a little botched."

"Daddy lets me be his private secretary," Sylvie explained to Judy. "Chief bottle-washer and full-time gofer for Winchester Aquaculture Incorporated."

"She's learning," Winchester said. "Slowly but surely. A little responsibility goes a long way with this one."

Sylvie lifted herself up onto the square toes of her cowboy boots. Rocking her head back and smiling at the darkening sky, her mouth clamped hard.

After a minute or two more of strained pleasantries, Judy refused for the second time Harden's offer of lemonade, and gave everyone a polite good-bye and with a private smile to Thorn, she got back in the pickup and left.

Thorn stood in the middle of the long sandy drive with Darcy's fuchsia overnight bag at his feet and watched the contrail of dust from Judy's truck rise up behind her.

CHAPTER 19

HARDEN STARED AT THE OVERNIGHT BAG, THEN BACK AT THORN.

"You're traveling pretty light, Lavery."

Fidgeting with her shirttail, Sylvie stood at her father's shoulder, faint worry beginning to ripen in her eyes.

"Actually," Thorn said, "I didn't plan to stay very long."

"But you *did* bring the money?"

Thorn glanced at Sylvie, but she'd bowed her head and was peering at the ground, all her playfulness evaporated.

Thorn glanced over at the long road out of there. Miles and miles from anywhere he knew. A half day's drive from home.

"Well," Harden said, "did you?"

Sylvie pawed at the sand with the toe of her boot.

Thorn said, "Look, Winchester, you think I'd come all this way, go to all this trouble and not bring it?"

Sylvie lifted her face, stepping back out of her father's peripheral vision, the impish smile resurfacing. Laced now with something new, respect maybe, or excitement. The smile gradually growing wider as her eyes feasted on his.

"Well, then," Harden said, his stance loosening. "I suppose you'd like to take a look at the operation, now that you're here."

"Of course."

"Then I can drive Mr. Lavery back to town. Get him situated."

Harden turned and glanced at his daughter, then back at Thorn.

"Can we call you Peter?" Sylvie said.

"Sure," said Thorn. "Why not?"

Harden said, "And you're still staying at the Ritz Carlton, Peter? Or did you change that part of your plan as well?"

"No. The Ritz is fine."

Harden hesitated, giving Thorn another careful inspection.

"Is there a problem, Mr. Winchester?"

Harden smiled, and raised his hand apologetically.

"Forgive me," he said. "You're not at all what I pictured."

"Daddy thinks rich people should dress rich."

"Well, I apologize," Thorn said. "But silk shirts make me itch. And I haven't found a pair of jodhpurs yet that don't rub me funny."

Harden hesitated a second, then smiled and clapped Thorn hard on the shoulder.

"Well, okay then, you're one of us."

"Yeah," Sylvie said. "Lucky him."

For the next hour, Harden Winchester led Thorn on a thorough and unhurried tour of the fish farm. The three of them walked around the perimeter of each of the large breeding ponds. Each one was surrounded by a two-foot high earthen dike. Thorn stopped to look at the fish swarming at the surface of the dark water. Doughy white, they were shaped like snapper, but glided about as lethargically as drugged mullet.

With quiet pride, Harden demonstrated the aerator, a large electrified paddle wheel that ran up and down the length of each of the larger ponds to force bubbles of air into the stagnant water. Thorn listened, made responsive noises, but said little.

Sylvie brought up the rear, and when her father wasn't watching, she poked Thorn playfully in the back with a stiff finger.

They halted at one of the smaller pools, the hatchery, Harden said, and he pointed out the filtering system he'd invented, all very low-tech, he was pleased to say. None of that Ph.D. Fiberglas indoor tank bullshit for him. His filter consisted of concrete burial vaults, three-by-seven-foot boxes that he filled with sand to screen out the algae and other impurities. Keep the water circulating, the thousands of fingerlings flourishing.

"Daddy doesn't like impurities," Sylvie said. "But he just adores burial vaults. They remind him of his career in the military. Don't they, Daddy? All those burial vaults full of your enemies."

Harden led them on.

"Daddy had to kill ten thousand fish in this larvae pond a few days ago. Now, that was what I'd call fun. Killing ten thousand of anything is a gas. Wouldn't you agree, Mr. Lavery?"

They were standing on the muddy bank of a dark pond. Twenty yards away was a stand of Australian pines, and through the pines Thorn could see the glitter of moving water.

"Why'd you do that?"

"This bank we're standing on," said Winchester, giving Sylvie a cold stare, "it had a crack in it. I felt it was about to go, so I had to kill the fish. Birds could swoop in, pick a fish up off the ground, drop it in a lake or canal somewhere nearby, and the fish and game people would be back here the next day blaming me for doing it."

"I see," Thorn said.

Sylvie said, "He killed all those fish with sodium fluoroacetate. It's a poison. A long time ago they used it to kill rats, but now it's outlawed. Isn't that right, Daddy? It's outlawed because it's so effective. But Daddy still gets it smuggled in from South America. A thimble full can kill a horse, and if a dog eats the flesh of that horse, the dog dies too. The fleas on the dog, and on and on. Outlawed, isn't that right?"

"It's a damn good fish killer," Harden said, and waved them

on. "But I'm sure we're boring you, Peter. You're a tilapia man. You know all of this already."

"My operation is a little different."

"Yeah, and how so?"

"It's much more high-tech," Sylvie said quickly. "All done indoors. Chrome-plated tanks, everything very clean. Daddy knows that. He's read about you, Mr. Lavery. He's just playing with you, aren't you, Daddy? Testing you."

Standing beside the largest pond, Thorn looked back and forth between the two of them.

"Is that right, Winchester? Are you playing with me?"

Harden held his eyes, but didn't reply.

Sylvie said, "In human beings sodium fluoroacetate causes ventricular fibrillation. A little bit of it in somebody's food, and look out, you better stand back before they fibrillate all over you."

Harden turned on her.

"Sylvie," he said, his voice under stiff control. "Go make us some lemonade. We'll have it on the patio."

"I'll shut up," she said.

"Go do it, girl. Right now. I'm tired of you baiting me."

"Aw, Daddy."

"Right now."

She ducked her head, held her ground for a moment, then she turned sullenly and stalked off toward the house. Halfway there, she peeked over her shoulder, saw that Harden wasn't watching, and she spun around, pretending she was holding an automatic weapon, gripping it at waist level, exuberantly spraying bullets at her father's back. Then she smiled, blew Thorn a kiss, and skipped on toward the house.

Thorn followed Harden through the completion of the tour, learning the rest of the gospel of tilapia according to Harden Winchester. Their sixty acres were almost completely circled by national park land with no access roads of any kind.

"We like living in the wild," Harden said. "It suits us. We can go weeks sometimes without seeing another soul out here. Except for our visits from Judy Nelson, of course."

Thorn remained uncommunicative as Harden led him past the shop, a storage lean-to. He saw the rump of a boat trailer behind the shop building, but couldn't see if it carried a vessel.

Finally Harden ended the tour on the keystone patio beside the house, and they sat down on some metal chairs in the shade of a white gazebo a few feet from the large swimming pool. A curved blue slide had been erected beside the pool, and a small waterfall tumbled across some coral boulders and splashed into one end. The pool seemed strangely shallow, a wading pool perhaps.

"Why all the lights?" Thorn said, motioning toward one of a dozen poles scattered around the grounds, a cluster of spotlights mounted on each one. More floodlights were fixed to the sides of the barns, the roof of the house.

"We have to work through the night sometimes," Winchester said. "You know how that is, right? Sudden fluctuations in the Ph balance. Cold fronts coming through. Can't have the water temperature drop too low."

Thorn met his eyes, but said nothing.

Sylvie brought out the lemonade on a Coca-Cola tray and they drank in silence for a minute or two.

Sylvie finished her drink, and smacked her lips. A laughing gull sailed past the umbrella and landed on the far edge of the swimming pool. It hopped up onto the lip and peered down into the shallow water. Harden stood up suddenly and waved his arms at the bird and it lifted off.

"Sometimes Daddy shoots the birds. He takes his Uzi out and machine-guns them. Anhingas, cormorants, gulls. Don't you, Daddy? You Uzi them to death."

Harden sat back down and had another sip of his lemonade. He glared out at the eastern sky where a small flock of laughing gulls banked in and began to circle around the largest of the fish ponds. Finally the flock scattered, taking up positions all along the opposite earthen bank.

"Goddamn vultures," Harden said, rising from his chair and staring at them. "Wait here. I'll be right back." He walked a few steps, then broke into a trot toward the pond.

When he was halfway across the yard, Sylvie stood and said, "Come quick, let me show you what you're up against."

Thorn pushed himself to his feet and followed her silently in through the back door of the house.

From the kitchen window, Sylvie glanced out at Harden, the man marching down the far bank of the largest fish pond, flapping his arms at the birds, flushing them back into the air. Sylvie took a key from a wooden rack by the back door and unlocked a narrow door beside the kitchen table. She swung it open, pulled the string on a light cord, and stood back.

The pantry was ten by ten, and the walls were hung with a wide array of military hardware. Uzis and M-16's, Lugers, .45 Brownings, a small rocket launcher, something that looked like an antitank gun. And there were some civilian weapons too, a MAC-10, a collection of automatic handguns. Thorn was no expert on exotic weapons, didn't know the exact names of all of those before him, but clearly it was a damn impressive collection.

On the floor just inside the door were four wooden crates. Nestled in the straw were neat rows of dark green hand grenades. Thorn squatted down and ran his fingers lightly across the cool thick steel. No bigger than pine cones, designed to spray their shrapnel in neat clouds for maximum carnage.

"Kaboom!" Sylvie barked. Thorn jerked his head around.

In the pantry doorway, Winchester stood just behind his daughter. He was breathing hard and his right hand rested heavily on her shoulder. The glass of lemonade was in his left.

"You're showing Mr. Lavery all our secrets, Sylvie."

"Oh, no, Daddy," she said, "not all of them. That would take too long."

"Got yourself quite an arsenal, Winchester."

Harden peered into Thorn's eyes.

"We have to stay prepared out here. You just never know. A

man can never be too well armed. Don't you agree, Mr. Lavery? Or are you some kind of gun-control nut?"

"I own a six-shooter, that's all. Never cared much for the automatic weapons."

"Yes. And why's that?"

"I've always thought that if you couldn't kill something with one shot," Thorn said, "you don't deserve to kill it at all."

Winchester smiled. Thorn cut his glance to Sylvie. She was giving him an encouraging look.

"You see," Winchester said, "in my former career, I made quite a few enemies. Some of them very violent individuals. And I'm afraid those kind of people have very long memories. Of course, one on one, I don't use weapons at all. But if they were to come in a group, Mr. Lavery, in large numbers, this room might prove to be most useful."

"Some people might call my daddy paranoid," Sylvie said. "But not me. He's just Daddy to me."

Harden continued to block the doorway, exploring Thorn's face as if he were trying to read the small print of his personality. Thorn could feel the pressure building in his throat, and he pictured for a moment spinning around and grabbing down one of those assault rifles. Find out if it was loaded.

Sylvie sighed loudly, broke the spell. She turned her back on Thorn, put her fingertips against her father's chest, and maneuvered him out of the way.

"So, Peter, maybe you'd like to go swimming," she said, tossing it over her shoulder as she walked into the kitchen. "Cool off after your long trip."

"Sylvie," her father said. A warning.

"Never mind, never mind. I forgot. Daddy doesn't like anybody to use the swimming pool. Might get the water dirty."

With his eyes still on Thorn, Harden drained his glass of lemonade. Then he formed an empty smile, and turned his back on Thorn and walked over to the sink and set his glass down.

"Okay, Mr. Lavery," he said. "How do you suggest we work our arrangement?"

He leaned his butt against the sink, arms crossed over his chest. Thorn came out of the pantry and stood near the back door.

Sylvie's lips formed a delicate smile. She was aiming her dark eyes out the window, off toward the stormy eastern sky. Waiting for Thorn's answer.

"To tell the truth, Winchester," he said, "I was thinking more along the lines of checking into my hotel about now. Taking a nap. I believe our business can wait till later."

Harden unfolded his arms, and set about limbering the fingers on both hands. He seemed to be fighting back his irritation, a man who was used to defining the moment, not liking it a bit that he wasn't in full command.

"Well, then," he said, keeping his gaze from Thorn, as if his mind were suddenly occupied with more important thoughts. "You want to get to your hotel. Then don't let us keep you here a second more."

Sylvie led him outside and across the yard to a shed near the river where a red '83 Oldsmobile was parked.

"You fooled him," she said. "So far, so good."

"I don't like this, Sylvie," said Thorn. "Not one bit."

"Oh, yeah, you fooled him, all right. Or else right now you'd be dead."

Thorn was silent, following a step behind her.

"You know, this whole farm," she said, picking her way past a muddy patch of ground, "it's all marshland. We're only an inch or two above mean high tide out here. And over there through the pines, that's the Okehatchee River. It's an estuary really, an arm of the Gulf. As the crow flies we're just a few miles from the coast. So whenever we get a full moon high tide, the Gulf rises, the Okehatchee backs up and floods its banks and we're knee-deep in water. Once a month the yard is underwater, the river climbs up the front steps. Water up to my crotch, sloshing around. It's really cool, you should see it. Almost to Sylvie's crotch. Can you picture that?"

"Let's go, Sylvie."

She gave him a dizzy smile as she unlocked the car.

Sylvie handled the Olds like someone who'd only just that afternoon come into contact with modern machinery. She switched on the ignition, gunned the big V-8 several times, then held the pedal to the floor for half a minute before backing off. She put the shifter in drive, clamped her hands on the wheel at three and nine o'clock, and steered the big car with a grim formality.

When they finally made it out to the main road, Sylvie floored the accelerator for half a minute at a time, then let off. And for thirty seconds that behemoth coasted down from around ninety to somewhere near the speed limit.

She slowed as a couple of oncoming cars approached, and sped up as a white plumbing van tried to pass. Sylvie raced the van for a mile, keeping it pinned in the lane beside her, almost forcing it off the road. Then suddenly she let off the accelerator and watched the van fly past.

Thorn tightened his safety belt.

A moment or two after the van incident, along a straight empty stretch of highway, Sylvie suddenly put both feet on the brake pedal, stood up on it, and the Olds's big tires squealed.

Thorn lurched forward, smacked his hands against the dashboard, and cursed. When they were stopped, Sylvie turned to him and pointed at a car halted on a dirt side road just ahead of them.

"Don't you see that guy?" she said. "He has the right of way."

She waved the astonished driver out onto the road in front of them.

"You had the goddamn right of way, Sylvie. This is a main highway we're on."

"Oh, sure. What the hell do you know? You're from Georgia. Everybody drives crazy up there."

She smiled at him, then floored the Olds, gradually caught up with the other car and sailed around it.

It took them almost an hour to get to the Ritz Carlton. Without all the unnecessary stops, and wrong turns, it might've been half that. She led them on a twisted tour of the city, up and down the same street several times, denying that she was lost, missing stop signs, her eyes continually drifting away from the road to stare at the suburban scenery.

As far as Thorn could tell, Naples had changed considerably since the last time he'd been there as a teenager. But it hadn't gone the way of most Florida towns. The folks over here had apparently circled their Lincolns and Rolls-Royces and had taken their stand against the plastic franchises, the massage parlors, the trashy bars. Every building and subdivision seemed less than ten years old. Freshly scrubbed and painted, all red-tiled, make-believe Mediterranean, even the downtown square was full of what looked to be Palm Beach boutiques. Tie stores, handkerchief shops, charm, charm, charm. It was the kind of beautiful sterility that only a steady gush of cash could create and maintain.

Golf courses everywhere, and each front yard was shaved as slick as a putting green. Carefully sculpted hedges, meticulously pruned trees. Apparently the perfectionist Disney World virus was spreading south. The city fathers probably even imported well-scrubbed teenagers armed with whisk brooms and dustpans to nab every trace of litter before it hit the earth.

As he watched the scenery slide past, Thorn recalled a story he'd read a year or two ago in the Miami paper. It was about a police action in Naples. Seems the manager of a restaurant that served one of the posh country club retirement developments had discovered a single Idaho potato in his kitchen with an obscenity carved in its skin. He called the police. Squad cars were dispatched and a thorough investigation followed, but the culprit was never caught. "We'll find the freak," a police detective said. "Don't you worry about that. It may take a while, but we're committed to this."

By the time Sylvie got them to the Ritz Carlton, Thorn was hungry for a little sleaze. A bait store painted garish purple, reeking of decaying fish for blocks around. A mom-and-pop motel with a neon sign out front that flickered on and off all day in the sunlight, offering free telephones and Magic Fingers for a quarter. Even a stray sheet of old newspaper blowing down the street would have made him feel a little more at ease.

Sylvie wheeled up to the hotel's elegant front entrance, missing the open door of a Range Rover by inches. While two doormen in black shorts and white shirts hurried out to the Olds, she switched off the car and swiveled around on the seat so she was facing him.

"You came for me."

She clapped her hands and smiled, and kept her palms pressed together as if she were offering up a loony prayer. She glanced over her shoulder at the doorman at her window but gave no sign she was ready to get out.

"Let's go inside, Sylvie. We have some things to discuss."

"You're good, Thorn. Damn good," she said. "I tell you my name, and a couple of days later, here you are. Even know who Peter Lavery is, where he lives. Thomasville, Georgia. Man, oh, man, a smart one. I got me a smart one. We'll take this one slow. Milk it out for a while."

She yipped, and beamed giddily at the windshield.

Outside her door a young man with red hair waited for her to finish her conversation so he could open her door.

"Finally," Sylvie said, turning her grin on Thorn again, "I found somebody who can give my daddy a challenge."

"And what does that mean?"

"Somebody good enough," Sylvie said, "you might actually be able to kill the bastard."

CHAPTER 20

"THIS IS PETER LAVERY," SYLVIE SAID. "HE HAS A RESERVATION, BUT IT'S not till later on this week."

Behind the curved marble counter, the registration clerk typed the name into the computer and stood back, watching the screen. He was a handsome kid of twenty-five or so, white shirt. Dark tan, blond hair trimmed neat, like a surfer gone legitimate.

"Now, that's strange," the kid said.

"Strange?" Sylvie was hugging Thorn's left arm, nuzzling her nose into his shoulder. Playing the newlywed. Thorn, seriously pissed, but riding it out.

"According to this, you already checked in, Mr. Lavery."

"You sure about that?" Sylvie said, dropping Thorn's arm.

"Yes, ma'am, right here, Peter S. Lavery."

"Great," Thorn said. "The more Laverys, the merrier."

In a bruised and far-off voice, Sylvie asked what room the other Lavery was in. The clerk apologized, but he wasn't allowed to give out that information.

"Well, what time did he check in, can you fucking tell us that much?"

The clerk looked at her for a moment, then hit a couple of keys on his computer and said Lavery had checked in an hour ago.

Sylvie asked the kid where the house phone was and he pointed at a table near the distant wall, and she marched over to it. Heads turned to watch this skinny girl with her chain saw haircut, muddy boots, and Raiders jersey tromp past.

Thorn turned back to the counter and began to fill in the registration card. According to the kid, the last available room in the entire hotel was a suite with a Gulf view. Thorn said that would be fine and the clerk asked him for a major credit card.

"Don't even have a minor one," Thorn said.

"Then you'll be paying cash?"

"Unless you'd barter for fishing flies."

The kid smiled wanly.

"So, that'll be two hundred and eighty-five dollars."

"Christ, I don't need it for the whole month."

The kid improved on his smile. Yes, sir, he'd met his share of kidders, wealthy wackos with seven-inch fingernails and beards to their belt buckles. And he was trained to be polite to all of them. You never knew when one might turn out to be Mr. Ritz or Mrs. Carlton. So, by god, when you checked into this place, you got treated right, no matter which mental hospital you'd just escaped from.

"That's two hundred eighty-five dollars *per night,* sir."

Thorn glanced around at the lobby.

"Hell, I've owned cars that cost less than that."

"So you don't want the room?"

Thorn looked over at Sylvie. She was sitting in a leather chair, curled around the phone receiver, her free hand shielding the mouthpiece. Completely focused on her conversation. He didn't like this hotel, and sure as hell didn't like Sylvie maneuvering him into this situation. But he had the very strong sense that he'd learn far more about the Winchester clan by playing along as Peter Lavery than by trying to strangle the truth out of them one by one.

For a moment, he had a painful glimpse of how Darcy might've felt living with him. Chafing in her limited role. Someone else defining the shape of her life. Thorn had just assumed his rhythms suited her. That silence and seclusion were as comfortable for Darcy as they were for him. He'd thought of her as his double, a complementary other half, his exhalations becoming her inhalations, hers becoming his. But probably she had squirmed inwardly for months as she searched for some challenge that could give her back her own identity, just as Thorn squirmed now, trapped in his role as Peter Lavery.

He turned back to the desk clerk.

"The Gulf view room then?"

"Look," Thorn said, "you sure you don't have anything cheaper? Say in the fifteen to twenty-dollar range?"

"Mr. Lavery, the only place in this town for twenty bucks a night is the Salvation Army shelter. I can call over there and see if they have anything available."

Thorn kept his face as pleasant as he could.

The kid said, "But as far as hotel rooms go, all we got is the Gulf view suite. Two eighty-five, plus tax."

Thorn pulled the wad of battered bills from his pocket. A few tens and twenties, mostly ones and fives. His savings for the last couple of years. Somewhere near four hundred dollars. It'd seemed like a huge roll when he took it out of a drawer at home, even seemed silly taking along so much.

He peeled off the cash for one night's stay, and didn't even bother counting what was left. Probably just enough to tip the bellman.

"So, you'll be staying with us for only one night?"

"Christ, if I spent two nights in this place I'd have to take out a second mortgage."

The clerk smiled tolerantly and tapped the silver bell on the counter. Thorn turned to see Sylvie coming back across the lobby, the fizz back in her eyes. Jauntiness in her step. She took hold of Thorn's arm and gave him a determined nod.

"Lights, camera, action," she said.

They followed the young black man in blue shorts and white shirt who was carrying Thorn's bag to the elevator. The bellman glanced at Sylvie as they all stepped into the elevator. He pressed the button for their floor, and smiled to himself as he stared at Sylvie out of the corner of his eye.

Man, you won't believe the one I had today, bony little thing, didn't weigh but ninety pounds, and her hair, holy shit, it looked like she'd just come in from a hair-spray hurricane.

"In the nick of time," said Sylvie when the door to his suite was closed, the bellman tipped and gone. "A minute later and Lavery would've been on the phone to Daddy, and hell, you and I would've had to spend the afternoon shopping for caskets."

"Sit down." Thorn pulled a desk chair away from the padded leather table. "We're going to talk."

"What's your rush, big fella?"

She began to prowl the suite. Thorn followed her impatiently. This time he wasn't letting her out of his sight till he found out what she knew about Darcy.

The suite was done in coordinated greens and blonds. Couches, leather wing chairs. A thick pile rug of a soft spun gold. On the walls were elegant watercolors of birds and plants, botanical drawings that resembled Audubons or some other primitive Florida naturalist. In the corners of the room were planters with silk plants of the highest authenticity. The Ritz people had also supplied the room with six telephones. A ten-foot-high glass-front secretary jammed with hotel stationery, a set of French doors leading to the balcony, another set connecting the living area with the bedroom. Four terry cloth robes hung in the large closet, and in the bathroom Thorn watched Sylvie paw through an array of brightly colored bathroom supplies, enough to last a normal person a good six months.

"You see this?" she said. "There's even a goddamn phone next to the john. You run out of toilet paper, just call the front desk. Jeeves, my man, bring me up another roll."

"Okay, Sylvie. Enough of this bullshit. I want to hear it. Start at the beginning. The whole story. How you met Darcy, everything."

Thorn followed her back into the bedroom and he sat down on the foot of the bed.

Sylvie walked over to the double glass doors and stared out at the wide stretch of beach and blue Gulf. She turned back to him, eyes blipping around the room. Since calling Lavery in the lobby she seemed to have tuned in to a new channel, this one piping even more frantic music than usual into her pulse.

"And what's Peter Lavery doing here? What's the deal?"

A half-serious expression washed across her face and she said, "Peter Stuyvesant Lavery, that's who you are. Grandson of Junius Lavery of Atlanta. The newspaper Laverys. You're a trustfund baby. An environmental kook, very big on sponsoring windmill research, harnessing wave action, lots of crackpot things like that. You got into tilapia a few years ago, threw a lot of money at a fish farm in Thomasville.

"Lots of people think you're a total loon. Got feathers for brains. In love with the snail darter, the spotted owl. Come to think of it, maybe that's why we hit it off on the phone. You and me, loons of a feather. We been talking to each other for the last three months. Negotiating this deal. My dad let me do it. He's very big on giving me responsibility, including me in his plans. Thinks it'll win me over. Make me into an adult."

"What's the arrangement?"

"You're here to give my daddy a million three in cash."

Thorn's heart faltered briefly.

Sylvie said, "I don't know why Harden made it such a weird number. If it'd been up to me, I'd've rounded it off to a flat two million."

"What's it for? He selling Lavery the farm, his land?"

"Oh, no. Not a chance. That's our little house on the prairie. Home sweet home."

Sylvie walked over to the French doors and drew them open. A warm rush of sea air flooded the room. And he heard the quiet sift of the Gulf waters washing against the long flat beach below. Thorn took a deep breath, the air so different here from the breezes on the other coast. Not the brawny, starched-shirt smell of the Atlantic coast. The air back home was always moving, buffeted by trade winds, those pure African breezes that arrived each day cooled and sweetened from their long journey across open ocean.

While on the Gulf coast the air was yeastier, a sulfurous brew tainted by swamp fumes from the nearby tidal marshes. And by millions of starfish and periwinkles and cowries that the tide dragged ashore each night, and which each morning lay in thick crunchy masses on the beach, rotting in the sun all day, the flecks of meat still inside them releasing a rank incense.

This was the coast where the ocean was not an ocean at all, but a large, shallow bay that lay stagnant and unstirred by powerful currents. No Gulf Stream here to keep things moving. Just a huge drowsy cove rimmed by Yucatán, the Cajun coast, by Texas. Out there beyond the horizon were the oil rigs and pots of bubbling crawfish gumbo, the steep Aztec pyramids. All of that giving its funky spice to the gust filling his two hundred and eighty-five dollar room.

Turning from the window, Sylvie stood with her back to the bright afternoon light.

"My daddy murdered Darcy," she said. "Or had you already figured that out too?"

His veins tightened down hard, and he stared at Sylvie but could not see her clearly for a moment, the blinding sun, the pressure in his heart.

"I was with him," she said. "We were on that other boat, the one anchored a couple of hundred yards away. Did you even see us over there?"

"I saw a boat, yes."

"I'm sorry," she said. "It wasn't my idea. I liked Darcy, she was nice. She was just trying to help me. I don't know how she did it, but she found out where the farm was. And one day she came over here just like you did.

"I got her alone for a while and told her about what Harden

was doing. His schemes and everything. Then she met him, the two of them talked. But he fooled her. Turned on his goddamn charm. So she left me there, drove off, completely twisted around about which of us was telling the truth, me or Daddy. But even if she didn't rescue me, I gotta say, she was a very nice lady. And now I wish I hadn't told her anything. Hadn't got her involved. Maybe she'd still be alive. I feel guilty about that."

Thorn came to his feet. He marched across to her, shoved her backward, pinned her against the wall beside the sliding door. Tipped her chin up, holding her with the other hand hard against her sternum.

She scowled at him and her eyes seemed to clear for the first time since he'd met her.

"You're sorry?" he said. "You're fucking sorry!"

She struggled to speak.

"Don't bullshit me, Sylvie. I'll strangle your skinny little neck if you do. I want to hear the goddamn truth. Every single detail."

She nodded, swallowing hard. He lessened the pressure.

"Harden killed her. He did. It's true. Just like I said. That's all there is to it. No details to it. She was sniffing around, Harden got worried, so he killed her. Followed you out to the reef, put on his air tank, jumped in, swam over there and killed her. He was going to kill you too, but he decided not to."

Thorn let her go. Stepped back.

"Jesus," she said, rubbing her chest. "I'm glad you finally got fired up. 'Cause, by god, you're gonna need every bit of that juice to go up against my daddy."

"I'm fired up, all right."

"So you up to it? Think you can handle a sixty-year-old man? A geezer in his twilight years?"

"If I had to."

"Oh, you can. I know you can. You're just the man for the job."

"Was Harden in the CIA, an agent, something like that?"

"Wow," she said. "Now, how in the world did you know that?"

Sylvie kept her back against the wall, rubbing her chest. Thorn, a yard away, staring at her.

"And what'd you tell Darcy that got her killed?"

"Just about the fish, about what Harden's doing, his big game plan." Sylvie pushed herself away from the wall, stepped close to him.

"Which is what?"

"I don't think I know you well enough to tell you that. Not yet anyway." Giving a flirty tilt to her head. Putting a coo in her voice, saying, "Listen, there's no reason to be afraid of Harden. He's dangerous, but I can fix it so you're on equal footing with him. Don't worry about that. Sylvie's got a scheme. It'll work."

She walked past Thorn, gave a little flounce as she passed, and went on into the bathroom. She came back out with a miniature bottle of mouthwash, twisted off the cap and poured the blue liquid into her mouth. She walked around the room swishing it, then went over to the balcony and leaned over the concrete balustrade and spit the stuff into the breeze. Then she tossed the bottle over the side and came back into the room.

"So, Thorn, what do you like to do? You know, in your secret life, what have you always wanted a woman to do to you?"

"What kind of boat was it, Sylvie?"

"Boat?"

"What kind of boat did Harden and you take out to the reef?"

She turned away from him, walked to the balcony doors.

"You're difficult, Thorn. Sylvie's gonna have to work extra hard on you."

"What kind of boat, Sylvie?"

"I don't know. A rental. I don't know anything about boats."

"Okay, listen," said Thorn. "We're going to the police. We're going right now."

Sylvie swung around.

"You're kidding me."

"I'm not kidding. We're going to the police."

"Hey! What happened? Where's your heroic spirit? It evaporate? Where's your goddamn primal urge for revenge?"

"We're giving it to the cops. You tell your story and that's it."

"Oh, Jesus Christ, Thorn. Look, first of all, I never said I actually saw anything. I stayed in the boat while he swam over there and swam back. That's all I can say for sure. I wasn't any eyewitness to what happened underwater."

"You tell what you know, and I'll fill in the rest. It'll be enough to put him away."

Thorn stepped over to her, took hold of her upper arm and started to pull her to the door. She jerked away. A wild look in her eyes.

"I don't believe this. You'd let a bunch of lawyers decide what happens to Harden? You'd just give up on this?"

"That's right. That's exactly what I'm going to do."

She paced around the room for a moment, mumbling to herself. Then she stopped and took a seat in the leather chair, and Thorn came over and pulled out the other one and sat across from her. She played with the fringe on her cutoff jeans, keeping her eyes down. She pinched loose some fringe, then looked up and stared at him, dark eyes, a look of sulky challenge.

"You ever see *Casablanca,* Thorn? Humphrey Bogart, Ingrid Bergman?"

Thorn didn't answer.

"First movie I ever saw. I was only eight, nine. My mother took me. I remember her crying in the dark. Me on one side of her, my sister, Gwyneth, on the other, and Mother crying between us."

Thorn watched Sylvie's eyes cloud, watched her begin to breathe through her mouth.

"We sat through that movie twice. The second time, all of us cried. Humphrey Bogart so bitter and hard on the outside, but turning out to be a hero after all. Ingrid Bergman making him love her, and turning him into a hero, making him do what she wanted him to do. All three of us sat there and cried and I decided right then, Thorn, right at that exact second that I was going to have to learn how to be a woman like that if I was going to survive in the Winchester family. I was gonna have to learn how to be Ingrid Bergman. That's what all three of us were thinking. How the hell do we turn Harden into Humphrey Bogart?

"But see, now I understand something I didn't know then. Some men are so mean and spiteful and cold through and through, nobody can make them love. No one can do it. Not Ingrid Bergman. No one. No matter what you do, no matter how hard you try."

Thorn stood up.

"Let's go, Sylvie. We're going to talk to the police."

"I can't," she said softly.

"And why not?"

"If I go into the Collier County police station one more time and tell them what Harden's done, they're going to strap me to a stretcher. 'Cause, see, I already been in there so much, they got a chair with my name written on it. They wave me right on in to see the county shrink, don't even bother to take a statement from me. Last time, they said, that was it, no more. Next time they're going to ship me off to the rubber prison."

She smiled bitterly.

"So, I'd say, as witnesses go, I'm not going to do you a whole hell of a lot of good. And even if you go along, they're just going to think you're under my spell. Just as wacko as I am. It won't work. You're going to have to trust Sylvie, get your own justice. Isn't anybody going to get it for you."

"I'm supposed to believe this hooey. Christ, I haven't heard anything coming out of your mouth yet that sounded like it was even a distant relative to the truth."

Her face clenched as if she were about to scream, but the words came out with a quiet hiss, like steam from a pinhole.

"Okay, so you don't believe Sylvie either. Just like the cops, just like everybody. Well, hell, I don't give two shits what you believe, Mr. Thorn. You aren't here to help Sylvie after all, are you? You're just another gutless dickhead, like all the rest of them. Coming on like Hemingway, but when it gets right down to nitty-gritty time, you got nothing inside your shirt. You got a mirage for a heart."

She snorted, and bowed her head, and her lips began to twitch with wordless curses. In her temples the blood churned.

Thorn rose and went to the bathroom. He washed his hands and rinsed off his face. He dried himself and looked in the mirror. His face seemed changed, eyes were heavy and mouth sagged. As if the grieving had burrowed deep below the flesh and had begun to leave its indelible mark.

Staring at his image, he ran Sylvie's story through again, and matched it against the facts he knew. On the surface everything corresponded. But Sylvie's loopy manner undermined it all. She seemed just as capable of telling a story about green midgets kidnapping her for a joyride in their Swiss cheese rocket ship.

Maybe that's what Darcy had thought as well. Maybe it's what had troubled her so much. Causing her to dismiss Sylvie's claims at first, then spend the next week second-guessing herself. A growing fear that someone was going to be hurt, maybe even be killed if she didn't do something soon.

But maybe Sylvie was right. He should shake off Sugarman's Dudley Do-right influence, forget the police, drive back out to Harden's farm, extract whatever truth he could from the man, then work out a quick, crude approximation of justice. Or else, he could return to Judy Nelson's office, pick up his car, drive back to the other coast. Just go home and forget it all. Hunker down once more behind his high, hard wall of seclusion.

He ran the cold water till he was satisfied it would not get any cooler, then he splashed another double handful on his face, dried off, and went back into the room.

She was gone.

He went to the balcony and for a dizzy second he looked down into the hedges eight stories below. Nothing.

He walked back into the room. Saw Darcy's fuchsia bag sprung open on the bed. Hurriedly, he went to it, dug through his stuff. Sylvie had her choice of three pairs of underwear, two rumpled shirts, his single-bladed Gillette razor, a worn-down toothbrush, a half-empty bottle of roll-on deodorant, or his loaded Smith & Wesson .357 Magnum.

She'd chosen the Smith.

CHAPTER 21

NOT AS NICE A ROOM AS THORN'S. THIS ONE MUCH SMALLER, DIDN'T HAVE the pretty artwork, and looked east out at the parking lot. The chintzy bastard. Worth nine or ten million dollars according to *Fortune* magazine, and Peter Lavery reserved the budget-plate special.

Lavery was on the phone with somebody, his stockbroker it sounded like. Joking around with the guy, but with a serious edge, money involved. When Sylvie knocked, he'd come to the door with the phone wedged between his cheek and shoulder, just covering the receiver long enough to find out who she was, then waving her inside. He'd been on the phone ever since, leaving her to browse, but Sylvie was aware of him watching her, while he jerked himself off, buying, selling, one company, then another.

Lavery was tall, thin, a bony face. One of those fast-growing beards that no matter how often he shaved always left a shadow, which in Sylvie's experience usually meant the guy had undesirable hair on other parts of his body. Sylvie not drawn to the type at all. Not that it mattered a whole hell of a lot. She wasn't planning on rolling around with this guy. But it was a strike against him anyway.

She could tell he was winding down his conversation, made enough money for today, got his blood a little redder from the excitement of transferring all that cash from pile A to pile B.

She sat down on the foot of the bed like Thorn had done upstairs. Seeing him in her head, how calm he seemed to be, how unblurred his eyes could get. Thinking maybe if she made her body do some of the same moves he made, her mind would follow, that Pavlov thing with the dogs. Body first, mind following.

Because the truth was, the whole cumulus thing was becoming a drag. Changing to suit whichever man she was with. Finding his buttons, pressing them long and hard. Speed-talking, witty comebacks. All it ever had been really was a defense. Like that shield they used on *Star Trek* to defend the *Enterprise* against enemy lasers, just an energy field, a lot of wired activity to block out the incoming shit. That's all she did, blurred her dragonfly wings real fast, made a bunch of static in the air and then hid behind it.

The truth was, when she met somebody like Thorn, somebody who'd apparently had his own major traumas but had worked them out, had found a wide, calm middle terrain, then it tugged at Sylvie, made her think maybe it was possible after all, maybe she could do it, mimic somebody like Thorn, imitate her way toward some kind of normal goddamn existence.

But then again, probably not. Probably she was cursed. Weakened down in the spirals of her DNA somewhere. Like circuits that had been so overloaded once with a power surge, they couldn't ever carry the proper voltage again.

Yeah, Sylvie was doomed. Not going to have a normal life. She'd fluttered those transparent wings too long, already worn deep grooves of habit in the air around her, and now there was no way to break the cycle. Sylvie was going to be Sylvie was going to be Sylvie was going to be Sylvie, forever and forever.

Sylvie the cumulus, Sylvie the dragonfly. Having to work every second a hell of a lot harder than normal people did just to keep herself aloft.

Finally, Lavery hung up the phone, turned on her and gave her a rude once-over. A rich man, blunt and smug, afraid of nothing. Probably been bossing people around since he was two years old, gotten real good at it.

"I guess I'm not what you pictured," she said.

"I was imagining older. Thirty-five, forty."

"It must be my mature telephone voice," she said. "It fools everybody."

"All right, so what's the plan? Go to the farm now? Meet the fisher king?" The man was all business, just flipping from one thing to the next.

"If I were you," Sylvie said, "I wouldn't make fun of Harden Winchester to his face. He takes himself pretty seriously."

"I'll try to remember that," he said. "So are we going or what?"

"What's your hurry? Aren't you tired after your long flight?"

"I drove," he said. "And no, I'm not tired." And he twisted his face into a condescending scowl. Guy had never been tired in his life. Pawing at the ground, always ready to go.

Strike two.

He was wearing a green flowery shirt. A Hawaiian variety, with a single green parrot over his heart. He had on a pair of khaki trousers, boat shoes without socks. Sylvie hated boat shoes, especially polished ones like his. Made her want to walk over, step on them with her muddy cowboy boots, grind her heel.

Sylvie came a little closer to him.

"So, Peter, tell me something. You ever save anybody's life before? Slay the dragon, climb the tower, rescue the maiden?"

He chuckled to himself.

"Not that I know of. Not intentionally." He chuckled again, amusing himself with his wit.

"Ever kill anybody? Hand to hand, like that? Or maybe even

seriously injure somebody? Back over someone in your Lincoln Continental maybe?"

"Certainly not. What're you talking about?"

"I didn't think so."

He scowled at her.

"What is this? Some kind of weird interview?"

"Yeah," she said. "That's what it is. And how it looks is, you're not going to get the job. I got one Peter Lavery lined up already, and he's actually a little more what I had in mind."

"Now see here."

Strike three. Talking British.

Abruptly Sylvie turned around and went out the door and into the hallway. She walked halfway down the hall till she located the glass box fixed on the wall. She reached under her Raiders jersey and took out Thorn's pistol. Looked both ways down the hall. No one. Sylvie raised the gun butt and smashed the glass, and pulled down the fire alarm.

In a second or two the sirens went off on the roof, whooping their two notes, low and high, like those European ambulances, the kind that always reminded her of *The Diary of Anne Frank,* the part where the Nazis came to get her and the rest of her family out of the attic. Anne Frank—now there was a girl Sylvie could identify with, a girl with her own set of dragonfly wings. Having to work awful hard just to do the normal things.

Sylvie walked back to Lavery's room. Lavery coming to the door, shaking his head at her, blocking the doorway.

She lifted the pistol, showed it to him, then aimed at his face, and he backed into the room. The hallway was beginning to fill with people, but she didn't think anyone saw her.

She stepped inside and closed the door.

"You bring the million three?"

Lavery was looking at the pistol.

"So this was all a trick? A robbery? You went to all this trouble simply to rob me?"

"Did you bring it? The cash, like we agreed?"

"Carry around that much cash, are you crazy?"

"I told you, Lavery, no uncertain terms, it had to be cash. Greenbacks, nothing else."

"The money's in the bank," he said coldly. "When we're ready to make the transaction, you'll have your cash."

Lavery took a step back from her, watching the pistol. She glanced down at his shiny boat shoes, thinking maybe she'd shoot him in the foot or something, get his attention. Then she looked back up and Lavery was flicking his eyes to the right. To the black plastic suitcase sitting on his bed.

"You fish slime," she said. "You brought it with you just like I told you. Good little Boy Scout, following instructions."

He walked over to the bed, stood in front of the suitcase, crossed his arms across his bony chest. Trying to puff himself up. But still looking like a sniveling brat, the kind of guy who when he was a kid, if someone picked on him, he'd holler for his butler, order him to go over and slap the other kid.

In the article she'd found on this guy, there'd been no photo of him. If there had, and she'd seen what a skinny bastard he was, she probably would've dropped things right there. What she wanted was somebody with some heft to him, some muscularity. A guy who could stay in the ring with her daddy for a round or two, give him a half-decent workout. Somebody more like Thorn.

"The fish samples," said Lavery, "the photographs, weeks of negotiations. All that was just some elaborate ploy to lure me here and hold me up?"

"Tell me something, Mr. Lavery. You got any secret fantasies you never had come true?" She'd decided, what the hell, give the guy one more chance. The least she could do, him coming all this way, bringing so much money with him. And plus, she wasn't a hundred percent sure she was going to be able to get Thorn to go along with her game plan. This guy might do as a half-assed backup.

She said, "Is there something Sylvie could do for you no other woman would do? Something of a sexual nature. Finger up the butt, something like that."

"Now, look here, young lady. This isn't funny. Put the gun away. You can have the money. Just take it and go. I'm certainly not going to risk my life for a few filthy dollars."

Gutless weasel. Strike four.

Lavery glanced at the door, listening to the commotion out in the hallway for a moment. Stalling, eyes beginning to float around the room, trying to figure out a plan of action. Maybe grab one of his platinum credit cards, charge her to death.

With the fire alarm still blaring, she cocked the chrome pistol. Muscles were starting to quiver around Lavery's eyes. She was pretty sure he was on the verge of bawling.

"Okay, all right," she said. "Now, here's what you're going to do, Peter Lavery. You're going to hand me that suitcase. Then you're going to get on the next airplane to Georgia and stay there and forget this happened. You try to call the police or anything, I'll come find you, and I'll make you dead. You understand, Peter? You hearing me?"

Peter Lavery nodded, getting all docile.

Sylvie was talking tough, watching its effect on Lavery, but not meaning any of it. Using words like she always did, just to make things happen. That's all they were with her. Truth, lies, what was the difference? You said whatever you had to say to get the things you wanted. Hell, everybody did it. From the president trying to get reelected on down to the guy trying to slide Sylvie into bed with him. Say whatever it took. Everybody conning everybody else. Words, words, words.

Lavery kept staring at the pistol.

"Pick it up," Sylvie said. "Pick up the suitcase and hand it to me. Real careful like."

A single tear appeared in his left eye. Lavery took a breath and let it out. He did it again, then he turned and took hold of the black case and came back around with it, uncoiling, flinging the suitcase at Sylvie and following behind it. Doing a brave thing probably for the first time in his puny life. Coming after Sylvie, going to knock her down, take her gun and turn her over to the police.

But Sylvie fired, hit the suitcase mid-flight, knocked it off course. And the slug must've gone on through, because Peter Lavery was knocked backward onto the bed.

A puncture wound in his chest. His eyes still open, right leg twitching, lying there looking at nothing, like a gaffed fish. A silver prong hooked through its heart but the thing still having spasms. The fish was dead, but hadn't figured it out yet.

Sylvie moved close, winced as she looked at the blood seeping out. Lots of blood, more than seemed possible for such a skinny guy. She hated this. Hated it. All that blood, the fire alarm throbbing like a killer headache.

Sylvie stepped close to Lavery's body. She leaned forward and pressed the barrel against his flowery shirt, aimed into the beak of the green parrot, shut her eyes tight and turned them away. A second went by, another second. She shut her eyes even tighter, and she fired. The fire alarm picked that second to shut off, the last moment of the siren just covering the loud blast of the pistol.

Nothing twitching anymore. Peter Lavery dead.

Sylvie's heart didn't know how to respond, whether to race or stop entirely. She stood there for a minute, trying to think. Her static shield seemed to have evaporated, feeling a dull ache begin to spread through her gut like she'd swallowed half a bottle of cognac. Killing someone, even to protect herself, it gave her a bad feeling. Even a priss like this, somebody probably cared about him, some other priss back in Georgia. There must've been a better way if she'd only had a little more time to figure it out.

But Lavery hadn't given her any time, and now it was done. She was standing next to the body, her own body stiffening more every second. Emotional rigor mortis taking over. And she knew she had to unlock herself from this position quick. Fight off this first stage of paralysis before it took root and forced her to stand there like a concrete shrine until the door came open, and she was discovered, her crime lying on the bed in front of her. But Sylvie's flesh continued to harden, chest filling with concrete, squeezing out her breath. Veins clotting, eyes going out of focus, brain dulled over. Those transparent wings tiring out, slowing. Sylvie, the dragonfly, tumbling out of the sky. Free-falling.

Scrambling inside, fighting it, Sylvie rocked herself forward onto her toes. Then back. Straining to loosen herself. Some sweat growing in her armpits, cold sweat, icy. Another rock, forward and back. Sneaking down a small breath. Letting it out. Little by little rocking some more and some more, easing the stiff grip, coming back, coming back to the limber world.

Finally, Sylvie could blow out a long breath, could make herself bend forward, stoop, touch her toes. And she was back. She was there again. Sylvie be nimble, Sylvie be quick.

She moved to the other king-size bed, sat down on the edge of it and got down another breath. Then she swiveled around and snapped open the black suitcase and there they were. Green blocks of cash with brown paper wrappers. A ragged bullet hole through the middle of them. Probably tore up a few hundred thousand, but there was still plenty enough to fool Harden. God, he'd love this one. This one was going to be her best yet.

She took the silver ice bucket off the bureau and walked out into the hall. People were chattering to each other in front of their doors, wondering if this was for real or just a false alarm. Should they evacuate? Sylvie passing by to the alcove where the ice machine was, no one paying any attention to her. She filled up the bucket, went back to Lavery's room.

She put the DO NOT DISTURB sign on the doorknob, set the ice bucket down on the bathroom lavatory. Then she called the front desk, made sure they knew that Mr. and Mrs. Lavery were on their honeymoon, and didn't want anyone walking in on them. Absolutely nobody. Not even to turn down their bed, put a chocolate mint on their pillow at night or bring fresh towels, for no reason whatsoever. Was that absolutely, utterly clear? Oh, yes. Yes, indeed, ma'am. Whatever you say.

Then with her hands in his damp armpits, she hauled Lavery

off the bed and dragged him into the bathroom and laid him out in the tub. She sprinkled the bucket of ice on his chest.

It was going to take thirty, forty trips down the hall for enough ice to keep the body from decomposing. She just needed to hold the smell down for a couple of days. After that, the trail that led to Sylvie would be too damn cold to do anybody any good.

She stood in the foyer and held her left fist up to her eye, peered through it, and cranked the camera with her right fist. She panned around the room, then brought the lens around to the bathtub, to Peter Lavery. Looking very relaxed now. A dreamy expression on his lips. Sylvie moved closer, cranked the film through the camera. Cranking it, she captured this moment, death, captured it for all time, for eternity. Death.

CHAPTER 22

SUGARMAN HAD NEVER CARED MUCH FOR THE EVERGLADES. OH, YEAH, HE knew how important the place was, all that groundwater evaporating, turning into heavy clouds, sucked east by the rising air heated by the city, all that water falling on Miami every summer afternoon at four. Same time every day, never varied. And the Glades wasn't just a source of rain for Miami and the Keys, but also the nesting place for a million different kinds of birds and all that. Important, yeah. But Sugarman always felt guilty riding across the place, 'cause he could never work up any real affection for it. Just looked brown and desolate to him. Nothing to do out there but traipse around in the muck, dodge alligators.

Fact was, he wasn't really much of a nature guy, except for liking to fish. He was definitely no Thorn, who lived without air-conditioning, hot water, TV, VCR, microwave, never seeming to miss any of it. Only reason Thorn had his house wired for electric at all was to power the refrigerator, and then mainly to keep his beer cold. But not Sugarman. He admitted it. He'd sold out, was a soft modern guy, hooked on conveniences. Loved microwave popcorn.

About the best thing Sugarman could say about the Everglades: it was nice not to have to look at billboards for a hundred miles. Driving the whole width of Florida, not a single advertisement. Probably the only hundred mile stretch like that in the state. That is, if you didn't count the alligator wrestling or airboat ride or bingo parlor signs. All of them put up by the Miccosukees, the only people with the right to advertise, it being partly their reservation land.

Mostly the Everglades made him sleepy. Two hours of that straight, empty two-lane blacktop road. You could just leave your steering wheel lock on, the Club or whatever it was called, not even give a twitch to the wheel for two hours. One slash pine looking just like the next, one wide open savanna an exact replica of the last one. Like your car wasn't really moving at all, the way they did it in movies, a guy holding the steering wheel but not really steering, landscapes showing outside the car windows, but dull scenery, nothing you'd really pay attention to.

Only today, coming across the Glades, he was wide awake. Major electrical current passing through him. He hadn't even exchanged a word with Doris Albright in the last twenty miles, but still, it was like they'd just finished having an intimate, revealing conversation. That's how it felt in his bloodstream, how alert he was, how aware of her sitting there next to him in the Mustang as he drove. Her scent in his nostrils, her every little movement registering in his peripheral vision, some crazy Gene Krupa–drummer going triple time in his pulse.

Sugarman was too polite to stare at her, too nervous to glance over, afraid she might catch him and he'd have to say something. Keeping his eyes fixed on the road, or taking an occasional look out his window. But all the while with a clear picture of her in his mind from when he'd picked her up at her house this afternoon, opening the passenger door for her, and Doris smiling, giving him a mildly surprised look like she wasn't used to men being so gallant. Which was hard to believe, seeing how striking a woman she was, and the social circles she must've traveled.

She was dressed in a lime linen jacket with turquoise Bermuda shorts, and some kind of silky white T-shirt under the jacket. Beige ballet slippers with little bow ties. A gold braided belt. Her hair loose today, thick and clean and white-blond. He could smell her perfume when he opened the door for her, a faint fragrance, clean with a crisp citrus edge.

All the trouble he'd had with Jeanne over the years, he'd been feeling the ties loosening between them, and lately he had to admit he'd been looking at other women more seriously than he ever had before. Been aware of their clothes, how they moved and smelled, letting his imagination loosen up a little.

But at the same time still hanging in there with Jeanne, being a hundred percent faithful. Despite her constant anger, her belittling him, her depression. And all her damn hobbies, most of them expensive in one way or another, that put more strain on the marriage. And, of course, there was that one hobby of hers a couple of years ago, her little fling at adultery.

Now, that had put a major stress on things. Sugarman having to suddenly study up on open marriages. What he found out was, Jeanne only wanted it halfway open. Her half. She'd told him she'd become convinced she could find religious salvation through vaginal orgasms. See the face of God from having a man's penis moving around inside her. And not necessarily Sugarman's penis either.

She took to having orgasms with whoever she could, including the preacher at their church, the very guy who'd given her that stupid idea in the first place. Also with a couple of the men in the congregation. All of them getting together for private prayer meetings every Wednesday and Saturday. That's what they called it, prayer meetings. Jeanne even admitting to Sugarman that on some of those occasions she'd tried it with a woman or two, and Lord knew what else. Sugarman wouldn't even let himself think about that. Damn, he was still reeling from that time, and here it was three years later.

"Want to listen to the radio?" Doris said.

"It doesn't work. Sorry."

He glanced over at her, met her eyes. She smiled again and he smiled back, then looked again at the road, having to jerk the wheel a quarter turn, bring the car back into their lane.

"I appreciate your doing this, you know. Though you didn't really have to. I could've brought my car. I know the way to the farm. It's just that I didn't realize he was still there. I thought he would've left that place by now."

"Oh, I needed to come over here anyway. I got a friend doing some work for me in Naples. Guy you saw in my office a few days ago. Thorn. An old friend from high school. We're working together on an investigation, and it just happened to bring him over here too, so I thought, why not?"

Not telling her the complete truth, that he was coming over here because Doris had finally told him her ex-husband's name. Winchester, Harden Winchester. Bingo, double bingo. Same name as the girl in the video, same as the man who raised tilapia. Sugarman not having any choice really. Having no luck locating Murtha, so he decided to follow the hottest trail, told Doris he'd drive her over to the west coast.

"Actually, me and Thorn go back even before high school. Old friends. I used to go fishing with him when I was six, seven years old. You don't find many friends you go that far back with. But Thorn's one. He and I, we're like brothers."

Sugarman thinking, shit, there he was again, babbling, filling the air with nervous noise. Like in high school, going out with girls, sitting there beside them, never having the first idea of what to say, and gradually concluding that hell, he must be IQ deficient, at least in communication skills. Then, after marrying Jeanne the year they graduated, it didn't bother him much anymore. Jeanne doing ninety percent of the talking for both of them. And still doing it.

But now here it was again. Sugar, the tongue-tied dullard, making absolutely no progress in twenty-five years.

She didn't say anything for a minute, and Sugarman could feel her looking at him.

Then she said, "Did you find out what Harden does for a living now?"

"He has a fish farm. Raises a fish called tilapia, I understand."

"Fish farm?" She stared at the side of his face. "Somebody can get rich raising fish?"

"Rich? I don't see how."

"But he said he was very wealthy. When he came to see me last year, he told me he'd made a whole lot of money and he assumed I'd be so impressed, I'd come back to him."

"But you weren't."

"That's right, I wasn't."

"I guess some women might've been."

"Well," she said. "That wasn't why I left him. Money never entered into it. Money's the least part of happiness."

"You tell him that when he was there?"

"No, I just told him to get his sorry ass off my porch before I took down my husband's twelve-gauge and filled him full of goddamn rabbit pellets."

Sugarman glanced over at her.

She said, "My language shocks you?"

"Well, coming from you, yeah, a little."

"I may buy my clothes at Neiman-Marcus these days, but part of me is still a girl from the hills of Tennessee. And I damn well know how to use that twelve-gauge too."

Sugarman watched the road for a minute. He passed a slow-going Winnebago. When he was back in his lane, he said, "You chased your ex-husband away like that, he might not be real friendly this time around."

Another boring mile went by.

"To be completely honest," she said, looking out her window, taking her time, "it's not Harden I want to see anymore. I should just level with you. I've decided I'd rather lose my business than take money from that man. I dread being anywhere close to him again. I loathe him, even after all this time. But what it is really, I want to see my girls. Want to talk to them, see if they're all right."

"Girls?"

"My two daughters."

"They still live with him?"

"From what I can gather, yes."

She sounded like she didn't want to go any further down that road, so Sugarman let the silence grow again. Watching the traffic start to thicken as they came out of the Everglades and into the outskirts of Naples.

"Are you married?"

Sugarman said yes, he was.

"You don't sound so sure."

Sugarman glanced over at her, back at the road.

"I think what it's called," he said, "is a dysfunctional marriage."

"God, I hate that word," Doris said. "You hear it all the time. But what does it mean? Have you ever seen a functional marriage? I mean, is that good, is that what marriage is supposed to be, a well-oiled machine or something? Why not just say bad marriage or good marriage? Dysfunctional, what garbage."

Sugarman looked over at her, the woman tapping her knuckles against her window, glaring out, getting upset over a word. Never met anybody like that.

"It's the word my wife uses," Sugarman said. "Came from her books, the ones she's always reading to see why she's so unhappy. Told me she's trying to figure out how she could have made such a stupid mistake, a white woman, pretty as she was, full of talent and pep, marrying a black man without any spark. A thing like that never could work. What was she ever thinking about? She uses a lot of words right out of those books to explain it to herself."

"Spark?"

"That's how she talks. Spark. Dysfunctional. Addictive personality. Toxic parents."

"Toxic parents!" She waved the phrase away like a bad smell.

"I know, I know. It's strange stuff."

"You're awfully casual about it," she said. "I think I'd be mad as hell, my spouse talking like that about me."

"I'm not mad at her," Sugarman said. "And not sad either. The way I feel, it's something in between. I don't know what the name for it is."

A half mile ahead was the first traffic light they'd seen for two hours, ever since entering the Everglades. Sugarman slowed to a stop. It was a relief to see some signs of civilization again. Houses, 7-Elevens, trailer parks.

"I think the word for what I am," he said, "is lonesome."

She was quiet, but he didn't need to look over to check if she'd heard him. He could tell the way her silence was, denser than it had been before. She was thinking about what he'd said. The two of them, right out of deep center field, having a conversation, a fairly good one, and Sugarman not even knowing this woman, feeling totally out of her league. But still, suddenly finding it easy to speak to her. Cured of his knotted tongue.

A minute or two later, he pulled off at a gas station to fill up. And when he'd drawn up to the pumps and turned off the ignition, Doris Albright reached over and lay her hand on his where it was resting on the seat between them. He looked down, her hand cool and slender and white, nails uncolored. A large simple diamond on her ring finger.

"I have one of those too," she said.

"One of what?"

"A dysfunctional marriage," she said, still holding his hand. "It wasn't that way before Philip got sick. Oh, no, just the opposite. But that's what it is now."

The look in her eyes held for a moment, sorrowful, then her face relaxed, and her mouth made something close to a smile.

"I really hate that word," she said.

"Yeah," Sugarman said. "So do I. I hate its goddamn sorry ass all to hell."

Thorn demanded to speak to the manager. In a minute or two a thirty-year-old kid with curly red hair and a blue silk suit came out of his office smiling broadly, and ushered Thorn inside, sat him down, and proceeded to assure him that there was no damn way he could reveal another guest's room number. It was hotel policy to insure all their guests' absolute privacy. Even if that guest is in danger? The manager lost a fraction of his smile. What sort of danger? But Thorn had no reply, nowhere to go with this without alerting the local cavalry, and he wasn't ready for that, wanted to peel away another layer before this went public.

As he stalked out of the office, an alarm siren began to sound somewhere in the hotel. The desk clerks looked nervously at each other and the manager hurried out of his office, glared at Thorn, then picked up a phone at the front desk and began to speak to someone.

Thorn located the stairway and hiked up the stairs to the second floor and marched down the long yellow hallway. He did the same on the third floor, the fourth, all the way to the top. No sign of her. He rode the elevator back down, checked the beauty shop, the sundry store, the bar and restaurant. Nothing.

By the time he decided to try the hotel grounds, the alarm had shut off and Thorn felt a headache beginning to stitch itself to the back of his eyeballs.

He walked out onto the spacious terra-cotta veranda, scanned the grounds for a moment or two, saw no Sylvie anywhere, then headed off at a lope past the putting green, down a wooden walkway that led into a thicket of trees.

It was a dense stand of buttonwoods, leather fern, gumbo-limbo and strangler fig. Mangroves, black and red, growing from a lagoon whose surface was coated with a bright green slime. Apparently that swatch of tidal marsh had been left intact by the hotel for the edification of its guests, because little wooden plaques were spaced along the walkway identifying some of the vegetation.

But no one was reading them. And Thorn didn't stop either. He went through the hammock and out to the wide stretch of blond sand, and walked along the water's edge to the south for a while, squinting into the distance. Then retraced his steps and walked north a few hundred yards. No Raiders jersey anywhere.

He crossed the tidal marsh on a different walkway, rounded the corner of the outdoor bar and there she was on one of the stools of the tiki bar. In her hand a tall frosted glass half filled with something pink, and Sylvie with her lips puckered around the straw slurping up the other half.

And as much as it jolted him to admit it, Sylvie looked stunning there. An untamed vitality about her. The sharp facets of her cheekbones, the porcelain skin, those tense black eyes. Even her disheveled hair that seemed plagued by a dozen competing cowlicks, seemed to enhance the charm. Until that moment he hadn't thought of her as a sexual creature. And even now this warm itch of attraction struck him as deeply perverse. She was little more than a child, certainly some fraction crazy. Darcy dead only a few days. Yet there it was. Walking toward her while she drank her cocktail, Thorn felt that familiar twinge in his gut, like something shifting deep inside him, some internal organ that had suddenly come awake.

CHAPTER 23

WHEN THORN REACHED HER, SHE SET THE GLASS ASIDE, PATTED HER LIPS
with a paper cocktail napkin, and gave him a loose smile.

"Where've you been?"

"Here," she said. "Quenching my thirst."

"Where's my pistol, Sylvie? What'd you do with it?"

"You don't need to yell."

"Where is it?"

"In a safe place, don't worry about it."

"Where, Sylvie?"

Slowly she lifted her Raiders jersey and let him have a peek.
The .357 was mashed against her belly.

"Your pistol's acquiring intimate knowledge of Sylvie."

"Give it to me."

She made a sulking frown, and glanced over his shoulder at
the other patrons.

"Now?"

He held out his hand, and after a hesitation, she tugged the
.357 out of her waistband and clapped it onto the bar.

The bartender and a couple of drinkers looked up at the noise, but Thorn bent forward and propped his elbow on the bar, managed to shield the weapon from their view. He slipped the pistol into his lap and opened the cylinder. Two rounds gone. He slid it under his shirt, tucked it into his jeans.

"So whatta you say, Thorn? Want to take the afternoon off, put your quest on hold for an hour, fool around with Miss Sylvie? Climb the stairway to heaven?"

"No, thanks."

"We got time. Doesn't take Sylvie that long. And I'm sure I can get you airborne pretty quick."

She picked up her drink, held it to her lips, and tongued some of the pink slush into her mouth.

"Looks to me like there might be some loose boards on that stairway."

Sylvie slammed her glass down.

"Jesus Christ, Thorn. You keep saying those things. Sylvie's crazy. Sylvie's a loon. But have I done anything that's fucked up? I got you out of all that gunfire at your house. It was my quick thinking that saved you out at the farm, turned you into Peter Lavery. If Harden had found out you were Darcy's boyfriend, you'd be dead right now."

"What'd you do, Sylvie? Where's Lavery?"

"I ran him off," she said. "Big baby. Took one look at your pistol and he started packing."

"You fired two shots from this."

"I know that. I went down the beach, a mile down where it's deserted. I knocked a tin can off a stump, working on my aim. I figure I might just have to shoot Harden my own self. Since it looks like all the men I'm surrounded by are so lily-livered."

"I don't believe you."

"I ran him off, is all I did. We couldn't have him hanging around, now could we? He'd screw up everything. Get us killed more than likely."

"You're lying."

"Look, I've got a plan," she said. "I've been thinking about this a long time, and now I know how we're going to do it."

She swiveled around on her stool and began to watch the kids splash in the shallow pool, chaises full of old folks turning red in the late summer sun. Thorn stood beside her.

Sylvie said, "We'll treat it like it was a drug deal. Which in a way it is. So what we do is, we put the million three in a suitcase, we rent a luggage locker at the Naples Airport. You meet Harden there, give him a look at the money, then close the locker back up and put the key in your pocket. He won't try anything with all those people around. Then the two of you go back to the farm in separate cars. That's so he can't drive you off somewhere, whack you and take the key. Then once you get to the farm, he delivers the fish to you. You hand over the locker key, back away to your car, and drive off."

"And where's all this cash coming from?"

"You let little Sylvie worry about the details."

"That's a pretty goddamn big detail. A million three."

"I got it covered, Thorn."

"Yeah? And when do I get to kill him?"

Sylvie shushed him, looking around to see if anybody'd heard.

"That comes next," she said quietly.

They watched as a muscled-up lifeguard passed by, giving Sylvie a close look. Not sure she belonged here, dressed like one of the Joads just in from Oklahoma.

Sylvie said, "On that long empty road near the farm, we're going to ambush him. You leave the farm, head back to town, Sylvie'll jump out and wave you down. You pull off on a side road and we wait for Daddy to come past for the money. When we see him coming, I'll pull Lavery's car out of the side road, drive into his path. He throws on the brakes, maybe even collides with the car. That's when you come out of the ditch and mow him down. Guns blazing. It's the only way. A sneak attack like that. Anything else is too dangerous."

"You're serious."

"Aren't you?"

Thorn stared into her black eyes and said nothing.

"Believe me, Thorn. You gotta shoot straight, gotta kill him quick, or else he'll find a way to put you away. Defunct. The man's a trained assassin. You gotta be quick. Mongoose quick. He's the best there is."

Her voice cheery, smiling like she'd just invited him to escort her to some formal ball where they would be the guests of honor.

He closed his eyes for a moment, massaged his forehead. When he opened his eyes, she was smiling expectantly.

"Forget it," he said. "I'm not going along with any of that crap."

"Why?"

"It's stupid."

"Oh, no, I know the real reason why. You're just a typical goddamn man. Gotta be running things. Can't give a woman any credit for having brains. That's what it is, isn't it? You're a sexist shit, Thorn. That's it. Admit it. Gotta be in control."

She turned around on her stool, picked up the remains of her drink, and took a petulant swig. She smacked the glass down.

"It's true," Thorn said. "I treat women different than men."

"I knew it."

"Because if you were a man, Sylvie, I'd have dragged your ass into the woods by now and slapped that shit-eating grin off your mouth, and I wouldn't have stopped slapping you until you told me the truth about what was going on. That's the kind of sexist I am. But you know, now that I think about it, I believe I'm having a major awakening. Yeah, I am. I've suddenly seen the light. And you know what? I'm going to start with you, Sylvie. You can be my first woman to get complete gender-neutral treatment."

She looked at him for a moment, the loony expression dying away, replaced with a flat, bland stare. The first time she'd let him see the face behind the goofy grin. She turned her eyes down, stared into the pink foam left in her glass.

"I need proof," Thorn said. "If you want me to believe what you're saying about your father, I have to have absolute proof."

"Proof he's a killer?"

Thorn leaned in close to her and spoke quietly.

"Proof he murdered Darcy."

"Proof?" she said. "You don't trust Sylvie? You can't just take her word for it?"

"No, I can't."

"You sure?" Sylvie climbed down off the barstool.

She tugged on the hem of her Raiders jersey, stretching the fabric tight over her chest. Showing him a little of what he was missing. Then yawning, lifting her arms into the air, a sexy little demonstration, loosening up all the equipment.

"You know, I'm awful sensitive," she said. "My tissues are just chock-full of nerve endings. I can be a bronco in bed. Some people have a hard time even staying on."

She crossed her arms and cupped each breast in the opposite hand. Gave them each a little squeeze.

"Not interested."

Sylvie let go and sat down on the stool again.

"You have some sex problem Sylvie should know about? Enlarged prostate, something like that?"

"I'm just as healthy as can be."

"Hey, I bet I know what it is, why you're being so cool to Sylvie." She edged close, a few inches between their lips, and whispered, "You don't want to have sex before the big game. That's it, isn't it? It's not that you got a problem with me. It's that game-day thing. Saving your sperm for the big fight."

"Did you ask Roy Murtha to kill your father too?"

She jerked back from him. Looked down, fiddled with her straw for a moment.

"Is that what he told you?"

"Maybe."

"Roy's a goddamn liar," Sylvie said, keeping her eyes on her drink. "Told Sylvie he cared about her, but he didn't. He didn't give a shit about Sylvie."

"He refused you, said he wouldn't have any part of it."

She stirred the pink foam with her straw. She said nothing, her eyes on his, but the sight was going out of them as she began to drift inward.

In a lazy voice she said, "I'll drop that airport locker key by your room later on. You be at that locker at three o'clock. Don't be late. Harden's a stickler for punctuality."

She turned from him and waved at the bar man and called out for her check.

"You're going to give me the key to some locker with over a million dollars in it?"

"That's right." She swiveled around to face him. "I trust you, Thorn. Even if you don't trust me."

"I'm not doing it," he said. "I'm not playing your game. I'll get the proof on my own."

"Tomorrow you'll have the key. Then you can decide if you want to play or not. Three o'clock at the airport. I'm telling Harden that Peter Lavery will be there. You got till then to decide."

"Tell him whatever the hell you want."

She hummed to herself and examined Thorn with a mixture of exasperation and respect.

Coolly, she said, "The way you live, Thorn, that house, no telephone, you're this real nature guy, aren't you? Granola, alfalfa sprouts. Walden Pond kind of person."

Thorn was quiet, watching a grim smile reshape her lips.

She said, "Well, Mr. Antelope Lover, you just might be interested to know what my father is going to do. Want to know?"

"I'm listening."

"As soon as Daddy gets Lavery's money in his hands, he's planning to let all the tilapia go. There's a few million fish in those ponds, counting the fingerlings, the larvae, and he's going to set them all free at once. Release them into the Okehatchee.

"A couple of days later they'll be in the Gulf, and by Thanksgiving they'll have migrated around the tip of the state and be in the Atlantic. And before the year's over, he says the only damn fish you'll find anywhere will be tilapia. They reproduce so fast, they're so aggressive, they'll beat out all the other fish and it won't be long, maybe a year or two, before they start to strangle the whole damn ocean, strangle it with themselves. That's what Harden's going to do, that's his plan. Cripple the whole ocean. Cause a major catastrophe. Whatta you think about that, Mr. Thoreau?"

"Why would he do something like that?"

"Why don't you ask him?"

"I don't believe you, Sylvie."

"The whole ocean," she said, her eyes bleak. "Tilapias, tilapias, tilapias. Just think about it, Thorn. 'Cause that's what's at stake unless you throw in with Miss Sylvie. The whole goddamn ocean."

Her eyes strayed off over his shoulder. Sylvie set her glass down.

"Oh, shit. End of conversation."

Her face drained as she climbed off the stool.

"He sees us like this, he'll know something's cooking. You're as good as dead."

She edged down the length of the bar.

Thorn looked around, following her stare, and it took him a moment or two before he saw Harden coming out of the lobby, start down the winding brick path toward the pool area. Thorn looked back for Sylvie, but she was already on the other side of the tiki bar, headed down the wooden stairway to the beach.

CHAPTER 24

THORN'S THROAT CLENCHED SHUT. HE COULD FEEL THE BRIGHT PING OF blood pressuring hard against his eardrums as if he were sinking deep and fast into a sunless sea. He stood his ground and forced down a long breath, held it, then let it out slowly, trying to decompress, reminding himself who he was now, his part to play. Not a man smoldering for revenge, but Peter Lavery. Rich boy from Georgia. An ecological businessman.

Winchester had changed into a white polo shirt, burgundy tennis shorts, and a pair of leather sandals. He had on a white Panama hat with a bright red band. Dapper guy. But moving with a fluid poise that Thorn recognized now was more than just athletic suppleness.

Standing next to him this morning, Thorn had registered the man's vigor, but he hadn't tried to give it a more accurate name. Now, seeing him from a hundred yards away, it was obvious. He probably worked out with weights, stretching, running perhaps. But that wasn't the point. What was unique about him was that all that strength was coiled around some volatile core. A lazy tiger stroll. Graceful and deadly.

As Winchester passed the Olympic pool, he spotted Thorn, and headed his way, and every motion he made was light-footed and precise. Carrying himself with extreme caution, as though the slightest jostle might cause the unstable gases bottled up inside him to detonate. Level everything for miles around.

They shook hands, smiled, nodded silently. A pantomime of civility. Winchester asked Thorn what he was drinking, then went to the bar and brought back two drinks and took the seat across from Thorn. Harden raised his shot glass and toasted Peter Lavery's health and the success of their enterprise. Thorn did not touch his beer, but watched as Harden took a small sip of his whiskey.

"The bellman told me I could find you out here. My god, Lavery, you've only been here an hour or two, and already you've made quite an impression on these people."

"Must be my Pepsodent smile."

Harden picked up the small box of matches sitting in the ashtray and rattled it like dice in his fist.

"I feel I know you already, Peter. That article Sylvie found about you in *Fortune,* very thorough."

Thorn shifted in his seat, touched a finger to the damp label on his beer bottle, then peeled it away, rolled it into a damp ball and set it in the middle of the table.

He tried for a hint of Georgia in his voice, honeysuckle and moonshine.

"Take it from the son of a newspaper man, Mr. Winchester, don't ever trust journalists. They're shitty listeners. Usually so full of themselves, they only hear every third word you say. What facts they don't get completely wrong, they find some way to twist."

Harden smiled, one skeptical man of the world to another. Thorn got a breath down and let go of it as casually as he could manage. The two of them sitting in the shade of one of the small umbrella tables. Both looking out at the beach crowd, the stream of handsome people strolling past. Three-hundred-dollar-a-day folks, scrupulously slim. While out in the western sky, huge clouds were foaming up, thick white concoctions that flirted with the sunlight.

"So tell me, Peter, is it true you and Warren Beatty are close friends?"

Thorn kept his eyes on the clouds.

"Everybody wants to talk about movie stars."

"Well, is it accurate?"

"That, Harden, is exactly why I never read anything they write about me. Just so much bullshit."

"Don't even know him?"

"Oh, I've met him. At gatherings. We've talked, but I would never call Warren a friend."

"You didn't invest in his picture? One about the gangster?"

Thorn inspected him carefully.

"Are we playing another game here?"

"What?"

"Because if we are, just tell me. Give me a couple of the rules, and I'll play with you. I like games. I'm good at them. But I like to know the rules."

"Hey, hey. I just wanted us to get to know each other better. No offense. I didn't mean to pry."

"Then don't."

Harden continued to smile, an unblended, hundred-proof grin. It seemed to be thriving on some deep-rooted pleasure he could barely contain. As if at any moment he were going to stand up, whoop out some patriotic song, try to get the whole bar crowd to join in.

Thorn glanced at the length of adhesive tape running across Winchester's right knuckles, and with brutal clarity he saw again the white, bloodless puckers on the back of Darcy's lifeless hand. And that image dissolved into another of Darcy underwater, thrashing, slicing at the bastard's hand that was gripping hers.

Thorn drew his own hands off the table, put them in his lap. Made two hard fists and ground them against the underside of the table. Wanting, by god, to throw the thing over, hurl himself on this cocksure bastard, tear flesh from bones. But no, he stayed still, kept the quiver out of his face, riding this thing out to its last stop.

"I'm a very happy man today, Peter. This is the final stop on a long, long voyage. The payoff for years of work. A celebration day."

Thorn took a sip of his beer and steered his eyes away from Winchester. Trying to cool the hot twist of anger growing in his throat.

"So, Peter, I'd like to tell you my story, how I got to this point. Would you like to hear it?"

Thorn looked at him squarely.

"No," he said. "Not particularly."

Winchester's smile emptied, but his lips held the pose, and while his eyes lingered on Thorn's, he lifted his shot glass and took a small, neat bite of the bourbon and set it down.

"Of course you do."

Harden slid open the matchbox and dumped the matches onto the table. He stirred his finger through them.

"Before I met my wife," he said, and shifted his gaze away toward the building clouds, "all I aspired to was a career in the military. I grew up in a drafty log cabin with a dirt floor, for christ sakes. A clodhopper from West Texas. I couldn't put two words together without one of them being fuck or shit. I was one coarse, uncivilized son of a bitch. But the moment I met Doris Carter, everything changed. I fell so deep and hard for that girl, everything changed. Christ Almighty, I started writing her poems, if you can believe it, poem after poem. Went to work on my manners, my deportment. God, I would have done anything for her."

"But she left you anyway."

His smile dimmed, eyes sharpening as he looked again at Thorn.

"And how the hell did you know that?"

"I could hear its footsteps coming across the stage."

Thorn reached across the table and tapped Winchester's bandaged hand.

"How'd that happen?"

Harden glanced at his knuckles and shrugged.

"It's nothing. I don't even remember."

Harden picked a couple of the matchsticks from the pile and positioned them meticulously behind his shot glass. He lifted his eyes, moved them off to the distance, head tipping back, a dreamy, self-satisfied smile surfacing.

"Yes," he said. "It's true Doris abandoned me eventually. And I have to admit now, she had every reason to. A lifetime in the military had made me cold down at the core. Add to that the fact that I traveled a great deal, left Doris for weeks, even months at a time, all alone out there on that desolate piece of land. And when I came home there was always a readjustment period. The nature of my work, the brutality of it, made it doubly hard to be a part of that feminine world."

Thorn took another taste of his tepid beer. Staring at that adhesive. Harden leaned back in his chair, took an expansive breath, and once more lifted his gaze up to the distance.

"First time I saw Doris Carter, she was only fifteen years old. I was thirty. Posted at Fort Campbell, on the Kentucky–Tennessee border. Doris was a high school girl, a cheerleader for her football team in Clarksville, Tennessee.

"I remember sitting in the bleachers with some of the boys in my battalion. Pimply kids not much older than she was. Taking some R and R on that chilly October night, watching the local hayseeds gallop up and down the field. And there she was in a sweater and short skirt. Doris Carter. Long blond hair and long slim legs. Everyone noticed her. She was like that. Walked onto the field, and every eye in the bleachers turned her way.

"And my god, I stole that girl from her big dumb boyfriend, from her Cadillac salesman father, from her cookie baking flirt of a mother. A couple months is all it took, but I walked off with her. That night in October, all my boys were whistling at her, stomping their feet, and I knew the very second I saw Doris Carter, I was going to make that woman love me."

"Stop it," Thorn said.

Harden turned his drowsy smile on Thorn. He ran a hand across the gray bristles on the side of his head as if he were combing the ghostly memory of a ducktail.

"What is it, Peter?"

Thorn drained his beer, set it down, and began to look around for the waitress. He knew he'd be better off encouraging Harden to ramble on through his autobiography. He just might learn something useful that way, some chance remark that provided the final proof of his guilt. But Thorn couldn't bear it, hated the dreamy rush of emotion in Winchester's voice. His talk of love. Hated the fever in his eyes, that sweet glow they took on when he spoke of his lost wife.

"Just spare me, okay? I don't want to hear your goddamn life story."

"What is it? Do personal matters make you nervous?"

"Look, Winchester, if it doesn't have a dollar sign at the beginning of it, I don't want to hear about it. Okay? I don't care who you are, how you feel about women. We do our business, get it over with, and we go our own ways. You understand that? We're not going to be bosom buddies, we're not going to bare our souls, or bond, or any of that shit. I got enough friends already. What we are is business associates, that's all."

"Well, you see," Harden said, "I have a slightly more complex view myself. I wouldn't be doing business with you at all, Peter, if it wasn't for love. Love and work, they're mingled for me. I mean, the only reason I've devoted myself to raising tilapia at all is because of Doris. Because of her and who she ran away with."

"I'm telling you, I don't give a rat's ass about who your wife ran off with, your philosophy of life, any of it. That clear?"

His smile had grown rigid. He looked down at the matches, removed another one from the pile and relocated it behind his shot glass.

"Are you, by any chance, a fisherman, Peter?"

Thorn slid his gaze out to the water, watched a shrimp boat move slowly across the horizon.

"I caught a couple of fish once."

"And why do you fish? For food or sport?"

"Neither," he said. Thorn met his eyes. "I fish to find out what's down there."

The last shred of Harden's grin was gone. Clearly Thorn had violated some ritual of his. Food or sport, the only options allowed.

"My wife," Harden said, very precisely, face under tight control, "Doris abandoned me, and married a commercial fisherman."

Thorn was silent.

"This man," Harden said, leaning slightly forward. "He filled my wife with romantic illusions about himself. He convinced her he was some kind of great white hunter of the seas."

"I'm having another drink." Thorn pushed his chair back.

"No, you're staying put," Winchester said. "I'm telling you a story. You need to hear this. You need to know who you're doing business with and why."

Thorn hesitated, then eased back into his chair, settled his gaze on the swimming pool, an old woman floating on her back looking up at the stream of passing clouds.

Winchester said, "This man stole my wife from me. Beautiful Doris. He seduced her soon after she left me, when she was very vulnerable, and then he took her off behind a big fortress of money. And he hid her there, kept her from me."

His eyes darkened, filling with acid.

"I've always thought," he said, "that it's infinitely more satisfying to beat an opponent at their chosen game. Give them home field advantage, every edge, and crush them there. Much more satisfying. Don't you agree?"

Thorn was silent, looking into those bitter gray eyes.

Winchester said, "Some time after Doris left, I devoted myself to the study of fish. I thought about them, I read, I became something of an expert. And I came to see, Peter, something that I'm sure you've seen as well. Before much longer, commercial fishermen will seem as silly as fur trappers do to us now, buffalo hunters. Silly, irrelevant. Quaint."

Thorn watched a passenger jet rising silvery in the eastern sky. Harden had another taste of his bourbon and set it down, removed a couple more matches from the jumble and set them precisely in the pile he was building.

"That man who stole Doris is crippled now. A sick, dying old fool." Winchester looked up from his work. "But that's not enough punishment for him. No, sir, before he dies, I'm going to take my Doris back before his very eyes, and then for a last measure, I'm going to wreak havoc on that man's world. I'm going to make him witness the destruction of his old way of life."

"Yeah? And how you going to do that?"

Winchester stared at Thorn for a moment, clearly wanting to divulge his scheme, but fighting off the urge. He turned away, focused on a flock of sandpipers whirring along the shoreline. The light had lost some of its hard-edged luster, taking on a lemon tint as the sun inched through a slit in the clouds.

"Oh, you'll see, Mr. Lavery. In due time everyone will see. Mark my word. Everyone will know about it. I'm going to write my name on the world. In great large letters. You could say I'm going to throw open the next Pandora's box."

Harden laughed bitterly, then suddenly closed his eyes and squeezed the bridge of his nose. He bent his head forward, and he suddenly seemed very tired.

Over the last dozen years, Thorn had met more than his share of lunatics. Men with drifting eyes and minds full of erratic molecules. You didn't talk with people like that. Reason and logic wasn't part of their world. You got out of their way. And if they continued to bore in and left you nowhere to dodge, you used whatever tools were necessary to save yourself. Chairs, tables, blunt instruments.

Thorn stood up and scooted his chair around the table and sat down again, shoulder to shoulder with Winchester.

Leaning close, he said, "When do I see what I'm buying?"

Harden drank the last of his bourbon and set the shot glass down. "Soon. Very soon." He smiled painfully and rubbed at the puckered flesh around the adhesive strip.

Clearing his throat, Winchester wobbled on his chair. The booze seemed to have hit him all at once, a hard clip on the jaw that had begun to dizzy his eyes.

"Tell me one thing, Peter. Do you believe a man can transcend his family upbringing? Be a better father than his father was, a better man?"

Thorn was silent. He didn't know the answer to that. He doubted it, though. Nature, nurture. Parents were both. No way to escape all the messages written in your own blood.

"Well, I'm certain of the answer," Harden said. "You see, my own father was a very brutal man, Mr. Lavery. He used to lay my brother and me facedown on that dirt floor in that cabin and thrash us in front of our mother with branches off Jerusalem thorn trees. Trying to teach us right from wrong, he said. But it was torture, plain and simple. Torture for his own amusement. I watched him beat my brother to death that way. Murdered his own son for smoking a corn silk pipe in the barn. I watched my father flog Stewart Winchester till he drowned in his own blood.

"That's the kind of family I'm from, Lavery. Not like yours. Not the good civilized folks in the newspaper business. Tea and crumpets at four. French artwork on the walls. No, sir. I've had a longer trek to make, a greater struggle to reach the point of triumph. A life harder than you'll ever know, Lavery. You and your easy smile, your shallow jokes. You don't know what it's like to have to construct your own existence. Build it all, plank by plank until it's a livable place. A place that a decent, civilized woman could call home. But I have done it now. I've changed myself into a man Doris will love. And when I have your money in my pocket, Peter, my transformation will be complete. I will have wiped the slate clean and begun anew."

Harden was smiling at him now, a boozy sway of his head, but his eyes had begun to pry hard at Thorn's as if he were only a membrane or two away from seeing into Thorn's mind.

Abruptly Thorn stood up, went to the bar, bought a frozen mug of beer for himself, another shot of bourbon for Harden. He handed the bartender his last twenty and carried the drinks to the table, set them down, Harden looking off at the western sky.

He went back for his change, and the bartender was talking to one of his regulars the whole time he was counting out Thorn's money. Having to start over twice before he got it right. When Thorn returned to the table, Winchester was no longer there.

Thorn stood for a moment and surveyed the lawn. A volleyball game among squealing eleven-year-olds, the pool quiet, a few tables occupied beneath the canopy of the outdoor café. But no Winchester anywhere.

He looked down at the table and there, sitting beside Harden's empty shot glass, was a neatly constructed log cabin of matches. The head of one match resting on the ankles of another, making a perfect square, then another on top of that. Five stories high. Twenty corpses.

Thorn scanned the grounds again, but saw no sign of Harden. He let go of a harsh sigh, sat down at the table, and raised his mug of beer and brought it to his lips. Then jerked it away. Sloshed half of it in his lap.

Floating on the foamy surface of the beer was a fingerling, a fish not more than two inches long, dead. It resembled the tilapias Thorn had seen at Winchester's farm. Looked identical in every way but one.

This tilapia was a vivid crimson.

CHAPTER 25

THORN TOOK A CHECKERED CAB TO THE FISH AND WILDLIFE OFFICE ON THE third floor of the Holiday Inn near the entrance to Alligator Alley. By the time he arrived it was after seven and Judy Nelson and everybody else at Fish and Wildlife had left for the day. He located a security guard sitting at the counter in the coffee shop downstairs and explained what he wanted. The guy took a quick look at Thorn and got back to his coffee.

"You want to leave them a fish?"

"This fish."

Thorn held it up by the tail.

The guard glanced at it. Unimpressed. He was in his late sixties and looked like he might've spent a few decades before retirement as a city cop in some rough Irish neighborhoods. He had a nose that was big enough and red enough that some creative chef might've been able to pluck it off, serve it on a bed of shortcake under a spoonful of whipped cream. Get raves.

"I know a lady works up there," said Thorn. "But she's gone for the day. I believe she'd want to see this first thing."

"And which lady would that be?"

"Judy Nelson."

The guard had a sip of his coffee. Grumbled in his throat. Judy probably had that effect on a lot of men. The ones who thought all women should be toy poodles. Stand up on their hind legs, do pirouettes for the guests. All cute and fluffy. Then get the hell back in the kitchen and serve the damn dessert.

"What's to keep you from bringing the goddamn thing back during working hours?"

"I wanted her to have it first thing."

"Not part of the job description, bud. Not even close."

"Is the coffee here that good? You can't get up, use your passkey, put the fish in a refrigerator up there."

"The coffee's pretty good, yeah." He smiled at a redheaded waitress passing by behind the counter. Toy poodle material.

"I guess what happened," Thorn said, "you found yourself a job lets you walk around with that Colt strapped on your big gut, it makes you think you're still cock of the precinct."

The man put his cup down. He wiped his mouth on a paper napkin and set it beside the cup. Slowly, he turned halfway around and fastened his yellowed eyes on Thorn.

"You got business in this hotel, boy, or you loitering?"

The redheaded waitress came over and poured more coffee into his cup, and said, "Look, I could take that fish, put it in a baggie, leave it in the fridge in back. When I come on for the breakfast shift, I'll see Judy gets it. How's that? Sound better than having a fistfight in a hotel coffee shop?"

The security guard was staring at Thorn, things happening in his eyes, twitches of light, as if he were seeing replays of a hundred nights on dark side streets, squaring off with some smart-talking kid. No holds barred. Waiting for what came next, and possessing all the skills to deal with whatever it was.

"Sorry," Thorn said to the waitress. "My testosterone's been acting up lately."

She nodded.

"Gotta watch that red meat," she said. "Stuff is filled with hormones, it'll give you wild urges. Make you want to lift your leg on other dogs' trees. Know what I mean?"

The cop wasn't listening. Still staring into the shadows of those hundred alleys. Everything that sent him out into the mean streets in the first place was looming up again in front of him, dressed like Thorn.

Thorn handed her the red tilapia and thanked her. He asked if she had something he could write a note on, and she tore off a page from her receipt pad. Thorn wrote a quick message to Judy. His room number at the Ritz, and that he'd call tomorrow.

He handed the note to the waitress, asked her to put it with the baggie and thanked her again. He told the cop good night, but the man didn't answer.

Outside in the parking lot, Thorn looked back through the plate glass window of the diner and the cop was staring after him. A thousand nights, a thousand dogs pissing on his trees, each and every one of them still haunting the guy, still vividly there. If Thorn wasn't careful, he knew he could wind up like that, a gruff and cranky loner, hunched over his coffee somewhere, just waiting for some young twit to come up to him, make some crack, set him off. All that testosterone simmering over a low flame for decades until it was reduced to a thick sludge of corrosive bile.

It was almost midnight when Thorn parked his VW beside a cow pasture and looked out his window at the Okehatchee moving golden through the distant trees. A nearly full moon was dusting the sawgrass and marshland, shrub and limestone outcropping with a fine film of white flour.

He got out of the car, walked over to the fence. He pressed a finger against the barbed wire, testing its tension. On a barb near his hand, a grasshopper had been impaled, and to his right at one-foot intervals a cricket and a caterpillar were fixed to other barbs. Thorn squinted up at the power line. There, directly overhead, was the moonlit silhouette of a loggerhead shrike. The bird was at attention, surveying his field. These were his insects, both his territorial markers and his rations for to-morrow. Such a damn thrifty creature, so disciplined. So fo-cused.

Thorn climbed the fence post, careful not to disturb the cricket and grasshopper, those lovely meals to come. He hopped down into the shrike's field and headed across the spongy soil toward the Okehatchee.

At the river's edge he headed east. Not sure exactly how far he had to go. A mile, maybe three. But he could take all night if he wanted, so it hardly mattered. He would get there. He would see what he would see. Find what he could find.

In the first half hour the only thing of note he passed was an abandoned pump building. An old concrete-block structure with the rusty remains of irrigation pumps and pipes. He stepped inside the building for a moment, resting from his walk, and saw a battered mattress lying askew on the dirt floor, behind it on the moonlit wall was someone's scrawl. Three on one, having fun.

Thorn pushed on through the scrub oak and thick palmetto and weedy underbrush, all of it densely clumped to the river's edge. Raw twigs scraped at his exposed flesh, thistles pricked his ankle. He might make better time doing a dog paddle up the Okehatchee. The ground slippery, the estuary brimming to the banks as it inched slowly inland like a golden lava flow.

After another half hour he was perspiring heavily and the mosquitoes had come in thick ravenous clouds to drink from him. Finally he could stand it no more and stooped down beside the river, scooped up two handfuls of mud and smeared it on his face and neck and ears. Another scoop to cover his shirt, front and back. Another for his hair.

He continued on with the swarm of mosquitoes and gnats in an angry tizzy at his ear. Thousands of them. And Thorn, the mud man, their only hope for blood, luring them further upriver. He had to stop again for a few more glops of rank sulfurous earth to cover some spots he'd missed. Then got back to his sweaty hike.

A mile or two later the night darkened suddenly, and Thorn looked up to see the moon sliding behind a heavy wall of cumulus. Muffled back there, the moon filling the clouds with gray light.

As he was feeling his way forward through the new murkiness, he missed a step. He lurched to his left and his foot slid down the bank. He thrashed his arms for balance, and by sheerest luck found a grip on a rough vine. He caught his breath and hauled himself back to safe ground.

Thorn bulled ahead through the thicket, branches snagging on his shirt, fingernails clawing at his cheeks. Completely blind, fumbling forward with outstretched hands, feeling foolish, thinking now this was a dangerous mistake. He'd lost his way, must certainly have passed the farm by now. He'd have to double back, cover those same arduous miles again, pay better attention.

He ducked below a heavy branch, pushed through a matting of vines and branches, and stumbled into a clearing. He caught himself, then started forward just as the moon broke free and lit the land before him. Thorn stopped, held still. He couldn't breathe.

Ten feet ahead in the center of the clearing were two very large alligators. One had climbed onto the back of the other and was satisfying himself with small thrusts. One hell of a beast with two backs. Both of them facing Thorn, oblivious. The bottom gator had some bloody meal in her jaws, munching the remains of an anhinga or some other hapless bird. Probably an offering from her mate.

Just then the moon disappeared again, and darkness rushed back into the clearing. Thorn waited a moment, then took a half step backward, and under his foot a twig cracked. He didn't wait to see how those two would react. He turned and dragged branches out of the way, scrambled back along the path he'd come, no longer concerned about noise, just retreating as fast as he could, to leave those two in their moment of delight.

He made fifty or sixty yards back along the riverbank before he stopped and stilled his breath and listened. And heard no rustle in the bushes, no scrabbling nearby, only the sweet ring of silence. Just the airless, empty dark. He stood there for a moment, letting his heart attune itself to the quiet. It was peaceful, utterly still, and Thorn felt at that moment some uninvited prayer begin to rise inside him. A benediction of thanksgiving to the goddess of moon and clouds for having seen fit to light his path at such a lucky moment.

With his breathing still ragged, Thorn leaned against a small live oak, the mud on his skin caked hard now. Brittle. He couldn't grin or speak without pinching his own flesh inside the rigid mask. With his weight against the tree, he listened to the night and felt himself sinking away into that absolute quiet.

When a needle scratched against the grooves of a phonograph record a few hundred yards away, it took a few seconds for Thorn to hear it, so far gone inside his own meditation was he. But then he stiffened, pushed away from the tree. It was an opera he didn't know, an antique recording, the lone soprano climbing steadily up a steep path to some lofty emotional peak.

He edged a few yards toward the music, passing through the perimeter of the pine forest, and halted beside a cluster of tree ferns and thatch palms. He listened to the woman sing, and stared into the blackness until at last the shape of the lightless house materialized.

Carefully, he headed forward toward the singer, the other buildings slowly taking form as he approached. The huge tilapia breeding ponds glittered in the shadows. With his eyes fixed on the darkened house, Thorn stumbled again, over some root or pipe, and he fell headlong onto the mushy ground. This time he stayed there, breathless, flat on his stomach listening for any sign he'd been heard.

But the diva sang on, her solo becoming slow and wistful. He lay on his belly and listened to the song for a moment or two more, then with a quiet grunt he pushed himself to his feet, and moved off toward the nearest storage building.

Halfway down the length of the building, he found three fifty-gallon drums. He pried off one of the lids, then wrenched his face away from the caustic fumes. White granulated chemical filled the drum, probably the thing Sylvie had mentioned, the fish killer. Eyes stinging, he replaced the lid and moved on to the other barn, and found what he had come this far to see. The boat trailer he'd glimpsed that afternoon.

Thorn wiped the tears from his eyes and listened to the opera spiraling on. Now two tenors were dueling over the heart of the soprano. He moved close to the boat and ran his hands along its slick hull. A new Grady White, twenty-two feet. Felt the salty crust of a recent day at sea. He came around to the stern, climbed the dive platform, and hauled himself aboard.

The barn hid the house from view, but the opera played on and Thorn felt himself mildly swayed by it, the tragedy, the yearning in that woman's voice. Felt some part of him that had hardened to ice in the last week, growing watery and warm.

He opened the storage box beneath the console seat. Found orange life vests and a compressed-air signal horn. A plastic whistle, boat hook, first aid kit. Standard gear. And there was nothing in the bow compartments but anchor line, fishing equipment, and a moldering towel. He walked back to the stern, squatted and drew open the last of the Grady White's storage compartments. Inside it were two fins and a single diving mask. He held the fins up to what light there was and fit his hand inside the molded shoe of one of the flippers. Then pressed the mask to his face.

"Jesus," he whispered. "Jesus Christ."

They were far too small for Harden, both the mask and fins. Sitting on the gunwale, he stared up at the murky sky, absorbing this. Trying to comprehend this family, the machinery of its madness. Getting nowhere. But it didn't matter anyway. The intricacies of the Winchesters' psychology, the reasons for the particular twists in their pathologies. He didn't give a shit about any of that. With a clever enough lawyer, a string of professional experts, even the most horrendous acts could be justified. Every culprit could be made to seem a victim of one brainwashing or another, a helpless casualty of negative conditioning. Poverty, race, drugs, sexual abuse. The great escape clauses of the age. But as far as Thorn was concerned, all that was bullshit. Only conduct counted. Behavior was everything.

With his heart floundering, Thorn set the mask and flippers back in the compartment, and he squatted down beside the one scuba tank in the transom rack. He fastened the buckles on the webbed belt and checked its girth. Less than twenty inches. Of course. Of course.

He rose and stood by the leaning post and listened to the music swell again. The opera seemed to be recounting some painful love affair where passion had died and been reborn as spite. Overhead the moon was moving in and out of patchy clouds, and in a moment of relative brightness Thorn caught the glint of polished metal on the console shelf. He came around the leaning post and stood before the wheel.

He didn't move for it immediately, just breathed, felt the air burn his lungs, savoring this moment. Darcy's Medlon diving knife with the serrated blade, the rubber handle. A grim little souvenir from a boating trip on an August afternoon. Not a murder weapon, so no one had bothered concealing it. Thorn could hear Sugarman's inevitable response. The knife was meaningless as legal evidence. And yes, even Thorn had to agree with that. No matter whose fingerprints were on it, no matter if the knife could be positively identified as being Darcy's, there was no jury that could convict anyone for merely possessing it. The thing was utterly without meaning. That is, except in the courtroom of Thorn's heart.

Finally, he reached across and picked it up, held it out to the moon, watched it catch a ray of light and fire it off into the dark. In the distance, the soprano's voice was aching, reaching beyond her human limitations, as if she were straining toward some ecstatic realm, past all pain and doubt. Reaching up for that golden place, Eden before the fall, some perfect summery childhood, a timeless, peaceful place that seemed to exist only in music and fairy tales.

Thorn tested the blade against the back of his hand, shaved away an inch of hair. Still razor-slick from hours against her whetstone. And as Thorn was wiping the blade clean against his leg, someone jolted the needle against the record, made a grinding scratch, then lifted it up, and the soprano was cut off mid-crescendo. The heavy silence once more filled the night.

Thorn hurried to the stern, leaned out to peer around the edge of the aluminum barn. The house was still dark. He turned and started down the dive ladder, was just about to hop to the earth, when the hard smack of a rifle sounded, and a half second later a bright hole exploded in the backside of the barn.

He sprinted for the woods while more shots tore through the leaves around him. With the knife in his right hand, thin branches whipping him in the face, he ran toward the river. Opened up his stride, thinking of those copulating alligators who lay in the woods ahead, and he veered away to the west.

Floodlights lit up the Winchester farm behind him. A beam of light panned jerkily across the woods, a few hundred thousand watts brightening the ground beside him, then passing across his back and moving on. More shots, several in a row, an autoloader, shredding the pines a few yards to his left.

Thorn dodged right, pushed through a clump of palms and stumbled into the clearing again. The gators had finished with their laborious love. They watched him halt before them, this strange dirt-covered creature. The bigger one, the male, took two quick steps, angling to Thorn's right. The female held her ground. A pincer movement. Neither seemed particularly drowsy from the afterglow.

A few hundred thousand watts probed the brush just to the east, working its way closer and closer to where Thorn was having his standoff. He watched the light approach, and set his feet, made up his mind. He took a good breath, then broke into a run, feinted right, and cut left—old swivel hips—and sprinted directly at the small gator, watched as it pushed its heavy body up off the ground and opened its jaws at his approach, and

Thorn cut left and broad-jumped over the gator's back, staggered once coming down as more shots sounded behind him. He found his footing and raced on toward the river.

A few feet from the bank he tripped again, and caught himself against a tree. His right foot was severely tangled in some kind of netting. He jerked and dragged his shoe half-loose, got to his knees, and clawed at the mesh fabric.

The beam of light shone in the trees above him, jerking in rhythm with his pursuer's stride. Thorn unraveled another strand of netting, ripped free from the rest. And the light passed abruptly across the ground where Thorn was huddled, illuminating for half a second a torn brown shirt lying at his feet. A shirt with a UPS label stitched to it. And on its next pass, the light flashed across the netting, and revealed beneath the camouflage a meticulous stack of corpses in various stages of decomposition. The stench of lime and decay instantly filled Thorn's belly, and acid brimmed at the back of his throat.

He dove forward into the brush and was suddenly at the river's edge. He stood for a second figuring the odds. Gunman versus gators. He watched the beam lighting up the opposite bank, heard the trampling draw closer.

Making his body as sleek as he could, he dove into the river, hardly a splash, and sank below the surface, and yes, oh yes, once again the goddess of the moon and clouds had heard his prayer, and in the last hour had turned the earth sufficiently on its axis so the tides were once more rolling out to sea.

He kicked his feet and churned his arms and stayed inside the dark current, kept his head a few feet underwater. A minute, two minutes, swept forward by the warm flow, doing only the small work of keeping his trim, staying a few feet down.

Finally, when his chest began to ache, Thorn rose to the surface, took a deep breath and listened. He could hear a voice calling out indistinctly far upstream. Another gunshot, and one more after that. He drifted on the surface for a mile, two miles. On his back, looking up at the great spray of stars. And at last, soggy and exhausted, he climbed up the slippery bank beside the same cow pasture where he'd left his car. And he heard the irritated scream of the loggerhead shrike. For after all, it was his field. And this made twice that Thorn had trespassed there.

Back at the Ritz, Thorn didn't shower. The Okehatchee had washed away most of the mud and anyway he was too damn tired to do anything but undress and fall into the huge immaculate bed, glance over at the clock, two twenty A.M., and settle his head against the pillow and disappear.

No rest for the last two nights, and only the fitful alcohol unconsciousness of two nights before that. Thorn tumbled down into the heavy dark, his body a thick weight around him. More a coma than sleep. He was too tired to dream, too tired to change positions, too blessedly numb to come fully awake, even when hours later he thought he heard the door to the hotel room squeak. Felt the room lighten, then go dark again.

Sensed it was happening, or dreamed it was, but didn't fight his way back up. Sluggish syrup in his veins, the dead weight of his muscles. Too tired and ponderous to resist when the bed moved, someone climbing in beside him. Down too deep in the narcotic haze. Not even caring when the hand touched him, the fingers, cool and bony, moved down his belly, down the slope of his groin, combed through the kink of pubic hair, found his penis and held it, stroked it alive.

Awake but not awake, asleep but deeper than sleep, Thorn rode this dream, caught in its magnetic surge, gave himself to it, feeling her there beside him, taking him into her mouth and holding him there, then moving him, swallowing his length into her throat, not a dream, could be no dream so real, and he stayed there, miles beneath the surface of his body. Inside some dark coffin on the ocean floor of slumber.

Wanting it to be Darcy, wanting her here, doing this, working him in and out of her throat, the tender head of his penis growing sore, had to be Darcy, and felt himself buoyed up through warm miles of ocean blackness, felt himself rising and rising to recapture his body, which floated on the surface of the bed where she was holding him in her mouth, then let go of him, swiveling onto his thighs and fitting him inside her compact body, a fit that was too tight, scraped, hurt him, made him groan with grief and pleasure. Moving up and down above him, a wriggle, a twist, rising and falling.

And finally she began to buck above him, a bareback gallop across a rutted field, Thorn doing his part, his eyes opening now, seeing her, seeing her above him, her boyish chest, her hair askew, not Darcy, not Darcy but this other one, her name coming to him out of the thick drone of sleep.

Sylvie.

Who wanted to bring him into her body for reasons having nothing to do with love, wanting to alter the orbit of his atoms, insert herself inside him, reshape him, seal their deal—Sylvie, who twisted and wrenched her body from right to left and back again, a corkscrew, throwing a single arm above her head like a rodeo rider, wringing what she could from him, which was everything he had stored away, everything he had kept hidden from Darcy, all that he had husbanded, the reserves he'd held back out of modesty or fear, whatever his reasons were, he didn't know anymore, but it seemed crazy to have kept anything from Darcy, especially the wildness, the savage howl of pleasure and the mad animal grind of his hips, giving it instead to Sylvie, trying to throw her off him, and trying just as hard to keep her on.

Until he hated himself for allowing this, and Darcy for not sensing that so much was still hidden in him, layers she had not discovered, and hated Sylvie for knowing it was there, knowing how to tap it, watching it gush. And hated her for climbing off him and hurrying out the door, pulling at her clothes, before he was finished.

Coming on himself now, the sperm thick on his belly and she, not an apparition, not a dream, but Sylvie, rushing out the door, slamming it behind her, running from him, and Thorn paralyzed on his back, still letting go, hating himself and Sylvie and even Darcy, but mostly himself, groaning at his idiocy, his mindless hard-on.

Thorn clutched the sheets until he was completely done.

CHAPTER 26

THORN WOKE IN A DAZZLE OF DAYLIGHT WITH SIX PISTOLS POINTED AT HIS face. It took him a minute to count them all, and it took him a minute more to see that this was definitely no dream.

Crowded around the bed were a couple of men in uniform and a couple more in street clothes. And behind them stood two more people. Another man, a woman. Revolvers and automatics, .38's and 9 m.m.'s. No one said anything for a moment while he woke, pushed himself up onto his elbows. Then a thirtyish guy in an oxford-blue shirt and dark pants, a John F. Kennedy haircut, holding a Glock close to Thorn's nose said, "This the one, Judy?"

In her neatly pressed green uniform, looking very official, Judy Nelson stepped up to the foot of the bed, looked up and down his naked body.

"That's him."

"Okay," John Kennedy said. "Get your clothes on, Mr. Thorn. We need to do some dialoguing."

"Oh, good," Thorn said. "Dialoguing is my middle name."

As he was pushing himself out of the bed, he noticed something in the ashtray on the table beside his bed. He leaned in that direction and saw a small silver key. Apparently a gift his visitor had left behind. The key to an airport locker.

"We're asking the questions here, Mr. Thorn."

"Am I under arrest?"

"Not yet."

"Then what the hell do you call this?"

"What we call this is a federal investigation," said the kid with the Kennedy hair. "Ever hear of one of those?"

Judy groaned and the FBI guys glanced at her in unison.

She gripped her nose by the bridge, pulled it loose, then pressed it back into place while a distinct pop filled the room. Her personal Bronx cheer. She slanted her eyes away from them, letting Thorn see she wasn't particularly on his side, but she wasn't fond of these guys either.

The rest of the posse was outside in the hall joking around. At the Holiday Inn again, third floor, the back room of the Fish and Wildlife office. Thorn sitting at the head of a long walnut conference table. To his right the single window looked out on a marsh. Egrets out there peeking through the sawgrass, holding their statue poses, poised to spear breakfast.

The federal guys were on their feet, prowling the room, their eyes continually darting to Thorn as though they were trying to catch him cheating on an exam. The two of them wore identical blue dress shirts and cotton slacks with pleated fronts. One pair was navy blue and the other khaki. The blond one was Bill and the brunette was Joe. Or Bob and Tom. Thorn wasn't sure. Interchangeable names, haircuts, clothes, faces. Eagle Scouts promoted directly into the FBI clone bank. Both of them with black leather waist pouches where their handguns were stowed for the moment. Something unseemly about that, having to unzip before firing.

There was a chalkboard on one wall, a plain institutional clock above it. It was ten past ten. A half hour so far in this room. On the other walls a variety of posters were taped up. Sierra Club and a couple of black-and-white Ansel Adamses. Snow-capped Sierras and a single saguaro cactus, peregrine falcons in flight, prairie dogs peeking out of their holes. These were a bunch of professional nature lovers, and let no one forget it. If you did, they just might pull out their Glocks and remind you.

"Go on, Thorn, tell us where you got that fish." Judy was seated three chairs down from Thorn, looking off out the window. "If we like the answer, you can be on your way."

"All right," he said. "You win."

The guys took a position across from Thorn. Eyes sparking.

"Go on," one of them said. "Let's hear it."

"I found the thing floating in my beer."

The FBI guys looked dully at each other.

"I was sitting at the Ritz bar with a draft beer. I think it was Michelob, but it might've been something else. I'm not that great at differentiating. But it was domestic, I'm pretty sure of that. And cold. Very cold. Frosted mug and everything."

"What do you think, mister? This is amateur night at the comedy club? Think if you can make us laugh, we'll let you go?"

"Hey, it's the truth. 'The truth shall set me free.'"

"In your beer, Thorn?" Judy said. "Come on."

"*You* come on, Judy. What's the fucking problem here? I'm so dangerous you gotta call up this platoon of geeks to bring me in and ask some questions? You tell me what the deal is, I'll tell you everything I know. How's that? Fair trade?"

"You know what kind of fish that is, Thorn?"

"Miss Nelson, it's not necessary to explain anything to this gentleman. He has to talk to us, we don't have to talk to him."

"It looks like a tilapia," Thorn said.

"Tilapia *nilotica*," she said.

"Only it's red."

"You noticed."

"Miss Nelson, we'll have to ask you to desist immediately. We're allowing you to sit in on the interrogation, but you're strictly in observer mode here. We can't allow you to discuss the situation with the subject."

"Observer mode," Thorn said. "Just your thing, Judy."

"Look," Judy said to the nearest clone. "You guys've been helpful. Great. We appreciate your support on this. I'll be sure to write a memo to my buddy Shanks in D.C. Get you all commendation plaques. But, listen, it's my jurisdiction here. At the moment all we got is a wildlife violation. It's my evidence, my bust. Everything about it is mine."

"Now *you* look, Miss Nelson," one of the guys said. But Judy stood up and the guy swallowed back what he was about to say.

She said, "I don't want to arm wrestle you people, but if I have to, I'll stamp on the floor three times and my guys'll be in here and we'll match judo skills. So, maybe what you should do is, you should go out, have a cup of java, take ten, fifteen minutes. I'm betting Thorn and I will've made some progress by then."

"You can't threaten us."

"Okay, then look at it this way," said Judy. "Maybe it's time for a woman's approach on this. You guys obviously haven't gotten anything out of him. Let's give the other gender a shot."

"Woman's approach?" John Kennedy said. For a moment he seemed to consider a smart remark, but took another look at Judy and thought better of it.

The Eagle Scouts stared at each other again. Then the one in khaki pants turned back to Judy, nodded curtly, and the two of them gave Thorn a glare with the full weight of the federal government behind it, and left.

"Christ, were those androids?" Thorn said when the door closed. "Are we doing that now? Making robo-jerks?"

Judy got up, moved to the chair next to Thorn.

"Look, old buddy, let's get this real straight. I knew you for a year or two when we were teenagers. But yesterday that whole scene out at the farm didn't feel right to me. So after I dropped you off, I made some calls. Talked to Sheriff Rinks in Key West, and some people I know in Marine Patrol in Key Largo. I asked them about you, who the hell you'd turned out to be."

"Those particular people, Judy—I wouldn't have listed them very high on my reference list."

"What I found out is, you've got a reputation as some kind of screwed-up cross between Daniel Boone and Bozo the Clown. Got a penchant for stepping in shit, and a habit of not giving a damn about whose rug you wipe it off on. Don't seem to have much use for the technicalities of the law. Don't own a social security card or driver's license, never cast a vote. And known to occasionally play it very loose with the safety and welfare of your fellow citizens."

"Oh, so that's it," Thorn said. "You barge into my hotel room, guns drawn, because I haven't ever voted, don't own a goddamn social security card."

Judy swung around in her chair and nailed him with her blue eyes flickering, mouth tight. Then things gradually began to soften as a thought grew behind her eyes. She grumbled, looked away, then rose and went over to the window and watched the egrets and herons stalk their nervous prey.

"You were trying to sell red tilapia to Harden Winchester. That's what you're doing, isn't it? Making a deal with Harden."

"Hell, no," he said. "I told you. I found that thing in my goddamn beer. Why in hell would I have dropped it off at your office if I'd been doing something illegal? I gave it to you, Judy. I gave you that goddamn fish. Is that what you think criminals do, hand over evidence of their crime to the authorities?"

"I don't know what kind of shit you're trying to pull, Thorn. But I'm gonna find out, one way or the other."

"Let me guess," said Thorn. "This whole thing has to do with what happened at Seamark, doesn't it?"

Very slowly Judy turned from the window.

She paced to the door and opened it, checked the hallway, then closed it, came to the table and sat down across from him. She took a breath, let it out. Took another one.

"So, I guess I said the magic word."

Her voice a whisper, Judy said, "Talk to me."

Thorn looked into those eyes for a moment. Seeing the girl in there, the stubborn one who'd knocked half the Coral Shores High School football team on their butts, and then was forced to sit up in the bleachers the rest of her life and watch the guys get the glory. That girl's eyes in this woman's face.

"A week ago," Thorn said, "a very close friend of mine was murdered. Darcy Richards. You may remember her, Gaeton Richards's little sister."

She made a faint nod. Still wary, but listening.

"Just before she died she mentioned a fish, a red tilapia. So I started scratching around, following the trail. And what I found out was there's no such thing as a red tilapia. But I kept on going and along the way, the name Seamark came up. I tracked the place down, went there. These days it's a nudist colony."

"I heard."

"People there told me what happened. Twelve dead people, their bodies stacked up, all the fish killed, place burned down."

"Did they tell you all the breeding stock was stolen?" Judy said. "A few hundred thousand cherry reds."

He stood up. Walked over to the window and looked out at the marsh. The toll gate for Alligator Alley was visible through the cypress. Cars lined up to make the dual lane straight shot across the state. That road had been damming up the sweet, clear water of the Everglades for decades. The Glades no longer flowed as it was meant to do, filtering for a hundred miles through the rough sawgrass and scrub pine. No longer cleaning itself. And now the polluted runoff from the farms and sugarcane plantations was collecting out there, tainting the virgin water. Mercury, sulfur, lead. Some of the gar and bass and bluegills were growing third eyeballs, extra fins. Gators dying of stomach cancer, herons and gallinules with cataracts. Just another trade-off. Sacrificing Eden so the Chryslers and Nissans could race each other two abreast across the doomed remains of the state.

Thorn left the window, glanced at the Ansel Adams prairie dog climbing out of his hole in the desert of New Mexico, West

Texas, or Arizona. Hell, the same thing was probably happening out there. Nothing so unique about Florida. Most likely there were prairie dogs with tumors too. No place was staying the way it used to be. Never as pure, as abundant. Corrosives leaching into every aquifer. And railing against it was doing no good at all. There were people who'd screamed from soapboxes for years, a hell of a lot more eloquent than Thorn, and nothing had changed. Even the good people, the smart people had gotten tired of hearing it. They'd tuned out. Turned cynical. One more lost cause. Pave it over and be done with it.

All a person could do anymore was cope. Keep touching the forehead, feeling for the lump beginning to rise. That third eyeball.

He looked across at Judy.

"Is there some way to tell if that fish I brought in is from the batch that was stolen from Seamark?"

"The lab's doing an electrophoresis on it right now."

"Sorry, but I'm basically a one- and two-syllable guy. I need help with anything longer."

"They run electrical current through a sample of fish tissue on a gel plate, study the patterns of the migrating charged particles."

"Now, that certainly helps."

"Like fingerprinting," she said. "DNA testing. Not a hundred percent accurate, but it'll tell us something."

"You can't be sure just looking at the fish? The markings?"

"Not with a fingerling like you brought in. If it was an adult fish, yeah, then probably we could tell."

"How?"

"The Seamark fish had black circles on their tail fins. Almost like a conventional red fish, a false eye shape. Very distinctive. No other tilapia has that marking. Apparently it just evolved in the crossbreeding process. Became a fixed feature."

"So fish with those marks, they'd have to be Seamark fish?"

"I'm not saying it would stand up in court or anything like

that," she said. "But, yeah, fish with that false eye marking would definitely be from the Seamark gene line."

"So let's go out to Winchester's farm and look around."

"You saying you got that fish from Harden Winchester?"

"I'm saying we should go out there and look."

Judy stared down at the table.

"Now listen to me, Thorn. I've been over every godforsaken inch of Harden's farm a hundred times. Taken samples, poked anywhere and everywhere I wanted to go. It's impossible he's got any stock out there I don't know about. Impossible."

"Maybe you let your feelings intrude. You like the guy. You like him pretty much. Maybe he steered you more than you thought, only let you see what he wanted you to see."

Her eyes floated up, settled on his. She tapped a finger against the edge of the table. Kept tapping.

"Tell me something, Judy."

She held his eyes but said nothing, kept on tapping.

"Tilapia, they're freshwater fish, right? Lake fish, that's what Ludkin told me. They wouldn't survive in the ocean, would they?"

She stopped tapping.

"Why do you ask?"

"I was just wondering about something."

"Well, you're wrong. The fact is, these fish go both ways. They're saline tolerant. They could live anywhere there's water."

"Is that right?"

"Miracle fish," she said. "Wonder fish."

"So what if they got loose? A whole bunch of them. A few million all at once, say into the Okehatchee. What would happen."

"They're not going to get loose. That's part of my job, to see that doesn't happen."

"But if they did. If they got free, swam down to the Gulf."

"If enough of them got loose at once, then we'd have us a serious problem."

"How serious?"

"They're a thousand times more productive, Thorn, don't forget. Four hatching cycles a year. In no time at all those fish would be a nuisance. And it wouldn't take much longer after that before you'd start seeing other species completely crowded out."

"Other species destroyed?"

"That's right. If a tilapia drives a fish out of its natural habitat, out into some unprotected space, it's not going to last long. And if tilapia are as good at living in an open saltwater environment as they are at living in the canals, I'd guess in a few years or so they'd dominate the environment. You'd have a hard time finding any other fish in the entire Gulf of Mexico beside tilapia."

"That bad?"

"Oh, worse than that even. Very bad."

Judy pressed the palm of her right hand to her forehead and seemed to smooth away the first stabs of a headache. She looked up at him, eyes working over his face as if she were trying to read some feature of his character. Finally, she stood up, told him to sit tight, and she left the room.

In a few minutes, when she returned, she carried a couple of eight-by-ten photographs. She lay them on the table in front of him. The first one was an aerial view of the shoreline of some tropical environment. In rich color it showed a lush green thicket of palms and bamboo and ferns that grew right to the shoreline of the bay. The water was six different shades of green, that many blues as well.

"Brazil," she said. "Six hundred miles south of Rio. Rain forest grows right to the seashore."

"So?"

"Seven months ago a dam broke five miles up the Sangre de Cristo River. A Brazilian fish farm was operating a mile downstream from the dam. They raised tilapia. The whole fish farm got washed out into the bay. A few hundred thousand fish. Look at the next photo."

The second photograph showed the same bay. The palms

were still there, but the ground cover was gone. It looked like Agent Orange had been sprayed on the jungle, or a hurricane had churned above the coastline for days and had mowed down ninety percent of the former plant life. What was left was closer to a desert than a jungle. The water was now a chalky white. Several large strands of sickly green wove through it.

"Tilapia did this?"

"Tilapia, yes."

"How?"

"You want the scientific explanation, you'd have to ask somebody else," she said. "But in my words what they did is, they rode the river down to the ocean. In just seven months they choked the water all along the shoreline. Overproduced to such an extent, they changed the whole balance of the system. Nitrogen levels grew dangerously high from all their waste. And all that nitrogen produced an algae bloom of giant proportions. Algae loves nitrogen, but that's about all that does.

"Sponges die, and sea grasses, and shrimp. The gulls leave, one by one the rest of the shorebirds desert the place. And those birds helped control insect pests. The bugs flourished. Termites, weevils, you name it. Chewed up all that vegetation along the coast, then marched off somewhere else.

"You know how the story goes, Thorn, right? The hip bone's connected to the thigh bone. I clap my hands in Florida, a sparrow falls out of its nest in Hong Kong. You know the story. Every little thing you do has effects you'll never see. Effects no one understands. We start playing around with Mother Nature, shipping a fish from its natural habitat to some other place, bad things can happen."

He stared at the two pictures. Shuffled them and stared.

"What'd they do about this?"

"Well, it was a little late by the time they got around to it. But the Brazilians poisoned the bay. Cordoned it off best they could, then killed every living thing in six thousand square miles so the tilapia wouldn't spread. That's what they did."

"Jesus." He looked up at Judy again. "So your people would do that? Or could they even do anything at all?"

Judy said, "Did you happen to read in the papers about the shrimp farm up in South Carolina? The Parker Project."

Thorn said no, he'd missed that.

"Okay, well, Fish and Wildlife had this giant research station up there, all these boys in white coats working with some kind of designer shrimp. Super jumbos. Raising these goddamn inter-bred genetic monsters in ponds and cages and big concrete tanks, similar in some respects to what Harden and others are trying to do with tilapia. But then along came Hurricane Hugo, taking aim on Charleston, and the Interior Department people up there flipped out, scared shitless. A few hours before the storm hit, they swooped in and destroyed all those shrimp. Burned a couple of the facilities to the ground."

"Burned them down?"

"Yeah, because if the storm surge reached that far inland, some of those hybrids could be dragged back out to sea. And none of the scientists could say for sure just what the hell would happen if those shrimp got loose in the general ocean population. And let me tell you, those environmental regulation boys don't like surprises. They're a paranoid bunch. They've seen pictures like those you're looking at. So they burned the place down. Destroyed a decade of scientific research, I'm told."

Thorn stood up, walked over to the window and looked out at the stream of cars lining up to roar across the Everglades.

"Talk to me, Thorn."

"I don't know if it's true. I'm not sure about the reliability of my source."

Judy said, "What're we talking about, Thorn? Specifically."

With his back to her, he watched a gang of vultures circling about a mile away, and said, "I think Harden's going to let his tilapia go. All of them. All at once."

"Bullshit."

"I believe he has a plan to do that. To let them loose into the Okehatchee."

"And why the hell would he do something like that?"

"I'm not sure. To get even with somebody. And because he's full of hate. I don't know. Maybe he just wants to leave his twisted mark. Piss on the world."

She considered it a moment, then shook her head.

"Now, look, Thorn. I don't know what you have against Harden Winchester, but this is ridiculous. A major crock of shit."

"He's gonna do it."

"First of all, his farm is landlocked."

"What about the Okehatchee?"

"His ponds are two hundred yards from the river," Judy said. She got up and came over to him, and they stood shoulder to shoulder looking out at the fringe of the Glades. "He'd have to dig several big goddamn trenches through solid limestone to get those fish to the river. It would require major earth-moving equipment. It'd take months to do that. And I'm out at his place twice a week. I'd see what he was doing. No way in hell he could manage that. Absolutely no way in hell."

"He's found a way to do it. Trust me, Judy, he's found a way."

CHAPTER 27

AS SUGARMAN WOKE, THE DREAM LINGERED LIKE A STRANGE FRAGRANCE, rich and earthy, full of sunlight. In the dream he'd been chasing a tall lithe woman, wildflowers rising all around them, up to their waists, chasing her in slow motion, following the path she left as she parted the thick green stems. From a movie he'd seen. That image of two young lovers in a field of flowers. The name of it coming to him out of a mist, though usually he never remembered movies, their titles. *Elvira Madigan,* some foreign film he'd seen long ago, not positive why or where. Maybe one of Jeanne's brief hobbies, a culture attack, dragging him to French films, some art cinema up in Miami, sitting in the dark reading subtitles and trying to figure out what the hell was going on.

And even remembering Jeanne, his wife of nearly twenty years, while he stared at Doris Albright sleeping beside him beneath the pale blue sheets, Sugarman felt not even the faintest sting of guilt.

He watched Doris and listened to the house waking up, the sound of coffee perking on the floor below, a toilet flushing, shower running. The Olde Island Inn, a bed and breakfast place she'd known about in a two-story wood frame house a block from Naples Pier. When they'd arrived last night at eight, the young woman at the desk had told them there was only one room left. Looking at them uncertainly. And without a flicker of hesitation Doris had said, "We'll take it."

The sexiest moment of Sugarman's life. *We'll take it*. Out of the deepest blue it had come. Just her hand touching his in the car before that. And then there was Doris Albright standing in front of him, opening her purse, counting out the money. Even filling in the registration card while Sugarman stood like God's own idiot holding their suitcases in the living room of the wonderful old tin-roofed beach house.

We'll take it.

My god.

And they'd said nothing going up the stairs to their room. Said nothing when he closed the door, remained silent when she turned around and came to him and he set the bags down and she stepped up to him, lay her head against his heart, circled her arms around his waist, and he held her and drew in her sweet orange blossom scent, found his lips pressing against the part in her hair, holding her that way, wordless, till finally, long minutes later, she stepped back, reached behind her, and began to unbutton her blouse.

We'll take it.

And they *had* taken it. Taken the brass bed and the sheets and the pillows. Twisted and grappled, fumbling in their haste, all of it as it should be on the first hot time. As it should be long after that. Wrestling, groaning, but still without a word about it, about what sins they were committing or obligations they were assuming. No thoughts in Sugarman's head, absolutely blank. For the first time in his life his mind as naked as his body. Wordless. Such a sweet relief. Such an instinctive fitting together of their strange and distant bodies.

As he watched her now, he could see something shift in her breathing, see her begin to rise up slowly through the layers of sleep and gradually reclaim her body. And at last her eyes twitched and she opened them, stared up at the ceiling for a moment, then looked over at him.

"I was dreaming," she said. Her throaty voice.

"Yeah. So was I."

"You go first."

"If we tell them before breakfast they may come true," Sugarman said.

She smiled.

"I think maybe mine already has."

"Then go ahead," he said. "Might as well."

"I was dreaming about Bermuda fire-worms."

"Do what?"

"They're creatures that live in the coral reefs off Bermuda. Shrimplike things. They may live other places, but that's where I saw them a long time ago."

"Oh." Sugarman lay back, pressed his head into the pillow. He stared up at the ceiling. "You were dreaming about worms."

"Well, these are special worms. They have a unique mating ritual."

"Okay," he said. "That's better."

"What happens is, when the females come into heat, all of them float in a huge mass up to the surface of the ocean at night. And they become luminescent. So picture this. Swarms and swarms of glowing female worms rising up through the dark water, and they begin to drift about on the surface of the ocean, and as the males see them up there and swim toward them, they also begin to glow."

"That's good," he said.

"There's more." She lay her head against the pillow, and closed her eyes. "Eventually they find each other and begin to mate, and just at the exact second that each couple joins in the darkness, they make a bright flash like a firecracker, or a flashbulb exploding. Then immediately afterward, each worm goes dark, completely dark. And then the ova and the sperm and all the exhausted worms drift back to the bottom of the ocean."

Sugarman was looking at her now. Her eyes closed, her hair in a blond tangle on the pillow.

"You dreamed that?"

She nodded, opened her eyes.

"So let's hear yours."

"Mine doesn't measure up."

He reached for her, his hand sliding under the sheet, touching her waist, then her stomach, a layer of soft flesh there, but with tightness just below. Not like Jeanne, who was all bone and dangerous angles. From hours at the gym she'd firmed herself into metallic perfection. Sugarman admired her condition, but lately he'd begun to think of her body as inhospitable, like hardscrabble farmland. Ground so tough and barren, no seed could possibly take root there. While Doris had a womanly lushness. Like the velvety dirt of a freshly tilled field.

Maybe not the pretty words a woman might want to hear about her body, but for Sugarman it seemed great praise. Doris was both strong and yielding, a woman who seemed fertile and abundant, a woman who made him, for the first time in his life, feel fertile too.

"Let me hear your dream," she said. "It's only fair."

Her hand moving out to touch him, nails tickling through the sparse hair on his chest. Scraping his left nipple, a fingertip against the tender nub, toying with it till it was firm.

"Wildflowers," he said. "A field of flowers."

"We were there, you and me?"

"Yeah," he said. "It was us."

She traced the line of his collarbone, then came slowly back to the nipple, hardened it again.

"What were we doing in the wildflowers?"

"I was chasing you. We were naked."

"I see."

"I woke up before I caught you."

"But then here I was."

Sugarman looked across the room at the antique oak dressing table, a small white vase sitting on it. Three roses in it, all of different shades of red. And the wallpaper was printed with small sprigs of wildflowers. His dream no dream at all.

"I've never had much imagination," he said. "Never learned how to dream."

"It takes practice," she said. "Like anything else."

Her hand going lower now as she snuggled close. Down between his legs. Finding him, that part which lately he had begun to wonder about. The part which had started to seem to him like some old pathetic war medal that still dangled there meaninglessly.

"Worms," Sugarman said. "I never met a woman before who dreamed about luminescent worms."

"Well," she said. "You're my first wildflower man."

"Good."

"Of course, I'm fairly inexperienced in these matters."

"Me too."

"Two husbands, and now you."

"That's all?"

"Not a long list by today's standards, I guess."

"Well," Sugarman said. "You're still one ahead of me."

Downstairs the coffee was finished perking. The toilets were quiet and the shower was off. Now there were voices, a breakfast conversation. Newspapers rattling. The pleasant clink of knives and forks, strangers meeting each other, talking for the first time over Danish and bacon, as Sugarman and Doris pushed away the sheets and began to improve in the gauzy daylight what they had begun so well the night before.

"I paid for the goddamn Sony video camera, I paid for the gold Maxell tape, I paid to have the whole fucking thing installed in my store. I think I'm fucking well entitled to have that tape."

"Sugarman said no. So it's no."

Roy Murtha glanced up at the cheap flicker of a fluorescent bulb. He expelled a breath, then eased down onto the green leather couch across from Andy Stutmeyer. The skinny kid had taken a minute to look up as Murtha came into the office, then he took another thirty seconds to pull his earphones off. Murtha in his black shirt, gray slacks, a beige sport coat.

"I don't get it. Are you saying Sugarman told you not to give the tape to me? He mentioned me by name?"

"That's ri-ight." Using a kindergarten singsong voice.

"I want to speak to him."

"No can do," Andy said. "He's out of town."

"He tell you where?"

"Over to Naples on business."

"And he left you to mind the store."

"You got it." Andy was bobbing his head, still listening to the music from the headset around his neck, his eyes jigging around the room.

"A lot of responsibility for a young man, running an office like this."

"I can handle it."

"What I want to know is where in Naples?"

"Beats the shit out of me. He just said Naples."

"Well, what'd he go over there for?"

Murtha crossed his legs, put both arms up on the back of the couch, getting comfortable, going to wait this out. Ask as many questions as it required.

"Sugarman doesn't tell me every piddly little thing he's going to do." The boy smirked.

"Do you know Doris Albright, Andy?"

Andy mumbled in the affirmative.

"When I called over to Albright's Fish House," Murtha said, "someone was kind enough to tell me that Mrs. Albright had gone somewhere with Mr. Sugarman. But they didn't seem to know where."

"Naples," Andy said.

"Yes, I think we've established that now." With a single finger Murtha touched the butt of the Ruger in the pocket of his jacket, getting a little lift from that.

He said, "But what we haven't established is the exact location in Naples. That's why I mentioned Mrs. Albright. I thought perhaps, being a smart young man, being left in charge, you might remember something you'd heard about Mrs. Albright, something about Naples maybe, and we could draw some conclusions about where the fuck the two of them might be."

"I don't see where it's any of your business."

Murtha uncrossed his legs. He could smell the rank chemical fumes of the beauty shop next door. That odor was settling in his stomach, curdling the coffee and six donuts he'd had for breakfast. And through the half-open door into Sugarman's office he could see through the spy mirror, a flurry of movement in the salon, and hear the blare of voices, phones and dryers and buzzing shears.

"Andy," he said. "Are you ready to die? Have you made your peace?"

The boy looked up. His head had stopped bobbing. His sneer melted away and in that moment Murtha could picture the face of the man Andy might become. His snarl taking root, becoming a mask of contempt. Murtha recognized the look.

He'd seen the same expression for years on the faces of men he'd worked with, the petty hoodlums, neighborhood gangsters who used those smirks to hide their stupidity, their crassness. Year after year, Ray Bianetti had climbed higher and higher up the mountain of their sneering corpses until finally he was three men from the top of his organization, his personal territory spreading from New York to Detroit, south to Baltimore. Swag and skag and hags. And then in June of '75, Ray Bianetti started seeing something in the eyes of his men. Holding his gaze a half second longer than they used to do. Challenging him. A half second, that was all. But it was enough to let him know things were over. Ray the Clink had gotten too fat; he'd softened, lost his grip. The hit was on. So he decided he'd just fucking well do it himself. And on the night of June thirtieth, Ray Bianetti was murdered. The grand style. Face in the pasta, a dozen bullets.

Shortly thereafter Roy Murtha was born, leaving behind in Bianetti's bank account over seven million dollars from his accumulated past sins. All he took along was a couple of hundred thou. Paying off one photographer at the *Post*, a couple of waiters at Tulipano, and a young intern he knew at Cedars Sinai, then vanishing into the giant tangle of highways and churches and fried food places that was America. Traveling, a week here, a month there, until he'd decided what he wanted to do. Be near the only family he had. His daughter. Maybe someday work up the nerve, try to make amends.

Murtha slid the Ruger out of his coat pocket, found a comfortable grip, raised it till it was pointing at Andy's face.

"Why don't you try thinking, Andy. See, maybe if you can remember anything might suggest a location in Naples, a place where Sugarman and Doris Albright could be."

Andy opened his mouth, seemed to form a word, then another one, but no sound emerged. He tried again, and this time said, "Fish farm. Something about a fish farm."

"Fish farm?"

"Mrs. Albright wanted to go see somebody who lived on a fish farm. That's all I heard."

"You have an address for this fish farm?"

"Christ, how many fish farms could there be?" Andy took another look at the pistol, paled, and said, "No, I'm sorry, I don't have an address."

"Could you turn that fucking music off, please?"

In a spasm of agreeableness, Andy fumbled for his Walkman, found the *off* switch and snapped it. Murtha taking another look at the boy. A few years past a teenager, but seeming younger now that he'd lost the sneer.

"Thank you," Murtha said. But he kept the unwavering pistol sighted on Andy. "Isn't it strange, Andy, isn't it fucking ironic how it takes guns to make people civilized? Like you. Now you're being a good boy. Now you're on your best behavior. Very well mannered now. Just because you know I'll kill you if you aren't. Isn't that strange? I mean, I drive around up in Miami sometimes, and it amazes me how polite everyone is. No one honks their horns. Nobody makes obscene gestures in traffic, no matter what stunts another driver pulls. Why is this,

Andy? Is it because people in Miami are more polite than people elsewhere? No, I don't think so. No. It's because in Miami everyone has a gun in their car. Everyone is armed. You have to be very polite, or you'll be killed. Guns, guns, guns. They've turned Miami into the most courteous town in America."

Andy stared down at the desk, wet his lips, looking queasy.

"I remember," Andy said. "It was a fish farm owned by Doris Albright's first husband. Winchester is his name. I just remembered that. Winchester."

"Isn't it remarkable how guns do that too? Great memory enhancers. Help us recall things we've forgotten. Like some wonderful goddamn drug."

Murtha was silent for a moment. Eyes on Andy, feeling the pistol begin to weigh down his hand.

In a faint voice Andy said, "I told you what I know. A fish farm in Naples."

"Do you know who I am?" Murtha said.

"Mr. Murtha."

"Sugarman told you, didn't he? He told you my real name."

"No," Andy said. "He doesn't tell me stuff."

"I'm afraid I can't take that chance, Andy. I'm afraid I'm going to have to push you over."

Murtha took another grip on the Ruger and pitched it underhanded out onto the floor. It clattered and slid near the side of Andy's desk. Two steps from the boy, six or seven from Murtha.

Andy looked down at the Ruger, then at Murtha. Then he slid his eyes around the room. Looked at the underwater photographs, Sugarman's police citations. He took a couple of deep breaths, his chin wavering, and then brought his eyes back to Murtha. Andy's face was sapped of color and expression.

"It's there," Murtha said. "Loaded. Safety off."

The boy rocked from side to side in the chair as if he had to take an urgent piss.

"You're trying to trick me. You got another gun."

"No, Andy. I'm just an old man. An old man who's sick of

pistols and bullets. It's yours if you want it. Go on, Andy, pick it up. Defend yourself from an old retired mobster."

Andy stood up, came around the desk, touched a tentative toe to the weapon. A sleepy look on his face. The boy was swallowing more and more. His eyes roved up to the ceiling and stayed there, squinting as though he were about to give blood and couldn't bear to watch the needle enter him.

"Why don't you just go on and shoot me?"

There were tears growing in his eyes. Years fell from his face. He looked seventeen, fifteen. A shivering child.

"The videotape," Andy said. "It's in his office. I'll show you where it is."

"It's a little late for that, don't you think, Andy? A little late to kiss and make up."

Andy's face was collapsing. The boy wavered, unsteady on his feet as he stared down at the pistol.

"All right," he said, the tears coming now. "All right."

From the beauty shop next door came the raucous laughter of a large woman. Others joined her. The beauty shop phone jangled. Someone dropped a heavy metal object.

Awkwardly, Andy stooped for the pistol, fumbled with it, the boy no athlete, no natural dexterity. Roy Murtha was out of his chair and behind the boy before Andy could straighten, the harp wire looped around his throat and Murtha drawing it taut.

There were those who used nothing but piano wire. Junior Monk, Mr. Sun Lee. They were the famous ones. But Murtha preferred harps for purely aesthetic reasons. He preferred the sound of harp music, so lush, not the piano, that noisy four-legged wooden box that men in tuxedos pounded on. But a harp, with its ghostly sound, played by loose-fingered women in shimmering evening gowns trilling their fingers across the strings, that was the true instrument of the angels.

His wire was two feet long, with steel ball bearings fused to each end. Similar to the steel balls Humphrey Bogart played with at the end of that mutiny movie, taking the steel balls out of his pocket in the courtroom and fondling them and giving it all away that he was crazy. Ball bearings like Bogart's, giving Murtha something to grip, and making it possible to use the wire like a bolo if necessary, sling it around the neck of his victim.

Murtha understood Bogart's fascination for the steel balls. Their weight, their perfect shape, the comfort they gave him when he rolled them in his hand. In his coat pocket the ball bearings clinked when he walked. It was how he got his nickname. The clink of death approaching. Of course, there were those who said it was the steel balls hanging between Ray Bianetti's legs that made the noise.

Gripping the wire tight across the boy's Adam's apple, feeling Andy squirm, then his slow giving in, Murtha held the steel balls, his arms crossed behind the boy's head, keeping the wire hard a few seconds more, the boy letting go, then the sudden weight of his body. And Murtha released him, let the boy crumple at his feet.

It was Ray Bianetti who stood still for a moment and listened to see if any noise had registered in the beauty salon. Ray Bianetti waiting till finally a woman laughed, and the others joined in merrily. He leaned to his left and looked at the one-way mirror and saw the group of women and hairdressers gathered around one of the barber chairs listening to someone's story.

It was Ray who turned around and locked the office door. Walked over to where the boy was sprawled, and stooped to turn Andy Stutmeyer's body faceup. Looked into the boy's slack face.

In a while Ray would get the videotape and destroy it, but first he wanted to spend a few moments looking at Andy. For he realized now who the boy reminded him of. Another bitter child from long ago, a boy from the Bronx who wanted to be good, wanted to win the love of his parents, wanted desperately to believe in the golden promise of America. But something had happened to the boy, something lacking in his diet had slowly stunted him, turned him ugly, poisoned his heart.

Ray Bianetti could remember spending hours and hours staring at that other boy's face, fascinated by it, that sneer starting to appear, the bitterness, the cold light of ambition growing slowly in his eyes. If the boy couldn't have love, then goddamn it to hell, he would have respect.

Hours and hours Ray had looked at the boy's face in his own bedroom mirror.

CHAPTER 28

SUGARMAN SWUNG OPEN THE SQUEAKY METAL GATE TO WINCHESTER'S farm. He paused for a moment and looked down the twenty yards of sandy road that curved around a sharp bend and disappeared. He took a leisurely breath and let it go, then turned, went back to the Mustang. He squatted down beside the open passenger window.

"Now, you sure you want to do this?" he said.

Doris touched his bare arm with a fingertip, left it there, as though she were testing the temperature of his flesh. She lifted her eyes to his, but said nothing.

"I mean, this old car still has a reverse," he said. "But whatever you want to do is fine. I sure don't mind turning around, driving right back to Key Largo. And I don't mind staying here and meeting this guy. It's completely your call."

"Is that because I'm the client? You have to do what I say?"

"Doris, Doris." Sugarman shook his head and smiled at her. "You're in a whole different category than client."

"I suppose that means this is going to cost me more."

"Probably," he said. "Probably cost you a lot more."

She smiled at him, seemed willing to accept that risk.

She was wearing her hair in a ponytail, a pink band tying it off. The pink matching the stripe in her white blouse. Lipstick a darker shade of pink. Navy blue slacks, white canvas boat shoes. Her eyes looking fresher, relaxed today. She seemed to be seeing more than she had yesterday when she was so lost in her head. Today she was a hundred percent right there. And that's how Sugarman felt too. Seeing it all in keen detail. Not having any more conversations with himself. Senses quickened. Enjoying each breath.

"No, there's no backing out," she said. "I have to find out what's going on. Something's wrong."

"People change," Sugarman said. "Winchester might not be as bad as the guy you ran away from. Might've mellowed."

"Or else," she said, "he could've gotten much worse."

Sugar lifted the finger Doris was touching to his arm, brought it to his lips and kissed it. Never thinking of himself before as that kind of guy, a finger kisser. But he kissed it, the tip, the middle knuckle, and Doris tried to tug it away, but Sugar held it tight, kissing across all the knuckles, till Doris suddenly tensed her arm, jerked her hand free.

Sugarman rose and stepped back. Doris staring at the windshield.

"What?" he said. "You don't want your hand kissed?"

Stiffly, she kept her eyes from him, and Sugarman could feel a hollow wind rising inside him, seeing in Doris's swerve of mood his wife Jeanne, the way her disposition so quickly and so often dissolved into a sulk.

"What'd I do? What's wrong?"

Doris's eyes were unblinking. She seemed frozen in the headlights of some memory. Then Sugar turned to follow her gaze and saw, at the sharp bend in the road, a man in tight jeans and cutoff sweatshirt, bald sun-darkened head, standing with his arms crossed over his chest. Legs spread. A handsome man of sixty with the sharp cut of an athlete. A gymnast who might've lost some limberness with age, but had managed to keep the spring in the steel. His face covered with a week's growth of silvery beard.

The man's eyes were pale, gray or blue, impossible to tell at that distance, but he could see Winchester was not looking at his wife from fifteen years ago, but the man's glare was fixed on Sugarman. Concentrating on Sugar's mouth, his lips, where the taste and scent of Doris Albright's hand still lingered.

Ray Bianetti drove his Firebird out of Key Largo, did the fifty miles north to Miami, exited the turnpike and went north along Dixie Highway, keeping well below the speed limit as he tried to spot one particular store in the dozens of rundown strip shopping centers lining the road. A poor area, blacks and white trash, check-cashing places, lots of liquor stores. He'd heard about this shop weeks ago, heard it mentioned in one of the clubs he frequented out on Miami Beach, stored away the name just in case. You want same-day weapons, beat the three-day waiting period, go to Guns B' Us in Perrine.

He parked, went inside, picked out a couple more pistols, a high-powered rifle, staying with the Ruger brand, making it the Ruger Number 1 H Tropical with the walnut stock, getting a quick lesson in its use from the hefty white woman behind the counter.

Bianetti peeled off the bills, handing them to the woman. Don't you want no shells? she said. Yeah. Yeah, of course, I do. Ray counted out more money. You okay? the woman said. You don't look too good. And Bianetti said, Does it matter how I am? If I'm not okay, if I'm fucking stark-raving nuts, would that matter to you? Would it keep you from selling me this shit? The woman said, How many boxes of shells you want?

Then Ray asked if by chance she carried any wire. Wire? she said. Piano wire, harp wire, garrote material. No, fresh out of wire, she said. Sold my last garrote just this morning. The woman so deadpan Ray wasn't sure, she could be joking him, she could be a hundred percent straight. It was Miami, after all, so who could tell?

Normally I use wire, Ray said, I was famous for it. But guns, they're still useful sometimes, when you can't work yourself close in, then a gun can be handy. But I prefer wire. Wire's better than a knife, not as messy. You get blood all over your clothes with a knife. I lost a lot of good silk shirts that way. You know how it is, right? Blood on silk.

The big lady looking at him, lost her case of wiseass, seeing this guy in her store, either a total lunatic or else what he said he was, a killer, a guy who'd spent his life perfecting his murder skills.

Then Ray Bianetti was on his way again, back on Dixie, a block or two, then pulling off at a convenience store and stocking up for the drive. Chee·tos, three bags of them, a can of mixed nuts, some Ding Dongs, three Milky Ways, a quart bottle of Miller, a box of coconut-covered doughnuts, still warm. Then with the beer between his legs, the Chee·tos open beside him, cramming it in with one hand, driving with the other, he got onto the Palmetto Expressway, north a while, then down again onto Southwest Eighth Street and aimed west out of Miami into the empty swamp with the guns jingling and Bianetti holding the car to the speed limit. Eating that salt and grease, eating his way across Florida.

Farther and farther, out there beyond the houses and stores and gas stations and gun shops, on that empty two-lane asphalt highway, out there in the wild place, the Everglades, the beer beginning to loosen his thoughts, and with nothing to look at, nothing to keep his mind from going inside itself, he was starting to consider things, and finally, after an hour of driving across that empty swamp, an hour of beer and Chee·tos, he felt himself sliding down a long, long tube into the kitchen of his mother's house forty years ago.

His mother's stifling kitchen. Where she spent her days and most nights cooking, making pastries and delicacies of meat and cheese, and stirring soups that clogged the house with the stink

of garlic, onion; Bianetti going down that forty-year tube, dropping out at the kitchen doorway, standing there and watching
her again, his mother, stumpy legs and arms, her stockings
gathering at her ankles, and not speaking the language of her
neighbors, but cooking all day, burying herself inside that
kitchen, inside all that food, hiding away inside the fat, until
when he embraced her, it was as though he were hugging an
ancient tree.

His mother was inside there somewhere, but the trunk
around her had grown very thick. The woman didn't even feel
alive. And there was no father to speak of. Off in the merchant
marines, sending money home now and then. But always gone.

So Ray stayed in his room for years, growing up in his room,
looking at his comic books over and over, bad guys, good guys,
finding himself drawn more to the bad ones 'cause they were
more fun, more interesting. The bad guys had imagination,
were the creative ones; the good guys just wanted things to stay
like they'd always been.

Then one winter afternoon, prowling the house, he discovered what he'd always suspected was there. Found it by endless
tapping for hollow places around the entire house. He never
understood exactly how he knew to look, but that afternoon he
located a loose floorboard in his absent father's closet. And there
it was, a single magazine.

On those pulpy pages, all the black-and-white photographs
were of very young naked girls. Even younger than Ray at the
time. Bianetti staring at them, girls with older men. Men his
father's age. Shots taken indoors against a wall draped with a
sheet. And Ray listened to his mother clanging about in the
kitchen downstairs and his face grew hot as he paged through
the magazine full of young girls. When he'd seen all of them, he
went back again through it, lingering this time. Stopping finally
at page six. The girl on page six was skinnier than the others,
looking famished, looking dark and Polish and terribly ashamed
as a man forced his face between her legs.

Ray knew who the girl was. An emaciated peasant girl who

had starved her way across Europe, starved her way to America. And did what she had to do to survive. Selling her nakedness in the streets of New York, until she met Ray's father, married him, and began to conceal her terrified child's body beneath great heaps of flesh. That magazine was hers, not his. A reminder of what she was hiding from. That little girl buried inside her. Hidden but not thrown away. That magazine, like everything awful that happened in a person's life, hidden but not thrown away.

As he drove that hundred miles across the skinny state of Florida, Ray ate all his junk food. While in his mind his mother never left the kitchen, never left the stove, all the pots bubbling, the oven full of pies and pastry and meat and melting things. And Ray, his mind clear, saw everything out the windows of his Firebird, hearing the hard jingle of metal, the rifle and the ammo on the seat beside him. Ray Bianetti driving to Naples with his cavernous belly. Devouring the nuts and chips and candy, and now glimpsing some part of the reason for his chronic appetite, his limitless capacity for food. Burying himself inside the food. Hiding from himself. Just like his mother.

But knowing the source of it all, its root cause—that didn't solve anything. Psychology was total shit. Ray was still famished, finishing the doughnuts, swallowing the beer, three Milky Ways, handfuls of nuts, licking the crust of salt from each finger, sucking them clean. Finishing everything he'd bought, every crumb, his belly full and warm, yet Ray Bianetti was still ravenous, still longing for something more, something he couldn't name.

"This *is* your car, Mr. Lavery. Isn't it?"

The valet was holding the door open for him.

"Yes," he said. "I suppose so."

Thorn stared at the burgundy sedan for a moment more, then walked around to the driver's side and handed the valet his last five, climbed in and settled into the deep leather seat. A Jaguar XJ-6.

He looked over the polished walnut dash, the instrument

panel, a host of switches and knobs, got his bearings, then slid the shifter into first. He let out the clutch and the car surged forward, wheels smoking against the expensive paving stones, the car sending back to Thorn a deep pulse of power. He swung the car out into the lot, oversteered into the main street, and was immediately gliding through traffic.

He'd never been a car person. Even as a teenager, when all his friends had lusted for cars, he didn't seem to have that gene. Cars were just for transportation, even something of a nuisance most of the time.

But by the end of the first buttery mile driving that Jaguar he was ready to convert. Handling that car was not so much driving as it was floating forward where mind and eye commanded.

He was at the airport by two forty-five, too early to park and go inside, so he circled around the loop and went back out onto the entry road to drive some more. Maybe it was pure distraction to enjoy that car so much. Something to dodge the inevitable look into the dark twisted heart of this situation. Or something to keep his rage at manageable levels.

But it was working. That car was giving its allegiance to him as easily and completely as a thousand-dollar whore. Beautiful and serene, whispering to him that she was his and his alone, always had been his, and would always be, to do whatever he wanted, satisfy his every driving fantasy. Soothe him, make him forget every car before her, every sad and imperfect moment he'd ever known behind the wheel before.

Thorn located storage locker 276, opened it, pulled out the briefcase, and had a look. He glanced around the waiting area, but no one was paying any attention. The million three seemed to be there, more or less. Old bills, hundreds mainly. It might have jiggled the heartbeat for some people, but holding that much money did nothing for Thorn. Maybe depressed him a little. A lifetime of wages for ordinary people, crushing years of drudgery and sweat. All that stored labor, that yearning for something better, was stacked before him in neat, orderly packets. Meaningless. Simply a prop in a madman's fantasy.

He put the briefcase back, found a seat on the padded bench a few yards from the lockers, and kept watch on the hallway. Three o'clock. Then three-thirty. And no one.

He thought for a moment of dialing the police, alert them to the pile of bodies on the edge of Winchester's land, take this cash and give it to someone whose life it would improve. A tempting thought. Just step aside, let the blue suits handle it. But he wasn't certain how that would play out, the probable causes, the legal niceties. And he wasn't sure what strings Winchester still had hold of from his years with the government. Whether they led to Tallahassee or even perhaps to Washington and beyond. No, the only indisputable proof of the man's guilt were those red tilapia, the ones that came from Seamark. And to discover where they were hidden, Thorn could see no other way but to play out his hand as Peter Lavery.

He walked over to the cocktail lounge, bought a draft beer, and had three handfuls of bar nuts, his only food all day. He washed the nuts down with a couple of sips of the Busch, then left the rest sitting there and went back to his seat on the bench.

Three forty-five. A tour group of elderly women in matching pastel pantsuits and shiny white purses were chattering on the benches nearby. A group of smiling Japanese teenagers sat primly in the plastic chairs a few feet behind the women, and two thin women with candied hair, red cowboy boots, and pearl-buttoned shirts chain-smoked Camels in the No Smoking section that looked out at the main runway.

Thorn decided to give it five more minutes, call it quits at four even, drive out to the farm, see what the hell was going on. Throw himself into the gears of this situation. He was just standing up to get another handful of nuts when Harden Winchester appeared at the end of the long corridor. Blue jeans, sleeveless gray sweatshirt, white running shoes.

He grinned when he saw Thorn and picked up the pace. Same tiger gait, slow, loose-jointed, poised to spring.

Thorn stepped over to the wall of lockers and waited.

"Peter, Peter, forgive me, please," he said, putting out his hand as he approached. Thorn shook it and Harden patted him on the back. Letting his hand rest firmly on Thorn's shoulder for a moment as if he were feeling for muscle mass. A probe of Thorn's potential for struggle.

"I know you said three o'clock, but something came up suddenly at the farm and I couldn't get away. I would've called and had you paged, but I didn't think you'd want your name echoing around the airport. Very sorry."

"It's okay," Thorn said. "Now let's get on with it. I want my fish."

"You pay your money, you get your fish."

Thorn dug the key out of his pocket and with Winchester standing at his side, Thorn opened the locker and took out the black suitcase. There was a ragged tear in the middle of it. Greenbacks visible through the opening. Thorn unsnapped the latches, looked around to make sure no one was watching, and then opened the lid.

Lavery reached out to touch a couple of the shredded packets of thousand dollar bills. The bullet had passed through the case, wiping out a few hundred thousand dollars.

"What the hell?"

"Don't worry. It's still negotiable."

Thorn closed the case. Left it resting on the edge of the open locker.

"Now we know," Thorn said. "It takes more than a million three to stop a bullet."

Harden let his arms dangle at his sides, hands open, poised, inching forward to within arm's length of Thorn, his smile disappearing. Thorn reset his feet, squaring off.

"So there's your money."

"Yes, there it is," he said. His eyes empty.

"Now we do the next part."

"Yes," he said. "But tell me something first. Would you?"

"All right."

Harden ticked his eyes to the right, then the left, back to Thorn.

He leaned close and said, "Is Thorn your first name, or your last?"

"What're you talking about?"

Harden smiled and pretended to watch a man in an electric wheelchair whir down the main concourse as though he were inviting Thorn to strike.

"You had me going for a while," Winchester said. He brought his lazy attention back to Thorn. "I actually fell for this one, god knows why. I have to hand it to Sylvie, that girl does keep on trying."

Thorn glanced around. No help in the waiting area.

"You know," Harden said, shifting his weight toward Thorn. "I've always admired white people who had black friends. I've never managed it myself. Just didn't circulate with any I wanted to get to know better. Though I suppose Sugarman is at least half white, isn't he?"

"You son of a bitch."

"Now, now. Let's don't get emotional. Let's keep this as businesslike as possible."

"What'd you do to him?"

"Let me put it this way," Winchester said. "I hope you weren't too attached to Mr. Sugarman."

Thorn wrenched to his left, and threw a clubbing right at Harden's face, but Winchester dodged inside the arc of it and secured a crippling pinch on Thorn's right triceps. He felt a shudder pass through the nerves, and his arm went dead midflight, fist coming undone, so that all he managed was a harmless swat against Winchester's shoulder.

Harden held the numbing grip on Thorn's arm as he took hold of the suitcase, then swiveled Thorn around toward the main concourse and steered him forward. Grasping him with his right hand, the suitcase in his left. The two cowgirls turned and puffed their cigarettes in Thorn's direction, watching this scene play out. But they didn't seem particularly concerned about Thorn's welfare. Seen too many bar fights to get worked up over a little scuffle like that.

"It'll be a lot easier if you're still conscious, Thorn. So do us both a favor and don't try any more asshole heroics. You're not major league material, my friend. Not even close."

CHAPTER 29

EVEN AFTER THE TWENTY-MILE RIDE TO WINCHESTER'S FARM, THORN'S right arm still hung lifeless at his side. Nerves in shock. When the car bumped across the rutted entrance road, his arm jostled and bounced, but it was a phantom arm now, the movement not his own.

The numbness reminding him of a gunshot he'd taken in that same arm years ago, winged by a redneck who was in love with Darcy Richards and thought Thorn stood between them. Thorn recalled that guy now, Ozzie, remembering that bullet wound, how the dullness in his arm had worn away quickly and the grim pain had begun. But at least then movement had been possible. Thorn would gladly accept that bargain this time, pain for movement.

This damage seemed far more acute than the gunshot. More fundamental. Winchester knew precisely where to press his thumb, how deep his gouge should be, how long sustained. The nerves in Thorn's arm felt torn beyond repair.

At the steel entrance gate, Winchester brought the car to a

stop. He got out, opened the gate, got back in, drove the car through and stopped again to close it. Dully, Thorn realized this was an opportunity to escape, a chance to throw open the door, stagger off into the sawgrass and marsh, see how far he could go before the man caught him from behind, tackled him and forever deadened all his limbs.

But he didn't move. Watched in the rearview mirror as Winchester closed the gate and started back to the car, coming up behind the big chrome bumpers of the Oldsmobile. Thorn leaned left, and with his good arm, tugged the shifter into reverse and with his left foot flattened the accelerator. The engine roared, and the car lurched but stayed put, wheels digging a trench in the sand.

Thorn wrenched the shifter into drive and floored it, trying to rock it free, but still the car did not move, wheels spinning, throwing grit into Harden's face as he continued to the car, not changing his pace or direction, squinting, walking into the fray as serenely as into a mild wind.

Thorn let off the gas and Harden stood by the driver's door and dusted himself off. He got inside. Stared out the windshield.

"I would've been disappointed," he said, "if you hadn't tried something."

He put the car in gear, eased it back and forth until it surged out of the gully Thorn had made.

"You know what this means," Thorn said. "You can damn well forget about me introducing you to Warren Beatty."

Harden kept his face forward as he steered them into the farmyard.

"That was you last night, wasn't it? Running through the woods. That was you."

"It was me, yeah. And I found your little funeral pyre back there. Got all your secrets now."

"A lot of good it's going to do you."

Harden gazed over at him again, shook his head and smiled without amusement.

"Your friend Sugarman fought much harder than you. He was a real scrapper, that one. A worthy opponent."

"You goddamn son of a bitch."

"When you reach my level, Thorn, it's impossible to find competition anymore. The only way to stay in condition is to shadowbox. Practicing against people like you only blunts my skills."

"They're coming for you, Winchester. They know what you've done, every detail. It's all over. You might as well put your hands up now."

"What people?"

"The people with guns. The people with badges."

The afternoon rain showers had begun. Coming down in a spiritless drizzle. A token rain, no heart in it. But growing gradually heavier, starting to thrum on the roof of the Olds.

"Guns make people dumb," Harden said. "And badges too. Someone with a badge and a gun together, they assume they're invincible. But let me tell you, it takes a lot more than that to make somebody invincible."

"Like special forces training school?"

Harden glanced over at him as they pulled into the yard. Sugarman's Mustang parked near the house.

"Who the hell *are* you anyway?"

"I'm Thorn."

"I know your goddamn name. But why're you here? You're not just another one of Sylvie's schemes, are you? You're not *that* stupid."

"I'm here because of Darcy Richards. Remember her?"

Harden's eyes retreated, going slightly out of focus as if he had moved inward for a moment to wander through a library of names. His private gallery of victims.

Thorn could feel the tingle of current draining back into his right arm. Out of view of Winchester he jiggled a finger. Opened his palm, pressed it hard against the seat.

"Darcy Richards?"

"The woman in Key Largo. The drowning woman."

He shook his handsome sun-baked head. Ran a finger back

and forth across the bristles of his cheek as if playing scales on the teeth of a comb.

"There've been so many," Thorn said. "How's a man to keep track?"

"Ordinarily, I'd crack your neck," said Winchester. "And pitch you out with the rest of the trash. But I believe I'd like to talk with you a little bit more later on. Hear exactly what else you know about me. A little private debriefing session. So I'm going to treat you with more civility." He turned his head, smiled at Thorn.

"It won't work, Winchester. Judy Nelson's coming for you."

"Oh, Judy," he said. "Yes, yes, you're the one who sicced Judy on me."

Thorn felt his head sag.

"Yes, Judy stopped by this afternoon. We had a nice chat. She and her men prowled around to their hearts' content. She even apologized to me on the way out. Apologized for bothering me when I had company. Doris had arrived by then, you see. So, if that's who you thought was coming to save your life, the men with the guns and badges, well, I hate to be the one to shit in your soup, Mr. Thorn, but Judy Nelson isn't going to rescue you. No one is."

Winchester smiled pleasantly and reached out and took hold of Thorn's left elbow, going to give him another dose of pain. But before his fingers could clamp shut, Thorn jerked his arm from his grasp. Then drew his arm across his body, and with a surge of strength, snapped it straight, a backhand punch to Harden's nose. It hit, drew instant blood, but Winchester caught hold of Thorn's wrist, immobilized it in his grip, and stared into Thorn's eyes while he pried open his fist, finger by finger, then bent Thorn's hand backward, straightening his elbow. All the while looking into his eyes, daring him to try anything more.

Thorn squirmed but couldn't break his grasp.

With his left hand holding Thorn's arm rigid, Harden used his right to probe Thorn's left triceps. After a moment he found the pressure point he was searching for. Thorn felt a tentative galvanic jolt. His vision darkened, then flickered on again as Winchester backed off the tension. Toying with him.

Then with a sly smile, a bead of blood rolling from his nostril, Winchester reset his grip, made a husky moan of pleasure, and sunk his fingers into the junction box in Thorn's arm, crushing synapses and circuits, and twisting his fingers like a pianist performing a complex chord, mangling crucial connectors, tendons, ligaments, the hundred strands keeping that arm intact.

Thorn roared and slumped back against the door. A dark tide washed across his vision, and his stomach rolled. When finally he could open his eyes again, there was only a dim yellow smog.

He blinked and squinted hard, and through a hazy stupor he was aware of Harden Winchester getting out of the car, walking through the light rain past the hood of the car, opening the passenger door. Catching Thorn as he tumbled out, standing him up, looping his arm around Thorn's waist, shrugging his dead left arm over Winchester's shoulder, and carrying him like a drunken guest to the middle of the yard.

Thorn looked up at the wobbling sky, a silver rain stinging his eyes. He took a painful breath and brought his eyes down. Harden was smiling at him, standing a foot away. In his hands was a shovel, which he gripped like a bat.

Thorn lurched forward, started a loose-jointed run, heading for the river, an awkward stride through the summer shower toward the Okehatchee beyond the pines, but he made it only a few feet before he stumbled, and caught himself, and heard a loud chime, steel against bone, and saw a shower of gold sparks. And his head became a great cathedral bell, cold and hard and weighing thirty tons. Gonging.

With perfect clarity, he looked down at his feet but they were not there, only black water, water coming up to meet him, rising fast, the earth seemed to be covered by a thin layer of black water, water coming up at him, splashing in his face, filling his nostrils with its dense perfume, the scent of primeval bogs, of tidal pools trapped far inland, those pools where tiny organisms first bred, the slithery one-celled creatures that swallowed each other and grew bigger, and swallowed each other again and fattened until they were large enough to stand, large enough to walk, to roam the earth, large enough and mean enough to swallow everything in their path.

Into the water he fell. Down into that ancient black water.

"Casablanca," Sylvie said. "You remember that afternoon we went to see *Casablanca,* Mommy? How we all cried. You remember that?"

Doris, on the edge of Sylvie's bed, looked at this young woman, her daughter. Her short black hair in a wild tumult, wearing blue jeans, torn at the knees and thighs, and a badly wrinkled long-sleeved cream jersey with smears of dirt, black tennis shoes. Sylvie trying for a mangled, grotesque look, but still beautiful to Doris. Still the smiling little girl, the mischievous one, the one who listened so intently to her bedtime stories. Tried so hard to please.

"I remember that afternoon very well."

"You remember how after that I got so hooked on Daddy's Super 8, started taking home movies all the time?"

"I remember." Saying it quietly, just beyond a whisper.

"Lights, camera, action. Remember how I used to say that all the time? Lights, camera, action. Lights, camera, action. It drove you crazy. You forbid me to say it anymore. Lights, camera, action."

"I remember it all, Sylvie. All of it. As though it were yesterday. Every second of it."

"No, you don't. You don't remember anything. How could you?"

The door to Sylvie's bedroom was locked, the windows covered with metal grillwork, a cell of a room. And Sylvie taking it as normal when an hour ago Harden had shoved her in with Doris. Told them both to stay right there, he had some things to take care of.

What have you done with Mr. Sugarman? Doris asked him.

Nothing yet. He's fine. We'll all talk later.

And Harden left them, locked the door. That's when Sylvie said, Well, look who's here. Mommy. Finally came back like she promised. Finally.

Doris tried the knob, rushed to the window, shook the bars.

So, Mommy, how've you been?

Doris rattled the solid bars. Holding back her tears, trying to think clearly.

You know, Sylvie said. I have an excellent idea how we can fill our time. Yeah, yeah. We'll watch a home movie. Wouldn't you like that? Catch up on old times. See how Sylvie got to be Sylvie. Get to know each other again. A home movie, yeah.

Now Doris turned from the window, watching as her daughter went about the room, hauled a projector out of a closet, set it on a small desk, erected the screen, told Doris that she looked at this movie a lot, once a week at least, it was her way of remembering how it had been, remembering her mommy, like a picture album.

"Remember how Humphrey Bogart turned to mush at the end of the movie? How Ingrid Bergman wrapped him around her finger? Is that why you cried, Mother? Thinking about Daddy, wishing you could turn him to mush. I know that's why *I* cried."

"Sylvie, we have to talk. Something awful is happening here."

"Awful ain't the half of it, Mommy. Not the half of it."

Sylvie fed the film through the slots and wound it onto the sprocket, and aimed the bright light at the screen leaning cock-eyed against the wall. Then she turned off the overhead light and switched on the projector and suddenly the screen was filled with garish color.

"Lights, camera . . . action!"

Two girls in frilly Easter dresses and wide-brimmed bonnets stood beneath a jacaranda tree blooming purple. Sylvie at ten or eleven, a gangly girl with rich black hair falling to the middle of her back. Her blond sister, a few years older, but already with the rounded body of a woman, not smiling like Sylvie, but staring moodily into the camera. The scene moved in the herky-jerky double time of Super 8 film, and it had a silent-movie graininess.

The Winchester family on one of their rare outings off the farm, on their way to Easter services. Sylvie, basking in the attention of her father, doing little half turns, a flounce of her skirt. Her sister not moving except once to touch her hat, keep it from being unseated by a breeze.

"Gwyneth and her little sister, two girls on their way to pray," Sylvie said. "One girl happy, one girl sad. Guess which is which."

"Sylvie," Doris said. "Please. We have to talk."

Sylvie said, "The girl with the black hair, she's the one that's happy, or at least she thinks she is. Of course, how it turns out is, you never know how happy you are till later, looking back. You think you're happy, but actually you're not. Or you think you're sad, and much later you see, that was as happy as you're ever going to be.

"But anyway, little Sylvie's all dressed up, new shoes, new purse, new underwear. She thinks the world was created just for her. But her sister knows better. Look at her, look at Gwyneth. She knows what's going on. She knows what's about to happen."

Doris sighed heavily and sat down on the edge of Sylvie's bed.

The Easter morning flickered and disappeared, became a sunny afternoon picnic in a grassy field. A thirty-year-old Doris sitting on a checkered tablecloth spread out on the ground. Doris with her blond hair long, in a simple white dress, opening a picnic basket, setting drumsticks on china plates. Her eyes weary, losing the battle with depression. Then the camera lifted to show Sylvie and Gwyneth in the field behind their mother, Sylvie in jeans and a T-shirt holding the string of a kite, Gwyneth in a shapeless dress standing by her side looking down at the ground. The camera lifted, showed the kite twitching in the wind.

"Sometimes when I watch this, I try to tell it different ways, make it come out a happy story, but that's usually too hard. Usually I just give up doing that."

The projector whirred. Doris felt herself falling away into the images on the screen as if she'd slipped through some weak spot in the here-and-now and was back there, completely gone.

"Now, there's a happy family," Sylvie said. "June, it was. Gwyneth's birthday party. A picnic by the Okehatchee, where the fish ponds are now."

Sylvie flew her kite for a moment or two more, then the screen went white for an instant then came back to color, the camera out of kilter, Gwyneth sitting with Doris on the checkered table-cloth now, a middle-aged, athletic Harden between them, his arms around his women. A roughly handsome man. That man who had swept Doris out of her small Tennessee town and taken her off to Florida and hidden her on this farm. Cut her off from her parents, friends. Forbidden the girls from going to school. Paranoid. Not allowing them any contact with the outside world, saying that his job in the military had made him a great many enemies. Very dangerous enemies. The only way to protect his family was to keep them totally sequestered from the world. Doris obeyed. Frightened that what he said was true, that they were in constant danger of being discovered, and frightened just as much of Harden's rage if she disobeyed.

She had little choice anyway. When Harden was home, they went nowhere but to the grocery. And when he was away, he hid the car keys, left behind a pantry full of food.

In the home movie, Doris's dark prince was sitting between two of his women, Harden the only one smiling. His black hair cut short. Doris speaking to Sylvie behind the camera, probably scolding her, telling her to be careful with that expensive piece of equipment. Gwyneth looking away at where the kite would have been if it were still flying.

"This was right after we saw *Casablanca*. You found where Daddy hid the car keys, and we drove into town when he was away. Remember? That was a big day. The day you found those keys. And after that I became Sylvie the movie maker. Sylvie the mogul. Remember? Lights, camera, action."

The camera held on Gwyneth as she stared off at nothing.

And then the screen turned white again. And came back on in brilliant overexposure, showing the lawn beyond the house, a white Ford parked out in the grass. A '63 four-door with its trunk open. Several suitcases sat on the ground nearby and Doris stood stiffly beside them.

"Now, who would that be?" Sylvie said. "Is that my mother? Doris Winchester? Yes, I believe it is. We're in August now. The day of the great escape."

"Oh, God, Sylvie," said Doris. "Please don't do this."

"The camera work is a little awkward, I admit. But Sylvie was having trouble keeping her arms steady on that day."

The camera panned to the side and there, standing in the shadow of the porch, was Harden, wearing his short-sleeved marine uniform, his left arm wrapped tight around Gwyneth, restraining her. She was in her Easter dress, two small suitcases perched on the edge of the porch in front of her. In Harden's right hand was his .45 service pistol. He was aiming it with great precision toward his wife.

CHAPTER **30**

THE CAMERA TURNED SLOWLY AND REFOCUSED ON DORIS STANDING twenty yards away beside the family car. Then the back window of the Ford exploded. A second later the rearview mirror shattered and spun off. Doris was crying. She wore a white summery dress.

"Daddy's a great shot, huh? He could've hit you. Could've blown your heart out your back, Mommy, but he didn't. He could've shot out the tires, exploded the gas tank, but he didn't do that either. He let you live, Mommy. Don't ask me why."

The Ford's side window ruptured, became a thousand diamonds and fell into the grass.

"Great stuff, huh?" Sylvie said. "Lights, camera, action."

The camera swung around and came into focus on Harden, standing on the edge of the porch. He was still pointing the pistol, screaming at his wife. His face contorted, the muscles in his neck cording up. Even from that many years away Doris could hear his voice, the curses.

"Daddy surprised you. He came home from Iran a day early.

Caught his three girls before we could make our getaway. You fucked up, didn't you? You really fucked up, Mommy. Didn't you?"

"Oh, Sylvie," Doris said. "Turn this off. Please."

"No," she said. "I can't shut it off. The switch doesn't work. Once it starts, Mommy, it never turns off. Lights, camera, action. Lights, camera, action."

"I was taking you with me," Doris said. "I was. You know that. Your bags were packed. We were all going together."

"But you didn't take us, did you, Mommy? You didn't. That's not how it turned out, is it? You changed your mind."

On the screen Doris stood at the rear of the car loading her suitcases into the trunk. And even from that distance, even with the grainy film and the bad lighting, she could see her right eye dark and bulging where Harden had struck her. Not the first blow of their marriage either.

Doris stood up, turned her back to the screen.

"Oh, wait, look," Sylvie said. "Here comes somebody. Who is it? Who could it be? Oh yes, look, it's the sad little daughter. Yes, here she comes now."

Slowly, Doris turned and watched as the camera followed Gwyneth sprinting to the car. She hurtled at her mother, and as she closed in, she balled up her fists, began to flail them at Doris. Windmilling blow after blow. Doris stood still, not defending against the punches.

From fifteen years away, Doris could still feel the blows, the memory sharp. She moved in front of the screen, the colors playing on her face as if she stood before an enormous bonfire.

"I had to get us away, Sylvie. We were dying here, shriveling up. You girls had no friends, I had no adult to talk to for months at a time. He made us suspicious of everybody. Always on guard. Believing every stranger might try to murder us. It was a terrible way to live. I was withering up inside. You were too, Sylvie. Both of you girls were."

"Down in front," Sylvie said. "Down in front."

Doris hesitated, looking helplessly into the fluttering light. Then she moved aside, sunk onto the bed again.

On the screen the young Doris in her white dress squatted beside the white Ford and held Gwyneth to her. The girl sobbing. They stayed that way for a moment or two until Harden lurched into the frame and seized Gwyneth and yanked her out of Doris's embrace. He dragged her back to the porch, yelling out over his shoulder as he marched toward the camera.

"He's giving you a choice, Mommy. That's what he's yelling. Leave or stay with your family. You remember, Mommy?"

"I remember," she said faintly.

The camera jiggled and jerked. For a moment or two the image was fogged over, then gradually it sharpened into view.

Doris stood in the yard midway between the house and the car. The sun was directly overhead, no shadows anywhere. Doris's arms hung heavily at her sides, eyes streaming as she spoke. She remembered. Oh yes, she'd relived it a thousand times. Reconstructed it, imagined a different speech, different words that might have sent her life down some other path.

"Now Mommy is telling Gwyneth and Sylvie that she's going to come back in a few days and take her daughters away. As soon as all the legal things get done, the divorce things, she says, she'll be back for her daughters, take them to her new life. But that's not how it turned out. That's not what happened. Is it, Mommy?"

The young Doris finished her speech, took a long sweeping look at the grounds, then stared dully at the porch where the three of them were standing. At last she dropped her head and turned her back on them and walked to the car and got inside. The Ford sat for almost a minute before it pulled away.

"I went to court, Sylvie, to get custody of you. But I had no money and Harden had a great deal. And he had connections. Powerful people he knew in the government. People in Washington he'd done favors for. They pulled strings for him. Found a judge who declared me unfit. A restraining order, everything.

I appealed, I appealed again. I tried everything I could. Years and years I battled him to get you back.

"But it was no use. He won, Sylvie. He humiliated me. Prevented me from ever seeing you again without his permission. It was his way of getting even, Sylvie. His way of forcing me to come back. He told me that. Told me that to my face outside the courthouse that last afternoon. 'You want your girls, you're going to have to crawl back, ask our forgiveness.' "

"But you didn't," Sylvie said quietly. "You didn't crawl back. You didn't come back at all."

"No. No, I didn't. I tried for years, tried every legal thing I could."

"You never came back," Sylvie said. "You gave up on us."

The screen was blinding white, a long strip of empty film with flecks and dashes of color. Sylvie staring into it. Silent for a moment, then harshly clearing her throat as if she were swallowing back her fury or her pain.

"So, that was August seventh," said Sylvie, her voice hollow. "And this next part is a little later. I don't know exactly, sometime in August. A week later, maybe longer. The two little Winchester girls fending for themselves. One of them is a little less happy, the other is a little more sad."

On the screen the colors were muted now. Shot indoors, bad lighting. The kitchen was in chaos. The round oak table turned over, pots, pans, skillets on the counters and stacked high in the sink, opened jars of jelly, peanut butter. Cans overturned. A large gray cat was hunched over a can of Spam, licking it.

"That's Mr. Boots," Sylvie said. "Early on."

"What's happening?" Doris said. "What's this?"

"This is when Daddy went after you," she said. "He tried to find you right after you left. Hunt you down, bring you back. Make us a family again."

"He left you alone?"

"Oh, yes," Sylvie said. "You never knew, did you, Mommy? You left and you didn't come back like you said you would. So you never knew what happened to us."

"I wrote to you every single day. For years and years."

Sylvie shook her head emphatically.

"You'll say anything now, Mommy. You'll lie, make up any kind of story to make it sound okay."

"You never saw the letters, did you? Oh god, I knew he'd keep them from you."

"You left us, Mommy. That's the whole story. You never came back. We learned how to do without you. We got very good at being without you."

Doris came close, peered at Sylvie through the half-light.

"How long did he leave you alone? How long was it, Sylvie?"

"A week the first time."

"And after that?"

"Oh, I forget," Sylvie said brightly. "The second time, it was a month, maybe two. He left lots of food, enough for a few weeks. That is, if we hadn't wasted so much of it at first."

"That bastard. That evil son of a bitch."

"He wanted to find you," said Sylvie. "He wanted to bring you back, make you our mommy again."

There was a long-distance shot from the yard, looking at the house. Everything looked normal. A slow pan around the property. The day windy, with heavy clouds off behind the pines.

"Lights, camera, action."

A bumpy walk across the yard, up the outside stairs, onto the porch, then into the house, the scene going shadowy, barely visible, the living room with all the same furniture it still contained. A walk down the dark hallway, the camera swinging to look into the kitchen. Very neat now. Everything washed, put away, the table upright. On the counter beside the sink sat a casserole dish. Lid off, a hunk of meat filling it.

"Mr. Boots," Sylvie said, "tasted a lot like chicken."

Doris felt the tears burn from her eyes.

"No telephone, a twenty-mile walk to town. We might've managed that distance the first week, but later on we didn't have the energy. And anyway, we couldn't leave the farm because we might miss Mommy coming back for us. So we stayed. We stayed to wait for our mother. We didn't know she'd given up on us. Though maybe Gwyneth knew. Maybe she knew you'd given up."

The picture went white for a few seconds, then a wooden chair filled the screen. It lay on its side.

"I don't believe this requires further narration."

The camera showed a pair of bare feet suspended a yard from the floor, and it traveled slowly up that same Easter dress that Gwyneth had worn in the earlier shot. Gwyneth's head cocked to the side, tongue showing, the noose tied off to a ceiling fan. The camera lingered on her face, lingered a long time until the dots and flashes marking the end of the reel appeared and the tail of the film began to slap against the projector, and the cock-eyed screen went white again.

"I buried her," Sylvie said. "But something kept digging her up. Something big, a bear maybe, a panther, I don't know. It was out there in the dark, and I could hear it scratching in the dirt. And all I could do was lie there and listen. I had to bury Gwyneth five times before she stayed buried, before whatever it was that dug her up got all it wanted of her. Five times."

Doris heard an automobile engine roar, then a few seconds later, heard it entering the yard. A door slammed, then another one. She felt the room begin a slow spin, and the bed seemed to be dropping from under her.

"Sylvie," she said, her voice strangling her. "You're a prisoner here, aren't you? He's kept you here all these years."

"What was I supposed to do, desert Daddy? Is that what I should've done? Like you did, Mommy? Run off."

"Yes," she said. "To save yourself."

"But, Mommy," said Sylvie, "you told us you were coming back. I couldn't leave. I might miss you."

Doris heard something out in the yard, a harsh scraping sound, and she stood shakily and walked over to the window. The sun was back-lighting the clouds in the west, a ruby glow spreading along the horizon. In the distance she saw Harden working with a shovel. She couldn't tell what he was doing.

Lifting the shovel and jabbing it down fiercely, as if he were trying to hack through a root. Doris gripped the metal grillwork on the window frame and shook it, but it was solid iron and mounted firmly.

CHAPTER 31

HOG-TIED. ANKLES AND WRISTS ROPED TOGETHER BEHIND HIS BACK. Thorn lay on his side, his left shoulder grinding against the soggy earth. Water covering half his face and rising.

"You awake?"

Thorn heard the voice but couldn't tell which dimension it came from, which century. Recognized it, but something had scrambled the wiring in his head, connected red wires to blue, green to yellow. Nothing computing, lights flickering, a sound somewhere, like the splashing of fish rising for the fly, rising and breaking the surface, flipping their tails.

Feeling water move across the side of his face, water near his mouth. And he thought he might be floating, thought he might be drifting out in the ocean. An eerie scrambled ocean, where a voice said, "Thorn, you hear me? You awake? Come on, man. Get up, we gotta move our asses."

Hog-tied. Curled backward, spine bent against itself, cheek in the water, having to lift his head slightly so he didn't breathe in the ocean water, smelling fish, smelling the rich green funk of the Everglades. A voice speaking, but Thorn unable to unscramble the words this time. A familiar voice, but with no name attached, like an old song, humming it without remembering the words, or a perfume, one of Darcy's perfumes he could never remember the names of, Darcy always asking him which one he liked best, but hell, he liked them all, if they were on her, he liked them. Darcy gave the perfumes more aroma than they gave her.

Thorn relaxed, rested his head in the mud, his face half underwater, held his breath, then blew bubbles into the water.

"Thorn! Wake up, goddamn it. Wake up!"

Yeah, now he knew whose voice that was. His old pal. What's-his-name. The cop. Out here in the twilight, the water up to his nose, over his mouth. Like here they were again at the bottom of the football pile looking at each other through their face masks. Giddy smiles. Happy as hell, until that arm came snaking down. That arm belonging to some asshole who resented anybody's accomplishment. The asshole who wanted to gouge anybody who was good at something.

"I hear you," Thorn said. "I hear you, Sugar."

"Jesus, thank god."

Thorn heard a splash and felt the water swirl around his face. It was almost night and he had his eyes open now and his eyes were seeing. Dusk. Just minutes of daylight left. Thorn scooched around to see his friend, and Sugarman was hog-tied too, a few feet away, halfway between the ponds and the farmhouse.

Sugar said, "We gotta get loose, man. Gotta do something quick. This guy's not fucking around."

Thorn rolled onto his back, brought himself atop his arms now. His body aching in places he couldn't identify. Sugarman rolled over onto his back too, water over their chests. But no more altitude in this position, just as close to drowning. At least Thorn's mind was clearing, the damaged nerves, the frail software of consciousness reconnecting.

"The knife," Thorn said. "It's on my ankle."

"You got a knife?"

"Darcy's knife. On my ankle. See if you can do it."

Sugarman squirmed toward Thorn. Sugar with a deep gash on his forehead, an eye swollen shut.

"What's going on, man? This a flood or what?"

"Full moon high tide," Thorn said. "The Okehatchee River running over its banks."

"That's one son of a bitching high tide. How much higher?"

Sugarman wriggling closer. Thorn rolled onto his shoulder again, presenting his ankles to Sugar.

"Could be just starting. Could get a foot higher."

"Great," Sugar said. "Great news."

He felt Sugar bump him. Felt his fingers struggling against the rope. Sugar's back to his back, doing it by feel. Hearing him blow into the water. Then rise up and take a long breath.

"I can't reach it, man." Sugar huffed for breath. "Angle's all wrong. Let me try this. Let me try something else."

While Sugarman gasped, Thorn stared at the horizon and saw against the last gray light in the western sky the silhouette of Harden Winchester with his shovel. Thirty, forty yards away, Harden with his back to them, breaking open the soft banks of one of his fish ponds. The water poured out.

And heard Sugar take three deep breaths, then go below again, felt his friend fumbling at his ankle.

Very clearly now, Thorn saw the shallow water spread across the yard, gleaming in the rising moonlight, the tight skin of water broken here and there by the flutter of fish. Tilapia were escaping into the yard. A splash near Thorn's face, a small fish frightened by the big men lying in its path, swerving off toward the river.

Harden was pitching shovelfuls of muck over his shoulder, deepening the furrow he'd already made through the wall of the largest fish pond. The water streamed across his shoes. Fish caught in the sudden current, flipped and twisted, riding the water where it was headed. To the Okehatchee, to the Gulf, to the Atlantic and the reefs and the great currents that would spread those fish to every inlet and bay and sound, every feeding ground, every reef and shoal. Pandora hacking open the box.

Sugarman choked and sputtered behind him.

"You all right?"

Sugar coughed and Thorn heard him splash. He twisted hard and rolled to his right, and watched helplessly as Sugar hawked up more water. When he had his breath back, he said, "Almost had it. I felt it. Almost had the knife."

"Take it easy, Sugar. Easy."

"Oh, sure. I take it too easy, we're gonna be dead."

Sugarman sucked air, lying on his back, arching his neck up above the flood tide.

"What's that son of a bitch doing? What's this about?"

"He's letting his fish go."

"Jesus Christ. How'd we get mixed up with these people?"

"Gotta get that knife, Sugar. Gotta get it quick."

"I know, I know. It's just that some of us can't stay under as long as others, okay?"

Thorn rolled back onto his other shoulder and watched as Harden continued to break down the walls of the fish pond.

"Why the hell'd you have to snap the scabbard shut? If you'd left it open, I could have the thing out by now."

"Sorry," Thorn said. "I'll do better next time. I promise."

Doris and Sylvie stood at the front window of Sylvie's bedroom, looking through the grillwork. Sylvie could see her father in the distance letting the fish go. And two men tied up in the yard, the water rising, still a foot to go before the tide started out again. It would climb to the top step of the front porch, then begin to slide back out to sea.

Sylvie didn't know how she felt anymore. Feeling very young, very old too. Her mother was there in her bedroom just like fifteen years ago when every night she'd sat on the edge of Sylvie's bed reading stories to her girls. Night after night, stories about giants, goblins, princesses, stories about children disappearing into their parents' closets, pushing all the coats and furs aside and finding a secret door in there and opening it and coming out in another place, a world much more colorful, full of danger and excitement, full of heroes and warriors, fools and monsters. Sylvie had searched for that secret door in her own house. Tapped the walls, feeling around. But never found it.

Loving those stories, loving the memory of them, the sound of her mother's voice. But the moment her mother left, the stories stopped. Everything else too. Her heart stopped. Body, biology, everything. All Sylvie could do was go over it again in her mind, go over those few years before her mother left. Go over and over that time again, looking for what went wrong, what Sylvie had done. Remembering the stories, trying to understand them. Trying to decipher that movie too, *Casablanca,* another fairy tale. Maybe that would explain. As though her mother had been trying to tell her some secret, leave a hidden message behind in those stories, that movie.

Now her mother stood beside her at the window and the two of them looked out through the darkness at the men. Thorn and the other one, tied up out there, about to drown. Sylvie not as good a storyteller as the ones who'd made up the tales her mother read. The heroes in those stories were smart and color-ful and ingenious. They escaped from danger, found ways to kill the monsters. Those heroes saved the children in that scary world on the other side of the closet. Not Sylvie's heroes. Hers were tied up in the yard, about to drown. Hers were stupid and slow and boring.

But it was Sylvie's own fault. Men only accomplished the things women urged them to. If it weren't for Ingrid Bergman, Humphrey Bogart would have stayed in that same bar forever. Cold and dead inside. Sylvie had tried. She had. Over and over, she'd worked to make the men into heroes. Her boyfriends, her father. But she'd failed. Look out in the yard. If only she could've gotten them to love her a little more.

"That guy there, the one beside your boyfriend, that's Thorn. He came to rescue me from the ring of fire. But he won't do it. No one ever succeeds against Daddy."

Doris gripped the bars, looking out at the darkness.

"Is there a way to get out? Do you know how to get out of this room?"

"There's always a way to escape."

Sylvie watched as a car drove into the yard.

"I'll take you with me," Doris said. "We'll go to Key Largo. I have a home there. We could be safe."

No, it was not a car. It was a pickup truck.

"Why did you come back now, Mommy? It was because of the money, wasn't it? Daddy made himself rich, so you came back. That's it, isn't it?"

"No, Sylvie. No. I came back for you."

Sylvie watched the truck plow through the water, its headlights shining toward the fish ponds, catching in its light her father digging in the dirt. The truck stopped, left its lights on, and Harden hesitated a moment, then continued to dig. The waves from the truck fanned out across the yard, glittered with silver like sparklers on Independence Day. Sparklers all over the yard.

Judy Nelson got out of the truck.

"Sylvie, answer me. How do we get out of here?"

Her mother's hand was on her shoulder, shaking her gently as though she were trying to wake her. Like that morning when she left, waking Sylvie from sleep to kiss her, sitting on the edge of her bed, Sylvie warm with slumber, looking up at her mother who told her they were leaving now, Sylvie's bag was packed. She needed to get up. They were going somewhere exciting. Shaking her shoulder, bringing her awake.

"How do we get out of here, Sylvie? What do we do?"

"You'll never make it," Sylvie said. "You'll never get out. You're here now and you'll never leave again."

"Show me how you do it. Please, darling. Please."

Sylvie turned and went to her bureau and dug beneath her underwear and socks and found the screwdriver she kept there, and she went to the window and reached through the grillwork with one hand and began to loosen a screw.

"Something big kept digging her up," Sylvie said as she worked. "I never found out what it was. All I could do was lie there and listen to it every night. Lie there and hate you, Mommy. I hated you. I did."

"I know, Sylvie. I know you did. It's all right."

"We don't need you anymore, Mommy. You didn't need to come back. Daddy and I are doing fine by ourselves. We don't need you. You shouldn't have come."

"You shouldn't be doing this, Harden. This is wrong. I can't let you do it."

Judy Nelson climbed up the embankment where Harden was digging. Twenty yards away, going closer.

Thorn watched Judy and Harden, and he felt Sugarman behind him, still sawing on the ropes, working on them now for a minute or more, holding his breath under the water, and Thorn could hear the bubbles of his exhalation coming to the surface, Sugarman pushing his limits of endurance.

"Please put the shovel down, Harden."

But the man kept on digging, water flooding out at his feet.

"Why'd you come back, Judy?"

She laughed bitterly.

"To apologize," she said, "for my rudeness this afternoon. Can you believe it? I baked you and Sylvie a cake. It's in the truck. And then here you are, doing this. Incredible."

"Go away, Judy. Don't make me hurt you."

"Put down your shovel, Harden. I want you to put it down now."

Thorn saw the dark glint of Judy's handgun.

The water had risen to Thorn's mouth. He was straining to stay above it, stretching upward, sucking in air through his nose, blowing bubbles out his mouth, feeling the ropes loosen.

Harden stopped digging and faced Judy. Thorn wanted to yell to her to be careful, warn her that her feelings for Harden were making her stand too close, love was taking the keen edge off her senses, letting her trust this man, making her soft. But the water was covering his mouth now, and he could only watch as Harden spoke to Judy, said something low that Thorn couldn't hear. And in the same second as Judy Nelson began to lower her gun, Thorn saw the shovel catch the light as it swung a half circle at Judy's face and whanged against her skull, and sent Judy tumbling backward down the side of the embankment.

Behind him, Thorn felt the ropes come loose at last, and he pivoted around and dragged the last knots free himself. Pushing his head above water.

"Way to go, Sugar. Way to go."

But Sugarman didn't respond.

Thorn pulled himself to his feet and turned, and saw Sugar floating facedown, his body caught against a white oak sapling, the water flowing silver around him.

CHAPTER 32

GRUNTING FOR BREATH, THORN PULLED SUGAR'S FACE FROM THE WATER, dragged him away from the tree. His body was bowed backward by the ropes, Darcy's knife still gripped in his fist. Thorn pried the knife free, cut loose Sugar's hands and feet, shoved the knife back in the leather scabbard and hoisted Sugar into his arms, then slogged as fast as his body would take him through the knee-high water across the yard. His heart was taking hard whacks at his rib cage. Bruised and sore to the marrow, he headed for the terrace of the swimming pool, which rose a few feet above the waterline, the stone patio glowing white and dry in the moonlight.

He stretched Sugar out on the deck and tipped his head back, made sure his mouth was clear. Took a quick glimpse across the yard at Harden, the man still absorbed in his digging, the gash in the embankment much wider, then he turned back to Sugar-man, pressed his lips to Sugar's and blew. And this time he would not leave the body for a second, he would make no radio calls for help, but stay until he had no more breath to give.

Tilapia be damned, oceans of the world be damned. He would do what he could to save the single thing that was in his power to save, the only thing that mattered to him anymore in that jinxed and twisted world.

Doris was back home. She was safely in their house again.

Harden listened to the rasp of his own spade cutting through the dirt, and that single sentence playing over and over in his head. Doris was back home, where she belonged. Doris was home.

Before him the tilapia flooded out, a thousand thousand thousand fish penned up no longer. Leaning on the shovel for a moment, he watched the tilapia swim across the lawn, the pickup's headlights giving them a ghostly whiteness. They darted like sperm searching for the great womb of the ocean, flitting in every direction, some of them heading inland, but more, many many more drawn to the river, to escape.

Millions of fish cascading from their pens, an avalanche of fish. He felt the power of their release, the pleasure of their flight, a great orgasm of fish, white fish and black ones, his years of penitent concentration, feeding them, nourishing, protecting them from the predator birds, the algae blooms. And the long grinding labor of transferring the fish from pond to pond as they matured, until they were finally ready to reproduce.

That was the key. Reproduction. The female tilapia made depressions in the sandy bottom of the ponds, then lay her eggs there, the males standing guard over them, watching the minnows hatch and grow, defending them at every stage. A thousand times more productive than other fish because of that, a thousand times more likely to pass their genes into the future, to outlive themselves, become immortal, simply because the fathers stood guard, protected their families, because the males were more combative, better fighters, more dedicated than any other fish.

The water rushed through the break in the last of the pond walls, everything that had been stored was now releasing. And

Doris was home, Doris was in their house again. Doris who had transformed him into something better than he was. Even in her cruel absence she had kept on changing him, given him a new identity. No longer the dirt farmer's son from Texas, no longer the civil service assassin, but now a creator, an artist who had brought into the world a new thing. A new beautiful conception.

Harden lifted his head and watched yet another car drive through the gate, watched its headlights sweep across the yard and house as it turned, as its driver must have seen Judy Nelson's truck, with its headlights still shining on Harden and the fish that came in a great gush from the pond.

The other set of headlights aligned themselves with Judy Nelson's, and a man climbed out of the car. A heavyset man lugging a shotgun. Harden picked up his shovel again and resumed his digging, keeping an eye on the man coming closer.

"Hey, you!" the man called out.

Harden kept on digging.

The man plodded into the path of the headlights, brandishing the shotgun at Harden.

"You Sylvie's father? Yeah, you. Answer me."

"I am her father. Yes."

The squat man sloshed through the water, coming within a few feet of the embankment where Harden worked.

"You been touching that girl?"

"What?"

"You know what, Winchester. You have sex with Sylvie?"

"Oh, Lord. Good fucking Christ. Is that the bullshit she's telling you guys? Is that how she gets you so fired up? Me, have sex with her? Jesus, what idiots."

Harden went back to his digging, and the man racked a shell into the shotgun.

"Listen to me, Winchester. I'm taking the girl away from here. You aren't going to stop me either."

Harden dug out another spadeful of the wet glop, and he looked over at the man aiming the shotgun at him.

"She's my granddaughter," the old man said. "I'm taking her away. As soon as I finish settling up with you."

Harden laughed at him, this man with his shotgun.

"Sylvie's grandfather! Now, look here, pardner, I met Doris's father a few times, and believe me, you aren't him. And you sure as shit aren't my old man."

Harden laughed, then laughed some more, watching the man's face change, watching it sour, watching him shift his hands on the shotgun, feeling for the right grip.

"Get on out of here, Grandpa, while you're still breathing through the right end of your body." Harden laughed again. "Sylvie's not going anywhere. She and her mother and I are starting our family again. Case closed."

The man moved closer, bringing the barrel up, the butt snug against his shoulder, aiming it halfway up the embankment.

"The fuck're you doing laughing at me? You crazy?"

Harden's laughter died, but he kept smiling, held still.

"I don't like killing crazy people," the old man said. "I'll do it, but I don't like it."

Harden reset his feet, watched the man's eyes in the dim light.

"Go on now, old man, get off my land. I'm too busy for this bullshit tonight. It's only a little longer till the tide turns."

The man lifted his aim, sighting on Harden now. But Harden believed he could see the barrel trembling.

"You can't do it," Harden said. "You're just like all the others. Believe me, I've seen a string of fools like you. Sylvie's thinned your blood. The girl's a genius at that. That's her great gift in life. Turning men into simpletons."

"I'm Ray Bianetti," the man said. "That name mean anything to you?"

"No."

"Well, it should. Ray Bianetti of the Petrosino family. Father of Doris Carter. Grandfather of Sylvie."

"Say that again."

Bianetti angled closer.

"You been abusing her," the old man said. "Having sex with your own daughter."

"The hell I have."

"Why would Sylvie lie? Why would she do that?"

"God knows why that girl does anything. Go ask her, why don't you? She's in the house there. Go on, go ask her why she lies."

Bianetti hesitated, glanced back at the house, then brought his eyes back to Harden. The old man took half a step forward, and Harden saw his trigger finger move, and didn't wait to see if the barrel stopped trembling. He dove forward, and in the same motion slung the heap of mud at the man and somersaulted down the bank, hearing the explosion of the weapon and another blast as he rolled, then found his feet and came up under the hot barrel and tore it from the man's grasp and hurled it out into the gleaming lake of his yard.

Bianetti stumbled backward, nearly fell. Mud coating his face, spattered across his dark sport jacket.

He was panting, clawing at the mud in his eyes. A man in his seventies, with gray hair, thick-waisted. And as he lowered his hands from his face, Harden could see his eyes were dazed and lost. He worked to catch his breath, then brought his slow eyes to Winchester's.

"There's something wrong with that girl. She's not right. You did something to her." A string of foamy spit hung from Bianetti's lip, twirled, catching the light. He put his hands in the pockets of his sport coat.

"It's 'cause she didn't have a proper family," Harden said. "But all that's about to change."

"No," Ray said. His voice was suddenly hoarse.

The old man's hands came out of his pocket. One of them drifted up to grip his own throat. Harden stepped back and watched as Bianetti's knees sagged. Then the old man stumbled to his right, threw his head back as though he were about to bellow at the moon. He clutched his chest with both hands as though his heart had ruptured, Harden watching, cautious. Then the old man caught himself, staggered, and changed direction as if he were about to spiral down into a heap.

But in the next instant, Bianetti was no longer old, not slow and helpless, coming out of his stumble, lowering his head and bulling forward, growling like a maniac, coming very fast, aiming at Harden's legs, tackling him and lifting him off the ground, then splashing him hard on his back. Harden swiveled quickly, blew water from his mouth, broke Bianetti's hold and tried to come around to face him, their bodies tangled, Harden's fingers groping for one of the vulnerable spots.

But something wasn't right. Harden Winchester wasn't totally alert, not focused, his muscles weakening swiftly as though he'd taken some buckshot without knowing it. Not feeling the warm damp of a wound, yet knowing something was wrong, something that prevented him from turning his head to either side. Kept him from drawing a breath, his face growing hot and swollen. And finally recognizing it, feeling it, a sharp burn cutting into his Adam's apple. Something he'd felt once before. A bad thing.

A wire at his throat. A goddamn wire.

Sylvie was right. Doris was too wide-hipped to slip through the opening. But Sylvie managed it like always, pushing one corner of the grating out, then prying her body past the sharp steel edge, only a few inches between the window frame and the angle of steel.

She hopped down into the water and Doris said, "Now open the door, Sylvie. Come unlock the bedroom door."

Sylvie stared off at the two men struggling by the bank of the fish pond. One of them throttling the other. A loud grunt. Recognizing Murtha's car, the red Firebird. Murtha coming all this way to fight for her, win her. Wow.

"Open the bedroom door, Sylvie. Hurry now. Hurry."

"No, Mommy. You stay there. I'm going to get something first, take care of some other business."

Sylvie started across the yard toward her father and Murtha where they were struggling in the headlights. She had an idea. A way to get things back to how they were.

CHAPTER 33

A CUP OF SOUR WATER ERUPTED FROM SUGAR'S MOUTH, AND JUST BEHIND it came a thin gruel of vomit. Thorn pulled his lips away, tried to keep his stomach down, but it took a second before he could get back to the cadence of his CPR, kneeling to the right side of Sugar's body, his left hand covering his right, the heel of his hand jamming into the soft flesh an inch or two below Sugar's sternum, one-pump, two-pump, three-pump, working Sugarman's heart from the outside, then leaning forward, pinching his nose and giving him three more quick blows of air.

Behind him he heard the splash of someone wading toward them, but he didn't turn. One-pump, two-pump, three-pump.

He heard the person leave the water, climb up the terrace onto the patio, and heard the click of several switches. And all around them, spotlights blazed from the poles scattered about the yard, from the roof of the house, from the barns.

Thorn glanced up quickly and saw an acre of harsh white light, saw the two cars standing in the yard, saw Judy's body lying on the pond bank, another body lying below it, head in the water. Dizzy now, his knees sore, Thorn leaned forward and blew three more hard breaths into Sugar's mouth. Heard the footsteps go quiet behind him, but didn't turn. One-pump, two-pump.

And felt Sugar's body respond, felt a weak tremble beneath his hands. Clumsy with excitement, Thorn's hands slipped, and he fell forward across Sugar's chest.

Sugarman opened his eyes, blinked, looked up at Thorn.

"Damn." His voice frail and hoarse. "You need a shave, man. Like kissing a porcupine."

Thorn sat up and eased the angle of Sugar's neck.

Sugarman closed his eyes for a moment, breathing on his own. He took a long breath, and his eyes came open again.

"And mouthwash too," Sugar said.

"Hush," Thorn said. "Just relax."

"Peanuts. Tasted them on your breath. Dreaming about baseball games."

"Don't talk. Just stay calm, Sugar."

Sugarman's gaze moved slowly over Thorn's shoulder. His eyes making the long journey back from his dream of baseball to this savage August night on the edge of the Everglades. Watching someone who stood behind Thorn, staring at that person as he would at a cottonmouth that blocked his path.

Thorn rose to his feet and turned. In one hand she carried a silver bucket, in the other, a shotgun. Sylvie set the bucket down and held the shotgun loosely in both hands.

"Now's your chance, Thorn. My daddy's over there. He's in a weakened condition."

Thorn stepped closer to her and said, "What I want to know is, Sylvie, what'd you do with his body?"

"What body?"

"Lavery's."

She came to attention, measured him with a long bland look. Finally in a sober voice she said, "It was self-defense."

"Oh, I'm sure it was. Everything you do is self-defense. Isn't that right? Your great all-purpose rationale."

"If you'd had my life, Thorn, you'd understand. Walked in my moccasins, full of broken glass, you'd see."

"So what happened to you, Sylvie? What was so goddamn awful it gives you permission to murder people?"

"It was self-defense with Lavery. I told you. He went for me, tried to kill me, and I had no choice."

"Did you ask him to rescue you too? That's what you do, isn't it? Find the Roy Murthas, the Laverys, twitch your spooky little butt at them, try to get them lathered up about what an evil man your father is."

"You seemed to enjoy Sylvie's butt pretty well last night. The way you heaved around. Never saw a guy get so worked up."

Thorn glanced back at Sugarman and shrugged his admission. Sugar shook his head sadly at the sacrilege.

"Darcy just stumbled into it, didn't she, Sylvie? She saw something that looked wrong, rushed in to help. And you thought, hey, why not? Maybe I should give a woman a chance to play the game. Might be a nice change of pace."

Sylvie's eyes were growing distant, coming unfocused.

"Nobody can help Sylvie."

"Maybe you don't want any help. Maybe that's not what you're asking for at all."

"Sylvie's in distress," she said. "She needs someone to step in the ring of fire and save her."

"Or maybe what she wants," Thorn said, "is to see people flame out trying. Maybe that's what gets you off. Lure guys to the blaze, watch them sizzle. Must be very gratifying having all of them so worked up they're willing to die for you. Must be an incredible turn-on."

Sylvie's eyes focused. She cocked her head to the side, a frigid smile coming to her lips.

"You're a deep thinker, aren't you? Just deep as can be."

"Not deep enough."

"I don't like you, Thorn. I don't see how Darcy ever put up with some navel-gazer like you. She deserved better. Somebody who could take her out to places, show her the world. Not some goddamn hermit. Some guy, you think it's a big deal to walk down to the end of your driveway and watch the traffic go by."

Sugarman inched to his right, but Sylvie noticed and flashed the shotgun his way and he halted.

"And that dragon guarding the cave," Thorn said, glancing out at the fish ponds, seeing just beyond the range of the lights the shape of a man slouching toward the house. "That's all bullshit. You don't want to escape from Harden. 'Cause you and the dragon have a sweet little arrangement, don't you? Sylvie supplies him with all the fresh red meat he can handle, and he demonstrates how much he cares, what he's willing to do on her behalf. A cat bringing home its catch for its master's praise. That's how it works, right? One hell of a happy family."

Her eyes twitched back and forth between Sugarman and Thorn.

"You don't know my daddy," she said. "He's not like you, Thorn. A man like him, he gets bored without challenges. He needs action. It's how he stays youthful."

"So that's your job, huh? You throw him nice slow pitches, and he belts them out of the goddamn park."

Thorn moved a half step closer to her, two yards away now. Sylvie tightened her grip on the shotgun, holding him there.

He said, "And it wasn't any rental boat either, was it?"

"What're you talking about?"

"That was you in the Grady White. Those were your flippers, your weight belt. Way too small to fit your father. That was you out on the reef."

"I told you what happened. My daddy killed her. Like he does all of them."

"You couldn't control Darcy. She didn't fall under the spell. Wasn't as gullible as the men. That got you worried. Maybe this one would actually succeed, bring your daddy to justice. You started sweating, thinking the whole goddamn fairy tale you'd dreamed up was going to come tinkling down. So you killed her, didn't you, Sylvie?"

When she didn't reply, Thorn said, "Supposed to meet her at

Snake Creek Marina so you could talk some more, but you didn't show. Instead, you followed us out there, looking for some kind of opportunity. Maybe you took along a gun. Ready to kill both of us if it came to that. But you saw your chance, swam over to her underwater, used a hand grip on her you'd learned from your father. I can just picture it. You and Harden sitting around the table after supper, father teaching his little girl some of his old military tricks, in case one day she might need to paralyze one of her playmates."

Sylvie shifted the shotgun, worked her finger toward the trigger.

"I should've never got involved with Darcy."

"Yeah. And why's that?"

"You can't trust women," Sylvie said. "You stand at the window watching for them, hour after hour, month after month, but they never come back. They pretend to care about you. But they don't. They don't care. Not really. They abandon you."

"So you had to kill her, didn't you?"

"Okay," she said, "I did it. I did it before she could hurt me. Women stab you in the back. Pretend they love you, then they do whatever they feel like. They go off. Sylvie had to defend herself before she was hurt again."

Sylvie shifted her feet, brought the shotgun level with Thorn's chest. A few feet to her right Sugarman inched her way, spreading her targets as far apart as possible. Sugar's right eye was bloated, only a slit of white eyeball showing. Sylvie cut a warning glance his way, then looked back at Thorn.

He'd shifted to the balls of his feet, had his weight cocked forward, and was estimating his chances for a dive at her feet. Out of the edge of his vision he saw Sugar trying to send him some kind of message with a flutter of his right hand, a countdown to attack or something, but Thorn couldn't read it.

Sylvie swallowed deep and started to speak, but a scream interrupted her. A woman's agonized voice. Then another shriek came from the house. The woman screamed again and Sugarman heaved out a curse and charged down the slope of the terrace.

Before Thorn could move, Sylvie had spun around and fired in his direction. But the recoil jerked her shot high, and Sugar continued to jog clumsily through the knee-deep water. Thorn lunged for her, but Sylvie stumbled away from him in time, swinging the barrel around till it was a foot from his face.

CHAPTER 34

"BACK OFF," SHE SAID. "BACK THE FUCK OFF."

Thorn did as he was told.

She seemed stunned by the blast of her shotgun. But after a moment her eyes gradually cleared, and she tilted her head, began to look curiously at Thorn, as if she'd just bumbled onto this stage and didn't remember which role was hers, had even forgotten the name of the play. Was waiting for Thorn to cue her.

But he said nothing, and as she stared at him, a winsome smile materialized on her lips and lingered there like lazy smoke. It was coming to her now. An old act she'd played so well, so many nights before.

"Oh, now, come on, Hemingway. Be honest," she said, her voice taking on a silky edge. "All that screaming and moaning last night, all that humping. Come on, Thorn, say it. Don't you love Sylvie, maybe just a little bit?"

He slid his eyes away from the black barrels of the shotgun, lifted them to the hazy sky above the floodlights. The night had cleared, the moon riding higher up the steep rails of its orbit, rotating from the earth, pulling away at thousands of miles an hour, that cold, barren rock loosening its hold on tides and lovers and the desperately insane.

Bringing his eyes back to her, he said, "Why don't you put that shotgun down, you little shit, and I'll show you just how much I love you."

Sylvie glared at him for a moment, then her eyes seemed to lose interest and swam inward like the eyes of a sleeper drawn back into the powerful currents of her dream. After another moment, Thorn was fairly sure she didn't even see him anymore. Just a murky shape, the outlines of a man. No longer one of Sylvie's soldiers, no longer of use, become now simply a faint annoyance. It must've been how she'd looked at Darcy at the end. The way she learned to deal with betrayals of every kind.

You were either completely devoted to Sylvie or you didn't exist. You either worshiped at the altar of her lunatic smile, pledged yourself to her every wish, tried to soothe each of her complaints, had utter faith in her, absolute loyalty, or Sylvie shunted you off into some dead part of herself, deposited you there in the cemetery of her heart, where you became, as Thorn had just become, a ghost.

Thorn turned from her and listened to the racket coming from inside the old wood farmhouse, grunts and scuffling, furniture overturning, a woman's voice pleading for them to stop. A large pane of glass broke.

"Get it out of your mind, Thorn. You're staying with me. Sylvie has some stoop labor for you." Her voice was remote, eyes frosted over, staring into the air above his head. "The fish are the money, and the money is what brought her back, so we're going to destroy the fish."

Sylvie kept the shotgun aimed at Thorn as she squatted down at the edge of the pool, plunged her arm elbow-deep in the water. She struggled mightily with something for a moment, eyes fixed on Thorn, then tugged up the edge of a sheet of plastic. It seemed to be a tarp tinted a deep blue, fastened by snaps to the walls of the pool a foot or two below the waterline.

"Now you finish it, Thorn. Pull it loose. This is man's work."

Thorn hesitated a moment more, the house ominously quiet now. Then he kneeled at the edge and patted the sides of the pool till he found the snaps and began to pull them free. As he circled the pool unfastening the tarp, Sylvie dragged the plastic sheet to her, and dumped the crinkly excess into a pile on the keystone patio. It was shiny blue, some kind of opaque camouflage, giving the pool its shallow look.

When Thorn was almost done, Sylvie moved to a panel on one of the columns of the gazebo and snapped on the pool lights, and Thorn saw them then, the swimming pool thick with fish. Tilapia *nilotica* swarmed everywhere, stirred into mild action by this sudden unveiling. Thousands of them, all a bright crimson, and all with those distinctive marks on their tails, dark false eyes.

"Now throw it into the pool."

She waved at the bucket brimming with white granules.

"Sodium fluoroacetate." Her voice seemed to come from a long way down inside her.

Thorn picked up the bucket and Sylvie stepped back, out of range, three, four yards away.

"Into the pool. Throw it in."

He stared at the fish for a moment, swirls of scarlet. All of them with the color the marketplace apparently craved. It was only skin, just a surface illusion. Because these fish were identical to all the other tilapia, the blacks and whites tasted the same, had flesh just as flaky as these reds. But men had died for these fish. They were the pretty blue-eyed blondes. The fairy-tale princesses. Born lucky, the Aryans of the sea.

Thorn hurled the chemical into the pool, and watched as the fish swarmed upward toward it, tricked, believing it was feeding time. They pecked at the dissolving powder, then backed quickly away, swam to the edges of the pool.

"It takes a while," Sylvie said. "They're tough bastards."

As they watched, the tilapia began to swim in faster and more erratic patterns as if some large predator had been dropped in their midst. Darting and diving, they bumped into the walls, splashed the surface.

"Now it's your turn, Thorn. I'm finished with you. Get in the pool."

He looked at her. The muscles in her face were slack, her mouth loose; all the blood was drained from her, her flesh a zombie-white. A bleak imitation of Sylvie aimed the shotgun at him. Aimed with her finger hard on the trigger.

He took a step toward the pool, Sylvie backing away, the shotgun steady. He considered the gymnastics involved in trying to disarm her, a feint, a dodge and roll. Some cinematic Bruce Lee kip and kick that sent the shotgun flying. But Thorn had never had the limberness for that, or the disposition. He was a bull-ahead fighter, the man who wins, if he wins at all, by getting back up and wading in one more time. Stubbornness his only talent.

"There's another way to do this, Sylvie. Nobody else has to die. But you have to put that shotgun down first." Trying to warm his voice, soothe the jumper back from the ledge. But Sylvie wasn't listening. Her eyes were cataracts of ice.

"Get in the pool," she said. "You're not sniveling your way out of this."

"If you testify against your father, Sylvie, they won't go so hard on you. That's how it works."

"I'm not testifying against anyone. Harden and I are going back to how it was. That's all I'm doing. Keeping it how it was."

Behind Sylvie, Harden was coming down off the porch. He had his arm slung around Doris Albright's waist and was hauling her along with him. They were headed toward the pool.

"Sylvie. It's never going to be that way again. All that's finished. You've got to give me the gun. Right now, Sylvie. It can't wait any longer."

Thorn edged forward into the line of fire, only a few seconds left before Harden was within earshot.

"Stop it, Thorn. Stop right there."

He drew a hard breath. It was too late. Harden plodded up the terrace to the pool, and Sylvie heard him then, and stepped back, keeping the shotgun aimed squarely at Thorn. She swung her head around and saw them approach, then cut her eyes back to Thorn and held him there.

"Good work, Sylvie," Winchester said. "Good girl."

Blood seeped steadily from Winchester's throat. A shiny metal wire seemed to be embedded there, the flesh of his neck was puckered and swollen around it. Dangling at each end of the wire were two bright silver balls slightly larger than marbles. They hung down to Harden's chest and swung like grotesque pendulums as he stepped forward with Doris onto the patio, then let her go.

"I must be a sight," he said, his voice a wet croak. "This thing." He touched a finger to his bloody neck. "I'd pull it out except I think it's all that's keeping me together at the moment. Be fine till I get to the hospital, have it fixed. The jugular's intact. That's what he was going for. Bastard cut some neck muscles is all. The Venter superior, the sternohyoideus. But I've survived worse. Much worse."

Harden took a long breath and it chattered in his throat as though he were sucking up the last of a milkshake.

He moved to the steps of the swimming pool, maneuvered himself awkwardly down the first two. The blood had stained his gray sweatshirt, leaving the shadow of what looked to Thorn like a tarpon diving in panic toward the ocean bottom.

"Doris, come here, come close." He waved at her. "I want you to see what I've done. See what I've made for us."

"Daddy, don't. Don't go in the water."

"What'd he do with Sugar?" Thorn said to Doris.

"Your friend," Harden said, "is staining my living room rug with his blood."

Doris swallowed. "He's alive," she said. "He's still alive."

"Daddy, don't go into the water. It's dangerous. You're bleeding, you're hurt."

Harden glared her way.

"Don't spoil this, girl. Don't try to sabotage this night for me. Do you hear your father?"

He waded into the pool, went deeper till he was waist-high, and he leaned forward, lowered his arms into the water and scooped up a half dozen fish, held them squirming in his embrace. Bright red tilapia, lifting them up, then opening his arms, letting them splash back into the water.

With a steady ooze of blood coming from his throat, he scooped up more, almost a dozen this time, cradled them to himself, giving Doris an elated smile, then one by one, let the fish go, let them slither free and escape back into the clear water.

"You see, Doris," he said. "See what I've done. So many people tried, people with unlimited finances, scientists with their Ph.D.'s. But I succeeded. I did it because I had a reason, Doris, because I had a just cause. I brought alive a thing that never existed on the earth before."

Doris seemed spellbound by the pool, the fish, by Harden Winchester splashing about, now grabbing up two large specimens, one in each hand, holding them heavenward like bricks of gold to the dark sky, beaming at Doris as the fish wriggled helplessly in his hands.

"They're ours, Doris," he said. "The most beautiful, the most fruitful fish in the world. Aren't they wonderful?"

Barely a whisper, she answered him.

"Say it, say those words, Doris. They're wonderful fish."

"They are," she said in her sad trance. "Wonderful fish."

The night was humid and a sluggish breeze carried the faint scents of pine and moldering vegetation. High overhead the moon was speeding along its trajectory, moving out of range.

"Do you realize, Doris, there are people who will pay great sums for these fish. Millions of dollars. Enough to wipe out all your debts, allow you to walk away from your dying husband, from that failed business, that pitiful life. That's how much these are worth. That's what I've done for you. For us. To free you of all your debts and entanglements, to wipe the slate clean for you, so you can return to us just as you left."

"I want you to let these people go, Harden," Doris said. "They've done nothing. They were only trying to help me."

Harden swept his hand through the water, stirring the fish into action. Some of them had already begun to die. In the corners of the pool they gathered, heads tipped up as if they were trying desperately to suck down some untainted air.

"What are they to you, Doris? Who are these people?"

"They're my friends. They were only trying to help."

"Friends? What do you need with friends? You have a family. That's all you need. That's all anyone requires."

"He didn't create those fish." Thorn stepped toward the edge of the pool.

Harden's hand fluttered through the water. He peered into a corner of the pool where some of the dying fish had clustered.

Thorn said, "He stole the fish from the government. Killed a dozen people in the process."

Winchester shifted his eyes to Thorn.

"Oh, he brags about it, claims he did it all himself. But he didn't do anything. He cheated. He murdered people who were in his way just like he's done all his life. Always got some noble justification. He used to kill because it was his patriotic duty, then he murdered to recover his family. But the man's just a goddamn killer. Just a simple lowlife son of a bitch who was raised by a murdering bastard and became a murdering bastard himself. And taught his daughter to be one too."

Harden glared briefly at Thorn, then his eyes dodged away, looking again at Doris. His mouth softened into a con man's smile.

Saying to her in a honeyed voice, "You know, sweetheart, pink is definitely your color. I always thought so. With your hair, your complexion. It's strawberries and cream. Sets everything off perfectly. I was telling Sylvie that just the other day. Pink is far and away your best color."

"Harden, this is enough. You've done enough now. Let us get you to the hospital. You're hurt."

"Those fish," Harden said, glancing at Thorn as he came up the steps, then back at Doris. "Do you realize, Doris, no one will ever need to go to sea again. I've rendered an entire way of life meaningless. No more fishermen. Because now we can create all the fish we want right here on land. Tasty and beautiful. I've made them for you. They are your homecoming present. Dedicated to Doris Winchester. My wife. This gift."

Obviously the poisoned water had not entered Harden's wound. He seemed fine. The tiger still fully alive inside him. While in the pool the fish swarmed in clumps, in their final frenzy as the toxin took effect. Harden stopped halfway up the steps, and glanced uneasily at them, then looked up at Sylvie.

"What's wrong with the fish?" he said. "What did you do?"

Sylvie struggled to speak. She moved close to the edge of the pool, a tear appearing on her cheek.

"I want it to stay how it was, Daddy. We had a good family. You, me. It's enough. We don't need her."

But Harden didn't seem to hear, the man preoccupied with his fish, and Sylvie just as absorbed in him. And for Thorn this was as good as it was going to get.

He sprang forward, knocked Sylvie aside, ripped the shotgun from her hands, but before he could turn, the big man chopped him behind the neck, and Thorn dropped the weapon. The light dimmed, and he felt himself going down, but Harden caught him by the arm, turned him around and stared into his face.

Roughly he crossed Thorn's middle fingers over each other and pressed his thumb into that cluster of synapses and nerves, and Thorn felt the arm go numb, felt his lungs contract. Harden using Dr. Ralph Mellon's grip—Mellon, the pathologist in the bright clothes. The big man holding Thorn's hand in the office of the funeral home and deadening it this same way.

Thorn was immobilized, his legs wilting, looking into Harden's eyes, only a dim flicker of consciousness. The twilight before everlasting dark. Harden's grip tightened, and Thorn stumbled sideways to the edge of the pool, the big man coming along.

Blowing out all the air in his lungs, Thorn drifted deeper inside himself. Clamped his eyes shut. Could feel the pressure in his ears, a hot twist in his chest, felt like he was drowning out there in the summer air, the last grains of oxygen consumed by his muscles, his arm numb and throbbing at once.

With his left hand he reached out, felt the clamp of Harden's grip, explored it, tried to peel away his hands, but it was hopeless, the man was far stronger than Thorn. And abruptly Harden tightened the grip. Thorn flinched, saw the fizz of lights, like bubbles in seltzer, exploding brain cells, the light show just before unconsciousness.

Thorn wasn't sure, but it felt like he'd stopped breathing. Lost in the dark undoing of his own chemistry, the self-consumption of his blood. Left-handed, blind from the pain, he reached out again, the last feeble seconds passing, extended his hand, eyes closed, felt his way up Harden's arm, patted him on the chest.

The man squeezed harder, jerked Thorn to the left, then right, shaking him like a shark tearing loose a chunk of flesh. Thorn patted Harden's chest again, gently. Breath gone, fading. Rocking on the edge of the poisoned bath.

Then Thorn brushed it with the fingers of his left hand. Not recognizing it at first. His mind loosening its hold on the moment. Mind going wordless and scattered. And once again he touched it, the cold thing, the round thing.

He considered it, tried to picture it as his mind grew gray. And yes, of course. He felt it, one of the pendulums, a steel ball, Thorn seeing it now with his eyes shut, closing his hand around it as the electrical current in Thorn's mind flickered and went off, flickered again and came back on. He gripped it, made a fist around it. Harden sensed what was happening and relaxed his hold on Thorn's arm, relaxing, letting go, but it was too late to back away, too late for forgiveness, appeals to reason. They were a long way beyond the reach of law, a long way beyond all restraints of civility.

Thorn yanked it hard. Like a parachute rip cord, and felt Harden fall away from him, felt himself dropping backward through some kind of watery sky, upside down, drift through the blue dangerous haze, a chute spreading open above him, slowing him down. Falling until he slammed on his back against the keystone deck.

With his eyes clamped, Thorn released the steel ball, let it roll away. And he lay there for a long time in the unhurried drowse of shock. Hearing only the nag of night bugs, the electric fizz of a hundred floodlights. Drawn down into silence by the irresistible undertow of his exhaustion. Lying still in the luxurious quiet. And then he felt himself let go as well of the rage, and finally surrender even Darcy Richards, the sweet terrible ache of her absence.

Thorn lay on the hard patio, with the dreamy night air bathing his face and filling his lungs.

CHAPTER 35

LONG MOMENTS LATER THORN WAS WRENCHED AWAKE BY A WOMAN'S WAIL. And began a slow breathless journey back to the surface. Fighting his way to the light. It took every fiber of his concentration to draw his eyes open, to lift his head, to push himself upright.

He sat for a moment and tried to slow the dizzy spin in his head. Blinking his eyes, rubbing them, the scene came into gradual focus. On the lip of the pool Sylvie was holding tight to Doris Albright's right hand. She had rearranged her mother's fingers into the same lethal grip Harden had used on him, the same grasp Sylvie had just a few days ago used on Darcy. And now Sylvie was tipping Doris backward toward the water. The girl sobbing silently as she leaned her weight into Doris.

"You lied," she said. "You never came back. You gave up."

Doris slapped her free hand helplessly against Sylvie's grip. Her eyes shut hard, wincing with the pain. Thorn hauled himself to his feet and stumbled toward them. Woozy, bewildered, a drunk staggering to the bar for one last shot.

With her eyes fixed on the pool, Sylvie cried out again, and threw all her weight against Doris, shoved her backward toward the water. But Thorn was there, and seized the neck of Doris's blouse, spun her around. Doris screamed, and Thorn felt the cotton rip in his hand, saw her twist away from him.

He thrust out his other hand, the crippled one, and snagged her arm as she was tumbling away. He gripped her hard, and threw himself backward, holding on to Doris Albright, yanking her against her own momentum, hauling her down roughly on top of him.

Doris landed on his chest, and lay there weeping quietly. Then he heard a splash. Heard Sylvie's voice, a babble of pain. He eased Doris to the side, lay her down on her back and stood up. In the pool Sylvie was thrashing through the mass of dying fish, splashing toward where her father floated facedown at the foot of the blue slide.

When finally she reached him, she grabbed the neck of his shirt, swung his body around. She looked dreadfully weary, her movements growing more sluggish every second. The movie she was in seemed to be turning to slower and slower motion.

Sylvie wrapped her arms around her father's chest, a clumsy embrace, and arduously turned him, then took one ponderous stroke toward the steps. But she faltered, and her head dipped below the water and she flailed her arms. When her head resurfaced, she sputtered, blew water from her mouth. As she lifted her eyes to Thorn, standing on the opposite rim, she seemed already to be disappearing into herself.

Her gaze was desolate and faraway, as if she had lost her balance and was beginning to fall backward from a ledge. Her eyes holding on to his as Sylvie began her long slow plunge into that endless ravine.

A moment later, Sylvie Winchester's body floated faceup next to Harden's. Both of them were motionless, surrounded by the carcasses of his red tilapia. Thorn watched them for several minutes, the water tinted crimson. He waited till he was sure they would not be moving ever again, then he turned around, checked on Doris, and staggered for the house.

*   *   *

"You can't do it. I won't let you. Thorn. I absolutely won't."

Thorn was backing Winchester's Oldsmobile, angling the boat trailer toward the edge of the Okehatchee. Judy Nelson waded through the water beside his open window.

"I'm telling you, Thorn, I can't permit this."

"And what do you suggest, Judy? Just let nature take its course, let the goddamn tilapia turn the Gulf into something like that bay in Brazil? Is that what you want? Let that million fish lay their five thousand eggs apiece? You want that, Judy?"

There was blood streaming from her ear, a gash along her temple. Her hair matted with muck. She was having trouble standing, had to prop one arm against the roof of the Olds.

Thorn set the brake and got out of the car. Behind them, Sugarman, in knee-deep water, began to run the electric winch, letting the Grady White ease back into the water. With both his hands badly broken, he was pressing the switch with his elbow.

"I'm telling you. You can't just go out there, Thorn, and kill wildlife indiscriminately. Fish, birds, reptiles. You can't do it. That estuary is chock-full of every kind of fish and animal. Some of them are even endangered species. There's manatees in there, birds roosting on the shoreline. I can't let you, Thorn. I can't."

She patted her hand against her empty holster.

"I don't like it any more than you do, Judy. But I don't see what the choice is. We wait till the morning, let the scientists and the politicians take it over, nothing'll ever happen. You know that. They'll decide to study the problem, write papers or some bullshit. A month from now, Judy, think about it, those fish'll work down to the Gulf, get out in that warm, shallow water, nutrient rich—it'll be a disaster, Jude, a total fucking disaster. We either do something tonight, right now, or it doesn't get done. You know that. You know it's true."

Judy reached up and touched her hair near the jagged tear in her flesh. She staggered. Then caught herself against the hood of the car and looked out at the silver water flowing west toward the Gulf. Fish flipped at the surface. All across the yard the shallow water was speckled with their presence. It was as though the surface of the earth were being peppered with an invisible rain.

An osprey high in the pines screeched three times, then four, its displeasure unmistakable. The off-key tone was grating at some ancient, biological level, warning every blood-filled creature below that it was not pleased. That it was on the verge of swooping down with its beak and razor-sharp talons extended.

"The boat's in!" Sugarman called. "You going to do this or what?"

Thorn came close to Judy. Her mouth opened, but she didn't speak.

"I hate it, Judy. I fucking hate this. But we have to do something. You know we do. And I haven't heard a better idea."

She closed her eyes and looked away from him, her mouth shut tight against all she wanted to say.

Thorn turned from her and went to the boat.

"You're going to have to do this alone, Thorn. I'm no good."

Sugar held up his bloody, mangled hands.

"Take Judy inside the house. Lay her down. Get Doris to look after her. Maybe there's a radio in her truck. You could try calling for help."

"You know how to work those things?"

"Not really," Thorn said. He hauled himself over the gunwale and stepped into the boat. "But how difficult could it be?"

"Good luck, buddy."

Thorn tilted the engine down, started it, and eased the Grady White backward out into the deeper water.

He swung the wheel around and headed downstream at an idle. In the rear locker he found a hand-held spotlight and plugged it in and shone it down into the water. The black and white tilapia were swarming near the surface. He washed the beam across the width of the river and saw them swimming everywhere.

He eased the throttle forward, RPM's up to two thousand.

Just short of a plane. Kept the spotlight on the water and moved downstream, watching until the fish began to thin, and then finally, a mile or so west of Winchester's farm, the river was clear of them entirely.

He went another half mile for good measure, then swung the boat about in the narrow channel, headed back upstream. He cut the throttle, turned on the anchor light, and squatted down beside the several crates of hand grenades.

There was probably another way. A sensible man would have stayed calm, considered creative options. A net strung across the river perhaps, something to contain the fish, keep them from moving downstream. Some ingenious solution that didn't involve killing every living creature for miles up and down the river.

A wiser man perhaps would have found a way to cull the tilapia from the other fish, separate them from the snakes and alligators, the frogs, the turtles, and river otters and raccoons, manatees and spoonbills, night herons, the snowy egrets, ospreys. Spare the innocent, execute the guilty.

But Thorn was not that man. No matter that he considered these river creatures his biological equal, their lives as rich and sacred as any two-legged mammal's on the shore, there was no other way to proceed. No time to sort the good creatures from the bad. The estuary was infected, a plague was loose. God help him, but the blameless would have to die.

The first pin came out easy. Thorn gripped the spring-loaded trigger, picked a spot out in the middle of the stream. He set his feet and hurled the grenade. It splashed and sank a few feet short of the spot he'd chosen.

Thorn waited. Seconds passed.

But nothing happened. A few moments more. A dud perhaps. Had sat in Winchester's humid pantry for so many years that the detonator was dampened somehow.

Then suddenly the water formed a huge silver bubble that lifted the surface of the river and rumbled through the deck of the Grady White, and a second later erupted in a massive geyser that broke the air into a thousand slivers of glass, put a bellow in Thorn's blood, river-spray coming down for minutes afterward like a short summer shower, the water rocking in the channel as if a tanker had passed by at fifty knots and left a tidal wave behind.

Before he could hurl the second one, the fish and a ton of other water creatures were already bobbing to the top. Their carcasses began to blanket the surface of the river like the flotsam from the shipwreck of Noah's ark. He threw another. And another after that. Working himself slowly, methodically back toward Winchester's farm.

He killed a million fish that night. A few million other things. And filled the dark with unforgivable thunder.

CHAPTER **36**

THORN KNEW A WOMAN ONCE WHO HAD GONE ON A SHOPPING TRIP TO
New York City, and among other things she had brought home
to Key Largo a necklace of shiny black beads. The woman put
the necklace away in her drawer, where it sat for months before
she remembered it.

When she tried to open the drawer again, it wouldn't budge.
Finally, using a screwdriver to pry it free, she found the drawer
was clogged with the vines and roots of a strange plant. Her
necklace had sprouted. It was made of seeds.

What might have remained dormant forever in the temperate
zone had gone haywire in the subtropics. If she had gone away
for a year, the plant might have taken possession of her house.

Then there were the catfish that had grown legs so that they
might climb out of canals and explore the adjacent shopping
centers. And the land crabs that flooded out of Biscayne Bay
each spring and invaded the neighborhoods for miles up and
down the coast. For days they clacked across patios, into bed-
rooms, caused pileups on the highway. And there were also the

termites that ate cement, and the lovebugs that mated in great black clouds along the roadways and brought traffic to a halt. Male and female attached, hovering with all their million relatives nearby, they squashed into an ecstatic gummy paste on every windshield. And there were also the roaches big as fists, and the flying ants that appeared suddenly and choked the air in random houses, then just as suddenly and inexplicably disappeared.

The list was far too long to recount in its entirety. South Florida was rich with short-lived phenomena. Naked twigs jammed into the earth became trees overnight, mold and mildew and pollen enriched the air till it was stifling and unbreathably dense. The climate was just too hospitable for its own good. The region was a giant petri dish in which everything, weak or strong, had an excellent chance to flourish.

And it was into that world that Winchester had released a million tilapia. Thorn had done the only thing he could. He'd headed off a disaster, saved the state of Florida untold misery and distress.

Why then could he not sleep? Why then did he hear the echo of those blasts every time he closed his eyes?

It was early December, the temperature had evened off to the mid-seventies. Tourists had retaken the roads and restaurants. Thorn and Sugarman and Rochelle Hamilton were out on Thorn's Chris-Craft, the wide-beamed thirty footer. They were tied up to an anchor buoy on Carysfort Reef, riding the swells like an ocean liner in drydock. Eleven miles out, too far from land for most of the party boats. Had the reef practically to themselves that Monday afternoon. Only two other open fishermen on the other side of the lighthouse.

For the last half hour Sugarman had been badgering Thorn to come in the water. But Thorn just kept shaking his head, sitting in a deck chair on the stern, nursing a bottle of Dos Equis, watching Rochelle standing at the fish sink, cleaning a grouper she'd speared a few minutes earlier. Every few minutes she threw more bones and skin and entrails back into the sea.

"I don't know why," Thorn said. "I just don't feel like swimming. Okay? Can you just accept that, get off my back?"

It was a partly cloudy afternoon, a small chop from a ten-mile-an-hour breeze out of the east. Humid for December.

Sugarman was standing on the top rung of the dive ladder, his mask up on his forehead. Both hands were still in casts, and those were wrapped in plastic bags for the diving trip today. The surgery was all done. Inside Winchester's house that night, Harden had crushed both of Sugarman's hands. Broken small bones and large, left Sugar writhing on the living room rug.

That's for touching the wrong woman, Harden told him, as he'd hauled Doris out the door.

Most of Sugar's movement would come back eventually. So said the bone and nerve physicians at Baptist Hospital. Sugarman asked them if they could put a number on it. Eighty percent, ninety, maybe a hundred percent? A hundred percent mobility? one of them said. What the hell's that? I don't even have a hundred percent, and I'm a goddamn surgeon. The other one going, Let me put it this way, Mr. Sugarman, I think your career as a concert pianist may be about to go into a serious decline. Drs. Laurel and Hardy. Sugarman smiled politely and said, How about twist-off beer caps? Think I'll ever manage them again?

Thorn had another sip of his beer.

Judy Nelson was deaf in one ear now. Hearing the chime of a shovel against her skull every minute of every hour. And Philip Albright passed on the week before Christmas. Thorn felt guilty admitting it, but Doris Albright had looked beautiful in black. The blond hair, the pale skin, those legs. Maybe if Sugarman wasn't going to take her dancing, Thorn would have to.

Sugar said, "There's an eight-foot hammerhead cruising around down there. A leopard ray. And a school of yellowtail you wouldn't believe."

"I'm happy right where I am, Sugar. Right here. Getting a little sun. A nice buzz."

"It's because of Darcy, isn't it?"

Rochelle looked up. Thorn tore loose the paper label on the damp beer bottle. He rolled it into a ball, dropped it into the garbage bin.

Sugar said, "You don't want to go underwater again because it's spooking you, isn't it? You can't do it 'cause you think about her. About not getting to her in time. That whole thing comes back and it's making you give up one of the things you've always loved."

"Jesus Christ."

"It's true," Sugarman said. "You know it's true. I asked my counselor about it. Guy I'm seeing about my Jeanne-Doris situation."

"You asked your shrink about me?"

"That's right, Thorn."

"He gonna bill me?"

"What he said made a lot of sense. You're punishing yourself. Not doing the thing you like the best. Like masochism. Marquis de Sade and all that."

"Marquis de Sade?"

"Masochism, sadism," Sugarman said. "Two sides of the same coin. But I don't know. I may not have that part a hundred percent right."

Rochelle was smiling to herself. Wearing a black one-piece. Very conservative. Trying to cover some of that body, though it wasn't completely working. A towel draped over her shoulders as she carved skillfully with the fillet knife. She had freckles on her back. Not as many as Darcy.

"Hurting myself to feel good. Like that?"

"Yeah. That's it. Like I am with Jeanne. Going back for more, over and over, even though it's all fucked up. Dog crawling back to the master that beats it. Same thing as that."

"We got the same problem? You and me?"

"That's right."

"Then you go snorkel, Sugar. And I'll sit here and drink beer. See which way cures the problem first. A little controlled experiment."

Sugar took his mask off, spit on the glass, rubbed it around and put the mask back on, pushed it up on his forehead again.

"What do you think, Rochelle?"

She jerked her head up, looked at Sugarman.

"You want to know what I think?"

"Yeah. You're a smart woman."

"Oh, smart," she said. "Yeah, I'm smart all right."

"I meant it as a compliment," Sugar said.

"Problem is, Sugar, smart doesn't count for much with things like this. Matters of the heart. Hell, I think being smart might just be a major drawback in most undertakings. There's so much racket going on in your brain all the time, it's hard to hear what your heart is whispering."

"Well, I sure as hell don't have that problem," Sugar said. "I've never been burdened by extra IQ."

" 'A temporary stay against confusion,' " said Thorn.

"What?"

"It's a line from a poem." Thorn shifted the deck chair so he was out of the sun. "I don't remember what the poem's about, but I like the phrase."

"You like the phrase," Sugar said. "He likes the phrase."

"A temporary stay against confusion," Thorn said. "That's the most we can hope for. To pretend that the temporary is going to last a while. 'Cause we know damn well it's still going to be temporary, no matter what we do to make it last."

"You understand what he's talking about?" Sugarman said to Rochelle.

"Yes," she said. "God help me, I think I do."

Thorn smiled, looked up at Rochelle, and she held on to his gaze, not smiling, not frowning either.

"I been thinking," Sugarman said, looking across the reef at the lighthouse. "Maybe I should get out of the detective business. Find a less messy kind of work. What's your view?"

"Give up Quidnunc Enterprises?"

"Maybe go back with the sheriff's department. Get the old job back. It'd make Jeanne happy."

"How about Doris, what's she think?"

"She doesn't care. She's happy if I'm happy."

"A sensible position."

"So take a stand, Thorn. I'd like to know where you come down on this particular issue. Think I should quit?"

Thorn considered it for a second.

"I never saw you happier than sitting in that office, eavesdropping on the beauty parlor."

Sugarman put his mask back in place. Turned around and faced the water.

Thorn stood up, stretched. Sugarman had his snorkel in his mouth, finding the right bite on it.

"Christ, Sugar, you're giving up Quidnunc just as I was about to volunteer to be your Sancho Panza from here on."

Sugar spit out the snorkel, turned his head to stare at Thorn. "My what?"

"Your partner."

"Don't shit me, Thorn. You? A job?"

He smiled at Sugarman.

"Well, yeah. When you put it that way, it doesn't sound real appealing."

"I don't need a partner, anyway. Christ, it's all I can do to make ends meet now."

"And by the way," said Thorn. "In case you're interested, I cast my vote for Doris."

Rochelle made a noise in her throat. A warning uh-oh.

"Yeah, I know. You didn't need to tell me. But it's more complicated for me. I mean, hell, even though I'm unhappy with Jeanne, and it never has been that great, I still love the woman for some reason. It's just not a simple thing."

"Love hardly ever is."

Rochelle kept her eyes on the hunk of grouper she was cutting free. Sugarman reset his face mask.

"So," Thorn said. "How big was that hammerhead?"

"Big," he said. "Damn big."

"Well, hell. Let's go on down there, see if the thing wants to wrestle."

"Now you're talking, Thorn. Now you're saying the words."

He watched Sugar splash feetfirst into the water. In a moment Sugar resurfaced and peered down at the coral and the fish. Then he took a breath and dove.

Thorn sat on the rear gunwale and pulled on his flippers and cleaned his mask. Then he swiveled around and looked out at the other boats bobbing above the reef. A couple of teenagers in white T-shirts were sitting side by side on the stern of one of the open fishermen. They were kissing, arms thrown around each other.

He looked back at Rochelle. She was watching the kids too.

"You coming?"

"In a minute," she said. "When I'm finished with this."

"Whenever you're ready. Whenever."

The breeze was warm and seemed drenched with cloves and nutmeg and the sweet, dizzy eucalyptus of distant lands. Visibility was almost unlimited. He looked again at the teenagers, lost in their embrace, melting into each other. This morning was going to last forever. That kiss. Nothing bad was ever going to happen to those two. Nothing. Ever.